Be Bold

A Novel of the Civil War

An advance printing of 10 review copies was made in 2020.
First printing, January 2021

LIBRARY OF CONGRESS CATALOGIN IN PUBLICATION DATA
Be Bold
1. Civil War—fiction. 2. George J. Stannard—fiction. 3. Gettysburg, Battle of—fiction. 4. Vermont Volunteers, Civil War—fiction.
I. Title.
PS3619.D47649F59 2014
ISBN: 978-0-9884597-7-9

Thunderbird Press
P.O. Box 417
Greenwood Lake, NY 10925
www.thunderbirdpress.org

AUTHOR'S NOTE: This novel is based on a real person, General George J. Stannard of Georgia, Vermont. All of the battles and soldier's accounts were taken from historical records. I have added appropriate dialog and descriptions of actual places to render a fully dimensional experience of the Civil War and some of the soldiers he served with have been combined or altered with regard to their enlistment time and place. Most of the social settings and home life, while also drawn on historical accounts, is fictional because there is not much primary or secondary material related to General Stannard and his home life. The author is not directly related to General Stannard. Any resemblance to persons living, or dead, is coincidental.

Cover illustration of General George J. Stannard courtesy National Archives, photo no. 111-BA-1575.

Be Bold

A Novel of the Civil War

by

E. Frank Stannard

Thunderbird Press
2021

For Isaiah

~ 1 ~

A bullet whizzed by his ear and punched a notch in the brim of his floppy hat but he walked tall among his boys, who lay crouched in a shallow trench behind a two-foot earthen wall. His stride was even, calm and he yelled, "*Men of Vermont! Stand firm!*"

George hollered with a tenacity that fortified the Union soldiers, who quickly reloaded and fired at General Robert E. Lee's main corps of Confederates, who were attacking for the third time in two days. Every available Rebel charged with fury on Fort Harrison, the outer most defense in a ring of seven forts. The Confederates needed to re-capture this key position, just five miles from Richmond, and fought a determined band of Union soldiers from Vermont, New Hampshire and New England.

Another bullet whistled by his ear and another snapped into a felled tree that was part of their low makeshift wall of timber and dirt that provided little protection. Charger, his fine white horse, was stabled in a lean-to on the other side of the fort with the other officers' horses. He and his boys were exposed.

A mini-ball glanced off his scabbard then Captain Converse cursed in pain from his crouching position. A bullet had stung Converse in the left hand and he dropped his Enfield musket. Private Lowe quickly set down his rifle, unrolled a wrapped bandage and spun it around Converse's bloody hand.

"*Keep it up, boys!*" he yelled then fired his Colt .45 steadily at a group of three Rebels dashing straight at them. He dropped one with a shot square into the man's chest, bloodying his gray uniform, clipped another in the leg as he ran then missed but finished him with a bullet to his pudgy face. The third Rebel lay still in the dirt. He either took a dive or was shot by Lieutenant Benedict, who stood next to him and fired his revolver steadily. Benedict was tall and thin with dirty blonde hair matted down with sweat. Under his spectacles Benedict's dark brown eyes scanned the field, found a running Rebel and smoothly shot him.

"*Captain Brydon!*" George yelled. "*Bring up—*"

A bullet slammed into his upper arm and knocked him down. Pain sent him into deep shock with a sudden loss of purpose. What was he doing again? Where was he?

He tried to roll off his throbbing arm but he couldn't move. His boys screamed, yelled and fought on. He felt proud of them but now what?

George had been the first person from Vermont to volunteer and he had led his Green Mountain Boys in every battle. He had led them at the first "big" battle at Bull Run, where his veteran leadership was in stark contrast to almost every Federal soldier. He had led them at Harper's Ferry, where they had a horrendous defensive position and were outnumbered by 48,000 soldiers but fought on for days. He was at the front of the Vermonters at Cold Harbor, where they attacked in the dark at a well-defended position and were butchered, losing 6,000 men in 45 minutes. He had also fought bravely at Gettysburg where 150,000 men killed each other for three days. He had been at the front of many battles, where each was considered *the* big battle to end this god-awful affair, and many felt he was the one person they could not lose.

Death felt close yet he feared for his boys, every friend and soldier and comrade, which he knew was a horrible position for any commander. Death took them daily. These were the best of the best and it would be a shame to lose any one of them.

He felt the warm Virginia earth as his wet blood pulsed from his arm. He thought he might be able to stop the bleeding if he concentrated, he had to stop it, but it was no use. Is this how it ends? Bleeding to death in far away Virginia?

The noise of the battle raged louder but over the din one boy screamed, "*General Stannard is dead!*"

His body rose from the earth. His arms flopped down, dead weight, his legs lifeless, and his head rolled back in spite of his effort.

Benedict pressed his thin hand down on the gushing wound. Four, five, now six men carried George back to the provisional hospital, where Federal army surgeon, Sam "Doc" Thayer, used a long metal clamp to pluck out a mini-ball from Private Wes Cauthen's neck. Corporal Reed Sullivan, Doc's assistant, stood ready to sew the wound shut. Doc Thayer, who was skinny with tired, gray eyes and pale skin with a long dark mustache, released the forceps, dropped the bullet and it clanked into a metal pan. Then Private Cauthen heaved, convulsed and shook in mighty spasms with his arterial blood spraying from his neck. Doc Thayer tried to stop it, placed both hands and gauze over his neck but Cauthen went stiff then collapsed into himself.

Doc Thayer, with a new sadness on his face of some blow he had taken, watched a crowd of soldiers bring in General Stannard. Doc Thayer moved on unruffled with professionalism, dipped his bloody hands into a pan of pink soapy water, wiped them on his bloody apron then picked up a scalpel. Doc Thayer turned to Chaplain Lucius Dickinson and, referring to Private Cauthen, said, "He's gone," then looked to the table where they lay General Stannard.

Benedict kept his hand pressed flat, tight against his upper arm inside his coat, while Captain Brydon maneuvered to take off his coat. Colonel Ripley, red-faced and anxious, looked on with deep concern. Ripley's dark brown eyes shifted from soldier to soldier then he unsheathed his knife and cut off George's coat and shirt, at first neatly then ripping them off his body.

Doc Thayer muscled his way through the growing crowd of soldiers, ten or more pushing into the hospital tent, and yelled, "*Alright, everybody out except Benedict, Ripley and Brydon!*"

Those ordered to leave stood motionless with a collective look of shock and gravity. Everyone was familiar with what had happened to Southern General Thomas "Stonewall" Jackson, who was shot in the arm exactly like this. Jackson's arm was amputated, pneumonia set in, and he died a few days later. No one moved.

Doc Thayer yelled again, followed by Benedict hollering in support as Ripley shoved people out of the tent. The Vermonters' chaplain, Lucius Dickinson of Cavendish, turned to leave and Doc Thayer said, "Not you, Father."

Private Frankie Sawyer saw the group of young men leaving the hospital tent. All were downcast and depressed. Sawyer hollered the news, "*General Stannard is dead!*"

~ 2 ~

George lay on a table and felt Doc Thayer probing into his right shoulder with a piece of metal. Benedict, quick and wiry, stood over him speaking words of encouragement then Ripley said something about Sergeant Lloyd but their voices were indistinct, vaguely audible and floating without meaning. He thought of the idle gossip of Mrs. Turner's soirees, of Helen's rants about fashion and the mindless chatter at intermission at a theater. What did they say? What? Did it matter? Doc Thayer's calm voice cut through the hectic noise and chatter, "Saw."

What did Doc say? What was happening? He couldn't open his eyelids and couldn't lift his arms. He tried to scream "*No!*" but couldn't move, dreamlike, then sharp metallic teeth cut into his arm, a wave of adrenalin rushed through him, and he pushed up off the wet, bloody table, and opened his eyes. His right arm was being hacked off and he screamed.

Benedict yelled, "*Hey!*" and another hand covered his nose and mouth with a gauze dampened with ether. He felt himself going limp everywhere at once and thought, Is this how it ends? What is Emily doing? I don't want to die, I don't want to die. How horrible—never to see Emily again. And the incredibly beautiful and incredibly frustrating Helen. I forgive you. I don't want to die. Father, mother, all dead. And me. He didn't want to let go.

He rocked back and forth and with each gentle swing more of his soul escaped. Now Sergeant Lloyd's pale face, dotted with sun freckles, was above him. Was Lloyd that heavy weight he felt on his chest, kneeling on him? He couldn't breathe! He couldn't breathe! What was happening?

He thought back to his boyhood when life was simple and wonderful. His father knew everything and took care of everything. It was a beautiful time. He relaxed, now comfortable, and felt the warmth of his father's care. He floated in memory.

~ ~

George sat on a small keg of molasses, using his right hand to support his head. He was tired from chores on their farm in the morning and then helping his father to stock the shelves of the trading post. He had just turned 18, was average height for his age but strong and athletic with keen eyesight. It had been a long day, it was almost dark, and yet Dr. Côté had not arrived.

His father sat on a stool behind the wooden counter, reading a catalog of dry goods from a large store across the border in Montreal, and said, "You can go up to the house and I'll tell you everything Dr. Côté says."

"No," he mumbled and shifted then leaned on his left hand. "I like seeing him."

Samuel smiled and turned the page. The prices in the catalog had increased since the last issue. The harsh winter and dry summer had made for a horrible year for crops, and farmers were in a desperate situation. "I don't know how anyone can afford anything anymore," his father said, then noticed his worried expression, gave a wink and added, "But we'll be okay. We always get by."

Samuel had settled his family in northern Vermont in a hamlet called Georgia, seven miles south of St. Albans, which had two streets with a common green between them. He built Samuel's Trading Post on the post road and travelers from Burlington to Montreal and local settlers frequented his store. About 1,700 people lived in the area and he traded furs and a variety of goods with the people around Lake Champlain including the Canadians. In their first winter, 1827, an epidemic of influenza took Samuel's wife Rebecca and their unborn child.

Samuel and George were regular attendees of the Unitarian Church. Afterward George ran outside to play with the other boys and enjoyed a variety of games and his favorites were buck-buck, lacrosse and wrestling. He grew up like most of the local farm boys, strong and fit for his age. When he was 14 his father encouraged him to join the local militia called the Ransom Guards, which gave him a good military education but he especially enjoyed taking care of the horses. Samuel noticed this, bought a few more, and they began breeding horses. For Christmas his father gave him spurs that were coin-sized, five-pointed rowels with short shanks. Samuel said, "These will last you a lifetime."

George was incredibly happy, gave his father a strong hug, admired the spurs and attached them to his boots. Later he asked to wear his boots to bed but Samuel smiled, said "No," and insisted he would not wear his spurs in the house again.

George also tended to a few cows, chickens and a large apple orchard but his chief task was to help with Samuel's Trading Post. Local Vermonters, Canadians, Mohawks, Irish and Scandinavian immigrants were all attracted to Samuel's sense of fair pricing and his treatment of everyone as a friend first and a trader second. In 1836 wholesale prices increased greatly and there was also a political movement in Canada led by a band of patriots who called themselves the "Sons of Liberty." They printed leaflets, organized demonstrations and fought against the latest tax imposed by the British. Samuel noticed an uneasiness in traders and suspected today's visit by Dr. Côté may be related to the political upheaval in Canada with the border only 20 miles away.

George folded his arms and rested his head against the countertop. He was tired from maneuvers the Ransom Guards had performed yesterday. His father enlisted him when he turned 14, four years ago, and he had gained a reputation as a smart, reliable sergeant. Yesterday the leader of the Ransom Guards, Colonel Asa Kent, a meticulous Englishman six feet tall, had asked him to state the manual's procedure for changing fronts. He recited it, forward then backward without missing a step. Colonel Kent was appeared annoyed, personally challenged, and ordered, "Draw your revolver."

His father had given him a pistol for his fifteenth birthday, a special order from an armory in Connecticut. Samuel had explained,

"You must always hold it with reverence," then handed him the Colt. "The aim is true and it carries all the seriousness of the world."

"See there," Samuel pointed along the barrel, "I had it engraved."

To G J S   Fight for Justice   S J S

Now, with the entire militia watching, Kent pointed to an oval notch in a tree 40 yards away and said, "Hit the notch in that tree."

George raised his arm, steadied his aim, exhaled, and fired. The shot pierced the center. "Anything else, sir?"

"Do 't again."

He again leveled the pistol but now he felt his father and all the others staring. He exhaled evenly then easily pulled the trigger. The smooth action of the Colt slid back, the hammer slammed down, the shot ripped through the air, and the bullet plugged a thick branch inches to the left of the notch.

"A-*ha!*" Colonel Kent scrutinized his uniform, which was clean and bright. He examined his three stripes and added with distain, "Perfect your aim, *Sergeant!*"

He fired again and again, and his third and fourth shots plugged then expanded the hole in the notch. He knew he could hit the target seven times out of ten but the colonel had made his point with that missed second shot and walked away with an air of superiority. That was the low point of yesterday's maneuvers. They had marched six miles with gear to perform a musket shooting exercise at a row earthen jugs in a clearing of pine trees, followed by

Kent's inspection and impromptu questioning, then marched back to their base camp outside St. Albans.

He closed his heavy eyelids and thought of feeding and caring for their horses. He could see each of their bright eyes and shiny coats, leading them with a line into the riding ring: Ariel, Bottom, Cupid… His father's voice awakened him from dozing, "D'you hear that?"

He sat up and heard a faint thumping of horses at a gallop. He bolted off the keg, ran to the doorway and looked north on the post road. Dr. Côté rode his chestnut mare named Joan, after Joan of Arc, and wore a long black duster and a floppy black hat. Another rider galloped next to him, dressed in sleeveless buckskin with a feather in his long dark hair. "Yes, I see him! And another rider, too."

Dr. Côté raised one hand off the reins of his heavy mare then called out, "*Hallo!*" The second rider was an Indian, who rode a white-spotted, gray horse with red rope reins. They eased back, brought their horses to a walk then stopped to dismount. They both stretched, led the horses off the road and walked the last 50 feet to the trading post.

Dr. Côté, a short, heavy Frenchman with round steel spectacles, walked with a stiff waddle. George did not recognize the other young man, who had long shiny black hair and his skin was a dark walnut color. When they came closer, he could see the Indian's eyes were marvelously strange, dark and unblinking. He wore a single turkey feather in his long dark hair.

Dr. Côté chuckled, tussled George's hair, clapped him on the back and spoke in his thick French accent, "Who's back?"

"You're back!"

"No, Georges! Theez iz *your* back!" The doctor laughed easily, looped the reins around a hitching post and stretched again.

The stranger was muscular with tribal tattoos crisscrossing his biceps like several leather bands. He had met Iroquois who had a similar complexion, with high cheekbones and large noses but this young man appeared unusually keen.

"Come in, Cyrille," Samuel stood in the doorway, holding a double candelabrum then nodded to the bronze-skinned man with long black hair and said warmly, "Friends. We're happy to see you!"

"We stay short," Dr. Côté replied. "Tonight we sleep by zee Nelson Inn."

"Oh la!" George said. "That's a two hour ride!"

Samuel and Dr. Côté shook hands vigorously, each with a big grin. Then his father bowed, clasped the young Indian by the forearm and spoke formally, "I am Samuel Stannard and this is my son, George."

He didn't know how to greet the Indian so he stood still. The young man was not much older than he was but he seemed to take in everything. Then the Iroquois spoke with a deep, slow voice, "I am Billy Caldwell from the land you call Niagara. I am Mohawk."

Dr. Côté unfurled his black duster with a sweeping flourish and the flowing black cloth flew around the room yet magically left all the goods on the shelf. The candelabrum flickered, burned brighter and was steady again. Billy copied him sans duster, twisting his sleeveless arms above his head to make a joke and all laughed.

Samuel patted the doctor's back and said, "You're looking healthy, Cyrille."

"Hey, hey! I am zee doctor here. *I* am to say who has zee health. I was in Napoleon's service, you know!"

"Tell us about Napoleon!" he said.

"Later, son," Samuel said sternly. "Let Dr. Côté and Mister Caldwell relax. They've had a long ride."

"Please. Call me Billy." The Mohawk spoke English very well and gave a good-natured punch to his arm then smiled. "We have been riding for five days around Lake Champlain because we have—"

"Show us zee latest from Montréal!" Dr. Côté broke-in, nudged Billy aside and walked around the room to examine the dry goods. The walls were lined with foodstuffs and farming implements, and on the floor were wooden crates and kegs of milled flour, oats, nuts, seeds, apples and gunpowder. Three new shiny muskets stood in one corner and a variety of powder horns hung nearby. Dr. Côté asked, "How iz zee busin`ess, eh?"

"Slow, but we'll be okay," Samuel said. "And yours?"

"Ach! There iz no shortage of sick *et* dying. You have zee luck to live *not* in Canada."

Samuel nodded. "The border's only a score miles so it's about the same here. Only the gov'ment's diff'rent."

"Ah-h-h," Dr. Côté's blue eyes gleamed. He gave a wry smile and pointed with his thumb, "*Et* zar iz zee cure!"

Samuel squinted his eyes then nodded and George understood his father's nod was due to the complex subject of politics, which he tried to avoid discussing with traders. As George became older and worked more in the trading post, he also knew the people of the region were not that different and trading connected them. Now Dr. Côté was about to discuss politics, which might connect them even more.

Dr. Côté stretched his short arms, put his foot on the small keg George had been sitting on and looked around with a smile of admiration. "Zees iz some place, *mon frère!* You have *avoir de la chance*, zee luck."

Samuel circled the room lighting candles but paused to bow. "Thank you."

Dr. Côté motioned with two fingers to a gunnysack of sugar and spoke to Billy. "We need *sucre, non?*"

The young Mohawk appeared surprised then nodded. George hustled over to the middle shelf, took down one sack and placed it on the counter. His father nodded.

Dr. Côté motioned to relax to Billy, who then leaned on a large barrel's edge, crossed his long legs and gazed at the wide, rough-hewn maple floorboards. Then the doctor pulled out a silver flask from his vest pocket and asked, "May I?"

Samuel brought out two shot glasses from under the counter and explained, "George recently eighteen but he doesn't drink." His father eyed Billy and asked, "He old enough?"

Dr. Côté smiled. "*Certainment!* Perhaps you know zee fazher of Billy? He fought in zee Eighteen Twelf War *et* made some name. Billy's fazher teached him *et* he has learnt a great many zeengs from Mohawk council. *Oui, oui*. Heez people call heem Black Eagle and now it iz Billy who iz leader of Mohawks. He may look young but he, *mon frère*, iz a man."

Billy raised his hand. "Thank you, Cyrille, but you say too much. Samuel, thank you for having us but no, thank you, I do not drink. I promised my father many years ago I would not."

Dr. Côté made a face and raised his eyebrows, as if this were surprising news then made a clacking sound. For him it was immoral *not* to drink yet there was something practiced to their routine. He turned to Samuel. "Tach. So it iz you *et moi, mon frère*."

Dr. Côté took off his black felt hat, showing his thinning gray hair. He held the silver flask at an angle and poured the golden liquor into two shot glasses. The flask had fancy engraving in French and glistened in the candlelight. "Theez cognac iz from zee estate zat supplied Napoleon. It iz zee finest in all zee world."

"My goodness!" he said and looked to his father, who also made an impressed face in the flickering candlelight. "Napoleon himself?"

"*Oui, oui,*" Dr. Côté ran his right hand over his thin, gray hair and patted it down. "Ah, Georges, eet iz hard to believe I was once young but, ah, zat iz anozher time. I have zee honor, Samuel, to share zees wif you."

Dr. Côté sniffed the cognac and sighed with satisfaction. He lifted one glass and spoke eloquently, "To liberty, equality, *et* . . ."

Samuel raised his glass and completed the toast, "Fraternity."

They sipped the cognac. The phrase reminded George of Napoleon and his light blue eyes stared with an intense pleading to his father, wanting to ask about Napoleon, but Samuel shook his head "no."

"It's always good to see you, Cyrille," Samuel smiled. "Your letter said you wanted to discuss something of great import. What is it, my friend?"

"*Oui. Merci, mon frère.* If you do not mind, I let Billy speak. Heez English iz so much more than mine."

Billy stood upright, bowed to each person around the room then paused. George sensed he was about to start an important speech, similar to one for his tribal council. Billy spoke slowly and clearly, "There is a rising movement in Canada called the Sons of Liberty. They have organized a revolt against the unfair government. I will tell you why and what needs to be done."

Billy made a fist, placed it over his heart then continued, "The Africans have come to the town of Niagara. Four hundred people who were once slaves, Harriet Tubman's passengers on her secret railroad, now live across the river from us. They are our neighbors. I know them and they are good people."

Billy cleared his throat, looked at Cyrille then George and lastly to Samuel then continued, "A man from the South named David Castleman came for a former slave named Solomon Moseby. The Canadian government made them give up the man because they said Mister Solomon Moseby stole a horse in his ride to freedom and that was why he cannot be free."

Billy's speech was having a profound effect on George and made him very upset. He had read of slaves in ancient Greece and looked to his father, who patted him on the shoulder and made a face "to listen."

Billy spoke with rising passion, "We, the Patriots, believe this is *not* justice. Slavery is *wrong!* It is an *evil* thing and we *must* fight it."

Billy waited for a long, dramatic pause and stillness filled the room. George could not stand it and looked at Dr. Côté, who raised his eyebrows to Billy, who gave a firm nod in return then continued his speech. "The Canadian government has abandoned its sense of *morals.* They are *wrong* in letting this mercenary Mister Castleman take away the former slave Mister Moseby. My tribe is *also* unhappy. The government treats *us* poorly. Remember, Mohawks fought *with* the Americans *against* the British in your War of Independence. And now, *now* the Canadian government grows *more corrupt* with each day. *Here* is the latest insult!"

Billy pulled out a newspaper from an oblong leather satchel. The paper had the headline, *Favoritism by Free Masons in Public*

Office. “This *shows* the high offices of government are only for Free Masons.”

Billy rolled up then tucked away the newspaper. “If you believe in *freedom* and are willing *to fight* in a revolution, we are here to raise an army of militia. We have been all across this great land and *we* will go back to Canada, to Montreal, and to Toronto, and *we* will fight those in power. *We* are *Patriots! We* will *fight* the British Canadian government!”

Dr. Côté raised his glass of cognac to Samuel. “So. It would zeem zat I am here for more zan *sucre.*”

Samuel engaged Dr. Côté with a level-eyed firmness and clinked glasses with Dr. Côté. “My sympathies are with you, Cyrille.”

“Sympathies are a marvelous thing, Samuel,” Dr. Côté said, finishing his cognac in a gulp. He took off his spectacles, revealing his bloodshot blue eyes, and polished the lenses with a fine silk handkerchief. “But sympathies do not change zee world.”

Dr. Côté replaced his spectacles onto his nose, wrapped the wires around his ears and looked to Billy, who stood tall in the glowing light. On cue the young man pumped his muscular arms and spoke loudly with passion, “*Sometimes a man must fight!*”

That outburst raised the hair on the back of George’s neck and he gave a pleading look to his father, summoning his bravado and let it burn in his fiery gaze. He had been involved in the Ransom Guards for four years and desperately wanted to prove himself. This cause, like the engraving on his pistol, was to *Fight for Justice!* When he could stand the silence no longer, he simply said, “Please, father!”

He sensed his father was thinking of all their friends, all the people they traded with regularly, before agreeing to bear arms and go into battle. He was considering this with "all the seriousness of the world." He had also heard his father tell stories about his grandfather, also named Samuel, who had served in the American Revolutionary War. Samuel Senior had lectured his father many times about how horrible war is and why he could not fight in the War of 1812. His father had also told his own stories, of war's effect on a community. Some men had missing limbs and some men failed to return home. He could sense this Canadian expedition was not something his father would agree to simply for his own eagerness.

Samuel's face was grim and he scratched his stubbly beard. After a very long pause of reasoning, he stared at Dr. Côté then Billy Caldwell, then back to Dr. Côté. He nodded once and spoke solemnly, "My son and I will join you."

~ 3 ~

He thought, What's happening? Why couldn't he move? A great pressure jammed his upper chest and his right arm but he couldn't open his eyes. Someone said something then another soldier yelled. Who yelled? Benedict? Good ol' Benedict. He and Benedict had been through so much together. He was always there, unstated, a known quantity like a given in mathematics. Benedict, sure, reliable.

Intense pain shot through his chest and right arm. Something was bobbled and a solid thud sounded when it hit the ground. "Pick it up! Jesus Christ almighty!"

"What's it matter? He ain't ever gonna use it again."

Another voice said, "Don't matter, he's dead."

Father Dickinson began, "Dear Lord, though I walk—"

"Quiet, Father," Doc Thayer said, his voice calm, then placed his thin hand around George's left wrist. No one spoke. All was still. "He's got a pulse. He's with us."

"Thank God!"

"Pour some whiskey over the wound." Doc ordered. "Goddammit Captain get out of the way!"

A cotton gauze tamped down on his nose and mouth but he was afraid to rest. He thought he may never wake again, felt this new fear, but everything was fuzzy, warm and comfortable. Was that a warbler singing? Or the happy song of a blue bird? Ah, the sweet blue bird of happiness. He thought of his father showing him how to whittle a bird while he spoke about his mother. They sat against a large elm near the trading post and Samuel whittled, talking softly but his voice was bold and full of certainty, "Your mother made me the happiest man in the world. But happiness is a home. Find a good woman and marry her. You'll be happy as long as you live."

Samuel's voice held some absolute truth, something sacred, but even in his dreamlike state George knew happiness through marriage was a myth. He had thought he had found a good woman in Helen, who would lead to happiness but. . .

He remembered meeting Helen on the Burlington common green, her dazzling blue eyes, her full figure and bold nature. He recalled their first intense moment of passion when they rode in his carriage in the rolling hills south of Burlington, when she had clutched his hands on the reins and pulled back sharply. Puck, a strong, responsive draft horse came to an abrupt stop in a small opening in the intensely colored woods with leaves of warm yellow, bright orange and crimson.

Helen said, "I need you now," wet her lips and gazed at him with her stunning blue eyes. He kissed her, gently at first, until she pulled him closer. He felt his groin becoming thick and she pulled back his coat, grabbed at his pants, buttons, and lifted her dress, revealing her soft dark hair, somehow glistening. He wanted to be with Helen so much he abandoned his thoughts of her virtue and for the first time felt her warm softness. Together they climbed into sensuousness, rocked back and forth on the carriage with building, firm strokes until she cried out, a murmuring moan, growing into a low throaty grunt then exploded into a great rocking scream of ecstasy, again, and again, and again. He felt an incredible intensity and the world was one, everything made sense, and everything had a purpose. He floated in the warm glow of their sensuous after-moment until his conscious bothered him, now, years later, for its untruthfulness. He had found a good woman, he thought, but Helen was not happy, not thoroughly happy. Now what?

He wondered, How many myths had his father told him, which he had believed wholeheartedly, were untrue? Or perhaps

Helen was *not* a good woman? Had he deceived himself about her? What other myths did he hold in his life?

It was comfortable to lay still and think. He wanted to remain conscious for fear of never waking again. Then he recalled the Canadian expedition with his father. He had desperately wanted to go and therefore it was *his* fault and he felt guilty about its result. So much of the Canadian invasion did not make sense. He floated on ether, on dreams, a kaleidoscope of thoughts about his life. He thought again of that huge, guilt-ridden expedition in another country.

~ ~

The group of men assembled by Dr. Côté, Billy Caldwell, and other leaders called themselves "Hunters" and included many men from the Ransom Guards and other militia groups from Vermont and northern New York. They planned an invasion of Canada to help free the oppressed citizens struggling under British rule. They would meet in Ogdensburg, New York on November 11, 1838 then attack the fort near the village of Prescott, Canada, across the St. Lawrence River. Once they had liberated this small town, the local citizens and free-minded patriots in Canada would rise up in rebellion.

George and his father began their trip on the morning of November 10th. They rode together on a strong mare, Diana, from their home in Georgia, Vermont and packed food and supplies for one week, and brought ammunition and four muskets. Samuel said, "We might be able to sell two guns, at cost of course, to other Hunters."

He liked riding with his father. Samuel talked more and pointed out different signs along the way like deer antler scrapings against pine trunks, an old pile of moose droppings, torn branches of a sumac bush, and various tracks in the melting snow from raccoon, beaver and a wolf. He recognized most of these signs but his father could point out an additional detail like the way the rabbit tracks circled back to the edge of the woods where it probably had its hutch.

At night, after they pitched their tent and made a small fire, his father spoke about Rebecca, his mother. He cherished stories about her and tried very hard to remember her pretty face but he was only seven when she died of influenza. It was also difficult to remember details of her personality and he knew she was a very good cook, she was kind and generous, but those were words he repeated to himself. He could not remember more but in his father's stories she was alive again.

"Your mother was quite witty, ya know. And she loved to dance and sing," his father's breath hung in the frosty air in their tent.

"She had blue eyes like mine," he said.

"That's right. Her eyes were as blue as the sky on a brilliant October morning, full of light. One time we went to a dance in the big city of Burlington. It was one of those big events with a lot of folks from near and far. She wore her finest white dress with tiny blue flowers that she made with embroidery. She was the most beautiful woman there," and then his father became very emotional and paused to swallow hard. "Her smile shined as brightly as her heart."

It wasn't much but he knew there would be no more tonight. He tried to sleep and imagined his mother and father dancing. Rebecca tilted her head back with a hearty laugh and they circled the dance floor. She said something witty, they laughed again, and went around and around, dancing happily. He fell asleep peacefully.

On their second day of travel they moved through Ogdensburg, a small town that reminded him of St. Albans although a little different. Ogdensburg was about the same size with a common green, a mill, a foundry and a few trading stores but there were also sailboats moored on the river and steamers at the docks. They met with a blacksmith, who boarded their mare Diana, and bought their two extra muskets. The blacksmith, a short Italian named Uno Agnello had long dark hair, thick arms and hands, and agreed to come later because he was waiting for his cousin's arrival from Albany. Agnello would also bring more supplies on Diana.

They continued on foot to a nearby open field, where the Hunters assembled. It was the largest gathering George had ever seen. He recalled a bear drive from Burlington to St. Albans with about 100 men, but here more than 250 men with guns had gathered and their mood was *very* different. These men were a rough bunch. They were large with heavy arms and broad chests, men who could clear the forest if given time. They wore fringed hunting jackets and lived like wild beasts in the open. Since they did not bother to dig "necessaries," the stench was already overwhelming. Many of them were drinking and singing old English pub songs, war songs, followed in spirited rivalry by old Irish pub songs, war songs, and then old Scottish pub songs and war songs.

Dr. Côté trotted his chestnut mare Joan into camp and spoke with several men who were dressed in blue-and-white uniforms. Billy

Caldwell arrived on his gray and white-spotted horse and wore a long-sleeve deerskin coat and leggings. A band of Mohawks and Africans walked around him and George asked his father if he could go talk to the others. Then Uno Agnello and his cousin arrived on their mare Diana, heavily loaded with supplies. Samuel replied, "Okay, I'll unload her. But come back here when they start speechifying."

Dr. Côté appeared busy, with many older people talking to him, so George went straight to Billy Caldwell, who had his back turned with his long dark hair braided into a single cord. George called out cheerfully, "Hello!"

Billy spoke with other Mohawks, Africans, and uniformed militiamen but turned and said, "Hey there George Stannard."

Billy appeared very serious with his dark, piercing eyes. He introduced several Hunters by name, including a young man named Abner Doubleday, who gaped with a stone-faced gaze. Then George realized many others had this same naïve expression, revealing their inexperience and brooding nature about this gathering. He wondered if his own face looked young and green.

Billy said, "These are some of my friends. We will help the Canadian Sons of Liberty and these men will fight with us. Then all the Canadians will join us when they see the time is right to fight for their freedom!"

"*Et* zee time *iz* right!" Dr. Côté came up to George from behind and clapped him on the back. Dr. Côté wore his black frock cloak but underneath was a crisp blue uniform with gold braiding and shiny buttons. "Eh, Georges! Who's back?"

"That's my back."

"*Non, c'est moi! I'm* back!" Dr. Côté laughed easily. George admired his French uniform and figured it must be from Napoleon's Army. He was anxious to ask about it, heard his father's reproachful voice, and knew this was not the time. Dr. Côté squeezed his shoulder, ruffled his hair then stepped around a small keg of whiskey, where another militiaman hugged Dr. Côté and began a serious conversation.

Billy Caldwell playfully punched his arm. "Here, I want to show you this. Come at me."

"What?" He took a short stick Billy handed to him.

"Pretend to attack me." George was still confused so Billy grabbed the stick from him, ran around, circled back then came straight at him with a mock scream. He met Billy head on, grappled with him but Billy's powerful strength won out and took him down, then he ran the stick across his throat. He was embarrassed but Billy smiled good-naturedly, jumped up and said, "Now. You come at me."

He took the stick, ran around, circled back and took aim to thrust the stick into his body but Billy swiftly took his arm, swung him over his hip, flipped him and he fell to the ground in a heap. Again Billy was on top of him with the stick, then he grinned.

"I learned that from a warrior from Ja-pan," Billy said, holding out his hand and helping him to stand. "I've forgotten their word but you step forward to take your attacker's force, turn it to your advantage, and *voila!* They are not in control. You are! It's good, eh?"

"Yes," he smiled.

Billy continued, "This Ja-pan warrior showed me many hand and arm holds, and leg moves, and many fighting skills. We must practice."

He offered, "Great! And I'll show you how to load and fire a musket."

Billy clapped his back with a broadening smile. "I know how to shoot. But I have heard of your excellent marksmanship and I can learn more. Thank you!"

Then Billy moved over to greet another group of Hunters and one of the young men he had just met leaned to him and whispered, "Are you really fighting in this?"

It was Abner Doubleday, who was very tall with dark hair and a heavy-boned frame. George replied, "Yeah, I'm fighting. My pa said so," which sounded boyish so he added, "I've been in the Ransom Guards four years. What about you?"

"My pa ain't, *isn't* here. I'm from Ballston Spa."

"Is that near Saratoga Springs?"

The young man nodded. "My name's Abner Doubleday."

"Pleased to meet you. I'm George Stannard. So, you fightin'?"

"I came to hear what they had to say. Give me a day and I'll let you know."

He laughed but then realized Abner was not joking. Then Lieutenant Falder approached them. He knew Falder from a time when the Ransom Guards performed joint exercises with a militia group from upper New York State. Falder was lean, middle-aged with shocks of gray hair on his temples and big jug ears that stuck out. Falder broke in, “Fighting is the best way I know to test your manhood. I seen plenty action in Eighteen Twelve. Killed a few lobster-backs myself.”

George looked to Abner, who was wide-eyed. He wanted to ask Falder questions about being in battle, about killing a man but Falder turned and strutted away, bragging to the next group about the War of 1812 and killing redcoats.

Abner then tried to show off his knowledge by using a stick to draw a map in the dirt. A squiggly line was the St. Lawrence River and Abner spoke down at the dirt map but his voice was filled with hesitation and pauses. “I’ve been accepted. . . to West Point. Here’s how I see it. . . The British garrison—”

Dr. Côté whistled loudly. He had stepped onto a whisky keg, put two fingers on each side of his mouth and whistled again. A crowd began to gather around Dr. Côté to hear his speech and he recalled his father’s instructions, said, “G’bye, Abner,” then made his way through the rough men to Samuel, who had moved closer with the crowd.

Dr. Côté looked portly on the keg with loose jowls and he was much more serious than he had ever seen him. He spoke for a brief moment then said, “Here iz our leader, Commander Nils von Schoultz!”

Dr. Côté stepped down and Commander von Schoultz took his place on the keg. von Schoultz took off his tri-cornered hat and showed his dark receding hair and long whiskers on the side of his cheeks thickening into a dark beard. He was thin and spoke with a heavy Swedish accent about their inspiration from God and of how beautiful liberty was in America and in France, and of how the Canadians should have liberty, too! The Africans and Mohawks cheered and Billy Caldwell's scream pierced the air in a high-pitched staccato. The cheering inspired George and he cheered loudly. His father stepped closer, put one hand on his shoulder, and held him with a grim look on his face. It appeared to be a look of disappointment, that *he* had made a mistake, like the time two years earlier when *he* had not ordered enough supplies, including enough feed for the horses, in the winter of 1835. He wanted to convince his father he could handle himself, he would do well in battle, and everything would be okay but the loud noise of cheering men made it impossible.

Then they all gave three strong "*Hurrahs!*" and Commander von Schoultz called the various company leaders forward, including Colonel Kent from the Ransom Guards and Billy Caldwell. They met off to the side but Abner Doubleday maneuvered his way into this small circle of eight men. George overheard Commander von Schoultz firmly giving instructions on how they would attack the British garrison across the river in a fortified windmill near Prescott at dawn. Then his father tugged his shoulder and guided him back to their tent.

As they settled in for the night they said very little. George lay still, trying to sleep, and heard his father's heavy, even breathing. He wondered what would happen in the morning, wondered how he would perform, and imagined what his father would do. His father was the best marksman he knew and everyone agreed that was a fact. His father would be fine but how would *he* do? Could he kill a man? How would it happen? Then the whole encampment stirred and awakened even though it was very dark. They were breaking camp *now!*

He swiftly ate some scrambled eggs from their neighbor Mr. Girod's small pan, washed it down with a cup of very strong coffee then helped his father pack up their tent and supplies. He took a plug of beef jerky from his gray militia coat pocket and gnawed on it nervously, watching hundreds of Hunters assemble on the riverbank where a flotilla of two schooners, a steamship, 15 canoes and 11 rowboats waited.

George followed his father then sat in the middle of a canoe. Their neighbor, Theodore Girod, paddled from the front and Samuel steered and paddled from the stern. He trailed his finger in the cool river and felt a rush of adrenalin in anticipation of what the day would bring. He felt giddy because the weather seemed to be on their side with a cold Northern wind bringing dark, heavy clouds and perhaps snow. Blocks of ice dotted the river and moved haltingly down the freezing flow then gathered in large chunks on the riverbank. The water lapped softly against the birch-bark hull and he thought of his father's story about his witty mother laughing and dancing and his father's trademark closing line, "Her smile shined as brightly as her heart," but he was too excited about the impending battle. He knew he should focus on his training from the Ransom Guards, where he had risen to the rank of master sergeant because he had mastered all the styles of combat, techniques of weaponry, and drills, but in his excitement with his heart racing he felt confused and much of his training was a rapidly circling blur. He decided he would simply follow orders and follow his father.

They pulled up their canoe on the Canadian shore and the Hunters gathered quietly around Commander von Schoultz, who spoke sternly but in a hushed, excited tone. Because of von Schoultz's deep, gravelly voice and his thick Swedish accent, George could not understand more than a few odd words and at first thought von Schoultz was no Napoleon Bonaparte. Then recalled his orders from last night and thought, Yes, von Schoultz had spoken firmly. He was a decisive leader with a solid plan.

It was still before dawn, becoming gray, when the Hunters moved out along the river's edge for Prescott, where they hoped to catch the Canadian garrison sleeping. He and his father both carried a musket and a pistol, and had left a heavy pack of rations in the canoe. Thick clumps of snow began to fall and he couldn't see more than a score feet ahead. His father marched next to him, looked out for him, and occasionally whispered, "Atta boy."

The wind blew piercingly from the northwest and snow crystals stung his eyes. The day became lighter even though the sun could not be seen through the heavy overcast clouds. Commander von

Schoultz found a path heading north and stood at attention under his snow-encrusted colonel's hat and pointed the way with his woolen mitten. The Commander's dark whiskers were speckled with snowflakes and tiny icicles hung in his beard. George followed his father, Colonel Kent, and the other men, weaving their way past very small pine trees and ferns toward a shadowy blockhouse.

"Puzh on, ladz!" Commander von Schoultz whispered, pointing with his stiff left arm toward the stone blockhouse. They made their way up the slope, through an orchard of leafless cherry trees, then came to an open meadow of snow-covered grass where a long wooden fence protected the blockhouse. Oddly, no guards stood near the entryway but its closed gate held a small lock.

Commander von Schoultz had caught up to lead the Hunters and motioned for Thad "Bear" Brisken to step forward. Brisken was the oldest of three sons of a hay farmer, who lived east of St. Albans. He had just turned 17 but Brisken was already huge at 6'7" with big powerful legs, a broad thick chest, arms heavy with muscle, and large hands that were meaty like a bear's paws, which inspired his knick-name "Bear."

von Schoultz pointed to an area of the wooden fence that appeared discolored and weak. Instead Bear Brisken ran directly at the locked gate, surprisingly fast, and bulled into the fence with his broad left shoulder, smacking into the wooden barrier and smashing it with a thunderous crack. The whole section of fence gave way with its lock in place and fell flat onto the snowy ground.

The loud crash caused a soldier in a bright red uniform to look down from the guard house. The redcoat's eyes widened in shock then he screeched a noise of panic, followed by frenzied stirring, and he and another soldier slid down a ladder in back and dashed for the fort further up the hill. The blockhouse was abandoned, along with a 12-pound gun pointing coldly over the icy river.

The Hunters moved through the fence opening, spilling out into the sloping field, over 100 men in a moment. A shrill northern wind blew then snow fell in heavy clumps.

"We are the lucky," Commander von Schoultz whispered. "We haff da snow, a shield." He exposed his rosy hand and pointed to the path of a covered road that led into town, "Thar de town," then motioned across the snowy field up the hill to the vague outline of the fortified windmill. "Ahead, de vindmeel fort."

The Hunters rushed in the direction of his command, following the trail of the fleeing redcoats through the snow. Their path wound around small mounds and up the gradual slope to the fort. George ran with them and thought, Everything is moving so easily like a dream. He heard Colonel Kent chuckling as he hustled alongside his father and Samuel whispered to Kent, "What?"

"I was just thinking of hunting a fox last winter," Kent spoke in a normal voice.

"Shh!" Samuel hushed sharply.

"It was a glorious time and the snow was my ally, just as it is here."

George thought it was odd, to think of a casual hunting outing when such a difficult task lay ahead. The fleeing soldiers would warn the others at the fort and what if they were now falling into ranks to fight? What if the soldiers used the snow to shield themselves, slipped out the back of the fort, and came through the woods on their side to flank them?

Kent stopped and yelled with great emotion, "*It's ordained by God!*"

"Shh!" Samuel whispered harshly and stopped next to him.

A smirk overcame Kent and he disregarded Samuel again and shouted, "*Push on, brave boys! Prescott is ours!*"

Alarm bells clanged frantically and soldiers stumbled out of the fort still buttoning their redcoats. They appeared shocked and unready for any action.

George whispered angrily at Kent, "What are you doing?" but his father put his hand on his chest to quiet him.

Kent stood stiffly at attention, imposing in the drifting whiteness, and said loudly, "*I'm rallying the men!*"

We don't need rallying, he thought. They had moved swiftly up the slope but Kent's yelling gave the redcoats a mark with their exact location amid the shroud of snow. Then, unbelievably, Kent shouted again, "*We'll be in the fort in two minutes!*"

George was lifted off his feet and slammed onto the icy hard ground. An instant later he heard fuzzy ringing, the repercussion of cannon fire. His ears stung and he felt woozy. He gathered himself, pushed off the snow-covered ground up onto his knees, and shooting pain ran through his lower back with a stinging jolt through his right arm. He thought, Where am I wounded? The earth wavered unsteadily and he knelt on one knee. He felt his blood pounding in his temples, pounding through his entire body. My God, he thought, what happened?

~ 4 ~

Slowly, moment-by-moment, George felt more aware of himself, of where he was, on the battlefield, although he was still hazy in his thinking. He caught his breath, picked up his musket in the cold snow and looked to the area where he had stood with his father and Colonel Kent.

Two bodies lay in the reddened snow with fresh earth sprinkled around them. The colonel was horribly disfigured. It was unclear if the two bloody bones were Kent's legs or arms reaching up for the sky but it was clear he was not moving again. Then he realized the colonel's back and head were buried into the ground so those must be what remained of his legs pointing straight up. Off to the side lay his father, on his side. He ran dizzily and stumbled next to him.

Samuel's blood oozed into the darkening snow from his shattered head. He tossed aside his musket and tried to lift his father but his body was heavy, lifeless. He gently eased him back onto the dark crimson snow then stared at his hands, almost foreign, wet and covered with his father's blood and bits of his bloodied brown hair. His father's skin had an unsightly bluish pallor.

He felt unsure, lost, and looked around. Scores of men wandered in every direction. Then he felt his father's presence and gazed into his calm brown eyes, already becoming milky white, and then he heard his voice, "Steady your nerves. You'll do fine. Remember, *be bold* and mighty forces will come to your aid."

He felt an immense deep loss followed by remorse burning with anger. The unsteady ground heaved left, titled sideways and his insides lurched up a brownish-yellow stew of chewed eggs, beef jerky and coffee. He heaved again then used the back of his militia sleeve to wipe his mouth. He was done and used his palms to wipe his tears. Inside, he ached with seething pain and growing anger, followed by an overwhelming need. It was a vicious rage seared with a consuming need for revenge. He stood, pulled out his shiny Colt .45, took a deep breath and hollered, "*Attack!*"

Another militiaman, Lieutenant Falder, rushed over, slapped his arm down and said, "Let's talk this over!"

Falder, who had been boastful around the campfire last night, had an unsure, crazy look in his eyes. Snow stuck to his gray woolen hat and he spoke timidly, "Maybe this isn't best!"

"*Onward!*" he shouted. The men looked around or gazed at the disfigured halves of Kent's corpse, or his father's lifeless body. Most were scared and nervous. Some yelled at each other but all questioned which way to go.

Two redcoats came running down the slope then turned right. He leveled his pistol, took steady aim, led one precisely, and dropped him with a shot straight to his head. The other man reacted, darted left and he again leveled his pistol. The second redcoat, a big man with large dark eyes, stopped, frozen in fear. He lowered his aim, from the man's head to his soft, large belly and squeezed the trigger, gut-shot him on purpose. The heavy-set man stumbled into the snow, fell to his knees and stared at him unblinking with a look that asked, Why? Then he collapsed awkwardly on the downward slope, rolled onto his side and struggled to keep his head up but continued to press his gut, oozing blood.

He immediately felt guilty for the terribly wounded man, recalling the one time he had accidentally gut-shot a deer. He considered shooting this man in the head to put him out of his misery but he was stupefied as to why he had gut-shot him. Then the brisk air and staccato sound of muskets firing drew him back to the moment.

"*Fall back to the river!*" Falder shouted, raised his arm in a windmill motion, skipped backward and called out again, "*Back to the river!*"

"*Press on!*" he screamed and heard his own voice, which sounded shrill and high-pitched. He flexed his abdominal muscles, made his voice deeper, more commanding, and hollered again, "*This way! Forward!*"

Billy Caldwell moved left, gathered and organized some Hunters, mostly Mohawks, and attacked the fort. Other men between George and Billy stood motionless then chaos ensued. Each man ran in a different direction or worse, dropped their musket and raised their hands to surrender. Very few charged the fort, some fled to the side for the woods, but most surrendered or dashed back around the fallen, running down the slope toward the river. Those at the base of the fort stopped and looked back.

Nearby one young man, Andre Benson from the Ransom militia, turned and ran for the rear. George jammed his pistol into his belt and reached out for Benson, who was plump with snowy ice dotting his colorfully-striped white Mackinaw coat. He stopped Benson with both arms then shouted, "*Goddammit get up that hill!*"

Benson twisted and jerked away then continued running downhill for the riverbank. Falder raced ahead of Benson screaming, "*Retreat!*'

That last cry, along with most of the men running down the slope, took the attention of those remaining, including the Mohawks and Africans, and all joined in a full retreat. They dashed down the embankment, kicked up snow and went through the collapsed gate. Random British musket shots rang out, whizzed by, and hit some Hunters, or snapped into the wooden fence. Another cannon blast exploded in the field, 20 yards to the right and took several lives.

Then a column of red-coated soldiers rushed onto their left side, pouring through the opening gate of the fort. They formed a squad on the downward slope of the hill, rapidly gathered in two lines with the first line taking a knee and the second line standing tall in their vivid red uniforms, then leveled their muskets. A distant cry screamed over the snowy field, "*Present!*"

George dropped to the ground an instant before he heard the officer scream, "*Fire!*" Musket balls ripped through the Hunters, cutting down several in mid-stride, their bodies falling clumsily legs over torso, and piled across the declining snowy slope, splattering it with blood.

He stood quickly. Off to the side a man had collapsed to his hands and knees, and he cried out, "*Christ, I'm shot!*"

He dashed over the snowy field to the man, who lay on his side. Bright red blood came out of his side and he clutched at the hole in his coat then pressed his left hand to his side, trying in vain to keep the blood in his body. A round hole had pierced his buckskin coat, now stained deep purple and he had a wild panic in his eyes. "What's going to happen to me?"

George pressed his hand over the man's bloody hand, over the wound, and looked around for help. The few remaining men made their way down the hill and through the fence. He asked, "Can you stand?"

The man winced, "No, it hurts too much." Blood oozed from his mouth, he spat, then used the back of his hand to wipe it. Sweat dribbled from under his black hair then his dark eyes became relaxed and he said calmly, "I can stay here."

"*Like hell you can!*"

"No, it's soft. Let me be."

He heard a sharp command across the slope, "*Second line. . . Fire!*"

He dropped to the ground again and bullets pelted the earth around them. He pulled on the wounded man's right arm and shouted, "*Stand up!*"

The man had no choice but to hold his gut while George pushed with his legs, lifting the man under his good side and the man grunted when his body fell over his shoulder onto his back. He jogged down the gentle hillside with the man's heavy weight pounding on his back and into his thighs. He noticed no one remained fighting on this side of the fence and one of the last men heading for the opening stopped and looked back through the swirling snow. It looked like George Benedict, the tall, skinny kid from Burlington. Benedict squinted through his spectacles at him, carrying the wounded man, flopping on his back and waited a moment. Then Benedict went through the opening.

He thought, That cowardly son of a— Then he heard a shout beyond the fence and a moment later Benedict returned with three men and one was Bear Brisken. They raced through the opening and Brisken and the two others fired their muskets at the line of redcoats atop the slope. The soldiers returned fired with the first line again and shots peppered the field, splatted against the wooden fence but remarkably missed everyone.

Benedict ducked but held down his black, tri-cornered hat and dashed to him but George continued running and stumbling under the wounded man's awkward weight. Benedict said in a high-pitched, boy's voice, "Set him down."

He jogged on but looked at Benedict from under the man's buckskin coat and flopping arm. Thick flakes of snow stuck to Benedict's steel-rimmed glasses with his dark brown eyes searching.

He was very thin and appeared even younger than himself. He sized up Benedict's youthful skinniness and said, "No, I'm almost there."

He stumbled a few more strides, turned to find the gap of the fallen fence then lost his balance and collapsed in a heap. The wounded man cried out in pain, "*Christ almighty! You're trying to kill me!*"

Benedict leaned over the wounded man then clasped his hands in an open cradle and said, "We can lock hands under Gatridge and carry him like he's sitting in a swing."

Most of the redcoats now aimed at Brisken and the other two Hunters, who moved rapidly and shot at the long line of standing troops on the slope.

George crouched over, slid his hands under Gatridge's rump, found Benedict's hands, and clasped them. They easily lifted Gatridge then went sideways through the fence opening and made their way down the slope where a few Hunters had gathered, ramming in musket balls and preparing to fire but most continued fleeing for the river. Another snow squall blew and clusters of icy snowflakes swept over the field and enveloped the whole area in a storm of white.

He and Benedict moved jerkily with Gatridge, then found their rhythm and jogged more smoothly. The slope was easier now and they ran past thin frozen cherry trees, around the small pines and ferns, to the clearing at the river's edge and set down Gatridge. He and Benedict breathed heavily and he shook Benedict's strong, wiry hand then huffed, "Good."

“My pleasure, sir,” but Benedict, now hatless with dirty blonde hair, hurriedly released his handshake then adroitly ripped long strips of cloth to make a bandage. Benedict’s dark brown eyes focused on treating Gatridge under his dripping, wet spectacles. Benedict had fair skin, a long straight nose and rounded cheekbones accentuated his boyish face. He pulled up Gatridge’s coat then shirt, placed a gauze pad over the bloody wound, then wrapped a long bandage tightly around Gatridge’s waist.

George doubled over with his hands on his knees, caught his breath, and again thought of his father, still in the snow with his hollow eyes gazing at nothing. He collapsed backward and sat down hard. My God, he thought. Father’s dead.

His entire body echoed emptiness, tears formed in his eyes and stung in the cold crisp air. He wiped his cheeks but more tears dropped down. He wiped those away but more fell again and again. He did not want to cry, not now.

Gatridge squirmed with discomfort while Benedict secured the bandage with a straight pin. He had a dark beard with a gray woolen cap pulled over his dark hair and he gazed about the clearing, at the icy river, then saw him weeping and spoke with a snarl, “You ain’t shot. What’s wrong with you?”

“Shut up!” Benedict snapped, tugged down Gatridge’s coat over the bandage and said brusquely, “You’ll need your strength.”

Then Billy Caldwell came into the clearing along with several Hunters. Billy had two black streaks of greasepaint down his face on each cheek, wore a heavy buckskin coat and a beaver fur cap, and his shiny black hair was braided into a single chord. They were all breathing hard but Billy hollered, "*Reload!*"

George stood, looked for his musket then remembered he had dropped it by his father. He thought of running to get it, thought better, and pulled out his Colt revolver.

Billy rammed home a mini-ball, swiftly put powder in the pan then spoke strongly, "You six men," he pointed with two fingers, "take a position behind that fallen tree up there. Wait 'til you see them up close, then shoot. After that, fall back to the river. You five—" he pointed again, this time to his right, "—and me will form a group by those cherry trees over there. Everyone else, go to the boat landing where Stannard will form a defensive line."

"But my father—"

"*Go!*" The first squad of six dashed up the hill for the fallen tree and five others sprinted for the cherry trees. The rest of the militia ran for the riverbank landing but George grabbed Billy's buckskin coat with his free hand, pointed his revolver up the hill, and demanded, "My father is up there!"

Billy's dark, unflinching eyes held a shared pain. "I went to him when you helped Gatridge. I'm sorry. He's gone."

"I know!" He choked on tears, now thick in his throat. "But I can't leave him!"

"He's moved on. The Great Spirit has him." Billy glanced toward the boat landing, measuring the distance then said to Gatridge. "Can you walk?"

Gatridge answered feebly, "No."

“We’ll carry him,” Benedict said.

“Good.” Billy jogged toward the cherry trees but then stopped to look back and check on him. George stared up the hill in vain with his jugular vein throbbing in his neck and his temples pounding. Then Red-coated soldiers advanced in an impromptu attack, stumbling down the slope and Billy shouted, “*Go!*”

Benedict held out his thin, bony hands. George tucked away his revolver then reached under Gatridge to once again clasp hands with Benedict. They lifted Gatridge but his backside was wet and smelled foul. Gatridge made an embarrassed face and said, “Sorry.”

Benedict snapped, “I told you to shut up!”

They carried Gatridge along the riverbank to the boat landing, about 40 yards up the river. Snow gathered in drifts but the icy wind was a welcome break from the stench of Gatridge’s stained pants. They splashed through the water and plopped him down inside a row boat then returned to the shore. Benedict hollered, “*Form a defensive line!*”

George took a few steps off to the side, still within earshot, knelt on one knee, and thought of his father’s kind voice, his gentle way of patting him, assuring him, and the wisdom of so many things he had taught him. All gone. His mother had passed away years ago but he wanted to somehow tell her then thought, They’re together now. Father will be so happy. He realized he would need to tell his Aunt Amelia, his mother’s sister, but there was no other family and that thought stuck in him. No other family. Father is dead and no other family. Now what?

Gunfire popped from the Hunters' muskets in random staccato bursts. Two dozen men had gathered in one long line as Benedict had ordered. Doubleday stood tall near the middle but there were odd holes of five yards or more. George knew this wouldn't work as well as two syncopated lines, stood and yelled, "*Benedict!*"

Benedict sprinted from the far end of the line. Despite being young and skinny, he was very fast and yelled even before arriving, "*Yes, sir?*"

He wanted Benedict to tap every other man on the shoulder to form two alternating lines but realized there was *no time!* The redcoats were sixty yards away, streaming through the fence opening above them and advancing down the hill. The battle took place at dizzying speed and crucial time was lost in their chaotic retreat.

Benedict stared at him from under his wet glasses, ready to act, with his deep brown eyes stark against his fair skin. Both knew time was passing.

"Never mind. We must hold this ground!"

"Yes, sir!" Benedict looked at him oddly. They must hold here, that was a given, so there must be something else wrong but Benedict dismissed it, somehow knowing it was too much to explain.

George ordered, "Fortify the men! Hold this line!"

"Yes, sir!" He dashed back to anchor the far end of the line.

Billy Caldwell stood among the cherry trees and his deep voice was loud and clear. He had organized his band of six into a unit and they jogged in a controlled retreat with two men stopping every ten yards to stand amid the thin cherry trees to fire then fall back. The second group of six Hunters fell back away from the log and came downhill randomly, dashing for their single defensive line gathered by the boats.

"*Fill in the gaps!*" George yelled. Then it struck him there were far less than the 250 Hunters gathered yesterday and wondered, Where are all the others? Where was Commander von Schoultz? Dr. Côté? Then he thought again of the dead and wounded on the hill and looked around the landing site. Most of the boats and canoes were gone and Lieutenant Falder was nowhere in sight. Falder must have convinced Commander von Schoultz to retreat and had taken most of the men and boats. If these 30 men were all they had, so be it.

He thought of the windmill fort, obscured by thickly falling snow, and imagined soldiers streaming out the front gate. The redcoats may bring cavalry and cannons. Then the last Hunters from Billy's group fell back, incredibly smooth and organized, and continued to the boat landing in rhythm and fell in orderly.

George hollered, "*Hold your fire until my command!*"

No one spoke but the frigid air was filled with the sound of musket balls being dropped into gun barrels, metal rods ramming them down, followed by the sound of paper cartridges being ripped open for their powder. Mist pumped out of the men's mouths. He deepened his voice and boomed, "*Steady boys!*"

The redcoats trickled out of the snowy air in ones and twos, and reacted to their line of muskets pointed at them and came to a sliding, skidding stop with snow piling over their black boots. Some soldiers scrambled back, slipping uphill and struggling to keep their balance with their muskets. A brief opening formed in the snowstorm and up the hill a score more soldiers poured through the fence into the clearing, and the 12-pound gun in the blockhouse had been turned and was now pointing down at them.

"*On my command!*" he yelled. Some of the redcoats banded together and tried to form a line. A few shot at them and their mini balls whizzed through the air.

"*Fire!*" A withering blast of musket fire filled the air and about 15 redcoats fell, collapsing in their place in line. Other redcoats turned, ran uphill and created a jam for the opening in the fence, blocking the soldiers' path.

"*Reload!*" George hollered. "*Hold your fire until my command! Reload!*"

The remaining redcoats ran in assorted directions and sought cover on the open hillside. Several men dove behind the far side of the fallen tree and others pushed at one another, trying to be the single person behind a thin cherry tree.

"*Steady!*" he yelled. More soldiers jogged out of the fallen fence section, appeared stunned and confused, but stepped around their fallen comrades then scrambled off to the woods on either side.

"*Fire!*" Another blast of bullets ripped through the soldiers and more men fell. Those soldiers not hit now ran like scared animals, giving every ounce of energy to flee. Some leaped over the fallen and ran clumsily through the snow up the hill.

George picked out a tall, gangly soldier dressed in his redcoat uniform, stumbling up the hill. He leveled his revolver, squeezed the trigger, and the shot landed squarely in the soldier's back. The man crumpled to his knees then fell face-first into the snowy field.

"*Reload! Pick a target and fire when ready!*"

"*Stannard!*" Benedict screamed from the end of the line with his high, boyish voice, crisp in its urgency, "*Enough! They're retreating!*"

Billy Caldwell split up the Hunters in an orderly manner then assigned them to board the remaining canoes and boats. Billy's dark eyes flashed above the black greasepaint streaked on his cheeks, scanning the area and counting the remaining Hunters then assigned them to boats.

"*Fire!*" George hollered and assorted shots of musketry peppered the cold air. The very few redcoats standing in the clearing ran uphill frantically then some dove through the fence opening. "*Reload!*"

Billy Caldwell scurried about, pushing men toward their assigned rowboat and a few more into a long wide canoe, then many more into another long boat.

George squeezed his revolver tightly, then realized only a few Hunters remained at the river landing. The loaded boats were moving away. Benedict stepped into the last of two remaining boats, sat down and wiped off his glasses with a small tan kerchief. Then Billy was at his side and put his solid, muscular arm around him, pulling him toward the last weathered rowboat, which was painted a faded blue. One of the Hunters sat ready with oars in hand. The man had a scruffy brown beard and dark, bloodshot eyes. Beads of sweat rolled down his temples, down his neck and made his buckskin coat wet around the collar. Benedict said something to the rower, who scooted over, then Benedict tucked away his kerchief and took up one of the oars.

George looked toward the snow-enveloped fort, thinking of where his father lay, then reluctantly climbed in and sat in the bow. Billy, in his long-sleeve deerskin coat and leggings, pushed off then hopped in behind him. He turned over his revolver with his knuckles white around the handle and didn't want to let go. He felt Billy's hand patting his back and saying something but there was a high-pitched ringing in his ears. He didn't care what Billy said. It couldn't possibly matter. The ghastly image of his father was in front of him again with his bleeding skull torn open and his crimson blood spilling into the snow with his mouth open and his eyes a lifeless, milky white.

A distant blast sounded then a cannonball from the 12-pound gun splashed into the river, sprinkling his head with water. What a god-awful day, he thought. Father's dead and it's all my fault. Now what?

~ 5 ~

He was hunting deer with his father. They waited silently in the woods with a soft breeze on their face as Samuel had taught him and the moment was filled with thrilling anticipation. When would a buck appear? Now he would show his father how well he could hunt. This would make his father proud!

Then, there! A vague brown blur and a gentle rustling at the edge of the woods, followed by a brief shower of loose snow falling from a bush and from low branches. A great buck with a large rack of antlers stepped gingerly into the clearing, its big brown body moved smoothly then stopped and looked back to the trees, its bulky neck holding upright a huge thick rack of antlers, twelve or more, and then he turned and faced him. Each did not move or blink. Its dark round eyes tried to gain some recognition. It smelled, snorted, and gazed without panic but was intensely focused. He was strong, bright-eyed and magnificent.

He readied himself with shallow breathing and slowly raised his musket. Then it suddenly bounded sideways, raised its white tail and fled with huge leaps of 20 feet or more, flying left, then right in amazingly long strides, zigzag through the underbrush, then one last glimpse of its white tail when it leaped and disappeared into the forest.

He awoke with his heart pounding and it was pitch black. He had been worried about never waking again so it was a relief to be alive but where was he? Then he felt himself bouncing in a covered wagon and his vision adjusted. Sergeant Lloyd, an immense man with his heavy arms folded over his thick chest, sat by his side and leaned against the tenting. He snored with his mouth wide open amid his thick black beard.

It was very dark. Where were the horses? Charger? Then he felt his left hand being held and turned. Benedict sat on the other side and in the immense darkness a slight smile creased over Benedict's pallid face.

"It's okay," Benedict said. His dirty, dark-blonde hair was greasy and his thin lips were dried, flaking and cracked. He said, "We're heading back to Washington City where you'll get better care. I'm sorry."

Benedict stopped and tears welled up in his dark brown eyes under his glasses then dripped down over his rounded cheeks.

He had an ungodly thirst and his mouth felt pasted shut. He tried to sit up but he couldn't move and the effort exhausted him. The wagon jostled over the bumpy road then Benedict choked out some words, "Doc had to take it."

He replied dryly, Take what? He thought he had said the words then realized his mouth didn't move with his lips parched together. He tried to convey the thought with his eyebrows pursed together: What?

Although he didn't speak he noticed Benedict was very upset, but why? He felt very groggy, similar to the morning after he had some of his neighbor James Lonegran's backwoods pop skull and ended up with an extremely bad hangover. His whole body felt numb yet he was somehow comfortable in spite of the hard jouncing of the wagon. Yes, his whole body felt wonderfully fine.

His thoughts returned to how his father had died, and how his pain and guilt had remained. It was his fault. If he hadn't pleaded to go, his father would still be alive.

~ ~

Through the harsh winter and into the cold spring following the Canadian expedition George felt horrible about his father's death. He often went for long walks, using the old footpath to cross the pasture, up the hill, where it first passed through open woods of oak, poplar, elm and pine then cut closer to the larger hill where timber somehow remained uncut with immense trees of white pines mixed in with hemlock and spruce. The path disappeared on more rocky soil covered with dead leaves and pine needles. An occasional huge tree lay felled by storm or old age, often pointing southwest as a result of Nor'easters. He found a peaceful rhythm in walking through his father's woods, now his. He continued uphill through the forest until he came to an opening, where the sun poured onto a small grassy clearing. He slowed for the last few steps then knelt next to the mound of his mother's grave. A simple stone marker read

Rebecca P. Stannard
(1786 – 1827)

He thought of his father, of how he should be alive, of how he had abandoned his body in a foreign land but mostly he felt a consuming, terrible guilt. Sometimes after crying he would relax in the serenity and comfort of the silence. This isolated clearing, surrounded by whispering pines, was his devout cathedral.

He recalled his father's wisdom, gazed about the idyllic clearing, and heard Samuel's soft, strong voice, "Someday it'll come to you. This is where your mother and I loved each other most openly, prayed for you. Never be afraid. Be bold and mighty forces will come to your aid."

Sometimes he thought of what his parents had expected of him and his life now. His meditation always had a simple answer. He was on his own.

He also thought of Billy Caldwell and wondered what had happened to him after the battle near Prescott? If it wasn't for Billy's expertise, more Hunters would have been killed. After the Hunters had returned to Ogdensburg, he recalled seeing Billy at a distance but then someone had told him to go home. It was all a blur and he was in shock. Yes, it was Lieutenant Falder, with a nervous shiftiness in his eyes, who had said something about home. Someone had told him the Hunters had suffered 53 dead, 61 wounded and 136 captured, which he wrote down. The battle itself had been a dizzying whirlwind with Commander von Schoultz among the captured and its result was a complete and devastating loss. He retrieved their mare Diana from the blacksmith Uno Agnello, took six dollars for the sold muskets, and went home in a daze.

He recalled Billy's passion for freedom, for the runaway slaves, for the Canadians, and for his Mohawk people. He figured Billy was fighting for someone, somewhere, but where? What had happened to Billy?

He also thought of Dr. Côté. He had not seen Dr. Côté since the gathering in the field before the Hunters attacked the fort at Prescott. He searched his father's papers, found a few letters from Dr. Côté, and wrote a letter to him at the address in Montreal. He explained how his father had been killed in the battle and asked how was his health? He closed by stating it would be grand if he could manage to come visit and to once again ask him, "Who's back?" Dr. Côté did not reply.

He also thought of the British-Canadian soldiers he had killed in the battle, especially the heavy-set man he had gut shot. How long did he suffer? What was his life like before he took it? Did he have a wife or children? Brothers or sisters? Parents?

It was his burden to sit in the woods and think these solemn thoughts. He sat through frigid weather as a penance for his guilt. As time passed he also became more uncomfortable with his idleness. He had 22 horses, 14 chickens, and four cows to feed and care for, and there were people who needed supplies from Samuel's Trading Post. The quiet times in his father's woods became less frequent.

He also kept up with his fellow militiamen and dedicated himself to the Ransom Guards, which became his new family. It was an odd sensation to be involved with a group tied to his father's death but these were his best friends. After the battle in Prescott, they shared a bond of brotherhood beyond friendship. Many would give all they had, including their life for him, and he would do the same for them.

The Canadian Rebellion fizzled out and there would be no war or military action. Still the Ransom Guards practiced for the event of war. Also, because he felt guilty he should have done more to prevent his father's death, including the execution of the battle plan and their chaotic retreat, he immersed himself in the study of warfare.

The Ransom Guards simplified warfare into two parts—preparing for battle and being in a fight. Preparing for battle required every man to know how to march in columns, how to close ranks, turn as a group, ride horses into skirmishing fire, shoot targets while standing and firing while riding on horseback, how to choose terrain, and how to use it to advantage. The fighting portion covered all known kinds of combat including hand-to-hand without weapons, the use of knives both long and short, the bayonet, swords both broad and narrow, pikes, staffs, pistols of every make and kind, and muskets. They drilled with two canons but rarely fired them to save ammunition. He also practiced his marksmanship frequently, sometimes twice a day.

Being in the Ransom Guards strengthened his friendship with George Benedict, Thad "Bear" Brisken, his neighbors Theodore Girod and James Lonegran but he also made many new friends including Charles Haskell of Wethersfield, Lucius Dickinson from Cavendish, the Ripley family from Rutland, Francis Randall of Montpelier, and Abner Doubleday of Saratoga Springs. In addition, he came to respect their new militia commander Colonel William Smith, who was 20 years his senior with an extensive military background. Colonel Smith had recently moved into the area but he had been schooled at West Point, the nation's military academy. Smith admired George's enthusiasm and gave him many of his military books and manuals to study, and spent hours answering his many questions.

George worked longer hours and relied on the knowledge his father had taught him to run the trading post and the farm. Even though he was young, he also became an expert at teaching horses.

He then showed his father's techniques, now his, to many neighbors and he gained a very good reputation for selling fine, well-trained horscs.

In all his years he and his father had never had any difficulty delivering a colt but that streak was broken the following autumn with a dark mare named Midnight. It was a clear, chilly October night and Midnight was still laboring after two hours. When it began, George called on his neighbor James Lonegran and his son Tommy. They spread a lot of hay around the stall, under Midnight, and washed their hands in very hot water, which took a few minutes to prepare. Lonegran's youngest son Timothy ran to the house of another neighbor, Theodore Girod, who came over despite the lateness of the hour. In the glow of two hurricane lamps George and his neighbors labored with Midnight. At first it appeared all would go smoothly then it was clear the colt was breach. After two hours of twisting, pushing, aiding, and pulling, then more firmly pulling with a looped chain, the newborn colt slid onto the bloody hay. The colt was white and appeared healthy. Midnight stomped, nuzzled, and licked it. The colt stumbled but stood on shaky legs with its white coat streaked with blood. It stepped on skittish, thin legs and fell again but stood quickly, looked around, then stepped under Midnight and nursed.

James Lonegran smiled with pride and slapped him on the back then Theodore Girod winked and made a clacking noise in approval. The boys Tommy and Timothy Lonegran gaped with awe. A few horses neighed from distant stalls, perhaps smelling the afterbirth, and seemed to understand some deep meaning of new life.

A chill raced over his spine for this wondrous moment and he felt connected to the farm. This was his calling. It was what he was meant to do with his life.

The next morning he checked on Midnight and the white colt. Both were fine. He did the farm chores and opened the Trading Post, then the following Saturday he trained with the Ransom Guards. His life had a routine but after the birth of this white colt, this brilliant new creature, he examined his life. He felt he needed to do much more than farm chores, to care for, train, and sell horses, and to run Samuel's Trading Post. He discovered he needed to be more involved with his community but how?

In November the mayor of St. Albans, Enos Littlefield, came to discuss an opportunity. Mayor Littlefield was a heavy, rotund man with round spectacles and he wore an old-fashioned powdered wig to remind everyone he was a lawyer. Littlefield approached on foot while George walked Midnight around the riding ring with a line and, as planned, the white colt followed them and learned he was the leader.

Mayor Littlefield gave a deep formal bow, shook hands then placed his thumbs in his vest and began with exaggerated pomp, "It is with extreme importance I call on you today Mister Stannard! Our schoolteacher moved with her family to Nevada in search of gold. Or perhaps it was California in search of silver. Or maybe the other way around. Well, regardless, Mrs. Ingraham left so quickly no one got the story straight!"

He looped the line to Midnight around a fence post and brushed her while Mayor Littlefield paced outside the ring. He stopped brushing and looked at the Mayor, who then gave grand motions like he was presenting final arguments to a jury.

"And so I ask of you, George Stannard, would you yourself, or do you know of anyone well-qualified, who would consider teaching our fair children?"

He wondered if he was "well-qualified." He knew how to read and write, he had been through school but he had never taken any advanced classes at the university in Burlington. Then he thought of his neighbors and none of them had any teaching experience. "I'll consider it but being away from the Trading Post will hurt business." He thought more and said, "I suppose I could close the Trading Post in the winter. It's slower then. But then again, that's when people need supplies desperately."

"Yes, yes. Point taken!" Mayor Littlefield's gray eyes flashed with enthusiasm under his wire spectacles then he waved his short arms for effect. "But! If they need them, as you propose they do, is it not true they will be able to find you," he pointed a single, stubby finger at him, "and then buy their supplies?"

"Yes, people could search for me, or they could go to Brownell's General Store in St. Albans."

The Mayor ignored this point, again tucked his thumbs into his vest so his short, stubby fingers stuck out, then adjusted his white wig and summed up his case, "Our children need a teacher!"

He felt he was being judged and thought for a few moments. He realized he didn't have anything in his life that couldn't temporarily be put on hold, or anyone who needed him daily. His horses were his chief concern but he could care for them very early, then very late in the day. He decided out of a sense of duty. "I'll do it for the children."

That same day he tacked a sign on the door of Samuel's Trading Post, "Closed for the Season" with a note explaining he could be found at the schoolhouse in St. Albans. The following Monday, on the first day of class, he did not hear the crowing cock in the coop 20 yards away. Sunlight shone through the icy windowpane and lit his bedroom. He hugged the warm quilt and rolled over. It was unusually cold and the warmth of the bed was comforting.

Then he opened his eyes wide, realized he had not heard the rooster crowing, the sun was up and he was still in bed! He quickly rose, pulled on his pants over his long johns and made his way into the main room. He knelt by the Franklin stove and carefully placed tiny shreds of tinder underneath the maple kindling. From the tin box nearby, he took a wooden match, struck it solidly then held flame to the tinder until it caught, moved the match, it caught again, and the wood burned. He closed the stove, paused to warm his hands above it, thought of his father and remembered a line of poetry,

Love comes and warms the soul, even for unseen deeds

He rubbed his hands together and put a small kettle of water on the stove, pulled on his black leather boots that came up to his knee, and stepped back into his room. The white marble-topped oak dresser his grandmother had brought from Suffield held his neatly pressed shirts and he took out one, buttoned it up then looked at himself in the faded mirror. His dark hair stuck up in back. He licked his hand, wiped it down several times, remembered how his mother did this when he was a small boy then brushed it for good measure. He went back into the main room where the Franklin stove popped with life and warmed the room nicely.

He took his heavy woolen coat off a peg by the door, swiftly buttoned it, grabbed a dark blue woolen hat, and stepped outside. It was snowing thickly with over one foot of snow on the ground. No wonder he hadn't heard the rooster!

He pulled down the knit hat over his ears and plowed his way through the snow to the outhouse. He had left his woolen mittens in the house by the door, he didn't need them yesterday, but decided to carry on. A drift of about 16 inches covered the base of the outhouse door and he used his boot to scrape it away. Inside, he hiked his coat, undid his clothes, and relieved himself. He glanced at the leather-bound Pilgrim's Progress on the shelf but knew there wasn't time plus it was cold. He buttoned up again and waded through the snow to the barn. Another small drift was in front of the door but he undid the latch and used his strength to wedge it open. He took a large armful of hay and spread it in the feeding trough then repeated it eight more times for the 23 horses. Then he gently opened Midnight's stall with the white colt and stroked Midnight with his palm tenderly and whispered, "Hey there, mama, easy," then he slowly went to the colt, offered his open palm as a friendly cue, and patted its neck softly. Its large eyes rolled to the side and examined him. He spoke softly, "How are you today little fella?"

He again offered his left hand to show no harm and stroked the colt's white nose, jowls, and reached into his coat pocket where he had placed a carrot from last night's dinner. The colt munched it from his palm, finished it, stepped forward, and nudged him affectionately with his poll.

"Hey, boy! You're a charger, aren't you?" he smiled. “Hm, that's not a bad name. Charger." The frisky colt bobbed his head twice then whinnied. "Charger it is!"

He spread more hay among the stalls then made sure the doors were all closed, latched, and milked the four cows rapidly while considering trading away three, this was too much work, then went outside into the falling snow. Another inch of snow had fallen in the doorway. He carried the tall milk churn to the house porch, put his hands in his pockets and made his way to the chicken coop, where he fed 14 hens and gave a stern glance at the parading rooster, gathered eggs and carefully rested them in his deep coat pockets. When he was leaving the coop, the rooster crowed.

"It's a little late in the day for that, Mister Redbeard!" He chuckled, made his way back through the snow to the house, made sure the tin milk churn was tightly sealed, and took off his woolen hat. Inside he imagined his father sitting in the wooden chair by the stove, reading the Bible, and heard his voice, "You better hurry. They're waiting for you!"

"I know, father." The kettle whistled and he used an iron hook to take it off the stove, set the eggs in a basket, picked up a bowl of oats off the table and poured in some hot water then immediately shoveled the hot oatmeal into his mouth. He thought of his father looking at him sternly, bowed his head and said, "God bless this food I am receiving—" blew twice on the hot oatmeal, dropped in some dried cherries and took another bite, "—and for all Thy gifts. Amen."

He gobbled down his breakfast, made sure the fire was out, again threw on his dark blue cap and mittens, picked up his satchel stuffed with books and papers by its leather strap, slung it over his shoulder but before he left he stood by the door and thought of his father again, sitting by the Franklin as he did so often, warming his hands around a cup of coffee in his large maple rocker now empty. When he was younger he sometimes wondered what to say to him but he had never expressed any words of appreciation.. "Father, I love you."

He imagined tears of happiness brimming in Samuel's kind brown eyes, the same tears of happiness that glistened when he told stories of his mother. He could hear his father responding, "I know. Now, git! You're late and good folks are waiting on you!"

He made his way through the piling snow to the barn and saddled Fern, a strong mare with a dark coat. He gathered some oats, his canteen, and headed out. Thick clumps of snow fell and the green boughs of pine trees hung heavy with glistening white snow. The road was pristine without a trace of any creature.

The heavy falling snow obscured the view of Grand Isle in the distance. The road stretched past Lonegran's farm, wound around Bengston's field of barren apple trees then down the small hill past Waite's farm. From there it was six miles to St. Albans.

Fern pushed through the shin-high snow and after two hours came to the main village green of St. Albans covered in a deep blanket of snow. On the northern edge was the one-room schoolhouse, where children filed through the door. It was a relief to see them because the weather was especially bad, even for November. He dismounted, tethered Fern to a post, unrolled his saddle blanket and spread it over her. He poured water from his canteen into a shallow pan, let Fern drink for a few moments then stroked her neck and fed her a pocketful of oats.

Inside the old schoolhouse were six rows of pews donated from the First Congregational Church, four small chairs, a larger chair and table for him, lesson books, a willow switch and a kerosene lantern for dark cloudy days. A large boy piled wood into small stove in the corner. George said, "That's fine, thank you! What's your name?"

"Orley Lloyd, sir." The boy was on one knee on the worn wooden floor then stood. He was very tall, hefty already, and offered a good-natured, infectious smile.

"I'll be your teacher," he said.

"Yes, sir, Mister Stannard." Lloyd had coarse black hair and pale white skin with freckles that was typical of his Black Irish heritage.

"Orley, how old are you?"

"Sixteen next April, sir." Lloyd was a big kid, polite, and smiled often.

Only a few years younger than me, he thought. "You don't need to call me 'sir.' Mister Stannard is fine."

There were many eager, young faces and he counted them quickly. Fifteen children were here, many of them politely seated at their desks and ready to embrace the world of learning despite the sudden early snowfall. Most of them were ready but some needed guidance, like Jimmy Freehan, who picked his nose and tried to wipe it in Megan Bailey's hair, who squealed and squirmed away.

Crack! He slapped the willow stick across his boot. "James Freehan! Would you like to begin today's lesson?"

"No," Jimmy laughed with a devious grin then wiped his finger on his pants. "No, I wouldn't!"

He realized he had made his first mistake. He had asked a student to do something instead of telling them what to do. His next order was clear and loud, "Multiplication tables, twos. Begin! One times two is two; two times two is. . ."

Orley Lloyd joined in and led the class with a deep but warbling voice. The students responded and even Jimmy Freehan joined. He handed some matches from the desk drawer to Lloyd, who lit a fire in the old stove. He smiled with pride at the class but knew hard work lay ahead. Most of the children stared at him, making him aware these students were already his, wholly and unquestioned. He looked back to Lloyd, who warmed his hands over the Franklin while his gray-blue eyes gazed dreamily into space while repeating the lesson. He wondered, What is Orley Lloyd thinking? How could he encourage each student to do their best? To be a fine person, to help their family, or help the state? Suddenly teaching became a mission he enjoyed.

He taught school in the winter, ran the Trading Post when people needed supplies, tended to the horses and farm as needed, practiced his marksmanship daily and trained with the Ransom Guards militia. All suffered a little but he knew he was growing. The town paid him a small salary for teaching but it was not nearly as much money as was lost in business at the Trading Post so in the spring he took a job at the foundry in St. Albans. A few of the horses, Ariel, Dancer, and Neptune became more skittish, although each had always been high-strung and needy, but they still performed well as partners, working together to accomplish any task he asked. He traded three cows to Colonel Smith for his library of military books, which he studied at night, and a small keg of ammunition and two antique muskets from the Revolutionary War. One chicken stopped laying eggs and another hen was lost to a fox but the following morning in the early blue light of dawn he used his Enfield musket and took down the fox with a single shot.

He learned he enjoyed serving his community. It left him tired and proud yet he wanted to do more for his friends and neighbors. He was so busy he rarely had time to hike through the woods but on one long walk he realized he was no longer young. In the blink of an eye, seven years had vanished in his busyness. He was a man of 25 but also realized something more important than his youthfulness was missing. Despite all the people he knew, he felt very lonely. He recalled his father's advice, which he had said often, "Marry a good woman and you'll be happy for the rest of your life."

Because of his increasingly demanding job at the foundry in St. Albans, where he was promoted to foreman, he had very little free time. Also, he knew almost everyone in the county and most of the young women were married. With each passing day he thought more often of his loneliness and decided to do something about it.

First he courted Catherine Wilhite, from north of St. Albans. She spoke continually of her first husband, who had died in a farm accident with a thrasher. Every time he was with Catherine, he felt her deceased husband stood between them.

Next George met Nancy Pells at church, although her family lived well north of St. Albans, near the Canadian border. Nancy had a very pretty face and loved to yodel, which she had learned from her grandparents who had raised sheep in the mountains of Austria. After a few meetings Nancy left home to study opera at Dartmouth College, where she wore boy's clothes and acted as a young man.

His next courtship was with his second cousin Winona Kellar, at the insistence of Mayor Littlefield. Winona was very plain and smelled of naphtha and underarm odor. After their first meeting, he wrote her a polite note and never called on her again.

Next he met Winona's cousin, Berthe, who was downright ugly with screwed up eyes, buckteeth and foul breath that smelled like a dead possum. With such unsightly cousins, he began to doubt his memory of his mother being beautiful.

Because of his awful experiences in courting women around the hamlet of Georgia and the village of St. Albans, he decided to take his Aunt Amelia's advice from her letter and would travel 20 miles south to Burlington, where she lived and knew eligible young women. It was his first visit to Burlington by himself.

~ ~

Burlington was enormous compared to the hamlet of Georgia, Vermont, and dwarfed the town of St. Albans. It was a grand city with broad avenues, where several coaches and horses with riders could easily pass, and more horses stood at hitching posts. Only a few large trees dotted the avenues. The timber men had cleared out the entire area long ago. Many buildings were clustered around the common green including several hotels, four banks, three blacksmith shops, six dry goods stores, an assortment of retailers selling tobacco, wine, hard liquor and dairy goods of milk and cheese. Farmers set-up makeshift tents around the green and sold their goods off their wagons loaded with corn, beets, carrots, flowers or eggs. More wide avenues held a few shabby boarding houses, three little grocery shops, two attorney's offices, and a number of restaurants and saloons that served clerks, lumbermen, farmers and ironworkers who flooded the growing city. A newly constructed opera house hosted traveling minstrel shows in a new theater on Church Street, where companies came to perform with famous stars Joe Jefferson, Charlotte Cushman, Edwin Forrest, or Edwin Booth. College Street had a few university buildings and a library but also a newspaper office. Many people strolled up and down the walkways, through the large common green and discussed politics or fashion under the few tall elms the timber companies had spared.

George walked leisurely through the common green and stepped up to the large gazebo where a poster advertised a traveling theater group performing *Hamlet*. The troupe of performers, The Essex Players, had "Bravo!" reviews from the New York *Herald Tribune* and would perform in Burlington on its way to Montreal this Saturday eve.

He was impressed by the number of buildings surrounding the green and more than 20 people were walking about! Carriages whizzed by without any warning from the driver calling out "Hey there!" or "Watch out!" Where were all these people going?

He noticed a lawyer's office across the green and thought of the attorney who came to the Trading Post when his father died. He stood in the shade of the gazebo and noticed a young couple sitting on a bench under the shade of two very large elm trees. He plucked a long stem of grass from near the steps of the gazebo and placed it in his mouth. Then two young women strolled by in large flowing dresses with big bonnets and one of them stared at him. She had dazzling blue eyes and coyly blinked above her lace fan. She paused, placed her white-gloved hand on her friend's forearm and fluttered her fan. Because he did not know what this meant, he simply nodded. She lowered her fan and smiled then the second woman glided over to him. She wore a white cotton dress with pink trim and curtsied demurely. She had small features but when she spoke her poor teeth had gaps and went in odd directions. She said, "Beautiful weather we're having."

George politely took off his floppy felt hat, removed the stem of grass from his mouth and examined the partly cloudy sky. A line of clouds hung near the horizon, sliding over the tops of the Adirondack Mountains across Lake Champlain. "Yes, but it may rain tonight. Of course, I may be wrong. I don't see any cows lying down."

The young women turned to each other and snickered with glee, and then he realized his ridiculous comment and flushed. He had not seen *any* cows in Burlington.

The pretty one with bright blue eyes, who had been holding back, again smiled sweetly then turned and walked toward the marketplace with waltz-like steps. He hoped she would turn to look at him but she cooed, "Come along, Hazel."

"Oh my!" Hazel said. Her small gray eyes stared fondly at him then she hustled away and called out, "Helen, did you ever hear such a thing about cows?"

Hazel caught up to Helen, who strolled toward the market area. He tugged on his hat, threw down the grass, went to the top steps of the gazebo, and watched the two women parade through a row of lean-to tents. They stopped to examine assorted bars of soap and candles then approached a cart of fresh-cut flowers. Hazel gazed at a bunch of dark red roses, picked them up then replaced them on the cart. Helen, the one with dazzling blue eyes, admired many flowers, first the daisies then tulips and black-eyed susans, then she lingered on the irises, gazing at the variety of yellow, blue or purple flowers. Helen touched the petals then lifted a single blue iris, delicately stroked it across her cheek then bent over to smell the bouquet but Hazel said something. Helen replaced the flower and they suddenly left the flower stand.

He watched them until he could not see them in the crowd and then the young couple on the park bench caught his attention. They were not speaking but their faces were very close to each other. The young woman giggled and blushed, then the young man leaned over and kissed her on the lips!

He could not believe he had seen such behavior! He cleared his throat loudly and knocked his boot against the top step of the gazebo but they did not stop kissing! He walked down the steps, away from them and toward the marketplace then glanced back over his shoulder. They were still kissing!

In the market he passed by the soap vendor, nodded to a man in a black derby selling cigars, then went to the flower stand, where he examined the various beautiful flowers before picking up the same blue iris Helen had admired. Its intricate petals were vibrant blue with golden stripes in the middle leading to the pistil. He stroked its soft petals and introduced himself to the portly florist, who responded, "I'm Abigail Linton, thank you kindly. I'm saving me money to open a proper shop."

He bought the sole blue iris and said, "Mrs. Linton, keep the dollar for your store!"

"Aw, that's right kind of you, Mister Stannard. I know yer Aunt Amelia, dear lady. Would ya kindly give her my regards when you give her this flower?"

He flushed because he had intended to give the flower to the pretty young woman, Helen, not his Aunt. He smiled, touched his floppy hat, and nodded goodbye then walked briskly to his Aunt Amelia's house, which was just off the common green.

Amelia lived in a small, two-room wooden house with a short porch. He rapped on the white door and she answered before he finished knocking. Aunt Amelia was very pretty but shorter than he remembered with auburn hair, dark brown eyes, and the same high cheekbones and quick smile he remembered in his mother. She spoke with enthusiasm, "Well, well, well! Georgie! So good to see ya again! Come in, come in!"

"Mrs. Linton sends her regards," he smiled and entered. Aunt Amelia's house smelled of spices and sauces, and dried herbs hung near the fireplace. The front room was spotless with a small table and chairs, and yellow and blue ribbons and bows hung from doorframes with a mirror by the front door. A calico cat rubbed itself against his leg and he bent over to pet it.

"Isn't Chessie sweet?" Amelia closed the door, he stood up from the cat, and she gave him a big hug. "Ooh, I see you bought a flower! Are you courting someone special?"

He blushed then felt he was being silly. "Well, I've seen someone I like but I don't know anything about her."

"Who is she?"

"I don't know," he smiled, trying to cover his awkwardness. "But maybe you know of her. But what do I do? How do I court her in Burlington?"

Amelia smiled broadly and winked. "You've come to the right place, Georgie."

"Please, call me George."

"Right you are, right you are! You're a full-grown man now, yes indeedy! And you've filled out quite nicely, sir!" She patted his muscular shoulders then squeezed his arms. "How is it you're so big? It can't be from teaching!"

Amelia laughed good-naturedly then motioned to the table, where he carefully set down the iris then sat. She poured tea into his cup, opened a blue-and-white sugar pot and plopped in a cube with another wink of her eye. "One? Two?"

"One is fine."

"Aye, because you're already so sweet! Right you are, right you are!"

"I've been working at the foundry a lot," he smiled then looked closely at his Aunt's face. Her skin was wrinkled and she wore a lot of powder with rouge high on her rounded cheeks. Her blue eyes were soft gray, not sky-blue like his mother's, but she was warm and kind. He wanted to know more about his mother but decided he would ask later. "School is out and I've been working at the foundry in St. Albans. I'm foreman now."

"I didn't know! Congratulations! You need to visit more often. You're staying for dinner, aren't you? I can make a pot roast."

"I'm staying at the Champlain Inn on Front Street," he said, wanting to keep some independence from her.

"Ah, Mrs. Ladd is a friend of mine and the Champlain Inn is nice." Amelia winked again, "But you can't beat my pot roast!"

He thought of Amelia's delicious pot roast with potatoes, carrots, stewed tomatoes, celery, onions, herbs and spices, and then realized Amelia's cooking used the same recipes as his mother's cooking. "That's true! Yes, I'll be back for dinner. I'd like to talk more about my mother, too, if that's okay."

Amelia smiled broadly then nodded yes several times. She poured hot tea into her blue-and-white porcelain cup then set down the matching pot on a thick, carved rose trivet, pulled her chair close to him and patted his knee once. "Now! Who's the lucky lady?"

"I think her name is Helen. I've only seen her. I spoke with her friend Hazel but Helen has dark hair and very pretty blue eyes."

"Ah-h-h, the fair Helen! My, you don't waste any time! And you go right for the bulls-eye, don't you!" He noticed how easy it was to speak with Amelia, who was lively and smiled warmly. "If it's the same Helen I'm thinking of, you've picked a peach!"

Then Amelia smirked and her self-satisfaction made him wonder, Was she enjoying this, or was she simply happy to offer mother-like advice? "So, you do know her?"

"Yes, indeedy! Everyone knows Helen. She's the prize of the county!" she leaned over to share a secret, "But the problem is, she knows it! Oh, she catches all the fellas's eye. Some say her father is an Austrian Count!" She chuckled loudly. She *was* enjoying this. "Or is he a Polish Count?"

"Hmm?"

"Well, he's a Count and that's all that counts!"

They laughed together. He drank the sweet dark tea, thought of who this mysterious Helen was, and listened closely to his Aunt's advice on how to court a lady, which were the fashionable events, and how to promenade with her through the common green. He imagined a lovely world where he and Helen were the toast of Burlington, although he wasn't sure why it mattered if she was a Countess or not. He had read of royalty in books and wondered, Did royalty still exist in America? In Vermont?

Then they spoke for hours about his mother, Rebecca. He was grateful to have his Aunt's advice, thrilled to hear more stories about his mother but it became late afternoon and he wanted to explore Burlington more and freshen up at the Champlain Inn before returning for dinner. He stood to say goodbye and reached for the blue iris but Amelia scooped up the flower then magically pulled a straight pin from her sleeve, slid the iris into his boutonnière, and pinned it to his lapel. She smiled at him and winked. "There! Now, you'll catch *all* the ladies' eye, George!"

He smiled fondly for her warm spirit and contagious confidence. Then he thought of Helen's beautiful smile and her bright blue eyes. Was she truly a Countess? When would he see her again? And would she allow a visit from a simple boy from the country?

~ 6~

He awoke to a hammer banging on nails. It was early morning, the sun angled through the nearby window, and across the aisle a large man in a gray suit visited with a wounded soldier. A wide-brimmed sombrero was tucked under his arm and he moved to another bedside, spoke kindly to another soldier then continued on with his charming grace, leaving a wake of smiles on the wounded. With some he sat down, took out pencil and paper, and wrote a letter for them. He was a stout, slow-moving fellow with a puffy white beard and thick, heavy-lidded eyes. After visiting with each man he offered a gift. To one man he gave an orange, to another some horehound candy, to Captain Male in the bed next to his, he gave some coins for the fresh milk vendor who would come later in the morning. Then he approached his bed, bent his large body over him, and said, "How are you feeling, general?"

"I've seen better days," his throat was parched dry. "I'll be fine."

"That you will. I read of your bravery at Fort Harrison, sir. It's a privilege to meet you. I'm Walt Whitman." He wore a sprig of cedar in his lapel buttoner and poured water from a blue pitcher into a tin cup then raised it to his mouth for him to drink. George took in the cool, refreshing water with Whitman's pale face inches above him. His worn, wrinkled skin was robustly scented with perfume and his light eyes twinkled brightly.

He nodded he'd had enough water and sat upright. "The pleasure's mine, Mister Whitman. I've read your *Leaves of Grass*. It's a fine book. I hope you haven't listened to your critics."

"I've had critics everywhere I've been and in every job I've had. If I listened to them, I'd still be suckling my mother's teat! Critics would say I did that wrong, too!"

They both laughed and the brisk movement caused a shooting pain to flash through his chest and right side. He clenched his eyes then gradually eased them open. Whitman's puffy face was over him, looking down with gentle concern. Then his soft, rosy hand touched his cheek tenderly and caressed his hair.

Outside the window the hammering banged on and he asked, "What's that noise?"

Whitman whispered, "It's the coffin maker. He's been busy with the recent battles but pay him no heed. He's as daft as my critics!"

"Has the news been bad?"

Whitman raised his white eyebrows. "It's often bad. Even when it's 'good' it's terrible. But Lincoln will steer us through. Would you like some pickles?"

"No, thank you." He thought of asking about the Vermonters but remained silent.

Whitman looked like a Southern planter with gentle manners but his straight talk and tender ways were different. He tapped two fingers to his thick lips and thought, then rummaged through his haversack. "An apple? They're quite good. Tasty 'Ben Davis' apples. I picked them myself yesterday. Here."

Whitman placed an apple on the table between his bed and Captain Male's, who lay on his side grinning. The bright red apple had a yellow streak near its stem and the sun's rays shining through the window made it glow majestically.

"Oh, thank you." He felt a powerful emotion both profound and complex. This was something more than a kind soul giving him a gift. He felt in some miraculous way this was a divine spirit from God, his own guardian angel. He didn't know how to respond and swallowed hard then a tear rolled over his cheek. He said, "I'll have it later."

"Atta boy. Your father would be ver-r-r-ry proud of you, sir."

Another tear rolled over his cheek. Whitman rose, gave a solemn bow all in one motion, and was off to the next soldier's bed across the aisle. The whole event reminded him of a well-performed theatrical play. This character had entered his downtrodden world, made a dramatic yet simple and kind gesture, and moved gracefully to the next scene. It was very like the theater. He ignored Captain Male's voice, closed his eyes and thought of the first time he attended a play, so long ago.

~ ~

Hundreds of well-dressed people crowded into the Burlington Theater for the Saturday evening performance of *Hamlet*. The cost of a ticket was an extravagant 75 cents. Each man wore their best suit and the ladies wore imported silk dresses with fine lace adornments, or crisp cotton dresses with tiny floral prints, with an assortment of beautiful, astonishing hats with wide brims highlighted with a fresh-cut flower or feather, plus the requisite fan by their side. There was an entire language to the opening or closing of the fan, a fluttering flirtation or a snapping shut, and each action was an unmistakable wordless signal. A few patrons held opera glasses and gazed about the auditorium.

George noticed most of the people watched other people with excitement and anticipation. From his seat on the main floor, he looked to the balcony and was awed by many couples in beautiful gowns and tuxedos or fine suits. From their high advantage, they looked down on the commoners in the cheaper seats with an air of interested disdain.

The crowd settled into their seats and the lights dimmed. Two guards in uniform appeared on stage, followed by a thin man in a black leotard, and the audience gave a rousing applause. The actor, Radcliffe Thames, was well known in England and had traveled to the United States to study with the famous Booth brothers, who were hailed as the world's greatest Shakespearean actors.

The actors on stage began their performance. They spoke eloquently but gave an eerie foreboding of events to come. George thought of the current political climate, of pro-slavery and abolitionists fighting in Kansas, of talk of secession or war, and nodded at the timeliness of the play. A musical instrument produced a chilling sound with vibrato followed by a dark illusion on stage. Then a growing commotion took the audience and the play stopped. A spectacular entrance was being made but not on the stage. Everyone gazed up to the balcony. It was *her!* Helen and Hazel made their way to their balcony box and they wore extravagant silk gowns, large hats with lots of feathers, and each had a fur boa and long white gloves.

Everyone stared at Helen, the Countess. Her blue silk dress was stunning with a very low breast line that emphasized her well-endowed cleavage. She turned to the main auditorium to allow everyone the opportunity to view her grand entrance, her royal blue dress, and even her friend Hazel gave a slight curtsy in deference to her position. Helen lowered herself ever so slowly, royally, in the first balcony chair, letting her large dress flow to either side. A small applause broke out from some of the patrons then a few men in the back laughed, which was drowned out by a great noise on stage.

He watched the play but his curiosity overcame him, turned to an older man sitting next to him, and whispered, "Pardon me, sir. Do you know that woman?"

The man had a sly grin under his pointed mustache and spoke in a hushed voice, "Yes, I know the Countess."

George was impressed. She *was* a Countess! He felt humbled by his status and thought, Should he admit he was from a rural village not far from the Canadian border? Should he admit he had never been to Burlington alone, or seen a play? "I understand she's well-known," he continued, "but I'm new to Burlington. What's her name?"

The man had a full smile now. His wife scowled and nudged him but he continued, "Countess Helen Bokowski. She is the most beautiful and perhaps richest woman in Burlington! Maybe all of Vermont!"

The man's wife cleared her throat with agitation. George gazed up at the balcony again and Helen looked through opera glasses, scanning the crowd below.

Then the older man used the back of his hand to cover his whisper, "Quite a peach, ain't she?" and his wife used her fan to smack his other hand, hard.

"Yeouch!" A sharp red impression welted his hand. "Whadja do that fer?"

His wife stared at the stage but spoke in a crisp tone, "The play is in progress!"

The play was entertaining, he had read *Hamlet* before, but sometimes he gazed up at the balcony to see whom Countess Bokowski watched. Quite often she surveyed the audience with her opera glasses and once he thought, She must be looking at me! Then she returned he focus to the stage. He also noticed other men stared at her.

The play was very good but he was distracted. It felt like hours and finally the curtain came down, the audience applauded, more torch lights were brought in, and the theater became illuminated for intermission. People stood and stretched. He walked with the crowd to the lobby, where he stood by the front doors to enjoy the fresh air. Then from the stairwell to the balcony came a growing sound of chatter and anticipation. Several men rushed forward with a group of gawkers and one said excitedly, "It's her!"

"She's coming this way!" said a young man. Then a young woman, who looked to be 15, inhaled and puffed out her chest like a competing hen but the men in the lobby had their eyes fixed to the stairwell for Helen's arrival. First came her friend, Hazel, pale with small features, gray eyes, and she gave a polite, closed smile. She raised her fan and spoke in a soft voice, “Pardon us. We’d like to step outside.”

Then came Countess Bokowski. She held her enormous blue silk gown by two side loops and floated down the staircase, over the marble floor of the lobby. Her sparkling blue eyes glanced about the crowd, gently nodded here, there and moved forward gracefully but with a knowing tautness of her own self-awareness on her thin lips. She gave a quick smile and her high cheekbones peaked with her dark hair flowing over her bare shoulders in a precise layering of curls that came to rest on her large bosom. A small crowd of staring men backed away, parting before her. George held his ground by the lobby doorway.

“Countess!” a rotund middle-aged man with a gray mustache bowed deeply then grunted over his great effort. His beefy face flushed with redness and he spoke haltingly, “What a. . . great honor! The play, it is, very special. Don’t you agree?”

“Yes,” Helen smiled, continuing on her way, “I need some air, thank you.”

The crowd moved instantly with a great opening made for them. For some reason, he wanted to perform some heroic act to impress Helen then thought of his father’s advice, “*Be bold* and mighty forces will come to your aid.”

Hazel led the way and they floated across the marble lobby then suddenly *she* was in front of him! He stood transfixed by Helen’s beauty and stared for a long moment into her wonderfully blue eyes. She stared back. Hazel cleared her throat, then cleared it again, and he became aware everyone was watching him! He felt warm with embarrassment, waved his arm with a flourish then extended it in a presenting gesture and opened the door, presenting them with fresh air and the great outdoors.

"Thank you, sir," Hazel said then added, "Why, you're the man who remarked about the cows!"

He flushed hotly, recalling their awkward conversation. He also remembered the way Helen brushed the flowers against her cheek and lingered over the irises. He unpinned the blue iris from his lapel and offered it to the Countess. "Excuse me, may I?"

~ 7~

The Countess, Helen, gazed at the deep blue iris with delicate golden stripes on the petals in his outstretched hand. Many theater-goers watched carefully. They needed to know what would happen. Helen seemed pleased but not surprised. This type of gesture occurred regularly for her and she spoke with disdain, "Yellow would have been better. This doesn't compliment my dress."

"But it matches your beautiful eyes," he said.

Helen licked her lips, smiled, then took the flower in her white-gloved hand to admire its beauty, delicately raised it to her small, pointed nose and sniffed.

"Ew, this stinks!" Helen flicked her wrist and smacked the iris against his lapel, causing a petal to break off and fall to the marble lobby. Then she whacked his right shoulder with the flower and more petals fell then tossed it aside but he swiftly caught the flower in mid-air. She turned a quick half-pirouette, slid out the doorway and said, "Oh, Hazel! Isn't the fresh air glorious!"

A few young men clambered past him through the open door and followed the two women into the darkness. Then an elderly lady with thick spectacles bumped into him, stepped on his polished right shoe, and tottered to the doorway. She wore a shiny black silk dress with embroidered red roses and carried a complimentary red silk fan. She said, "That was quite a first act!"

When he realized no one was with her, no one responded to this well-dressed older woman, he said, "Yes, the performances are very lifelike. I particularly like the acting of the Prince and Ophelia."

"I meant your gentlemanly gesture. A splendid first act. But, yes, the play is respectable." She spoke loudly in a frail, old voice and looked up at him. He was fully grown at five feet eight inches and was much taller than this curious, elderly woman. She leaned closer then used her fan to shield her voice to share a secret, "One dies and one goes crazy from unrequited *lo-o-ove!*"

Her oval face was heavily powdered with white makeup and dust coated her small glasses but she was alert and quick-witted. Then he realized she was having fun with him.

"Yes, a lot of dead bodies at the end," he chuckled. "That's what makes it a tragedy."

"A bit like life, no? When will *this* gifted young prince take action?" She raised her eyebrows, repeatedly tapped his forearm with her fan then cackled a laugh.

“Mmm.” He pulled a handkerchief from his coat pocket and dabbed his brow. He didn’t realize he had been sweating and imagined what a dreadful site he presented to the Countess. His reflected image gleamed in a mirror across the lobby where his brown hair stuck out in a cowlick. He used his sweat-dampened handkerchief to pat it down.

A husky man, wearing a vibrant red hunting jacket with black trousers, tapped a staff on the marble floor. He had a mustache that ran across his face from one ear below his nose to the other ear, and he called out in a very deep voice, “The second act is about to begin!” paused then bellowed in his bass voice again, “The intermission is over! The second act is about to begin!”

Some of the women, who fanned themselves near the mirror, snapped their fans shut, hoisted their large formal dresses, and hurried for their seats. He thought of waiting for the Countess to return and outside the darkened night sky was dotted with twinkling stars. The elderly woman called out, “Come now! You don’t want to miss all the dying!”

He smiled, gave a quick bow and said, “After you, ma’am. Beauty first.”

She curtsied, smiled, and fanned herself. “It’s a pleasant surprise to meet such a gracious gentleman!”

“Thank you, ma’am. It’s *my* honor.”

“The *most important* soiree of the season is tomorrow afternoon at one!” She offered her carte de visite. It was unusual for a lady to have a carte, which showed her wealth and social standing. “You are cordially invited to attend.”

“Thank you,” he said, “but I’m visiting from out of town.”

“All the more reason you should attend!” She leaned closer to him and he noticed her dusty spectacles. “My niece *Helen* will be there.”

“The Countess?”

She cackled loudly, laughing so hard she flushed maroon through her thick white makeup then composed herself. “Please. Do try to attend, Mister Stannard.”

“Yes, I’ll be there,” he read her carte aloud, “Mrs. Ethel Turner. How did you know my name?”

“It’s a military secret,” Mrs. Turner smiled coyly, entered the auditorium without him, and tottered down the aisle. She stepped on the toes of a skinny tall man who jumped out of the way and his tuxedo tails flew up behind him. She plowed down the aisle, startled men in tuxedos or suits avoided her, and she took her seat in the front row.

He looked back across the lobby but did not see the Countess or any of the many men and women who had followed her into the night. He thought it was odd they would miss the start of the second half of the play but he returned to his seat. The house lights were extinguished, the orchestra began a whirling romantic recap of the first act of music, and soon the exciting drama began. Instead of focusing on the play he kept thinking of this incredibly beautiful and outrageously direct woman, Helen.

~ 8 ~

He awoke with the sunrise. Captain Male slept quietly in the next bed. Captain Male had arrived days before him with a serious leg wound, which had become infected with gangrene and had it amputated. He was partially covered by a navy blue blanket embroidered in gold with 'U.S. Army.'

George made his way to the washroom, where he stood in front of a large oval mirror. His missing right arm was bound by a clean white bandage just below his shoulder and he recalled a nurse had come in the middle of the night to change his wrapping. After a few moments of gazing at what wasn't there, he noticed shaving utensils and awkwardly used his left hand to dab water from a basin on his face then used a brush, soap, and the straight razor, which he set down to stare at himself for a long moment, considering whether this life was worth living. Then he picked up the razor and continued. It was tedious, he nicked himself in several places, and his frustration and anger mounted. When he finished he clutched the straight razor and again stared into the mirror. His brown hair had receded and drops of scarlet blood dotted and ran in tiny rivulets down his face. He looked hard into his eyes and thought of all the tedious tasks to be learned left-handed: reining a horse, feeding the horses, all the farm chores, writing, my God *everything!*

The straight razor shook in his trembling left hand. Why was he so angry? With whom was he angry? He set the razor on the cool marble top then scooped sudsy water onto his face and again wiped the linen towel over his smooth, stinging face. He made his way back to his bed and thought of his friend Cranston Selzer, who was a barber in Burlington. Perhaps he could make a deal with Cranston to shave him regularly?

He walked by Captain Male, who had rolled over onto his back. His left leg hung over his bed but was amputated below the knee. His face showed no pain and he wondered if he was sedated with morphine.

He made his bed with his left hand then sat down. He thought of the first time he met Cranston, the barber in Burlington. It felt so long ago, a different era. When he was a young man he had examined his own appearance closely and felt it was extremely important to look his best and to smell fresh. He desperately wanted to impress Helen.

~ ~

He had worn his only suit to the theater so he meticulously brushed it to remove lint and hair. He took out the folded, one-sheet playbill from his inner coat pocket and placed it on the dresser. Next he shined his boots with bees' wax and spit. He dressed, looked into the mirror and gave a confident smile. He felt good about himself but his cowlick stuck up in back and wings of wispy brown hair sprouted in curls around his temples. He checked his pocket watch, nearly 9 a.m., and decided he had time to get a haircut. He closed the door of his room behind him and went downstairs.

George crossed by the dining area to the lobby reception where Mrs. Ladd, the owner of the Champlain Inn, sat at an open secretary desk. Mrs. Ladd had thin dark hair in a tight bun in back and small dark eyes behind short spectacles.

He recalled Mrs. Turner had said this was the "most important soiree" of the season so he announced proudly, "I'm going to Madame Turner's."

Mrs. Ladd raised her eyebrows, examined him over her glasses, and said, "Honestly, you don't seem the type! We have a ten o'clock curfew, Mister Stannard!"

He didn't understand. What type was he? The high-society type? Also, the soiree began at 1 p.m., so why would she comment on curfew? He was confused but smiled politely, "Of course."

Mrs. Ladd gasped, rubbed the end of her nose then composed herself. She pointed a crooked finger at him and blurted out, "I know your Aunt! It's not too late to honor your mother's wishes!"

He turned his head and squinted his eyes, unable to fathom what Mrs. Ladd meant or why she was so upset. Did she mean he should not court Helen? Confounded, he walked out of the inn and thought, Burlington has its share of odd folks.

Across the wide roadway, a barbershop had a newly painted red-and-white striped pole and two horses were tethered to hitching posts. With the same color of flat red paint, a poorly painted sign read, 'Selzer Cut Hair & Shav' and he crossed the road.

Inside the shop the barber took off a black cotton cape from a young blonde man and sent sheared golden locks flying onto the wooden floor. The young man wore a white suit, bounded out of the chair then snapped a silver quarter-dollar into the air and said, "Thank yee mightily!"

Cranston Selzer, the barber, snatched at the silver coin, bobbled but then caught it. He made a clucking sound and said happily, "Any time, Winston!" Selzer was very tall with dark, neatly trimmed hair smoothed-down with tonic. He turned to face George in the doorway, smiled with a crooked eye-tooth and offered cheerfully, "Haircut, sir?"

He stepped aside but the young man in the white suit brushed past him, humming a peppy tune. He went inside and sat in the still-warm chair. Selzer cut his hair short, trimming down the cowlick and removing the side wings, and they spoke about the weather then Selzer turned the conversation to the latest news, "I've read the newspaper accounts of the martyrdom of John Brown, ya know, the fella hanged at Harpers Ferry. Yep, in all likelihood we'll be at war soon."

"Very likely," he nodded, to which Selzer raised his hand with the scissors then straightened his posture to the front. George did not want to talk politics and, keeping his head still, said, "I'm going to my first soiree."

"Yep, newspapers say the Southern states have a 'growing displeasure' in Congress." Selzer clipped his hair as quickly as he talked, "And I have a few notable customers. They come from Boston, Hartford, New York, all over, but the point is they're abolitionists, ya see. Yeah, I know lots of people who favor the politics of Henry Ward Beecher or even this John Brown fella. Yes indeedy, war is a certainty."

He had read the Burlington newspaper account of John Brown's raid on Harpers Ferry and remembered seeing Brown give a speech on Main Street in Vergennes a few years ago when he had traveled to Port Henry to pick up supplies. His first impression was of Brown's passionate nature. Brown had wild, light-blue eyes that made him appear like a crazed fanatic, preaching on a street corner, spitting his words with fury through his scraggly beard. He seemed capable of *any* horror and would justify it by saying it was God's will. He didn't want to engage Selzer on this topic because he was new to Burlington, just visiting, and said, "I'd like to go to Harpers Ferry some day. It sounds scenic, being on the river and in the mountains."

"Yes sir, near as I can tell. There's an engraving in the paper, or maybe it was the *Weekly*. It's 'round here somewhere if you want to take a look-see. Lovely indeed." Selzer finished and held up a small mirror for his approval.

He examined his trimmed brown hair and nodded. "Can you give me directions to Madame Turner's?"

Selzer's wide grin showed his crooked eyetooth and a dimple-like crevice in his chin popped. "Gettin' spruced up for Madame Turners? Ha! Ya don't need a haircut to get yer short 'n' curlies but I sure 'preciate yer bus'ness! It's the big gray house, Victorian, right over yonder. Ya can't miss it."

He wondered why Selzer would say those things, paid him five cents and thought of his dwindling money. This trip of leisure had become expensive. He had only three dollars remaining. He put on his felt floppy hat, touched two fingers to the brim and said, "Thank you, Mister Selzer."

"Cranston. Call me Cranston," the barber smiled again and shook his hand.

He walked out refreshed, strolled past many stone buildings, and soon came to the gray Victorian house with white trim and a big porch. A heavy, large-breasted woman in a very low-cut, red silk dress sat in a wicker chair on the porch. She appeared to be the very picture of a flirty queen on a Roman throne. He walked up the steps, bowed slightly, and said, "Madame Turner's?"

"Go right on in!" the woman said with a good-natured grin. She wore silvery-black eye makeup, rouge, lipstick and fanned her big bosoms with a black lace fan.

Inside the Victorian house, several women sat on a round velvet settee and all said "Hello!" One of the women approached him. She had brick-orange hair, very fair skin and freckles, and spoke seductively, "What's your name?"

"George." He took off his hat and cleared his throat, "Ahem, George Stannard."

"Well, come this way, Ahem George Stannard." She wore a green satin dress with black lace around the trim and led him by the hand to a stairway on the right. From upstairs he heard several people moaning and groaning like cows during mating season then he stopped. "What is this?"

“This is Madame Turner’s,” she cooed, smiled and stroked his hand then raised it and placed it on her cleavage where her delicate porcelain skin was heavily perfumed. “My name is Ruby and I’ll give you *anything* your heart desires.”

“There must be some mistake.” He pulled back his hand and circled his hat by the brim. “I wanted Madame Turner’s house.”

“You’re in it, silly boy.”

He chuckled over his embarrassment, thought of the barber’s comments about “short and curlies,” then recalled Mrs. Ladd’s remark of “it’s not too late to honor your mother’s wishes!” They thought he was going to this house of ill-repute! He reached into his coat pocket and pulled out Mrs. Turner’s carte de visite. Centered at the bottom was the address 31 Shore Road. “Is there another Mrs. Turner?”

The women on the settee all laughed like this had happened before. A thick-boned woman with blonde hair called out, “Let him be, Ruby! He’s meant for Madame Turner’s sister’s place.”

“Yes, that must be it,” he said and cleared his throat again. “Ahem. This isn’t the Shore Road, is it?”

The big blonde woman laughed huskily. “The Shore Road, Ahem!, is down by the water!” All the girls laughed again and a man coming down the stairway also laughed. He was short with a thin moustache and held an unlit cigar with a thin blonde woman in tow.

“Ya looking for me, Mistah?” the blonde called out then raised her dress to show her black lacy stockings and a garter on her shapely leg.

Then a dark-haired woman with dark eyes, who lounged against the back of the settee, hoisted her purple dress to reveal black garters on her thin legs then spread her legs open and said, "How 'bout me, Mister Ahem?"

He turned quickly, headed for the door and considered looking over his shoulder and laughing but instead he put his head down and went outside. He paused on the porch to find the direction of Lake Champlain with its clear blue waters visible through the tall elm trees down the hill. Then the short man from inside exited behind him, lit his cigar with a matchstick and spoke with a French accent, "Hey boy, good times, eh?"

He chuckled out of embarrassment, put on his hat and walked down the hill for the lake. He wondered if he should explain his mistake to Mrs. Turner? He stepped onto the shore road, glanced at his vest pocket watch, nearing eleven, and walked leisurely.

It was a beautiful day with a few puffy clouds high in the brilliant blue sky. He strolled along the Shore Road, gazing at a calm Lake Champlain with gulls cawing and following above a boat where fishermen pulled in their nets overflowing with many fish. The sun was warm on his face and he enjoyed the thick woods of pine, oak and elm with an occasional large house nestled among the woods.

After twenty minutes of walking he began to wonder why he had stabled Puck, a draft horse he had ridden from Georgia, at Peck's Livery. Then he recalled many of his neighbors had said, "everything ya need is in the city," which he took to mean all the businesses and homes were within walking distance but it was expansive.

Then he came to a large white stone building modeled after an Italian villa that sat high on a hill with a superb view overlooking the lake. An entry lane was lined on each side with evenly spaced planted poplar trees about fifteen feet high that led to the huge villa. An archway above the lane had a large iron "T" painted black, with vines hanging down and with their green leaves shimmering it made the arch appear alive.

He had never seen such a fine mansion. It had manicured gardens, a small stream that took a long turn into a small pond, and Greek statues in various heroic or graceful poses.

No one was near the front door and he checked his pocket watch, a few minutes before twelve, so he sat on the grass at the base of the archway and admired the southern view, over the rolling hills to the shoreline. In the distance, a farmer moved sheep onto an open pasture and cows grazed nearby in another field of deep-green grass. He picked up a short two-inch poplar branch, took out his pocketknife and whittled. A small bluebird chirped in a nearby pine and he noticed its bright plumage with dark eyes and tiny feet, and whittled.

The bird flew off but in thirty minutes he had fashioned a tiny bluebird that fit into his palm. He thought he would take it home, paint it blue with dark eyes and gift it to his Aunt Amelia on his next visit. Then he heard the thumping sound of several horses approaching in the distance. A carriage with two horses in elegant red-and-gold dressage was followed by a young man on a chestnut horse, riding with good speed, and galloped past him, turned into the lane, went under the arch, and up to the mansion. Another carriage came around the bend in the road and also turned under the archway. They also did not wave but he now understood people here do not converse easily like they do in Georgia or St. Albans. He put away his whittling knife and bluebird and strolled up to the enormous white stone villa with a second floor terrace with small pillars. Tall bushes grew by the front entrance and also at the corners, next to the carriage port on the left.

The second carriage unloaded its passengers, a young man in a white suit followed by a heavy-set, middle-aged man with a shiny red face. He appeared very hot in the warm weather and used a handkerchief to dab sweat off his face then repeated dabbing any remaining sweat. A tall African American in a red vest, white pants, black boots and black top hat took the nearest lead horse by its halter and steadied them.

George nodded hello but the dark man looked down and walked the horses toward the carriage house in back. He had rarely seen a black man. There were scores of black men with the Hunters before the Battle of the Windmill and one other time when he was a young boy at the Trading Post he saw an older black man, who was silent. Now he stared after this man and noted he was tall with broad shoulders. Halfway to the carriage house the dark man looked back and George waved but the man looked down again. Then another black man called out from the front doorway, "*Sir! Hey there, sir!*"

He was amazed by this man's very dark skin. He was short, had a straight nose that flared at the nostrils, brown eyes, and short dark hair that was kinky. He wore a shiny black suit with a bright white shirt and a white linen cloth was over his left forearm. “Come in here, sir!”

The curving walkway was lined with red and yellow tulips but he was still amazed by the richness of the African American’s skin and again recalled the group of ex-slaves from northern New York who had joined the Hunters. This man had extraordinary, dark skin. He placed the carved wooden bluebird in his pocket, approached the man then offered his hand to shake but instead the man bowed.

George bowed slightly but kept his hand extended until the butler rose. Rather than shake hands the servant turned and gracefully held out his white-gloved hand, meaning he should enter, and said, “Welcome to Mrs. Turner’s soiree.”

“This is the second Turner soiree I’ve attended today!” he chuckled. The butler remained placid with his arm extended.

Inside was a grand entryway lobby. The ceiling was covered with a beautiful painting of the constellations in the Northern hemisphere with rosy-cheeked cherubs and cupids with bows and arrows at the ready. Fresh cut lilies were in two large vases on marble-topped plant stands on each side of the sitting room doorway which he entered with an immediate sense of déjà vu. Five elegantly-dressed ladies sat on a large round settee, including Hazel, whom he recognized from the common green, who wore a bold yellow dress. Three men stood over the ladies in tuxedos or fine dark suits but this group discussed the Nebraska Land Act, while most of the women appeared bored. He had read about the Act in the newspaper but, being new here, didn’t want to engage in politicking.

Mrs. Turner stood up from an impressively carved mahogany chair near the settee, extended her white silk-gloved hand and said, "Mister Stannard! It's so delightful of you to attend!"

"I'm George, and it's my pleasure," he replied with a bow and kissed her ring, mimicking a novel he had read about how to approach the Queen of England. Then he felt awkward, to be unequal and below her status. He rose and shook her hand vigorously.

"Oh, aren't you strong!" Mrs. Turner cackled while massaging her gloved hand. She had thick powder over her reddened nose and shiny green eye makeup around her eyes with dark eyelashes. She wore a large, red silk gown with black embroidery in a fleur de lis pattern.

"Your dress is *incredible!*" he said but he was quite shocked. Its box-shaped, low cut revealed her ample bosom bouncing like two hens settling over eggs. He did not know what to think of such a display from an elderly woman, he figured her to be sixty or older yet she openly displayed most of her bosom!

"Thank you. It's French. It was made by *the* designer to the Empress Josephine!" He thought of Dr. Côté's stories of Napoleon and watched Mrs. Turner, waiting for another complement, then she smiled and turned to the people around the settee.

"These are my friends," Mrs. Turner said, then shut her fan and extended it with her silken-gloved hand.

A dashing young man with dark hair and a full mustache rose, stepped forward, gave a half-bow and spoke directly. "Sam Thayer but everyone calls me Doc."

"Pleased to meet you, Doc Thayer." He shook Doc's hand vigorously and noticed his light gray eyes, high cheekbones and trimmed dark mustache. He wanted to make a good impression and thought it would be humorous to tell his story of visiting the wrong house but instead asked Mrs. Turner demurely, "Do you have any relations in the city?"

"Yes, that would be my *step*-sister. *Lady Eve* she calls herself." Mrs. Turner chuckled. "I can assure you she is neither a *Lady*, nor is she *Eve!*"

Everyone laughed loudly. Mrs. Turner then asked, "Did you meet her?"

"No, not exactly!" he smiled good-naturedly then added, "No, I haven't had the pleasure!"

Doc Thayer and a few of the men chuckled but one laughed robustly. He was uncommonly handsome with dark hair and dark eyebrows. When he laughed his teeth were brilliantly white against his tanned skin then he spoke with a deep bass voice that was clear and practiced, "Titles are cheap around here. Some people have 'em and some people could care less. Title or not, she's made quite a reputation for her *entertainment* despite the law. I, of course, prefer the theatre where the *acting* is more refined."

They all laughed again and the handsome man tapped his cane on the floor. "Here, here!" he said, gave a very strong handshake, and said, "Wheelock G. Veazey, Esquire."

"Pleased to meet you, Mister Esquire."

Veazey laughed good-naturedly and the others followed. Hazel, in her vivid yellow dress, snickered on and on, then doubled over in laughter. Hazel had a tiny nose and small features, and her laughter made her entire face scrunch into a knot of convulsion with her gnarled and gapped teeth showing. She continued laughing while the handsome man explained, "No, it's Veazey. Wheelock Veazey. I'm a lawyer. Esquire is my *title,* legally, that is."

"Yes, I'm unfamiliar with so many titles," George said and chuckled with them. "I'm a little nervous."

"No need to be," Veazey said. "We're all friendly. Except Doc over there. If you're not paying attention, he'll take out your appendix!"

Doc Thayer laughed heartily and the men chuckled. Then the young man in the white suit from the barbershop entered the drawing room and, wishing to draw attention away from himself, George spoke quickly, "It's a pleasure to see you again, Winston."

The young man had a questioning look on his face. "Do I know you, sir?"

"Please don't tell me *young* Winston has been to *Lady Eve's!*" Mrs. Turner said. The men roared with laughter along with a few women, including Hazel, who wiped tears from her eyes with a fine lace kerchief, unable to control her convulsions of laughter.

"No, we share the same barber, Mister Selzer." He ran his palm across his recently cut hair and some of the women giggled with excitement.

Then the short Frenchman with a thin moustache who *was* at Lady Eve's parlor entered the room and several women caught their breath and stared at him. The Frenchman's cigar was very short now but still lit. He wore an impressive gray suit with blue piping that swirled in a decorative design on the cuffs and a gray top hat he kept on, white gloves and a matching white silk ascot. Captain Henri de La Salle introduced himself but because La Salle remained near the women George did not cross the room to formally meet him and he did not say anything about seeing him at Lady Eve's parlor. Wheelock Veazey again tapped his cane on the floor and Mrs. Turner smiled with satisfaction that her soiree was going well.

Veazey's dark features complimented his refined manners and he told interesting stories from his law practice in Montpelier. Veazey seemed to know everyone's business in the state but when he related a story he spoke in a firm yet soft voice but it was filled with kindness and joviality, and not to gossip about the people.

The clock on the mantle struck six and George felt he should return to the inn for dinner, rose and shook hands strongly with Veazey, Doc Thayer, and Winston then went around the room shaking hands politely with La Salle and several of the women. Then he approached Mrs. Turner on her mahogany throne chair and said, "I should get back to the inn because I leave for home very early tomorrow."

Mrs. Turner, in her elegant red dress with a black fleur de lis design, motioned for him to come closer, pulled on his lapel to draw him still closer then whispered in his ear, "You haven't met Helen!"

He stood upright from her clutches and spoke openly, “Yes, but she has not arrived and I must eat dinner and prepare for my travel.”

“We have food! *Obadiah!*” Mrs. Turner raised her gloved-hands, clapped twice and caught the attention of the African American butler, who rushed over and gave a slight bow. She spoke in a haughty manner, “We’ll eat directly, in the dining room.”

“Yes, ma’am, it’s ready,” the butler, Obadiah said. “How many?”

Mrs. Turner looked over her glasses and counted everyone in the room with her gloved hand, “Fifteen, sixteen, and seventeen, Obadiah. And serve the good burgundy.”

“Of cou’se, ma’am,” Obadiah again bowed formally. “With pleasure.”

Veazey stepped over from his conversation with three women on the settee and said warmly, “I know we said our goodbyes George but I do hope you’ll stay for dinner. Mrs. Turner’s meals are the best in New England!”

George smiled to Mrs. Turner. “It will be my pleasure. But I must leave at eight.”

“Excellent!” Mrs. Turner said. “Mister Veazey, have you seen *Hamlet?* George and I attended a fine performance last night.”

“Not yet but I will. My plan is to attend with Helen.”

“Yes!” Mrs. Turner said. “You’ll need to discuss that with her.”

“Yes, of course.” He was distracted by Veazey, who twirled his cane on its point, making the glass facets in the handle sparkle. “Will she arrive soon?”

“*Obadiah!*” Mrs. Turner exclaimed. “Mr. Veazey’s champagne glass is empty.”

The servant came swiftly. Obadiah used the white towel over his forearm to cradle the neck of the bottle and poured champagne with a precise, graceful movement into Veazey’s glass. He then offered George more but suddenly he was gone, having returned the champagne to a silver ice bucket, and once again stood motionless like a soldier at attention at his station near the doorway.

Another African American servant entered the room and whispered into Obadiah’s ear, who called out in a clear voice, “The first course shall be served in the main dining room!” Then Obadiah bowed and extended his arm to the side, suggesting the partygoers should go through the hall to the back of the mansion.

George turned to offer his forearm but Wheelock Veazey had already taken Mrs. Turner’s gloved hand and aided her rise from her throne chair. Veazey escorted her past the butler then the ladies followed them, some of whom were escorted by men while others waltzed by in groups of two or three, followed by the remainder of the men.

The guests strolled past the fragrant lilies on marble-topped stands and into the beautiful lobby with its gorgeously painted ceiling of cupids, cherubs and stars, and then through an open, large oak door, where another dark-skinned servant, who also wore an immaculate black suit, stood at attention in the dining hall, which held a long dark table elegantly decorated with white linen, fine china with gold emblems of "T" on the plates, crystal glasses and highly polished silverware. The men pulled back the chairs for the women, who curtsied and puffed out their large dresses then sat and the men pushed in their chairs. He noticed *two* empty place settings, one of which was to the right of Mrs. Turner and reasoned that setting must be for Countess Helen Bokowski and then went for the next empty seat, sat, and smiled in anticipation.

A delicious dinner was served in six courses with an orange-flavored sorbet to cleanse the palate before the main course, which included pheasant, venison with carrots, beets and onions, with a strong, flavorful burgundy to accompany the meal.

At eight o'clock George again apologized to Mrs. Turner and said he must leave. After some protestation, he was persuaded to adjourn to the library, where the men smoked cigars and drank cognac. The women, according to Mrs. Turner's wishes, were allowed to join them. They reclined on large sitting chairs but Mrs. Turner sat next to the still fireplace in a mahogany deacon's chair which was a gift, she explained, from the Old Ship Church in Hingham.

Doc Thayer, who had lively gray eyes and a pale complexion, told the story of an old woman he met in the back woods who knew all types of herbs and plants used for remedies and assorted ailments. George sipped some fiery cognac from a cut-glass tumbler then Doc Thayer concluded, "The last item this creaky old woman pulled out of her basket was a small bottle of backwoods white lightning. She said, 'If nothing else works, this is good for what ails ya!'"

The story of doctoring reminded him of Dr. Côté and he wondered where he was tonight. He decided to re-tell a story Dr. Côté told often, of serving on Napoleon's staff and aiding the Emperor on his long trek from Moscow back to Paris in the bitterly cold winter of 1812. When George finished his tale, he lifted his glass of cognac the way Dr. Côté would have raised his silver flask, "Dr. Côté said, 'A good gulp of cognac at bedtime is not scientific… But it helps!'"

Everyone laughed and then Helen entered the library, also laughing at some other joke, and everyone watched her. Helen wore a pink dress that exposed her neck and arms and her dark hair curled alluringly on top of her heaving bosom. She was with another woman and two men dressed in dark suits. One man was the barber Cranston Selzer, who beamed a large grin, showing his missing eye tooth, then he collapsed into a chair. The other man was Radcliffe Thames, the actor from Britain who had performed in *Hamlet*. Thames was tipsy but engaged the party, "Ah, cognac! I spend ninety percent of my fortune on good times, wom'n, and cognac. The other ten percen' I probab-b'y *waste!*"

"Here, here!" Veazey said, trying to catch Helen's attention. Veazey raised his glass in her direction and gave a polite half-bow. Helen giggled, which made her high cheekbones even more pronounced and accentuated her bright blue eyes.

"I do hope you haven't been waiting on me and Alyssa!" Helen said then turned to her friend, who had curly blonde hair with a few strands of red hair mixed in. Alyssa had very white skin but a few freckles dotted her face in a captivating way. She wore glaring dark-red lipstick and smacked her lips.

"Ah-*ha!* The men are drinkin'!" Alyssa said then laughed and used her closed fan to slap Cranston's knee. Cranston giggled but when she fell into his lap, he also laughed and held her. Alyssa responded with a spastic drunken laugh, spraying spittle into the center of the room, and slurred her words, "Who's gon' gin me a li'l drink?"

Three of the men offered up their snifter glasses but Cranston wrapped his long arms around Alyssa's waist to keep her from falling onto the floor. Helen snickered then warmly slid her white-gloved hand onto George's forearm! She whispered, "Thank you for coming," then more loudly for the entire room to hear, "We were delayed at Alyssa's Aunt's tea. There was cream pie to be tasted before the Fair tomorrow!"

Alyssa burst out in laughter, which puzzled George. Mrs. Turner rose out of her chair and offered her hand to Thames, who took her lead and gave a grand, deep bow with a fluttering hand. Thames then kissed Mrs. Turner's gloved knuckles and spoke in an overly dramatic tone, "Never a face more fair than sweet…" Thames's awkward compliment was left hanging and he searched his drunken memory to get her name right then guessed, "Mrs. Turner?" Thames's compliment became a question and a few men laughed nervously.

"Mr. Thames, it's an honor to have you join us," Mrs. Turner offered.

"The honor is mine," he said. Thames again bowed deeply, rose and burped, then laughed to cover it. A few people laughed with him, including Helen, Alyssa and Cranston, while others looked on with shock and mild disgust.

Wheelock Veazey stepped to Helen and with one smooth motion took her gloved hand from George's forearm. He bowed and kissed her gloved hand while his dark eyes stared directly into hers. "At your service, Countess Bokowski."

The Countess giggled again then looked at George. "Well, there is at least one gentleman in the room."

He bowed and held out his hand but Veazey would not let her go. Veazey continued to stare into her eyes then smiled and said, "Only the moon has such radiance on this special eve!"

He rose from his bow and glared at Veazey, who smiled brightly with his tanned skin. He felt he was losing some type of competition, which made him upset but also he could not blame Veazey. What would he give to hold Helen's hand? What clever phrase could he quote? Then from across the room, Captain La Salle smiled to Helen and arched his eyebrow then smiled more broadly, making two dimples in his cheeks pop. Helen blushed.

Then he noticed Cranston's grasp slide up around the front of Alyssa's dress and across her bosom. Alyssa gave a half-startled "woo!" but complained no further. She turned to look Cranston in the eyes with a big smile, clutched his face, and kissed him deeply, which caused great embarrassment in the room. Veazey let go of Helen's hand and tapped his cane on the floor at the impropriety of this act. When the couple parted, their faces were inches apart and Alyssa's face again glowed with a radiant, full smile. She beamed, "Cranston has an announcement!"

Cranston turned crimson and smoothed back his greased-down hair then tapped the sides to ensure all were in place. "I, well, we, that is Alyssa has decided, um consented, to be my wife."

The guests gasped with excitement then applauded but George noticed Helen appeared stunned. He carefully watched Helen, who had tears brimming in her eyes. After a moment a very slight smile came to her, followed by polite applause.

"Ah, of course!" Veazey said. "Three cheers for the lucky couple!"

It was not until the third cheer that Helen spoke, adding a half-hearted "hoo-ray" before she turned briskly and hurried out of the room with her pink dress flaring out and flowing behind her. He turned to Mrs. Turner and discreetly asked, "What's wrong?"

~ 9~

A tense stillness followed in the wake of Helen's sudden emotional departure. Everyone appeared flustered of how to respond, then Wheelock Veazey made another robust toast, "To the joyous news of Cranston and Alyssa's engagement!"

Mrs. Turner flexed her fan to conceal her words from the room and said, "Helen is often upset when she is *not* the center of attention. I can only assume she thought *she* would be engaged before Alyssa. After all, Helen is seventeen and Alyssa has only recently turned fifteen."

Veazey tapped his cane twice, cleared his throat and launched into another story. When it ended Mrs. Turner chuckled and the party was lively again. George slowly finished his glass of cognac, walked around the room again, shook hands good-bye, returned to Mrs. Turner and said, "Farewell. I enjoyed your soiree very much."

"Thank you so much for attending!" Mrs. Turner said, using her gloved-hands to shake both his hands warmly.

He exited the front entrance and the African American butler, Obadiah, gave a very slight smile. He winked and smiled back and Obadiah bolted upright, staring into space like a motionless statue as if the exchange never happened.

"So long," he said and waved. Obadiah didn't move.

The next day he rode Puck, a strong draft horse with light points, back home to Georgia. Along the way he reminisced on his adventures in Burlington, enjoying the cool autumnal breeze, and thought. Those few days were the most fun he had ever had, even if it was very expensive. He rode along, gazing up at the high October sky and was filled with a feeling of vast hope and unlimited potential. The bright color of the sky also reminded him of Helen's beautiful eyes and he recalled other details of her stunning beauty—her high cheekbones, her buoyant laughter and the way her dark hair curled around her ears and flowed down in ringlets past her shoulders to her full bosom. And she *is* a Countess!

He also recalled Wheelock Veazey, the very handsome lawyer with dark features and wondered what he was doing now, at this very moment. Was Veazey courting Helen? How could he compete with a clever, rich lawyer? Then he thought of the dandy Frenchman, Captain Henri de La Salle, who had made a fortune in shipping and was said to be one of the richest men in the state. Was he also courting Helen? What secret did they share for his smile to cause her to blush? How could he compete with a wealthy and experienced man like Captain La Salle?

Then he thought it might be best if he returned to Burlington to be closer to Helen and perhaps see her at social events? Maybe he should have a big event of his own, or some big news to make a grand impression upon his return? He reasoned if he was able to make a grand impression then Countess Bokowski may be attracted to him because of his great potential. What event could he offer from his home in small Georgia, Vermont?

He thought for days about what he could do to impress Countess Helen Bokowski. Then he received a letter from Dr. Côté. The writing was stylish with many swirls, flourishes and, because of Dr. Côté's awkward English, it was difficult to read:

Dear Georges —

Many, many gracious Bows et Humilite. Thank You for Your Leter—it Touchd et Warmd my Heart et Soul. It is an Oddity but I Receivd Your Leter today. I was in France for 5 Years. Oui, Your Father passing still Troubles Me Greatly! Samuel was th rare Gemstone—a Brilliant Man—so Kind, so Considerate, so Steadfast in Noble Virtues—Willing to Help Others—for Foods or Supplys, et Oui! To Fight for Liberty et Freedom! Non! A Great Man like Samuel Does Not Walk this Earth so Often! Please Accept my deep Apology for Me Not at th Funeral et for Your Aid. I was to France for Personal Reasons—My Family—Mais, Not to Worry You!

I Live near th Saratoga Springs where mon Health is tres bien! I do not Travels so much theese Days. Mais if You Come,-Please Ask for Me! Oui, Oui, it would be Grand to see You Back, mon Frere!

With Utmost Honor et Your Humble Servant,

Dr. Cyrille Côté

He was very happy to receive Dr. Côté's letter and wanted to visit him but placed the letter on the shelf behind the counter of the Trading Post. It was not a good time to visit but perhaps next spring. He returned his thoughts to making some kind of grand impression for Helen. What could he do?

When Abraham Lincoln was elected President an uproar came from the people of the Southern states declaring their intention to secede from the Union. It felt inevitable war was coming and then an idea came to him. He packed his bag, hitched Puck to a carriage in order to escort the Countess around Burlington, and returned to the Champlain Inn in Burlington. Then he sent a note to Mrs. Turner's mansion and asked if he could speak with her. A reply came to the Champlain Inn the same afternoon:

You are cordially Invited to
Tea at 3p.m.

He steered Puck and the carriage toward the Italian-style mansion. As he drove up the poplar-lined lane, the dark-skinned stableman hustled out from the back to arrive at the front door at the same time he arrived. The stable hand took Puck's halter without a word but George smiled to him and the man smiled back then took Puck's reins.

The front door opened, where Obadiah bowed and said, "Good to see you again Mister Stannard," but he avoided eye contact and did not shake his hand. Obadiah led him through the entryway into the receiving room, where Mrs. Turner sat in a red silken robe in a deacon's chair, which had one armrest carved with a lamb's head and the other a lion's head. From a distance she looked like a Catholic Cardinal. Another African American servant arrived with a silver tray with steaming tea but then left without serving them. He noticed a sweet-smelling smoke filled the air and a hookah pipe rested on the small table next to Mrs. Turner, who had a contented, Buddha-like smile creased on her lips.

Mrs. Turner spoke languorously, "Helen was most pleased when I told her that you had inherited your father's estate and Trading Post near, um, Saint Albans. *But!*" she paused for dramatic effect then passed her heavily veined hand across her red silk robe, "Because the Countess is young and her father is in Poland on business, I must inquire on her behalf. You *do* understand, don't you?"

He nodded. It was an odd beginning to their meeting. He poured himself a cup of tea and placed one sugar cube in it. He remained standing, awkwardly, and Mrs. Turner spoke authoritatively from the deacon's chair. "Exactly how much land do you own and what is your chief source of income?"

Mrs. Turner's words hung in the air but he continued to think of how awkward their conversation was. Was there to be no exchange of pleasantries? No talk of the weather, social events, or the most popular subject of the day: the possibility of Southern states seceding from the Union? He brushed aside his frustration and took command of the situation. "Good afternoon Mrs. Turner and thank you for receiving me. In response to your direct question, I'm sorry but I don't know."

Mrs. Turner frowned, arched her eyebrows above her glasses then glanced at the hookah pipe and fidgeted. A nervous smile slid across her face.

He understood his answer was not sufficient and he did not wish her to feel uncomfortable for her lack of pleasantries then thought of estimating the acreage, or perhaps stating he took pride in raising and training the finest horses, or even of how he missed his father dearly. Instead he added, "I'm a simple man. I own twenty-three horses that my father and I raised, and I may sell many of them if there is a war. My father *had* a Trading Post but my father was killed in the Canadian Rebellion of Thirty-eight and not too long after that I started teaching. I'm also the foreman at the foundry in St. Albans. It's difficult to run the Trading Post on my own, raise horses, work at the foundry, and teach children in the winter but I manage. No, I love them all. I have some money from my father's estate but mostly I raise and sell horses, work at the foundry, and teach."

The summary of all his activities seemed to help. Then Mrs. Turner spoke without emotion, "Mm. I had heard of your father and I am sorry for your loss. He was an organizer in that Canadian revolution, wasn't he? But as Shakespeare said, 'That was in another country!' "

"Marlowe wrote that," he said quietly, not wishing to be disagreeable.

Mrs. Turner harrumphed with exasperation and returned their conversation to an accounting procedure. "As you should know I am obliged to look after my niece's welfare. I *must* give a full report to my sister's husband, the Count, in Poland. I regret to be direct but this is what we need to know. What would you estimate your worth to be?"

He had anticipated this would be discussed because he had read novels of wealthy society, of how people are married where one side adds up the goods on a ledger and the other side reckons if the total is worthy of an exchange. With this system, he wondered how he could compete with a rich lawyer like Veazey from Montpelier, or Captain La Salle, who was one of the wealthiest men in the state. He responded by reciting a phrase he had practiced, "My wealth is little in relation to my enormous concern for the Countess and in comparison to my vast potential to care for her and love her."

Mrs. Turner grumbled, "Love is a troubadour's song!" Something seemed to trouble from her own past and she gazed at the hookah pipe for its comforting sedative. "An odd choice of words, Mister Stannard. This is how you intend to care for my niece? *Love*, you say?" She had pronounced the word "love" like cursing a dirty word, then repeated it for effect, "*Love*, you say?"

He flushed over her disparaging words and decided to switch tactics by making his "grand impression" announcement, but how could he do that smoothly? This meeting was quite awkward so he decided to simply announce it. He spoke boldly, "I intend to raise one thousand men to preserve the Union!"

"Hmm. Now *that* is interesting." Mrs. Turner raised her eyebrows and rubbed the lion's head armrest. "One thousand men? The father of our country did that. Of course, General Washington was a very rich man and he *paid* for such support. Yes, that would be impressive. You can do this? You have this much such support?"

"I'll do it before the year is out," he responded with bravado but then thought it was too soon. Why didn't he say "next spring" or "April first"?

Mrs. Turner leaned onto the left armrest and tapped her fingernails on the ornate carving of a lamb's head. Her red silk robe rustled with her movement and she kicked her short legs, dangling off the floor. Her tiny black boots stuck out from under the hem and he felt the impropriety of seeing her ankles. He was about to retreat, to announce his departure, when she made a grand pronouncement, "You have my permission *to court* my niece!"

Mrs. Turner extended her left hand for him to kiss and he thought of an engraving he had seen in a book about the Queen of England, grasped her hand dotted with dark spots and lumpy with bulging blood veins, and kissed it then noticed she wore a large Free Mason's ring. It reminded him of the problems the Free Masons had caused in the Canadian government then thought more about the ring itself. Because Masons don't allow women, how would *she* have *that?* She added, "Bring in a list of the men by January first."

He bowed but wanted to be clear in their "deal." "Do I understand you correctly, that my success in courting the Countess is dependent on my raising one thousand soldiers for the Union?"

"No, no, no, dear boy. Of course not!" Mrs. Turner snickered, took off her glasses and rubbed her reddened eyes then replaced her spectacles. "It will demonstrate you are so admired, men would be willing to *die* for you. It's all very romantic!"

He felt queasy at the vulgarity of making war sound romantic and glorious, and recalled the Battle of the Windmill and the death of his father. Samuel had died, in essence, for him but also for the cause of freedom, along with many others. Then the Canadians viewed their "freedom" on their own terms and went on with their British system of government. War was often ugly and far from glorious. Yet he rcmained silent for the opportunity to court Helen.

Mrs. Turner closed her eyes for a long moment then a thin smile came over her face. She again looked at the hookah pipe longingly then returned her intense gaze to him. "It also shows you are a man of your word. Surely you understand being enormously well-liked, respected, and a man of your word are important values?"

"Of course. Good day, Mrs. Turner." He made another quick bow and left the room. He drove Puck and the carriage back to the center of Burlington and thought of all the places he could enlist men. He would go to the common green, the taverns and livery stables. He thought of the foundry where he worked in St. Albans then thought of Burlington again and Selzer's barber shop, boarding houses, shipping docks, general stores and the market area. He knew he would need help so when he arrived back at the inn he went into his room and wrote many letters asking for assistance in raising a Vermont brigade to all his friends, to fellow officers from the Ransom Guards, to Wheelock Veazey, the lawyer from Montpelier, who knew everyone in law and politics in the state's capitol, to Edward Ripley, who was involved in the Rutland militia, to Dr. Côté, who knew anyone of importance from Montreal to Albany and also asked him for an address in order to write Billy Caldwell, who also knew a lot of people in Burlington and around Lake Champlain.

Next George went to the *Burlington Free Press* to speak with George Benedict, whose father ran the newspaper. He recalled

Benedict's help in carrying a wounded soldier at the Battle of the Windmill but now Benedict's dusty blonde was hair thinner and he had lost his boyish grin. He told Benedict of his plan to raise volunteers for a Vermont brigade but Benedict explained that the newspaper, with his father Editor-in-Chief, would not run an editorial calling for volunteers for an army while an opportunity remained for a diplomatic, peaceful settlement with the South. He was disappointed but, with Benedict's help, they ran a daily advertisement calling for volunteers.

Next he spoke with the local shop owners, who put up posters in support of the Union then talked with men around the common green and in the market area.

When he had time, he courted Countess Helen Bokowski. Unlike most eligible women, she did not like to walk through the common, which she considered a public announcement of her courtship intentions. She preferred, she said, to keep that information private. "It's no one's business whom I court. The gossip mongers can find another sacrificial lamb for their petty stories and allegations."

"People will talk, regardless," he said. She agreed but they kept their meetings secretive and spontaneous, for which she would not plan more than two days in advance.

On Saturday evening they met, along with Alyssa and Cranston, at the Opera House to see La Traviata. The next time they met, along with Hazel, on a Wednesday evening after the sun had dipped below the horizon of the late autumn sky, to listen to a quartet of men singing in front of the Wilson Hotel. The following Sunday they met after service at the Unitarian Church, where he shook hands with all the men and discussed the growing Vermont regiment of volunteers.

At Helen's impromptu request, without Hazel, or Alyssa, or Mrs. Turner, they took a ride in his carriage. When they were in the undulating hills south of Burlington, she clutched his hands on the reins and eased back. Puck, a big draft horse, slowed into a trot but then Helen tugged briskly and Puck came to an abrupt stop.

They were high on a hill slope in a small opening by a meadow in the brightly colored woods. Far below was a tiny, cedar-shingled house by a creek and he wondered whose farm this was, then thought of using an organized system of riding through the countryside to enlist soldiers. Then she grasped his collar and kissed him strongly on the lips—a very direct and improper action! Her mouth was sweet and wet, and he kissed her back. He had dreamed of this, wanted it intensely, but in one month of courting he had not made such an advance. He wanted things to go properly, to gain her confidence in his righteous intentions, and now she was being passionate! His heart pounded in his chest and his mind raced. They continued kissing and her lips parted and her tongue probed, tickling his lips with tiny flickering taunts. He responded, held her close, and clutched her waist, feeling the tightly drawn silk of her dress, moving with her heaving chest. Then Helen broke from their fiery kiss and pointed to the meadow on the side of the hill, and spoke coyly, "There's a hay stack, just over there."

He was stunned. Did she mean it? Wait, what did she mean by it? She unbuttoned his jacket, tugged at his shirt tucked in at the waist then fell back onto the buckboard and raised her leg over his lap. Her wet mouth kissed his lips, his bearded cheeks, his neck then she pulled him closer, on top of her.

"Please," she said and gazed up with her radiant blue eyes and an eager slight smile on her face. "Please! I need to know."

~ ~

The following Sunday after the service at the Unitarian Church he again spoke with a small group of men about a Vermont regiment while he waited for Helen outside. When she exited he stepped away from the men and said brightly, "Let's go for a walk in the common," but she ignored him without looking in his direction. He felt hurt and went after her but she stepped into a waiting carriage, where Mrs. Turner sat in an elegant, dark gray dress with a pattern of red embroidered roses.

Helen spoke sharply, "I told you. I don't take walks in the common. That's where trolls and gossips thrive."

"Very well. Would you like a ride into the country?"

"My Aunt," she nodded in Mrs. Turner's direction, then puffed out her yellow silk dress on the seat, "has a tea later this morning—"

"G'morning, Mrs. Turner," he removed his floppy felt hat.

"—and then I'm going to Montpelier."

He thought of Wheelock Veazey. "Are you seeing that lawyer?"

“That’s none of your concern, or anyone else’s business.” Helen raised her open fan to his ear and spoke under her breath, “The actor Radcliffe Thames asked me to elope with him to Montreal! I said no, of course! He’s a drunkard and has no money!”

The Countess folded up her fan, a smirk crossed her lips then she nodded to the African driver, who looked at George with kind, compassionate eyes and snapped a whip. The carriage drew off with a start and jerked away from his hand, twisting his knuckles away from the door handle. He watched Helen, Mrs. Turner, and the carriage bounce over the cobblestone road. This is how she is, he thought, then recalled the behavior of skittish horses like Neptune or Dancer that startled easily and frightened with any little sound or movement. He felt Helen was similar except she was high-strung and she *needed* constant excitement. How would he keep up this energy?

He decided to make a bold effort in his courtship. He would keep his carriage at Peck’s Livery but returned his draft horse, Puck, to Georgia, then rode back to Burlington on Charger, a fine white stallion that was now three years old, impeccably trained and very responsive. He knew riding high on Charger made a gallant impression but he also decided, much like a battlefield plan, to integrate a coordinated series of events instead of one chance meeting at a time.

When Helen agreed to go to the theatre to see a traveling show called *Hiawatha*, they also stopped for a glass of sherry at Renard’s Tavern where they chatted about the play and laughed at how bad it was. When she agreed to go to the waterfront ferry landing to see a race between two paddlewheel boats, *Queen of the Nile* and *Star of Champlain*, afterward they went to Swinson's restaurant for hot apple pie with freshly grated cheddar cheese.

As their courtship continued, he felt inspired. He wanted to do important, good deeds like raising the Vermont Brigade but he also felt inspired for himself, to be even more than *he* had dreamed of being. He felt strong with her, he could do anything, and he felt a renewed sense of purpose deep within himself. He wanted to fight for justice, to make the world a better place. She made him feel special. *He* was the most important person in the world and he loved that feeling. He wrote her poems and passionate letters, and she whispered delicate words of inspiration, often in public! He *always* wanted to be with her and hated when they had to part. Seeing Helen gave him a grand feeling he wanted to have *forever*.

It was a wondrous autumn with both the excitement of courting and the serious work of raising troops to uphold the Union, with an incredible mix of beauty and purpose. He felt invigorated with passion in every moment of his life. When January 1st came, more than 850 men had enlisted and he knew one day he must go with the troops to Washington City. Before that happened, he decided he would ask Mrs. Turner for Helen's hand in marriage. He was incredibly excited, prepared many wonderful phrases, then asked for and was granted permission to call on Mrs. Turner and the Countess Helen Bokowski on the second of January.

It was a crisp, clear, cold day. He handed the reins to Charger to the stableman and then Obadiah, the African American servant, greeted him at the door with a big smile. He wondered, What did Obadiah's sudden smile mean? It wasn't a smile of joy, or of nervous humiliation. Not knowing Obadiah's motivation, he decided to ignore it then realized he must know something of how he would be received, which bolstered his confidence. "I'm here to see Mrs. Turner and the Countess."

"Yes, sir, Mister George! It seems like every time I see you, you have a different horse!" Obadiah stepped closer and whispered, "I wish I could go with you."

He was very confused and wondered, Why would Obadiah want to be in his meeting with Mrs. Turner? "What?"

"To Wash City, sir. To serve the Union."

"Oh, yes. I see." He looked more closely at Obadiah. His smile was replaced by a look of earnest conviction. It was the same look he had seen on hundreds of other naïve Vermonter's faces. Why should this man be any different? Obadiah appeared strong and fit and he had probably never fired a gun in his life but he could be trained. Almost all of the Vermonters would need to be trained to be a soldier.

"But what of Mrs. Turner, this household?"

"Well, that's it, to the point precisely," Obadiah paused, delicate of the situation of a servant speaking with a guest then continued, "and, of course, me being Colored."

"Well, maybe you'll get the chance. Who knows?"

"Yes, sir, *you* know. *You* the Colonel, right?"

He now considered him with seriousness. Obadiah knew nothing of the intense frenzy of battle, of witnessing a comrade suddenly horribly disfigured, or lying wounded, awaiting help during a long, heated battle. No, he couldn't aid Obadiah in his whim plus he was needed to run this household. "I am the Lieutenant Colonel."

"Yes, sir! You know." Obadiah's eyes glistened with hope. "I'll announce you directly. Please wait in the parlor to your right, Colonel Stannard."

"*Lieutenant* Colonel," he corrected him again then sat on a tufted, cream-colored chair but then rose and paced the room, staring at the green floral pattern in the cream-colored carpet. After a moment, Mrs. Turner entered wearing a solemn, black dress with long black gloves and the Mason's ring over her glove. She went to her deacon's chair and motioned for him to sit in a high-backed wooden chair opposite her.

"Please explain your situation," Mrs. Turner demanded gravely.

"Hello," he said. No response came. "It's been a very good year but, well, ah, won't Helen be joining us?"

"Yes, in good time. First I *must* say, you were to have been here yesterday. I distinctly asked you to bring the muster roll January first," Mrs. Turner pointed a finger authoritatively then pushed her glasses to the bridge of her nose, all business.

"I didn't bring the muster roll," he said. "I didn't know you needed proof. It's about my word, isn't it? And when will Helen, the Countess, be joining us?"

“She’ll be along, by and by. You know *the Countess!*” Mrs. Turner burst out in a robust laugh.

He wondered, What is happening? Her dress and demeanor appeared serious yet she joked about her niece’s title. He looked over but Obadiah was not in the doorway. The closed door felt like a casket lid and he was alone. He began again, “We’ve raised eight hundred and fifty men.”

“General Washington had one thousand.”

“Yes.” He had given his word to be here on the first, to bring the muster rolls, and to raise 1,000 men. He had failed on each count.

“Well, what else?” Mrs. Turner said. “I hope you haven’t pinned your plans of being with Helen by outshining General Washington!”

“That was to my goal. To make a grand impression.”

“Yes, that would have been *grand!*” she snickered. “Come, come, Mister Stannard,” and again she sang “*love*” for emphasis like an opera queen, “Last time you used the word “*love!*” Then she shifted to the lion’s armrest and stared at him with a level eye. “Tell me. What are your intentions?”

Mrs. Turner asked so bluntly he felt introspective. How did he feel? Did he love Helen? Did he wish to marry his soul to hers for eternity?

“Why should *I* consider your proposal?” She tapped her fingernails on the lion’s head armrest to punctuate the silence. “You are proposing, aren’t you?”

"Yes, yes." He thought of all his rehearsed phrases but none were intended for Mrs. Turner, then considered various gestures of supplication but decided to remain still.

Then Helen came into the room playfully, like a refreshing breeze on a hot day, and the atmosphere of the room changed, becoming cheerful and bright. She smiled warmly with her radiant blue eyes sparkling and rushed to him, took his hands, and kissed him flush on the mouth! "Hello, my darling!"

He smiled broadly and stared into her captivating blue eyes. After a moment he remembered Mrs. Turner was there, waiting for him, and Obadiah stood just inside the doorway. This is the moment, he thought, and went into his suit coat pocket, took out a dark blue velvet ring case, dropped to one knee, and said, "Helen, please. Would you give me the honor of being my wife?"

Helen looked to Mrs. Turner and burst into laughter. He looked up at Mrs. Turner, confused and opened the ring case. A sparkling five-carat diamond mounted on a thin gold band gleamed on white silk.

Helen took out the glistening ring, slipped it on then held out her hand. "It's a little small."

"It can be made larger."

"No, it fits fine. The stone. The diamond is smallish," she said and extended her hand again to see the ring at a distance. "Of course on my wedding day I will wear our family jewels, right Aunt Ethel?"

"Yes, of course, dear, *but!*" Mrs. Turner paused for dramatic effect. "On your wedding day! And *we* will give this question our utmost serious consideration, won't we? Mr. Stannard has *failed* on several matters of grave importance. Yes. Well! We must give it serious consideration. That is all. *Good day*, sir!"

He felt vulnerable and awkward, rose off his knee, and closed the empty ring box. The room felt larger than ever, such a long distance to cross in embarrassment but he walked silently past Obadiah, who stood motionless. He stepped out of the mansion into the fresh, brisk air, where the dark-skinned stableman handed him the reins to Charger, nodding and nickering.

~10 ~

It was oddly quiet. A few soldiers snored. Across the aisle a doctor in a blood-stained white coat held a young man's wrist, shook his head with taut lips then folded the soldier's arms over his chest. He slid a navy blue blanket over the gaunt-faced soldier then walked toward him.

He lifted himself onto his left side, turned around to see if Captain Male was awake but his bed was empty and unmade. He wondered if Captain Male had passed away and looked around anxiously.

The doctor walked by swiftly so he called out, "Doc! Hey there!" but the doctor never broke stride and continued on his way.

"No generals in here," a clear voice said. Captain Male sat in the open window across the room.

"Thank God, you're alive!" he said.

“Near as I can tell,” Male smirked then winked.

“You a Vermonter?”

“No, I picked it up from your visitors. ‘Near as I can tell.’ I’m kind of an authority on oral history and speechifying.”

He smiled amiably and asked, “What visitors?”

“There’s been a steady stream.”

He was confused and thought he must be very ill. He only recalled Whitman and thought he had arrived the day before Whitman visited. “How long have I been here?”

“A spell. You seem to be doin’ better, thank God.” Male spat out the window. “The doctors would just as soon let you go to make room for the next. They push ‘em out near as fast as they bring ‘em in. You’re lucky it’s been quiet so I reckon they don’t need your bed.”

He realized the coffinmaker’s hammering was still. He looked around again and wondered where Whitman was today. Perhaps he only came when a large number of ambulances arrived? Very few people stirred so he figured it was early in the morning. Should he try shaving today? Then he thought, Why? He didn’t have any appointments. He decided to let his beard grow. “Where’s my horse? Is there any mail?”

“Your horse?” Male chuckled and shook his head. “Fine, I reckon. They bring mail ‘round when it suits ‘em,” Male scoffed then raised one boot onto the window sill and rested his cheek on his bent knee. The other leg was simply not there with the nub of the knee wrapped in a bandage and pointing toward him with nothing below it.

"Your best bet for news is from vis'tors. You've had more 'n most." Male sang off key, "They'll be comin' 'round the mountain, when they come."

"What's your name, captain?"

Male looked up with surprise. "It's me. Captain Male."

"What? No your first name."

"I was with you at Fort Harrison, sir," Male said and his eyes went back and forth, searching for some sign of recognition.

"I'm sorry," he said, feeling foggy. "I'm, ah, I'm a little not myself."

" 'at's understandable. No one here is." Male slid off the window then stood at attention but wobbled on his one good leg and announced, "Captain Mercury Dodgson Male, sir! New York One Hundred Thirty-Ninth!"

He looked at him from his bed. What was Captain Male expecting? Orders? "Captain, may I call you Mercury?"

"If you like, sir, but my friends call me Pete." He bounced on one leg in an attempt to stand rigid.

"Okay, Pete. Relax. Sit down." Pete leaned against the open window and George continued, "I'm not feeling well."

"I know, sir. I'd be happy to assist you in any way you see fit."

"Very good. What are your wounds, Pete?"

"Me?" The captain looked at him strangely—couldn't he see the obvious? Then he answered in the style of a military report, "Missing one leg, sir. I got a Reb mini-ball in my left thigh, shattered the bone and they had to take it. A few broken ribs. Mac, my horse, threw me, landed on me, I don't remember right. It feels like my insides been kicked out. I got the dysentery. I ain't shit solid in a week, maybe more. 'Course you know that ain't nothin' new. *Passing well.*"

Then Pete looked down, perhaps ashamed or unsure of what to say. A moment passed before he spoke again. "Most of all I got the jumps."

He walked over and looked at Pete evenly until he looked up.

"Any little noise can set me off to crying like a baby. I cain't help myself," Pete said then added, "Sir!"

"Okay. Okay." He rested his left hand on the young man's shoulder. "I'm putting you in charge of making your bed. . . when you're not in it," he chuckled but Pete was stone-faced, "and getting the name of every visitor of mine. Do you write?"

"Yes, sir, and I can give an oral history of our family, if you like." Pete smiled, showing a dimple in his left cheek. Then his jumpy, hazel eyes glistened with alarm. "I ain't got no paper! No pencil neither!"

"Find Mister Whitman. He's got 'em. Or maybe a doctor. We're going to get this unit into shape. Is that clear?"

"Yes, sir!" Pete puffed out his chest and stood at attention on his one good leg.

"One more thing. When's your birthday?"

"Sir?"

He knew most people had fond memories of their birthday and knew Pete could use a few of those good memories now. He assumed Pete had a good family somewhere and someone who would celebrate his birthday in the future.

"Seventeenth of March, sir." Pete smirked then winked, "Near as I can tell!"

He chuckled and nodded at the irony of that particular date. He squeezed Captain Male's shoulder again and patted him once for good measure. Pete hobbled off in search of paper and pencil. He thought again of that date and a faint smile came to him. It was years ago, impossibly far away. In 1861 March 17th was a beautiful day.

~ ~

The wedding took place on Saturday March 17, 1861. It was a clear, warm day after a particularly cold winter with vibrant spring foliage budding green, with all of Burlington green, in bloom, with green maple and elm leaves, and deep forest green pine boughs that dappled the avenues against a high bright blue sky. The steeple of the Unitarian Church glowed luminous white.

He felt it was the most wonderful day possible for this grand occasion but many thought the groom was not worthy of this radiant girl, after all she was a Countess! By all accounts he had a fine physique, stood five feet eight inches, but there was nothing impressive in his bloodline and nothing impressive in his amiable face. His patriotism was remarkable and he wore his soldier's blue uniform with a crisp, white-plumed hat, and rode his remarkable white horse. People whispered all together he *looked* the part of a fine groom but was he *worthy* of the Countess?

At the Unitarian Church on Pearl Street a long line of carriages moved slowly forward and a footman helped passengers alight. Mrs. Turner, stout, ermine-clad, stepped down from a coach with aid from Obadiah, her African American butler who was there to assist her but would not attend this event for the upper society of Vermont and New England. White lace and streamers swirled over the entrance of the church. Jewels gleamed on the white gloves and dark gowns of the women. Vivid beauties shone for attention including young Miss Clarissa Welch, the newly-arrived daughter of the British Ambassador, Miss Constance Highsmith, an actress from Boston who settled here, Miss Catherine Aniston, an opera singer, and Mayor Leeds' lovely daughter Ophelia. Still, the people were not satisfied. They wanted to see the Governor.

It was 5:30, the time set for the ceremony, when Governor Fairbanks arrived solitary without escort, which created a stir. The Governor wore a simple black suit, stepped from his carriage and slipped into the church. People whispered he looked weary, overworked and speculated on what could cause him so much worry.

In the entryway of the church hung the national colors and the flag of the State of Vermont. A buzz of excitement electrified the crowd, anxiously awaiting the start of this spectacular event.

Standing in the back room of St. Michael's, George felt proud and so honored, he wanted to give a speech but there was no one with him. He had thought of many friends to name his "Best Man.

Perhaps Billy Caldwell but Dr. Côté had lost track of him, George Benedict, Cranston Selzer, Dr. Côté himself, even Wheelock Veazey. But in thinking carefully of each, no one had been as close to him as his father. He recalled the tender way Samuel tucked him in bed and told stories to ease his thoughts into sleep, which was his favorite part of the day. As a boy he often lay in bed, unable to sleep, and thought on the lessons of Samuel's stories and of life's incredible adventures to come. In this moment, now, he realized he missed his father much more than he had known.

He clasped his hands together in the cool back room of the church and listened to the organist playing something light by Chopin in honor of Helen's Polish ancestry. It was a romantic piece, dancing softly through the chambers of the old church. He thought again of his father, felt Samuel's presence and heard his voice speaking to him with confidence, "Steady your nerves. You'll do fine."

Then the music stopped and he realized he was late entering! They were waiting on him! He squeezed his fingers into the palms of his hands, rolled his shoulders and spoke to himself, "This is a wonderful day!"

He walked down the hallway adjacent to the altar where a stained glass window reflected bright colors in honor of the drowned soldiers of the *Philadelphia*, a gondola-shaped fighting ship sunk in Lake Champlain during the Revolutionary War. That's not comforting he thought then turned to the wooden door and entered the main chancellery. Then the organist, a rail thin woman with protruding eyes, energetically played "Bridal Chorus" by Wagner.

Aunt Amelia sat in the front row. She wore her best blue silk dress with a corsage of white roses and smiled joyfully with tears running over her rouged cheeks. Amelia looked a little like his mother, as he remembered her, except much older. Aunt Amelia was slow to accept Helen but after she saw how taken he was with Helen, she approved whole-heartedly. Would his mother have approved of Helen? Suddenly he felt very emotional and wondered, should he go through with this? Then Amelia turned away from him and the entire congregation stood to turn their attention to the back of the church. The double doors swung open and there was Mrs. Turner, alone. Then gracefully sliding to her side—Helen stood motionless to let everyone admire her. It occurred to him they were *alone*. Helen's father, Count Bokowski, was not there. They had said the Count would come to America for the wedding but, no, he was *not* there.

Helen stood motionless and allowed everyone to adore her in this, her finest moment. She wore a lovely silk white wedding gown with a lace veil clasped to her brow by a parure of pearls, a gift of Mrs. Turner. Then Helen boldly stepped forward, stopped in rhythm to the music, practiced so many times from childhood on, then stepped forward and stopped. A thin veil covered her face but her radiant blue eyes gleamed with tears. Mrs. Turner walked graciously one step behind her. It was the Countess's grand march and she beamed with pride. The audience gasped in awe: She was breathtakingly beautiful.

Helen's wedding dress was adorned with pearls and lace, and elegantly flowed to the floor and formed a silken train behind her, where little Rose Anne, her four-year-old niece with long blond hair, held the gown from touching the floor. A stern look of studious effort caused tiny creases on Rose Anne's forehead, showing her duty was of the utmost importance, and she bit her lower lip in concentration.

The moment streaked by like a shooting star in the night, one instant an attractive apparition and the next moment Helen stepped beside him.

"Who presents this woman for holy matrimony?" Pastor Gabriel Keyes, in his silken white robe, had mysteriously appeared from somewhere behind the altar. He was a large man with spectacles at the end of his nose and he held a Bible.

Mrs. Turner said, "I do," and her words confused him. His mind was a whirl of emotional turmoil and he thought, Was Mrs. Turner getting married? How could this event happen without Helen's father? Had the Count given permission by way of some parchment document sealed with a wax stamp from Poland? And how he missed his own father!

Helen looked at him through the thin white veil with her cheeks rouged, her sparkling blue eyes lovelier than ever, glistening with tears of joy and her smile beaming with happiness. He gazed transfixed by her loveliness and could not look away.

Pastor Keyes said something to the congregation, then said something to Helen, who nodded. He nodded too and smiled. Then the pastor's words rang clear, "Do you George J. Stannard take Countess Helene Marie Bokowski to be your lawful wedded wife, to have and to hold, through—" his smooth voice melted into a sonorous wave while he was again captivated Helen's radiant beauty. Then Pastor Keyes stopped and everyone was waiting for him. He spoke clearly, boldly, "I do."

They exchanged rings with her warm fingers swollen and trembling, his hands steady and sure, and the ceremony was completed. They kissed but he pulled away after a brief touching of the lips, everyone was watching!, and his life was inextricably changed.

George and Helen beamed with happiness, turned to the audience and paused then walked down the aisle. Aunt Amelia and Mrs. Turner, each in the front row and across from each other, wept softly with profound happiness and used fine lace kerchiefs to dab their eyes. The congregation stood and Alyssa and Cranston grinned broadly and applauded. On the groom's side Dr. Côté winked to him with a big smile, Wheelock Veazey whistled, George Benedict clapped loudly and Billy Caldwell whooped with joy. Billy was here! Somehow, probably through Dr. Côté, Billy had learned of his marriage and he was here! Billy wore a dark suit with a vest, a black bow tie and he whooped again! Everyone all at once exploded with great hurrahs, cheers and loud applause!

The guests surged jubilantly around the bride and groom and they made their way in one joyful mass to the back of the church and out the wooden double doors, where a four-piece brass band played a Polish march and led the crowd down the street to the Burlington Hotel Ballroom for the festive reception. At the hotel they were met by a string quartet that played more music by Chopin. They waltzed into the grand hall adorned with crystal chandeliers, white linen tablecloths, and red velvet chairs on a black-and-white checkered marble floor.

Strains of beautiful dance music filled the night air. The gentlemen moved stiffly upright and the ladies revolved circularly around them and together they went around the dance floor. The quartet played the "Countess Helene Bokowski Wedding March," composed for the occasion, and the glamorous couple held center stage. He and Helen danced on, and on, through the night and received many well wishes.

He felt wonderful to see Aunt Amelia and so many great friends again. He hugged and spoke with Billy Caldwell, Dr. Côté, George Benedict, Bear Brisken, Mrs. Turner, Wheelock Veazey, Doc Thayer, Alyssa and Cranston—all of his good friends and family were here! The hotel trembled often with explosions of laughter, frequent tiny showers of tinkling glasses, and recurring toasts of long happiness to the young couple. Throughout the reception, Helen danced only with him. In his bold military uniform he swept Mrs. George Stannard, a languid smile on her full lips, across the dance floor then later, out into the dark night.

He and Helen rode in a hired shiny black coach to a Victorian house on the west side of Burlington. A few weeks before the wedding he had purchased a modest, slightly run-down house built in 1829. He and five workmen spent 12 days of long, hard labor and spruced it up. It was a freshly painted, grand white house with dark blue trim with a new large porch that wrapped around the side of the house.

The coachman had been paid in advance but he tipped him handsomely and smiled. He heard Charger neighing from the small stable behind the house and helped Helen alight from the carriage, offering his arm to escort her up to the front entrance. The coach driver clicked his tongue twice and said, "Git, Mabel!"

As they approached the front of the house, he felt romantic and took Helen's white-gloved hand and together they stepped up the porch stairs. He opened the front door, turned to Helen and easily lifted her in her silken white gown and carried her over the threshold.

Inside the front entryway was a brilliantly stunning, cut-glass chandelier lit with a dozen white candles and dozens more white candles flickered romantically and illuminated the house, courtesy of George Benedict, who had ridden Charger after the ceremony to light them. A long blue velvet Victorian sofa was off to the side and a curved mahogany staircase led upstairs.

"You can put me down," she giggled.

He held her aloft, spun in a circle then started up the curving staircase. He felt strong and happy, and looked passionately into her amazingly blue eyes. He wanted to memorize this moment to make this feeling last forever.

He charged up the staircase steadily. The master bedroom was the first door on the left and he pushed the door open with his left leg then carried her into the room where more white candles gave the bedroom a soft, romantic glow. A large bed with a thin white canopy was gorgeously decorated with green pillows and fresh white linen sheets. He tenderly placed her onto the bed and eased her down. She tossed aside his white-plumed hat then pulled him down to her and kissed him fully on the lips, ran her fingers through his hair, and pulled tenderly on his upper back. He lay gently on her, feeling the warmth of her body. Her silken dress rustled slightly. He felt the curve of her waist and her plump bosom pressed against his chest. Her legs were exposed, revealing white stockings and a single white garter belt, just above her knee! He smiled with pleasant shock, gazed at her again and drank in her beauty deeply. She pushed herself up, eased back against the pillows, arched her left eyebrow and stared into his eyes. He felt himself becoming very hard and pressed himself against her. She was incredibly, radiantly lovely. He knew this moment and this night would last forever in his memory.

~11 ~

Captain "Pete" Male combed then wetted his hair with his palm, over and over again. Pete was dressed nattily in his uniform with one shoe shined to a bright glow. He held a small mirror and examined every inch of his appearance, stopping at each of two rows of four brass buttons on his coat then gave them an extra polish with a soft white cloth. He turned to George and said, " 'Bout time, sunshine!"

"I needed my beauty sleep." Pete did not respond but continued to examine himself meticulously so he asked, "What's the occasion?"

"There's a wing-ding of a dinner party at the Willard," Pete said. "They say Gen'ral Grant may come. I'd sure like to meet him. Maybe he'll give me an office."

"As what?"

"As anything! I need a job."

"Ah." He watched the captain pick lint from his uniform with his right pant leg pinned below the knee. "Why Grant and not Lincoln?"

"Lincoln done gived out all the jobs he had. All the plum ones anyway. Shoot. I'm thinking long term."

"You mean next term, should Grant be elected."

Pete made a final inspection of his smoothed-down hair then placed the mirror next to the apple on the small table between their beds. "Yeah. Grant's gonna be somebody, yes-sir!"

He sat up in bed and scratched the bandage around his stump of a right arm. His skin was very tender from the surgery and it hurt to touch the area. He felt weak and wondered how Captain Male had the energy to attend a party. "How will you get there?"

"Oh. Major Hench has a carriage, right outside."

"Ah." He thought more of Pete's ambition for a post. "What skills do you have?"

"Heck, I can do anything. That's what my pa always said. Well, I got to go if I'm gonna get a good seat."

"Did you find pencil and paper?"

Pete opened the drawer of the small table, took out a single piece of paper and placed a pencil on top of it. At the top of the page was written,

Visitors of Gen. Geo. Stannard, Vt. Vols.

"Ain't been no one since you asked. You jinxed it."

He chuckled then noticed Pete's neatly made bed. "Very good. I know you want to go but I was counting on your help to write a letter."

Pete tightened the corners of his mouth then pulled out another sheet of paper. "There ya' be. Go at it."

He thought of writing with his left hand and looked up evenly at Pete, who clearly had no interest in helping. Then he considered military protocol. What authority did he have in the hospital? Was a captain from New York under his authority? What did all of this have to do with the war? He understood how someone like Pete could be focused on a social function and nodded for him to take his leave. Besides, to whom would he write? Aunt Amelia? Mrs. Turner? "Enjoy the party. And that's an order!"

Pete smiled, showing his dimple, and gave a jovial salute then bounced swiftly on two crutches down the aisle between the cots of the wounded. His energy was astounding. It was only last week Male was wounded, so how has he adapted so quickly? Then he thought of people in civilian life who showed great excitement for parties and balls, which reminded him of Helen and of how desperately she wanted to climb the social ladder. Social functions dictated her life—

where she would be and what she wore. She followed protocol more strictly than any well-trained soldier.

~ ~

George and Helen were still in their first months of marriage but it was the high point of the spring season, of coming out soirees and social balls in Burlington. Helen was a-titter with emotion and tried on one dress after another. He sat in the front room reading a book of Keats's poetry when she entered with a rush of silk.

"Does this seem appropriate for the occasion, for my figure?" She made a swirling pirouette in a light blue gown.

"Yes, you look splendid, darling," he smiled then closed the book, keeping his finger on the long poem. "You're absolutely radiant."

She looked puzzled then lifted the blue dress up and raced up the curving staircase, showing her bare feet. He chuckled and returned to the poem, which was an intriguing ballad describing an ailing knight-at-arms.

After a few moments, Helen stood before him again, breathing excitedly. She now wore a stunning green dress with a very low décolletage that showed off her ample bosom. "Tell me, honestly. Do you think this is better? For my figure, I mean. I know my eyes look better in blue but somehow this seems better. Is it?"

She stared at him for his decision. He closed the book and looked up at her then said warmly, "You've never looked better, my dear."

"Truly? I think the blue may be better. I could have the blue altered to this cut, couldn't I?"

He observed the low-cut breast-line that hugged her cleavage and wondered what was so important about *this* party? "Of course you may."

She turned and ran for the stairway so he called out, "Which party is this for?"

She slowed on the staircase, clutching the railing. "This is for the Governor's Ball! I can't believe you had to ask!"

"Oh, of course." He lifted the leather-bound book and said, "I guess I'm a little pre-occupied with this poem."

"It's only *the* event of the season! Sometimes you act like nothing I do matters!" she huffed and was crying before she reached the top of the stairs. He set the book on the end table then went after her, catching her as she closed her bedroom door but he forced his boot into the doorway to stop it.

"Helen! My darling, I'm sorry."

"You should be! You don't understand me at all!" She sobbed then slammed into the door, pinching his boot but he kept it in place.

"Tell me, what more do I need to know?" he spoke calmly.

"Everything! You act like none of this matters when it matters *entirely!* Of all the balls, theater, soirees, teas, functions, this is it! I can't explain it. You're a simpleton!"

She threw all her weight into the door and a crack sounded. It may have been the door hinge but it felt like a broken bone in his foot and he cried out in pain, hopping around on one foot, and slowly came to rest, holding his ailing foot in his boot. She slammed the bolt lock then called out through the door, "You deserved that!"

Pain throbbed in his foot but after a moment he was able to limp on it then tenderly made his way down the staircase, leaning heavily on the railing. He eased himself down the stairs. Afternoon sunlight streamed in the windows and beautifully lit up the cut-glass chandelier in assorted gleaming colors of yellow, red, and bluish purple, filling him with awe. On the landing, he admired the sun just above the crest of the elm trees and stepped to the front door, calling out, "I'll be on the porch, dear. We can talk about the Governor's Ball," then to himself, "or my achin' foot."

He eased into the first of two Adirondack chairs, painted red, then took off his boot, crossed his injured foot over his knee and rubbed it. He took out a cigar from his vest pocket, struck a match on the box and puffed away. The spring sun inched closer to the horizon and beautiful golden light streamed through the budding trees and shimmered on Lake Champlain. He puffed, exhaled with a sigh, and watched the bluish cigar smoke hang in the fresh, fragrant air. He wondered how many of these important parties made up "the spring season"?

During their winter courtship, he and Helen had attended 31 social functions in the 10 weeks between Christmas and the first day of spring. During that time he learned about high society, yet always found himself bored at these events until he met up with anyone who could discuss the latest news and political events.

During the spring season the men spoke almost exclusively on the possibility of war. After Colonel Robert E. Lee hanged John Brown for his abolitionist-led uprising at Harpers Ferry in 1859, it felt like it was only a matter of time until the entire country would be at war because people were willing to die for and kill for the abolition of slavery. Then in 1860 Abraham Lincoln was elected president and shortly afterward the news focused on the seceding states. One state tumbled after another, following President Lincoln's taking office. After South Carolina's secession, Mississippi, Florida then Alabama withdrew from the Union.

Meanwhile he and Countess Bokowski, for she enjoyed using her title, attended her niece Catherine Anne Beauchamp's grand soiree for her 14th birthday, where the men discussed the admission of Kansas as a free state into the Union. Later, for the opening of Rigoletto at the Opera House, Helen bought a new hat with peacock feathers and she was envied by all the women in attendance.

They were married March 17th, enjoyed a romantic honeymoon in their home in Burlington, and eased into the functions of high society as a married couple. She bought a Japanese silk fan, painted with two Geishas demurely holding fans, and showed it off along with her altered, low-cut, light blue gown, at the Governor's Ball on Saturday April 13th in the State Capitol Ballroom. Attendees were unaware that the previous day Southern Rebels had fired on Fort Sumter in South Carolina so when he and Helen entered they received warm, robust applause. Then Mrs. Turner took his arm and Helen spun off gracefully to the host, the Governor, and they floated across the black-veined white-marble dance floor. Mrs. Turner proceeded to give him a report on every arriving couple and every lady's style of dress.

"Oh, look at those mutton chop sleeves," Mrs. Turner said, drawing in a deep breath of admiration. "It must have taken days to sew. Oh, there, ah-h-h! That material is French watered silk. And look at that fichu. Belgian lace." He tried to learn but soon realized he had little interest in the names of the frills of women's dresses.

That night Helen danced with 16 men, including Alvan Herndon and Captain La Salle, before he cut in on the newly-elected Judge Wheelock Veazey, who appeared to be holding Helen's waist especially tight.

"I thank you, Judge," George smiled stiffly, gritting his teeth.

"It's your honor," Judge Veazey replied with a graceful bow. Veazey's dark features and bright smile made him quite handsome, and he spoke with a velvety, practiced voice. "Countess Bokowski was telling me how much she enjoys your escorting her to these events."

"Indeed. It's my pleasure to bring *Mrs. Stannard* and please allow me to congratulate you once again on your judgeship." He bowed with a swift, agitated nod then spun Helen away, dancing hurriedly around the crowded ballroom. She followed his lead effortlessly, a very skilled dancer who needed little guidance. Her tender white hand lay motionless on his thick, warm palm but tension filled his jerky steps.

"What has gotten into you?" she snapped.

He held his temper and remained positive, feeling somehow this discussion was vital. “I needed a dance with the most beautiful woman here.”

“Yes, that is me, isn’t it?” After a moment, when she looked up at him with her radiant blue eyes, he winked at her and with some effort he smiled. She noticed the strain in his face but responded cheerfully, “Thank you for letting me alter this gown. It is perfect this way, don’t you think?”

He stared into her eyes but could wait no longer. He spoke passionately, “I don’t care about the dress. I love you.”

“Yes, of course,” she said, spun herself under his hand and admired the way her dress flared out in a gleaming, light blue arc. “My gown is *quite* lovely.”

He grasped her hand and spun her back then pulled her tender waist tight to him. The music ended and she curtsied deeply, with her bosom pouring out of her low-cut dress and showing her round, pink nipples. She rose then gave her oft-repeated phrase, “Thank you for the dance.”

“It’s time for the Governor’s Waltz!” the conductor called out and a greasy-faced young man pushed up and held out his smallish pink hand.

“It’s my dance,” the young man’s voice quivered. It was Alvan Herndon, an apprentice at the bookbinder’s office. Acne dotted his forehead around his dirty, dark-blonde hair.

“I’ll get us some punch,” George said, “and you may meet me on the veranda.”

"No." She licked her lips, forced a smile, and curtsied again. "I regret to inform you I have another three dances before a break."

Helen glided away, tossed her head back in joy but then held up her dance book with her stone-white hand in Herndon's hand and called out, "But you enjoy yourself!"

He watched Herndon lead her, swirling them across the dance floor, remarkably graceful for a young man and he swept them around the room to beautiful effect. Helen laughed gaily and leaned back her head again, causing her dark curly hair to bounce over the large white bow on the back of her dress.

He made his way to the punch bowl table where several men in dark suits, or navy blue or gray militia uniforms milled about, watching the dancers. He picked up a ruby-colored cup filled with punch and went out on the veranda, where white paper lanterns hung in trees and on poles, illuminating the veranda against the dark, bluish-purple sky. A streak of thin clouds, orangish-pink on the horizon, made a last hurrah to the setting sun and the warm spring air smelled lovely, full of fragrant flowers blooming.

Across the veranda was a commotion of agitated men, who stood in groups and spoke excitedly of telegrams received. They discussed the news of the Southerner's bombardment of Fort Sumter, South Carolina, where Rebels had attacked and the Federals defended, led by Major Anderson with Abner Doubleday second-in-command.

George drank his punch in large, restless gulps and worried about Abner Doubleday's fate. He felt the inevitability of the swirling events, knew it would carry him into duty, finished his drink, and placed his empty cup on a silver tray carried by a waiter, who circulated through the growing crowd on the veranda.

He went to the stone railing, gazed past a large open field of mown grass to a thick copse of tall elm trees and enjoyed the last flare of reddish-orange sky. Then he thought of the coming of war. He needed to prepare almost 1,000 volunteers to be soldiers and would devote his time and energy away from home to serve his country. It would be a major undertaking. He had experienced terrible, gruesome horrors in battle and vowed to do everything in his power to train these Vermonters to become excellent soldiers. He thought of his father, of how Samuel had taught him to love his country and to do what is right, to *Fight for Justice.* He nodded solemnly with his mind resolved and embraced the challenge. To no one in particular he said, "I'm ready."

"Here, here!" several men called out in response and he turned around. Two dozen men stood on the veranda, each with their attention riveted on him. He glanced down, thought of Helen dancing through various spring balls without him, then looked at the expectant faces of the men. With pursed lips he again nodded firmly.

~ ~

On Monday morning April 15th George entered the Governor's office in Montpelier and officially tendered his services to Governor Fairbanks and the United States of America. He was the first Vermonter to volunteer for his country.

~12 ~

Captain Pete Male returned from the Willard Hotel after dinner but before nightfall and was intoxicated with a slowed, staggered gait to his one-legged walk with wooden crutches. He slumped down onto his made bed with a thud.

"What happened?" he asked. "Did you see General Grant?"

"No. Word was he weren't comin'. Wasn't comin'. He di'n't show." Pete let both crutches fall to the floor with a bang. "He's prob'bly out somewheres 'n drunk more 'n me! 'Sides it wouldn't do me no good no way. Who in th' *hell* am I kiddin'!"

"Captain! You are to stop this manner of talk *right now!*"

"Yes-s-s sir!" Pete laughed, raised his one leg and took off his muddy boot then his white sock with a hole at the big toe. "It ain't no use. I ain't never gonna meet Gen'ral Grant no way."

"Suppose you don't. Does your future depend on meeting him?" He waited for a response but the captain collapsed back onto his cot. After a moment he continued, "Let me tell you this. I've met him and it didn't improve my life. Quite to the contrary."

Pete looked over with a quick jerk and his bloodshot brown eyes searched then focused on him. "You met Gen'ral Grant?"

"Yes, a few times."

"*You.* You met Genr'l Grant?" Pete struggled to sit up then propped himself up on his elbow and swung his leg over the bed. "Com'on, tell me! Where was ya? Is he great like everyone says? I bet he is!"

"No, I'll save that for another day. But look how your interest picked up. Your whole demeanor changed over a few words and you probably felt better, at least for a moment, didn't you?"

"Yeah. So?"

He nodded slightly. "A few words of hope and you raised yourself up."

"So?"

"So, why can't you do that all the time?"

"What fer?" Pete said.

"To improve yourself. Give yourself a better attitude." He didn't think his words landed and added, "To make yourself productive instead of hoping a social connection will solve your problem."

"Connections 'ill get ya where ya need to go."

"That's not what I was taught, although I've seen the truth to your claim. But by using my tact at least you'll have a job well done."

Pete scratched the back of his head then looked around the room. Here and there a few young soldiers moaned in pain but were sedated. Overall it was quiet. A male nurse carried a full bedpan down the aisle of beds then turned out to the hallway. Pete pointed at him and spoke sarcastically, "Lookee tha' boy with th' bedpan. He's doin' a job *well done.* 'Cording to you, he'll be the next Sec'tary of War!"

He laughed and Pete laughed with him. Another full bedpan carrier hustled by and George said, "There goes the next Secretary of the Navy!"

"An' here comes the Sec'tary of State!" They enjoyed a good laugh together.

Outside the window birds called in the trees, nightfall settled in, and the large room grew dark except for a single candle on a table across the aisle, where a recovering sergeant read a book. Then an orderly entered with two lit hurricane lamps and placed one on a table near the hallway door then lit candles here and there.

Two hours passed while he re-read yesterday's newspaper in the dim light. Captain Male sobered up and his attitude improved a little. Despite the passage of time, he couldn't let go of their earlier conversation. "Why is your faith so grounded in connections?"

"My cousin works for Sec'tary Blair. He's goin' places."

"Oh?" He raised his eyebrows, impressed. "Yes, okay, Secretary Blair is an important man. What does your cousin do?"

"He's a butler. Most of the time he don't *do* nothin'. He's met all kinds of famous people. He even met Bobby Lee."

He turned his head with doubt and thought, How was that possible? Secretary Blair was one of the most powerful men in the Federal government but how had his butler met General Lee? "How'd that happened?"

Pete explained how his cousin had worked for Secretary Blair for several years when the entire household became anxious over the visit of Virginia's most prominent soldier. Pete's voice slowed to a steady cadence, then he told the story, perhaps for the one-hundredth time, and it carried the weight of fact in his practiced recital:

“Colonel Robert Lee is a short man with a sturdy build. Everyone knew he was the best soldier in the entire country because he was one of the top graduates of West Point and he served in the Mexican-American War, um, with great honor.

“At West Point, Robert Lee taught tactics and warfare. His pa was Harry “Lighthorse” Lee, a general in the Revolution. We all know who General George Washington is. And it is a well-known fact General Washington was lucky to know Lighthorse Harry Lee.

“Now when John Brown captured the Federal arsenal at Harpers Ferry in Eighteen hundret and fifty-nine, it was Colonel Robert Lee who had to recapture the fort. He done it, despite John Brown and his gang of hooligans. For Bobby Lee it was just another honorable duty and he served his country.

It was April, Eighteen hundret and sixty-one, right after the Fort Sumter, um deal, and the newly elected President Abr’am Lincoln needed a commander to lead his Army. He wanted to put down the Secesh. Everybody knowed there wasn’t but one man to call on ‘cause one man was superior to all the others. President Lincoln wanted Robert Lee to lead his Army and be Commander in Chief of all the armed forces.

Now Ab’ram Lincoln, um President Lincoln, didn’t have the nerve to speak to Mister Lee. No. He knew Colonel Lee was from Virginny, so there was a chance he’d say no and side with the Southerners. So Lincoln,” Pete made the noise of a chicken, “ba-gawk, needed to save his own face so he asked around and weren’t long ‘til he found Francis P. Blair, the most powerful man never elected president. Mister Blair was good friends with Bobby Lee so Lincoln, ba-gawk, asked Mister Blair to ask Colonel Lee."

Pete took a deep breath, he seemed to be tiring, but continued, "So, it was on Thursday the Eighteenth of April, an unusually warm day in Washington City, when Colonel Robert Lee, rode his white horse, Traveler, across Long Bridge, over the Potomac River. On the bridge were posted militia men and they had carts with iron jars of cartridges, grapeshot, and ammunition shells. Some Federal officers, with their blue capes a-flowing, carried bundles of hay on the pommel of their saddle and dropped them on the Virginny side of the bridge.

"So now then, Colonel Lee rode his horse Traveler right up to the front door of Mister Blair's three-story, yellow house on Pennsy'vania Avenue. He tethered Traveler's reins to a fancy hitching post. He walked with purpose right up the stairs, a-wearing his best uniform with medals and ribbons from the Mexican War and let loose a barrage on the knocker. Of course, being a veteran tactics man he knew what Francis Blair was gonna ask him. Heck, everybody knowed he was the top choice to be commander of the Army of the Republic.

"Now then, a tall butler with a handsome face, Erastus J. Male, greeted Colonel Lee with all the grace and charm he could. The butler, that's my cousin by the way, showed Mister Lee into the front parlor, where he sat on a red-velvet upholstered chair. The butler, Erastus J. Male, closed the door behind them and stood nearby while Mister Blair talked with Colonel Lee. They chatted for a spell with the butler right there. He weren't listening in, he was just doing his duty right there by the door. Of course everybody knowed it would be no. Still, Mister Blair started off by saying, 'Colonel Lee, you are the most experienced and qualified military man in the entire United States.'

Now Francis Blair, he liked to eat so he was a big feller but he was also near-sighted so he looked over his glasses at Colonel Lee. Bobby Lee said, 'No, Mister Winfield Scott has the honor of being the most qualified military man.' So right off, Bobby Lee set Mister Blair straight.

Ol' man Blair he pressed on and asked if he wanted some tea or somethin' to drink and before Colonel Lee could answer the butler was sent for Madeira. You may not know this but Madeira was the favorite of General Washington and, of course, *Harry Lighthorse* Lee, Robert's pa.

Colonel Lee bowed and smiled, and waited for Mister Blair to finish his speechifying. Blair said somethin' like, 'Yes, but General Scott is old and frail, and so fat he can't even mount a horse! So, he can't be counted on to lead the troops.'

Then their conversation stopped while the butler, Erastus J. Male, poured them each a glass of Madeira. Then Mister Blair made Erastus leave the room and he closed the French doors behind him. Mister Lee sipped the dark wine with brandy and showed his ease of conversation and Southern charm. Mister Blair tried to tell one of his favorite stories of a man who stumbled upon a polecat in the woods and now, engaged against his wishes, the man didn't wanted to fight the polecat or let it go!

Course that didn't help none. Colonel Lee chuckled politely. Then he stood up, smoothed down his neatly-trimmed, graying beard, and said, 'Mister Blair, it is difficult to tell if you are engaged in the situation with me as the polecat, or if you are suggesting that I am in a difficult situation because I am a Southerner. Let me say it was with great honor that I was called here today and you have been exceedingly complimentary of my qualifications.' Then Bobby Lee paced over to one of the tall windows and gazed out to the distant, tree-covered hills. 'But I am *first* a Virginian.'

Colonel Lee pointed out the window to the land over the Potomac, to Virginny. He smiled easy-like but his gritty, gray eyes showed determination. 'I owe it to my right-honored forefathers to serve their cause and to be true to the reasons they fought.'

Mister Blair approached Colonel Lee and stood next to him at the window. 'The President has given me his consent, with authorization from the War Department, to ask whether any inducement can be offered that will prevail upon you. Colonel Lee our great nation asks for your service, that you should be given full command of the Army of the Republic with the rank of Major General.'

Colonel Lee had his defenses ready and said, 'May I speak candidly?' and Mister Blair said yes. Then Colonel Lee said, 'I look upon secession as anarchy. If it was me who owned the four million slaves in the South I would sacrifice them all to the Union. May I ask,' Colonel Lee stood his ground and looked hard into Mister

Blair's cool blue eyes, and offered some bait. 'How would I use this Army, sir?'

'To put down this rebellion of Secesh, Seceshion, um Seceshonists, and to preserve the Union, of course.'

Bobby Lee grinned because Blair done took the bait. 'As a Southerner, it would seem this Army would be used to invade Virginny, our land, and destroy our homes.'

Francis Blair still did not see his error because some say he chose the *legal* argument rather than the *military* consequences. He said. 'This group of a few people, these rebellious few, challenge our Constitution. They challenge our central government. It is the good people of the various State legislatures that are being taken to task by these few rebellious youths. They have no legal authority. They are using nothing but force. Therefore, we must meet their dividing force with our uniting force. It was the rebellious South that *provoked us* with an unlawful attack on our federal Fort Sumter.'

'Mister Blair,' Bobby Lee turned his shoulders away and again pointed out the window. 'My home is across that river. You can almost see Arlington House from here. My family is well-landed and lives all over Virginny. If yo' Army crosses that river, you will not be crossing into foreign soil but onto my father's land, and my Uncle's, my dear cousin and brother's land. How can I draw my sword upon my family, my Virginny?'

'This is *all* our country, Colonel Lee.' Mister Blair walked away from the window and put his hands on the back of the velvet-upholstered desk chair. 'It is for our nation's sake, the very nation that your forefathers fought to unite. This is why I ask you, *our nation* asks you, to serve as Commander of *our* forces.'

Bobby Lee would not be intimidated. He stood at ease, not moving an inch. He rested his hand on the guard of his sword. 'Beg pardon and with the greatest respect, sir. I must consider both my country *and* my heritage.'

Francis Blair scratched at his white beard, which was a new fashion after the President, although Blair's beard was kind of patchy. Then he again approached Colonel Lee. Mister Blair was over sixty but he knew what the stakes were. Mister Blair set his hand on Bobby Lee's shoulder to get cozy with him. 'Colonel, may I call you Robert?'

Colonel Lee gave a gentlemanly bow. 'As you wish, Secretary Blair.'

'Yes, Robert. Please call me Francis. We've known each other too long to stump on formality. You know my son. He brings me much joy, so I can appreciate your heritage and your concerns for your family. You are in an uneasy position, not unlike a beautiful bride being courted by *two* suitors. One is your charming neighbor, whom your father adores and whom you have admired all your life. The other is this great, sprawling behemoth that is most powerful and filled with immense riches, great beauty, and filled with vast potential but one cannot *see* potential or hold something vast and powerful, like this country of ours.'

'I understand your story, sir. I admit this is a difficult situation.'

Francis Blair squeezed his shoulder. 'This is not something we take lightly. We know what war is. It is not a pleasant thing. It is not all glory that youth sings with drunken passion. It is vicious and it kills both the honored and the scoundrel equally.'

'Yes, sir.' Bobby Lee nodded and his lips were taut. Then Colonel Lee bowed in order to break free from Mister Blair's grip, marched to his left, flanking Blair by the window, and stood by his side. Bobby Lee said, 'Sir. In the War with Mexico I sent thousands of young men into battle and I knowed not all would return. The brutal killings at Harper's Ferry are fresh in my memory. War *is* a horrible thing. It is to be avoided at all costs and *this* government should try to avoid it. You may be certain this is not something I enter into with any sense of lightheartedness or with blind thoughts of glory.'

Mister Blair put both hands on Robert Lee's shoulders, in his best dress uniform, and he faced him directly. 'I understand your dilemma, your sense of duty to Virginny, but you must know there is no greater honor than to serve the United States of America.'

There was a long silence. Then Bobby Lee turned away from Mister Blair's grasp again, put on his military hat, and bowed. 'I am sorry Francis. I never thought that I would live to see the day the President would raise an Army to invade our own people. No, I cannot lead such an Army.'

'I'm sorry to hear you cannot lead the *United* States of America, Robert.'

Colonel Lee walked for the doorway then turned to face Mister Blair, who had sadness in his eyes. He understood the trouble his friend would have when he must tell the President he had failed so he said, 'Please convey my deep sense of honor and gratitude to the President but I must decline his offer. I have never taken my duties lightly. But I have no greater duty than to my home and my family. My Virginny.'

Mister Blair smiled feebly. His face flushed and he swallowed hard.

Colonel Lee clicked his boots together at attention with full respect for his old friend. He gave a formal salute, bowed again, and left the room. The butler opened the door for him.

Then Mister Blair's aide, Sanderson Griffey, an arrogant, pompous arse of a young man wearing an ill-fitting suit, turned in the hallway to gawk after Colonel Lee. Mister Blair done told Griffey to let him be, but he couldn't leave well enough alone. Griffey followed after Bobby Lee, got his autograph, and it weren't long after that he signed up with the Secesh. Got himself kilt at Manassas.

Anyway, Mister Blair waved to the butler to close the parlor door but the butler saw him sit on his red-velvet desk chair. Mister Blair knew he had failed and knew his failure would prolong a potential war that would now have Colonel Lee leading the *Reb's* army. And that fact would cause the deaths of thousands *more* men and perhaps would cause the *entire* Union to dissolve. Mister Blair let his heavy head sink into his hands and he was depressed for a very long time. Who could possibly lead this country better than Bobby

Lee? Tears welled up in Mister Blair's sad eyes and then spilt out onto his hands because he thought of the thousands of young men who would die facing Colonel Lee's soldiers. A tear for each dead soldier."

Captain Male clapped his hands once to signal the end of his recital, fell back onto his bed exhausted, and fell asleep, snoring. George scratched his beard stubble with his left hand and thought about Pete's story. For the most part, it sounded true.

~13 ~

He awoke with dawn's light. Pete slept heavily in his bed and it was very still and quiet. He made his bed and put on his uniform, awkwardly doing it all left-handed, single-handed, but it also was not *that* difficult, only more time-consuming. He went to the window and gazed at the grassy hospital lawn and the dawn's slanting rays, unable to burn off the heavy, misty haze. He sat on the ledge and waited for Pete to awaken. Two hours later, after several bouts of tossing and turning, Pete rose then relieved himself in the bathroom and hobbled back to his cot.

"I was thinking about your story about Robert Lee," he said.

"Ain't no story!" Pete exclaimed, his voice rough from morning congestion and without its even cadence in spilling out a memorized speech. "You can ask my cousin. He weren't tell no lie."

"No, I'm not saying your cousin would lie. I'm saying, ow!—" Suddenly his missing right arm ached! It was a strange sensation to feel pain in his right arm, from below his shoulder with pain shooting down. There was nothing there yet his right forearm and right hand hurt badly. Then, just as suddenly, the pain subsided and was gone. "Oh. Oh. No, I'm saying it's remarkable. I was the first Vermonter to volunteer for my country and here Mister Lee was asked directly and he refused. It's remarkable. Well. Your cousin. Does he enjoy working for Secretary Blair?"

"Nah, he hates it." Pete looked around at the many wounded soldiers who lay on beds to see if they were listening. None were. He spoke candidly, "He smells old! His health is peaked and he needs a lot of care, if you know what I'm saying."

"A lot of folks need care these days." He looked at Pete's pinned-up pantleg, then his own empty sleeve, then every wounded soldier in their ward and returned a hard stare at Pete until he fidgeted with self-awareness. "So why is a position as an aide something you'd want to do?"

"It ain't the doin'. Don't nobody want to *do* nothin'. It's the power."

He had witnessed ambition in Mayor Littlefield in St. Albans, who meant well but was officious and pompous; the lawyer and now Judge Wheelock Veazey, who was suave, a good leader, had great instincts, and seemed to always do the right thing; Colonel Whiting, who relished the idea of leading the Vermonters in battle but didn't have any experience in war; and several politicians in Burlington who wanted to be governor. He thought more of Pete's story, of the beginning of the war, and of how Colonel Lee refused to serve his country when asked. It disturbed him greatly. Lee had refused his country's request. He remembered what it was like for him at the beginning of the war when he heard the news of the firing on Fort Sumter and recalled the feeling of knowing his country was in need and, unlike Colonel Lee, he did not wait to be asked. He was the first person from Vermont to volunteer and his actions were not guided by naïve provincialism.

~ ~

He sat on the porch swing in a quiet conversation with Helen when a boy with an armful of one-sheet newspapers ran down the road screaming, "Fort Sumpter Fired On!" and tossing one-sheet papers in the air. He had discussed his patriotism with Helen on the way home from the Governor's Ball then again in more detail before he rode to Montpelier to volunteer, and now he explained he must do his duty for his country. A worried smile crossed Helen's face. Neither one said anything more.

He then went to the *Burlington Free Press* to speak with George Benedict, whose father ran the newspaper. Outside the building a gentle breeze wafted off Lake Champlain, filling the air with the scent of blooming flowers but despite the perfumed breeze Burlington was abuzz with talk of the impending war. He recalled their conversation last autumn when some people still held hope for a peaceful resolution and therefore the newspaper would not run an editorial calling for volunteers for a Vermont Brigade. He also recalled Benedict's courage in his help in carrying a wounded soldier away from the Canadian Battle of the Windmill but upon seeing Benedict now he noted his demeanor had changed from last fall and he had a slight smile at the corners of his thin lips like he knew something. They met near a loud printing press in the back of the large room, where they needed to raise their voices to be heard. He told Benedict, "I'm adamant in my sense of duty and I hope you'll serve, too. Will your father write an editorial now?"

"How 'bout this?" Benedict pointed at a row of backward type which upon printing would create the headline, **Call for Volunteers!** Benedict spoke loudly, "He's writing something now."

He smiled and spoke with authority, "Using my experience in the Ransom Guards, I will organize and train the boys. We have almost one thousand volunteers!"

Benedict looked impressed then hollered, "Tell you what. I'll let Pa know you're organizing it. Maybe he'll put your name in it. We can make camp at the Fairgrounds." The racket of the printing presses made so much noise it was difficult to hear so he stepped closer to Benedict. His brown eyes expressed loyal confidence. Then Benedict clapped his shoulder with his slim hand, pulled him closer and shouted, "*It'd be an honor to serve with you!*"

~ ~

Helen was occupied with preparations for the latest spring ball to be held at the lavish home of Captain Henri de La Salle, one of the wealthiest men in the state. Captain La Salle, only 31, was a bachelor although it was rumored he had more than one wife in foreign ports of call. La Salle had a small thin mustache, a long aquiline nose, and had made his fortune in shipping, having been based in New York with long trips to the West Indies and London with cargoes of rum and slaves. Then he settled in Vermont to enjoy the clear air and scenic views of mountains over Lake Champlain.

Captain La Salle's Spring Ball would be the highlight of the social season, Helen explained, and attention must be paid to every detail of her appearance. She went to two different dressmakers then consulted with Mrs. Turner and visited often with Hazel.

It was a warm, lovely afternoon in late April when George made final preparations for his departure, then trimmed the hedges around their home when he overheard Helen and Hazel talking on the porch. They chatted about the dashing Captain Henri de La Salle, who was very rich, not unhandsome, and had gentlemanly manners.

Helen took Hazel by her hands and said, "Oh dearest, you must meet Captain La Salle! He has such sad, dark eyes. And he's a very good dancer, too!"

"Yes, yes! Tell me more!" Hazel squeezed Helen's hands then bounced them on her lap. They eased the porch swing back-and-forth.

"At the Akin's Ball, Henri and I danced to the Emperor's Waltz," Helen smiled fondly then her tongue traced lightly over her full lips. "It's a very long piece and honestly I was beginning to tire. It was my twenty-first dance of the evening, so I asked *Mon-sieur* La Salle if he would mind resting and do you know, he looked at me with such hurt, puppy-dog eyes! I could have died!"

"Oh!" Hazel raised Helen's hands to her cheek, smiled dreamily then spoke with hushed excitement, "How romantic! Go on, go on!"

"Henri looked hurt so I explained the rest was only for my feet because I had danced all night but I would be happy to converse with him for the remainder of the Emperor's Waltz." Then Helen paused and George stopped trimming the hedges. He noticed the fine blonde hair of Hazel's tweezed eyebrows and the sharp curve of her cheeks. She had become prettier with womanhood.

"What did he say about me?" Hazel begged.

"I'm getting to it, dearest. Hold your horses!" Helen again wet her lips.

"Oh I can't! I'm about to explode!" Hazel kissed Helen's hands excitedly. "Please, please hurry!"

She smiled then raised one dark eyebrow, feigned a look of distraction and gazed out over the yard, past George, to the large tulip tree with buds near bursting.

"Ahhnnn!" Hazel cried.

Then Helen continued, "He said, 'You look beautiful.' "

Hazel shrieked. "He said I'm beautiful?"

" 'And your friend Hazel is quite charming.' "

"He said that about me? I'm quite charming!" Hazel sighed. "Do you suppose he ever killed a man? For his honor, of course. Or maybe for a lady's honor?"

"Oh, I'm sure of it," Helen said.

"No! Did he?"

"He must have. He looks so brave and he's the captain of a ship. He must have!"

"Oh, yes, of course!" Hazel giggled. "His ship was in Port Au Prince and there was a ruckus in town. A sailor had gotten into trouble with a drunken bartender over a servant girl and Captain La Salle was called to settle the matter. Oh, his name is so dreamy, Hon-*ri!*"

"Yes! Yes!" Helen said and picked up Hazel's story, "The Captain knew the lady in question from his many trips to Port Au Prince. She was secretly *his* lover, so he knew she could not have been involved in an affair with another man! So Cap-i-tain Hon-*ri* de La Salle challenged the barkeep to a duel! They met at dawn on the beach, with palm trees swaying in the salty sea air."

Hazel said in a husky voice, " 'Take ten steps!' The second called out, 'then turn and fire at will!' " Her voice returned to its romantic pitch, "The two men stood back-to-back. Captain Hon-*ri* could feel the barkeep sweating against his back. The other man trembled but Captain Hon-*ri* was calm because he did not fear death."

Helen now spoke in an affected French accent, " 'I do not weesh to keel you,' Capt-i-tain La Salle said, 'but I will keel you to protect my lady's ho-nair!' "

"Eeek!" Hazel cried out. "One. The duelists began separating. Two. The barkeep trembled and stepped again. Three. It was happening. Four. Five. Hon-*ri* called out, 'Pleez I do not weesh to keel you!' "

Helen continued, "Six! The pistol felt heavy in his hand. Seven. Eight. Nine. He raised it near his shoulder. *Ten!* They both turned and the barkeep could not keep his hand still. He shook like a leaf in the wind and *Bang!* The pistol fired! But the bullet whistled by Henri's ear!"

"No! It struck him in the chest but the bullet missed his heart!" Hazel said, "He took the blow and he nearly died, tragically, because his lady's honor would be forever soiled. Blood dripped through his shirt and down his side but with his last bit of energy he raised the gun and aimed. Cap-i-tain Hon-*ri* found the frightened barkeep in his sight but he heard him cry out, 'It's true! I lied!' so Henri did not shoot."

"*No!*" Helen said firmly, raising one eyebrow. "The barkeep cried out, 'It's true!' but Henri fired, ka-*bang!* and the bullet struck the barkeep. He fell to his knees clutching his bleeding heart. 'Yes, I lied!' the barkeep said, and he fell to the ground, dead."

"Hon-ri was very sad," Hazel said. "He turned to the sailor and said, if only the barkeep would have spoken sooner and told the truth, he would be alive today. Hon-ri miraculously recovered but justice was served!"

Helen laughed. "Yes! And to this day, Captain Henri de La Salle carries a bullet *near* his heart. It's too close to be removed and he feels its weight."

Hazel sighed again and brought Helen's hands to her cheek once more. "But what of his secret lady in Port Au Prince?"

"She died of malaria!" Helen said.

The young women laughed and hugged each other then Hazel said, "Oh if Captain La Salle was my husband, I would greet him so romantically after his long voyages! 'Oh, my dear love! Light of

America! You're in safe harbor now. Rest in my arms!' And then I'd give him the best, most caring and loving hug, and the sweetest, most tender kiss he's ever had in his life!"

Helen smiled coyly and again raised one eyebrow. She then brushed Hazel's long hair and started another story, this one about Mr. Astor, the married millionaire who had a carriage business in New York City. She braided Hazel's hair while she envisioned a tale about the dashing Mr. Astor, of how he single-handedly won the Mexican American War and became rich doing it.

Helen and Hazel spent the afternoon chatting and laughing while George finished then gathered up the trimmings from the hedges. When the dinner hour approached, Hazel excused herself, returned home and Helen went inside to freshen-up.

He took up a small, fallen branch and sat on the porch steps whittling. A moment later a courier arrived with a sealed note. The courier was a young boy, no more than 12, and he wore a blue sailor's suit. He did his best to stand still, smiled then looked out longingly at Lake Champlain.

He opened and read the note, then told the boy no response was needed but gave him a nickel and sent him on his way. Now he had to break the news to Helen. He sat on the porch steps with his back against a post and continued to whittle the small branch. Twenty minutes later a small pile of wood shavings surrounded his boots and Helen returned, eased herself into the porch swing then gave it a big push. He stood and placed the unfinished carving of a bird's head and body, without defined feet, on the porch railing. He sat next to her, stopped the swing from rocking, and stared into her eyes.

"They've called us to Washington City," he said with a slow, serious tone. Helen bit her lower lip and gazed at his wood-stained hands so he wiped them on his pants. "We leave in the morning."

"I knew it," she said harshly and stomped her feet down then stepped off the swing. She acted injured and this was his fault. He had let her down. After a long moment she faced him but her emotion burst out and she cried, "I'll have no one to take me to the Captain's Spring Ball!"

"I can arrange for a coach to take you, there and back."

"I can hire a coach!" she snapped with her full bosom heaving. "I can't go *alone*."

"Ah." He rose and stepped to her then held her hands tenderly, admiring the fine trace of blue veins under her skin. "Perhaps Hazel or Mrs. Turner may accompany you?"

"You don't know this because you're a man, and because you're not from here, but my Aunt is not as highly regarded in society as you would think. But I suppose going with Hazel would be *acceptable.*" She gazed at the trees' ripening green buds. "Although Hazel is inexperienced and she has no idea of how brutish men can be."

"All the more reason for you to escort her and introduce her to Mister La Salle."

"Yes. I suppose so." Her bright blue eyes glistened with this thought and a plan seemed to be forming in her mind.

Amid another long pause crickets chirped slowly then a blue bird flew out from a pine tree and landed on the porch railing, staring oddly at the wooden bird-like carving. Then the blue bird turned its head to examine the wooden creature from another angle, blinked then looked at it again from another angle.

"I must tell you," he said, "I overheard you and Hazel talking about Captain La Salle."

"Oh?" Helen flushed. "You shouldn't have been listening to our conversation. That was most improper!"

"I was working in the yard. I meant no ill will. Although I must tell you, your adventurous story of a duel, and death, it's all overly romantic."

"Ha! What would you know about the life of a sea captain?"

"I don't. I meant about war and killing someone. War is ugly and vicious."

Helen looked away and fanned herself briskly. Then she turned back and spoke passionately, "Promise me you'll come back alive! I, I'm too young to be a widow!"

He felt uneasy at her choice of words but pulled her close, kissed her warmly then swept her up in his arms and entered the house. He climbed the curving staircase and remembered carrying her up these stairs on their wedding night, only six weeks earlier.

Helen playfully slapped his muscular chest but then became solemn. "Promise me you'll take in a sermon before you leave."

"Of course," he said, mounting the last few steps then slid sideways through the doorway and lay her down on their bed. She sank back into the goose-down pillows and unbuttoned her blouse feverishly. She stared up at him, smiled slyly then opened her corset to expose her beautiful large breasts.

"I know this may be our last night together," she said, "so I want to remember every moment."

He kissed her gently on her neck then made his way down her body, opened her corset fully then kissed her often, slowly, all over her shapely body and returned to her tender face. She arched her back then pulled his head down and drew his mouth to hers, kissing him fully.

They kissed passionately for a long time. Then he said, "I love you."

She did not say anything but closed her eyes. The room was quiet, except for their soft moaning and the creaking of the bed.

~14 ~

A nurse came by and examined his dressing caked with dried blood and scar tissue. The nurse, a tall man with soft hands, used fresh warm water to gently take off the bandage, cleaned the wound with some alcohol that stung but swiftly put on a salve then wrapped a new bandage around the stump of his right arm. The nurse did not speak during the whole procedure but gave a kind smile and left.

Across the aisle a priest knelt by the bed of a soldier and prayed The soldier's body was ashen with his eyes fixed unblinking into nothingness. The priest, clad in black with a white collar, rocked back-and-forth, prayed and clutched a Bible, rosary beads and a silver cross.

The ward was quiet. No one stirred except the priest, who continued to pray devoutly. George rose and made his way down the aisle of cots then down the corridor to the latrine to relieve himself. When he returned, the priest no longer knelt but now hunched over the bed and cried. He thought perhaps there was some family connection or a special bond between these men. He sat quietly on his bed and watched. The priest in his black robe was genuinely involved with the deceased soldier and grieved for him.

It reminded him of Pastor Keyes' sermon for the volunteers before they left Vermont for Washington City and the coming war.

~ ~

The heavy-set preacher waddled up to the mahogany podium with quick small steps. Pastor Gabriel Keyes had long gray, mutton chop sideburns and dark eyes that blazed with fury. He was known to have the gift of words and people came from the entire area surrounding Burlington to listen to him preach. Over 100 soldiers in uniform filled the aisles and stood in the back. The choir's final note resounded and Pastor Keyes gazed over the congregation, sizing them up.

"*Sin!*" Pastor Keyes yelled, in unison with a smacking sound of his Bible blasting the podium, ". . . of the flesh!"

Pastor Keyes had everyone's attention. "Today Nathan Jervis pays for his sin of the flesh, a sin he committed years ago!"

"Yes, indeedy," an older woman in the front pew called out and re-arranged her false teeth then pushed them up onto the roof of her mouth.

"*What'd he do?*" a soldier hollered from the back.

"*Tell us!*" another called out.

Pastor Keyes nodded. "What led young Nathan down his sinful path? Clearly—" he paused for dramatic effect, "—he did not have the good book in his life!"

George recalled differently. He remembered meeting Nathan Jervis, originally from Montpelier, shortly after he had moved into the area and recalled Jervis carried a small Bible in his vest pocket. He had also attended this same church on occasion.

"Without God on his side he was lost. . . Lost to the ways of the flesh! Poor Nathan Jervis has only lived on this earth for nineteen years, but his life will not shine much longer, nay!, for he is dying of that vilest disease whose name shall not be spoken *and*. . . he will be *damned* for all eternity! No, in his brief, brief, *brief* nineteen years he did not *learn* to keep God in his heart. Foremost in Nathan's heart, two years ago, was the pursuit of the flesh! And so he was easy prey to lewd women. He cavorted with any hussy who showed an ankle, God forbid, a stocking. Nathan sought out the adventure of the flesh and *now* he is paying the consequences!"

"*Tell it, preacher!*" the elderly lady in front said with her false teeth clattering. She rocked and fanned herself in the stuffy church.

"Yesterday I visited Nathan Jervis in his parent's home. Nathan told me, two years ago he went down, down, *down* into the belly of the whale! Where? Nathan Jervis went down to Lady Eve's, that house of ill repute! He said he often attended Saturday night parties, where he frequented the company of lascivious women. Nathan told me of one particular woman. *He* called her a *lady—"*

"*Harlot!*" the elderly woman called out then rocked back-and-forth righteously in rhythm with her fanning.

"*I* will not judge!" Pastor Keyes continued. "A certain Miss Cassandra Hiccox, a pretty young lass of fifteen, works in this despicable house of Satan. Nathan went to *her* every Saturday night and *she* led him astray!"

The congregation gasped, a few groaned, and several called out "*Harlot!*" and another "*Whore of Babylon!*"

"Last night I visited Miss Cassandra Hiccox," another catcall of "Harlot!" rang out, "and indeed she has a full-blossomed figure despite her tender age. Also, if you can believe the devil's words, Miss Hiccox assured me she was as *pure as the driven snow!* Why should we *not* believe her? Her skin is soft and fair. Her dark brown eyes are convincing."

The rotund preacher paused to look around the assembly. Everyone was attentive and ready for him to preach. "Then Miss Hiccox, a tender lass of fifteen mind you, told me to my face, 'My legs have not parted for any man.' "

"Oh!" Many in the congregation gasped. George noticed some of the men fidgeted in the pews and several women looked around nervously.

Pastor Keyes used a pristine white kerchief, dabbed his forehead then held onto it while resting his left hand on his Bible on the podium. "Miss Cassandra Hiccox told me she worked there in order to take care of her sick Aunt, who lives in Plymouth. Yea, the land of the Pilgrims! We spoke for some time and she touched my hand with gentleness, her tender words falling upon me like flowery petals."

"*Then what?*" A young soldier in uniform called out from the back.

Pastor Keyes dark eyes burned with a brimstone fire but he paused and poured water from a blue pitcher into a glass then drank it. "That lass told me her whole life story and I squeezed the good book tight in my lap. The devil, *Cassandra,* what a perfect name the devil has taken!, moved to Burlington with her uncle two years prior, after her parents died of disease. Cassandra's uncle was an *unkind* man, she needed employment, and Lady Eve's was the only place she found to work. She has no skills in sewing, or caring for animals, or farm work. Cassandra asked me, What was she to do with her parents dead and she so young?"

Pastor Keyes nodded then became somber and gazed around the congregation but stopped to stare at him. His words were meant for him! "Dear friends! Cassandra took me to her small room—"

Most of the congregation gasped in startled awe while others called out "*Dear Lord!*" or "*Never lay with the Devil!*" or "*No!*"

"Her room was barely large enough for a small straw mattress." There were more calls of disgust and prayers. Pastor Keyes paused for a long time. His hand trembled, sweat beaded around his face and he used his kerchief to dab his forehead, temples, bushy mutton chop sideburns and his brow again then continued. "And *she* lit a candle for *my* health! *She* cried soft tears *for me!* And I received her confession."

"*Oh! Praise God!*" several in the congregation shouted.

"When I wiped that poor girl's tears, she looked up at me with the most angelic, dark brown eyes. She thanked me for saving her soul and asked if there was anything that *she* could do to help *me*. Her cheery, dark eyes sparkled in the candlelight and she showed me the quilt her mother had given her before she died. She spread it on the straw mattress and asked me to *feel* how soft it was. The top side was made of silk. Then she asked me to *try it* and Cassandra lay me down on the bed. She caressed my shoulders, thanked me, and this child of God sealed my lips with the kiss of a sweet, dear angel."

The entire congregation was in shocked silence. "I did not know why God had this young woman in front of me but I could see that *He* wanted me to hear her story."

Then Pastor Keyes's voice thundered, "*I was in the belly of the whale! I was in the hands of the Devil!*"

Pastor Keyes's voice shifted to a whisper, soft and low, in a confessional tone, "She lay me back and kissed my flesh. It made the smallest hairs on my body stand on end. And then she swirled her soft hair around and around my torso and—" he bellowed, "*God spoke to me!*"

Pastor Keyes's voice thundered in a resounding bass and vibrated to the pews in the balcony. "*Sin of the flesh! Repent! Yea!* He took me to the mountaintop and *He* showed me the way of Eve's transgression. *His voice* spoke unto *me* and *behold!* I could see the entire valley of mankind."

Pastor Keyes gazed around the congregation and George also looked at the many startled and shocked members, who held a mixture of bewilderment, entertainment, and piousness. The heavy preacher used his kerchief to absorb beads of sweat from all around his portly face then continued in his thunderous voice, "*Yea!* I have lain with the Devil! But now I see the light! Thank God, *He* has shown me His wisdom. Dear friends, never go the way of the flesh! For in the flesh lies slothfulness, the sin of adultery, the sin of all mankind! I went there for you! Just as *He* gave *His* life, *I* went there for *you* and now I can say, faithful friends, go *not* into temptation for that way lies ruin!"

The assembly gawked at each other but Pastor Keyes motioned to the choir and they broke into a rehearsed song of forgiveness and devotion. The faithful followed.

George stood with the congregation but did not sing the prayerful song, both gracious and powerful. He made a mental note to avoid placing himself in any such situation of regret with a woman then thought back to his early meetings with Helen and realized the way of flesh had led him into the position he was in, of being married. He loved Helen, had confessed his transgression, and wanted to live his life purely. He vowed whenever he was with a woman he would keep his thoughts chaste.

The congregation emptied into the common green and several people discussed the worthiness of Pastor Keyes's sermon. Some said it lacked scripture while others said it was an appropriate sermon on the sin of the flesh because many of the soldiers, who were about to be shipped off to Washington City to do their duty and possibly fight in a war, had never been out of the county. Many said Pastor Keyes had given these young men sound advice.

George considered everything these young men were to encounter, of the horrors of war from his experience in the Canadian Expedition, and his prayers focused on the boys of the Vermont regiment. He prayed they were ready and he prayed they would fight honorably.

~15 ~

He made his way down the hospital corridor for the mess hall. At the end of the hall were two double doors, which opened into a very large room with long rows of tables. Inside and near the door stood Walt Whitman with his large sombrero hat tucked under his beefy arm and several reporters standing around him. The newspapermen had pencil in hand with pads of paper to write on.

"Here he is now," Whitman said. "Gentlemen, General George Stannard."

Were all these people here for him? What did they want? After a pause, a reporter said, “Can you give us news of the attack on Richmond?”

Whitman looked him in the eye. “I asked a few of my fellow reporters to come by. I hope you don’t mind.”

He tightened his lips and felt the emptiness of his right sleeve. “No, I don’t mind. It’s okay.”

“How is the war progressing?” another reporter asked.

“Tell us about your experiences,” another said. “How were you wounded?”

Some were older, wizened men, and some had disfiguring wounds of their own but most were city folk, out of shape, or cocky with bravado and pseudo intelligence. All awaited his report on the war but where should he begin?

“Have a seat gentlemen,” The cafeteria had two very long rows of tables with high-backed dining chairs. “I’ll tell you what happened to our fine boys, mostly from Vermont. But I’ve led many men, from several states, in many battles.”

“Tell it all,” a reporter with wire-rimmed glasses said loudly then placed his hand to his ear, perhaps he did not hear well, then added, “General. Sir.”

He nodded to the reporters and a few fellow wounded soldiers, who had gathered in the cafeteria. As they were being seated, it reminded him of teaching children in St. Albans. Then he thought of the entire conflict to date and decided he would tell them everything about this god-awful war. Everything.

He regretted not pinning up his right coat sleeve, to make it more formal, and the empty sleeve hung by his side. He remembered the first time he had put on this same uniform and recalled the anxiety of leading the Vermont volunteers into battle. This uniform carried great responsibility and he always wore it with pride. He remembered the early days when he first wore this uniform and spoke in a clear firm voice, "The Vermont volunteers assembled in a field near the Burlington fairgrounds. It had been a long day of organizing raw volunteers, making arrangements of who would be in which regiment and where they should set up tents. The entire Vermont regiment was under the command of Colonel Whiting, who graduated from West Point almost 20 years earlier, in 1841. Colonel Whiting was appointed to lead the Vermonters, not only for his schooling at West Point but also, and more likely, due to his friendship with the Governor and other prominent Vermont politicians.

"Whiting was plump with a long white mustache curled at the ends and he appeared unsteady with his horse but he didn't wear gloves. He had soft pink hands. He preferred to shuffle among the boys with his flashy spurs jangling. It was soon evident he had not been in a military situation in a long time and he had never seen any conflict.

Whiting's first order was to make Lieutenant Colonel George Stannard responsible for molding the volunteers into one effective fighting force. He had done similar duty with the Ransom Guards militia but that was a group of 50 enthusiastic, easily organized men. This was a colossal assortment of 868 volunteers, wide-eyed boys, hunters, ruffians, wild men from the forest and every other sort of man and boy, most of them motivated by their bounty money and wanted it paid in advance. A handful had some militia training but there were very few trained soldiers among them. Many had volunteered to "Save the Union!" but the majority had never been out of their county, although some were from western New Hampshire, or northwestern Massachusetts. Almost all saw themselves as a general. Privates slapped their company officers on the back, called everyone by their first names, and thought saluting was pure nonsense. These volunteers were independent-minded Americans who answered their country's call and were ready to fight but they were not ready for strait-laced discipline or irksome military formalities. Yet the politicians and newspaper reporters predicted it would be a brief war.

George was officially the first to volunteer from Vermont and received one of the few blue uniforms, which he always wore with pride and honor. He was appointed the rank of lieutenant colonel and designated Lieutenant George Benedict to be his Aide and Thad "Bear" Brisken was Master Sergeant. Benedict had proven himself an able soldier in the Canadian Rebellion, enthusiastically followed orders, was detail-oriented and could write well. Benedict organized the men, using each region's militia unit as a core, and arranged them into companies from West Windsor, Woodstock, Burlington, Tunbridge, Bennington, St. Albans, Northfield and Rutland. Master Sergeant Brisken, who was the strongest man he had ever met, would be charged to instill discipline into the boys and to train them as soldiers.

They set up camp outside Burlington near the Fairgrounds with the green hills to the west and not far from the river. Hundreds of tents dotted the meadow while George and Benedict signed up the volunteers. It was clear some volunteers were boys of 15 or younger who lied about their age and some were well over 60 and frail, but those volunteers were persuaded to go home and guard their home front. They also had every type of volunteer in-between including short, tall, fat, lean, out of shape, or hardy. Some were inexperienced with a weapon or fighting, and others were crack marksmen from their militia or deadeye hunters of squirrel who could fire nine shots out of ten into a tree knot from 50 yards. They had every sort, from lawyer to misfit to backwoods hunter. They were an unsightly band brought together by the notion of defending their nation with a code of honor handed down with the legend of General Ethan Allen and the Green Mountain Boys of the Revolutionary War.

Colonel Whiting arrived on his gray horse, skittering sideways, well after mid-day and pronounced their location fit for an encampment. Whiting had two aides, both majors, who helped him with his mare to dismount, whipping it from both sides and then staking the hostile horse. Next they set-up his large, spacious tent on a rise overlooking the meadow, after which Whiting resigned himself to a long nap.

After a long day of signing up volunteers, with the sun sliding behind the western hills, dusk fell quickly. George decided to mingle among the troops to see how the boys were doing, pulled on his uniform coat and mounted Charger, his white horse now fully grown at 17 hands. Charger was strong, quick, and easy to handle like an extension of himself. They were partners. Together they began a casual walk among the volunteers.

Tents were set-up in helter-skelter fashion with some ripped in tatters. Campfires drew small crowds to stand or sit around blazing branches, where they told stories, jokes and sang pub songs, which reminded him of the encampment of "Hunters" near Ogdensburg before the Battle of the Windmill.

One older man with a long gray beard sat on a small keg and cleaned his musket with an oily rag. He eased back on Charger's reins then patted his neck. "That's some musket you got there."

"Aye." The old man glanced up but remained seated on the keg, probably not aware he should stand and salute an officer. He was haggard-looking with white hair and tired pale-blue eyes. He focused on cleaning the flintlock. "But it'll sure blast a hole in any Secesh."

"Where'd you get it?" he asked.

"It was my uncle's." The heavily wrinkled man closed one eye and squinted with his open eye then wiped the flashpan with care. "From the war of our independence, un-huh. Care for some potato and sausage soup?"

"No, thank you, sir. Do you mean the Revolutionary War? Eighty years ago?"

"Aye, that's the one." The elderly man squinted his eyes and tilted the flashpan to get a better look at it in the dying light. "It was quite a to-do, near as I can tell."

He raised his eyebrows and made a mental note to have Benedict instruct all company leaders to inspect *all* weapons and to replace any gun more than 10 years old. "I don't recall you signing up today."

"Figured I didn't need to. I'll blend in. Stand and fight with the others."

"Un-huh," He didn't wish to confront the old man, not tonight but would let him stay for the evening and made another mental note to have every company sergeant double-check the muster role with those in camp. He nodded goodbye then weaved Charger through the tents on a zigzag path. Very few saluted and most wore civilian clothes. When he rode past the large tent of the temporary mess hall, a pair of rowdy young men tumbled out with their arms flailing at each other. One screamed, "Northfield!"

The other grunted, "Rutland!" and landed a punch to the gut.

A number of drunken onlookers watched them brawl and a growing crowd gathered around. One officer, Captain Ichabod Upham, who George knew from the Rutland militia through Edward Ripley, pointed at one brawler with his silver flask. "A dollar says Cromartie takes 'em!"

"*Hey! Stop!*" George yelled.

There was a brief murmur from the dazed spectators. A few returned to watching the fighters, who scrapped at each other crudely. Most were confused on what to do. One of the fighters, Cromartie, with a dark-haired wild look, from Rutland, appeared to be winning. He wailed on his opponent with his right fist while also choking him in a wrenching headlock. The other man had bitten off part of Cromartie's ear and blood dribbled down his cheek, along his neck, to his sweat-soaked shirt.

At first he sat in the saddle in amazed disbelief but when it was clear he was not being obeyed he dismounted swiftly and pounced on both brawlers writhing in the mud. With one powerful arm he encircled Cromartie's throat and with his left hand he seized the sweat-matted hair of the cannibal. He wrenched the young men sideways, shook them then dragged them to their feet, apart, and cursed them.

Master Sergeant "Bear" Brisken, fully grown and very tall at 6'8", barrel-chested with thick arms and a short blonde beard, pushed his way through the crowd. He released the brawlers, who brushed themselves off and examined their wounds until Brisken swatted each of them with his huge hands and their faces registered shock. Brisken clamped down on a wad of shirt at the scruff of their necks, put them under arrest and pulled them further apart.

George realized they would need to build a stockade but who would have thought they'd need it on the first night? Then he examined the crowd. Some were drunkenly dazed the fight was suddenly over while others stumbled to a resemblance of attention and a handful saluted pitifully. Captain Upham wavered under wobbly, drunken knees.

George didn't bother to dust off his coat, saluted to Sergeant Brisken, who nodded upward in recognition with his hands full then shook his head with a smirk and winked one of his large brown eyes.

He mounted Charger, swung up easily into the saddle and looked down at the soldiers. Captain Upham's hand trembled, attempting to screw on the cap to his flask, fumbled it and glanced up at him on Charger.

"Captain Upham!" He spoke loudly so all could hear. "I expect a report on this by eight a.m.!"

Upham jumped nervously, saluted with the flask still in his hand and doused himself with whiskey, and everyone laughed. He saluted back sharply, turned Charger and eased him away, then heard Upham yell with slurred speech, "Get t' yer tents! Ya got a long day t'morra!"

A few more laughs broke out and after Charger had taken a few more steps he turned in the saddle. The boys were breaking up, heading in different directions. He considered more severe punishment for Upham, perhaps even going through the show of a court-martial but decided it was only the first day. If the captain's report showed he had learned his lesson about keeping his company and himself under control and showed remorse, he would not punish him. Upham deserved one warning.

The rest of the night was peaceful. He admired the thousands of brilliantly twinkling stars, the swirling expanse of the Milky Way in the dark sky, but thought, This is the beginning of a long, difficult journey.

He awoke with dawn the next morning, went to Benedict's nearby tent and called out, "Benedict!" but there was no response other than his slow shallow breathing.

"*Benedict!*" he shouted then he heard a grunting, snoring sound and a brief moment later again heard deep, shallow breathing. "*George Benedict! Wake up!*"

"Yes, sir!" Benedict responded in a raspy voice. "What time is it?"

"Time to get up! Why hasn't our bugler called reveille?"

"We don't have one," Benedict said. He heard the sound of clothes and boots rustling through the tent, followed by Benedict emerging through the opening. He scratched his light beard then readjusted his glasses on his thin, long nose. His dark brown eyes were partly bloodshot. "Morning, sir! None of our boys know how to play."

"The Collins boy didn't sign up?"

"No, sir. His mother didn't approve."

"Alright. Have the officers wake the boys and assemble. Quickstep! And we *need* a bugler!"

The troops fell in slowly, sleepily. Captain Upham turned in a respectful, regretful report on the two young men fighting and his lack of command over them and his inappropriate excess in drinking. George let Upham know this would not be tolerated and next time he would be punished. Then he saluted him sharply to dismiss him.

Benedict instructed each officer to make a list of the volunteers still *not* present. Colonel Whiting was absent. The long lines of boys and middle-aged men stood unevenly, in various colors of militia uniform or plain clothes. He knew Benedict had the same thought he did, but Benedict said it under his breath, "It's not much to go on."

He said quietly, "I hate giving speeches but I guess on our first day something official needs to be said." He glanced at his pocket watch, 7:58, replaced it then walked casually among the boys, eying their general demeanor and forgiving their lack of uniform and cohesion in standing in straight lines. He waited a few more moments hoping Whiting would arrive and recalled a discussion with Benedict about Whiting's lack of recent military experience yet both remained optimistic he was a skilled leader. Then he decided he would start and hand things over to Whiting when he arrived. He moved to the top of a small rise and began with a strong voice. "*Good morning, boys!*"

A few responded and a few saluted but most were quiet. "I'm Lieutenant Colonel George Stannard. Colonel Whiting is our commander. We're volunteers of Vermont! I *thank* each and every one of you for your service. I know some of you, others I know by name, but most of you I do *not* know. I've had conversations with some of you, but most of you I have not. What I have learned from my own, hard experience is that you're about to encounter the most dangerous time of your life. You appear to be good, stout men," he caught himself. Many of the volunteers were boys of 16 or 17, hardly ready for a rough scrap much less a full-blown battle. "Let me rephrase that and be completely forthright. You are all fine young men but most of you lack the skills of a soldier. You are very, very raw."

A few responded in disbelief and one shouted, "*I can whup anybody here!*"

"Step forward, private!" he said. No one answered but a young man stared with a challenging face with dark eyes. His grizzled chin jutted out, looking for trouble.

He shouted louder, calling out the haggard young man and a burly, dark-haired, bearded youth lumbered forward with a cocky gait, knocking a short private out of his way then stood before him with a sly grin on his face and staring up with angry eyes. His patchy, youthful beard was at odds with his chin, set at a tense angle and ready for a fight, with his right hand relaxed on his rope belt next to a small, well-worn blackjack. He appeared familiar but couldn't place him. "What's your name, son?"

"Cromartie." The young man looked around with his smirk widening through his dark, patchy beard. A few of his friends gave shouts of encouragement.

"From last night?" he asked, examining him closer. This man had both ears intact.

"No!" the young man barked and his grin was replaced by a snarl. "That was my brother Asa. I'm Burt."

"Damn right!" Another man called out. "Bad Boy Burt!"

He nodded to Burt's friend and smiled. "Small world. What a coincidence."

"How'd you like your teeth bashed down your throat?" Cromartie said.

He unholstered his pistol, flipped it around handle first then gave it to Benedict, who spoke through clenched lips, "Are you crazy?"

Although young, perhaps 18, Cromartie was muscular with broad, heavy hands with thick, pudgy fingers and black fingernails. He projected power, coiled tightly and set to explode, with his venomous gaze unflinching and focused on any opening to strike.

He took a few sideways steps into the open and noted he walked up a slight rise.

Sergeant Brisken, tall with blonde features and imposing, stepped through the ranks into the front line then stood next to Benedict, ready to stop Cromartie with any signal but George waved for Brisken to stay back.

"*Git 'em, Cro'!*" one of his friend's called out.

Another shouted, "*Go, Burt!*"

"I ain't sign up to fight you but I will," Cromartie said.

"*Ah!*" he hollered. "Cromartie here has recognized *I* am not the enemy! *And* I am his superior officer! He needs to take *orders* from a superior officer. *Me!*"

"I ain't said that," Cromartie said and a few laughed. Benedict again jerked his head to the side with widened eyes to stop this.

Cromartie spat into his palms then rubbed them together, perhaps a good luck charm to help him fight better, and clenched his fists. "Let's go!"

Cromartie's backers cheered him on with crude remarks. One smart aleck made it clear they were not taking orders from any one.

He waited another moment for the catcalls to clear but they continued so he spoke loudly, "*If we are to accomplish anything in this war, we* must *work together as* one *unit!*"

More catcalls rang out then Cromartie rushed him bull-like with his big broad shoulders, head down and his thick burly arms reaching out, all muscle and force. He used a throw Billy Caldwell had taught him, grabbed Cromartie's left arm, kneeled slightly and spun him over his hip, slamming him to the ground. Then he slid on top and pressed his left knee down into Cromartie's chest and throat, staring into his shocked brown eyes. He playfully tapped his bearded cheek and stood up. "Cromartie here has learned he's not the most skilled fighter after all!"

A few young men clapped and cheered but Cromartie was up again and pulled back his right fist into a solid haymaker then flung it wildly. He ducked then stuck a quick left hook into Cromartie's mid-section and bent him in two. Rather than punch him again, he pushed him downhill to the ground. Cromartie didn't quit and scrambled crablike after his legs.

"*Don't let 'em do that, Burt!*"

"*Take 'em, Cro'!*" another man hollered.

He stepped out of the way, he wanted this over and kneeled on him but Cromartie clutched his legs with his strong arms then twisted and took him down. Now he was in a rough-and-tumble wrestling match with a young man who had fifty muscular pounds on him. He slipped under Cromartie grip, grabbed his left wrist then twisted it behind his back and pinned him down. He leaned over Cromartie, sweating through his greasy dark hair and unkempt beard, and whispered into Cromartie's flushed ear, "Why don't you quit before I hurt you?"

"Blow it out your ass!"

He twisted his wrist further, higher, until Cromartie yelped with pain then cursed through clenched teeth and said, "Alright! Give!"

"*You'll obey orders!*" he yelled. Cromartie grunted animal-like with resentment flowing from his wild eyes. He twisted his shoulder higher, "*You will obey orders!*"

"*Yeah!*"

"*Say it! You will obey* all *orders!*"

"*I will obey all orders!*"

He let go and stood up, eying Cromartie then looked past the regiment of volunteers. With the fight over, most of them stood placidly but a few had turned and gazed across the open field at Colonel Whiting, in full uniform, who pushed dramatically out of his incredibly large tent like an actor thrusting back a curtain to walk on stage.

Whiting stumbled into a hole his horse had pawed then went over to the stake where his gray mare was tied down. He attempted to untie the line but the white-socked horse nipped at his hand, which he waved downward in agitation. After another attempt to untie her and being nipped, Whiting gave up mounting the mare and walked with his spurs jangling, staggering over the uneven ground toward the volunteers.

George stood up straight, saluted and called out, "*Attention!*"

Benedict and Brisken echoed, "*Attention!*"

All of the officers, less Whiting's majors, followed suit. A moment later Whiting called out from across the grassy field, "*What in the devil's name is going on here?*"

"*Training, sir!*" he said loudly and held his salute. "The boys need to understand protocol, take orders, hand-to-hand combat—"

"Why, we haven't had breakfast!" Whiting spoke with a congested, nasal tone. He gave a broadening smile, arrived at the top of the slight rise and stood by George's side but did not salute. Instead he twisted the long white whiskers of his waxed moustache with his pink hands, again smiled goofily, then turned to the regiment. "These boys need to eat! Three squares, yes indeedy! And we *ain't* had number one yet!"

"Damn straight!" Cromartie said. Many laughed and a few others called out. Any progress he had made was lost. The volunteers gaped at each other as individuals and murmured about where they would eat.

Whiting turned to him and Benedict and spoke in a lowered tone, "Who's making breakfast? Where's the mess hall?"

He relaxed his salute and shot a glance to Benedict, who reported, "We have two cooks, sir! Men who have cooked for an inn and a restaurant but we're still working out the details, supplies, and so on, sir!"

"No, no, no. You need to do that *first!*" Whiting gave a self-satisfied smile then announced to the volunteers, "Napoleon said, 'An army travels on its stomach!' By God, I won't have our boys going without food!"

"*Three cheers for Colonel Whiting!*" one man called out. The boys of Vermont responded with three cheers and huzzahs. When it quieted down, Whiting continued loudly like an overly dramatic actor. "*You're all fine young lads! Fine indeed! You're all free to go. Go find some food! What do you say we meet back here in a couple hours?*"

George shot Benedict another glance then turned his eyes back to Whiting, who stood slightly taller than him and spoke with a nasal tone, "Get this organized, Stannard. I'm making a note of this. I won't stand for another slip-up!"

He stood dumbfounded. Whiting grunted then waddled back toward his tent with his silver spurs ringing. He saluted again then hollered, "*Return at ten! Dismissed!*"

He again looked at Benedict, who burst out laughing then added, "Sorry, sir. It struck me as, well, amusing."

Sergeant Brisken grinned under his blonde beard with his big brown eyes glistening. Then he lumbered off with the others in search of food.

He took back his pistol from Benedict and saw Cromartie stood nearby but his eyes glowered under his dark hair, staring at him. He walked over, patted Cromartie on the left shoulder and shook his right hand vigorously. "No hard feelings, Burt. We *all* need to follow orders, even me. This afternoon I'll show you those holds and throws. Deal?"

Cromartie appeared confused but gave a thin smile and looked at him out of the corner of his eye. "Yeah, okay." Then Cromartie shook his hand hard and hustled off to join his friends, who baited him with various rowdy comments, then he looked back over his shoulder once.

He and Benedict organized the camp and with Brisken's help trained them but some of the volunteers became very ill with flux. Fortunately Doc Thayer was also in camp. They prepared a very large tent to be the hospital with several cots brought in from Burlington along with other supplies. By the third day, 23 men had flux, severe dysentery, or heat exhaustion from learning military maneuvers in the very warm spring sun. Overall these boys had spirit and some had raw ability but they needed to be trained in military maneuvers and drilled into shape. Some needed weapons and almost all needed uniforms but those would be issued when they went to Washington City.

After the first week Colonel Whiting told him he would have a horse for his use in Washington City and should send his horse back home. Whiting explained each of the officers, Veazey, Benedict, and Ripley would also be supplied horses. George then sent a telegram to his neighbor, James Lonegran in Georgia, to "Pls get Charger in Brlngtn." It was with great reluctance he boarded Charger in Peck's Livery, where Reinhard Peck ran the best stable in Burlington. He took some solace in the thought Charger would be safer from the dangers of war but he would miss him.

Three weeks later Colonel Whiting on his unruly gray mare led the Vermont brigade of almost 900 boys and men on their march to the nation's capital. They carried their packs and gear but many also carried at least one parting gift from a mother, wife, sister, aunt, girlfriend, loved one, or neighbor and staggered under the weight of a Bible, pipes, tobacco, pills, needle and thread, towels, soap, slippers, water filters, portable writing desks, stools, fishing poles, tackle and gear, and books and magazines of every sort. Despite all these items, they marched well and were among the first regiments of volunteers to arrive.

The Vermonters joined the encampment called the Army of the Potomac, where they were given huge piles of tents, haversacks, knapsacks, blue wool overcoats and navy blue blankets. Some of the officers received hammocks or cots, but the large and growing Union Army of 20,000 men still did not have a commander.

~16 ~

George paced slowly in front of the reporters, who were seated at two long rows of tables in the hospital's dining hall. One reporter fetched himself a bowl of bean-and-cabbage soup, a colonel walked by, saluted and he instinctively raised his right stump, waved the empty sleeve and thought, The war has done this. Why was there such discord between *this* reality and the beginning of war? He recalled the patriotic fervor just before the nation went to war. Almost everyone felt righteous in their thinking. He dismissed his stomach's growling, and addressed the six reporters and four soldiers seated before him.

"President Lincoln had issued a call for 75,000 volunteers and, although Colonel Robert Lee had declined to command the Union troops, there was no shortage of well-trained West Point officers or other well-known leaders capable of commanding the army of volunteers. General Winfield Scott, over 70 years old and in declining health, had met with the President and suggested many brilliant men for the position. Several generals were considered including Joe Hooker, Ambrose Burnside, George McClellan and George Meade. Other leaders considered were the popular frontiersman Jim Bridger and James Lane, the senator-elect from Kansas who had made a name for himself fighting Missouri bushwhackers in their border war over slavery. Also, many state militias had a well-known officer in charge. The Massachusetts militia was under the command of Brigadier General Benjamin Butler, a stout successful businessman who had done a remarkable job organizing their troops efficiently. After much deliberation, President Lincoln, in counsel with General Winfield Scott, the grand elder of the military, decided the command of the Army of the Potomac would go to General Irvin McDowell, who was a well-known, scholarly West Point leader.

General Irvin McDowell was a favorite of General Scott and had served on his staff during the Mexican War. McDowell was a sensitive, robust man, 43 years old with short dark hair, a thin graying beard and hardy build. McDowell had received additional education in France and was well-versed in historical and theoretical military maneuvers.

When a report arrived stating the Confederate Army was gathering near Manassas, less than 30 miles from Washington, President Lincoln called a meeting at the Executive Mansion with the newly appointed General McDowell, the elder hero General Scott, and select members of his Cabinet including Secretary of War Simon Cameron, Secretary of the Navy Gideon Welles, Postmaster-General Montgomery Blair, Secretary of the Treasury Salmon P. Chase and Secretary of State William H. Seward.

The leaders filed into the entryway receiving room led by General Scott dressed in his elaborate uniform with gold epaulettes. President Lincoln's little boy Willie ran to him and jumped onto the general's leg, nearly knocking him over. General Scott caught the boy, tried lifting him but failed, then set Willie on the marble floor with a grunt.

"My boy's anxious to get started," the President joked. "He's been marching up and down the hallway in uniform!"

Willie, 10 years old, wore a homemade uniform of dyed blue wool complete with a black stripe down the pant legs. He gazed up at the general with great admiration, smiled with beaming eyes, and saluted with his left hand then, remembering the proper hand, changed to the right. Everyone laughed, Mr. Lincoln patted the boy on the back then turned to his African American caretaker, Mrs. Keckley, who was a favorite of Mrs. Lincoln, and motioned to escort Willie outside to play on the lawn.

The leaders made their way to a second floor office, filed into a powder blue room, and sat in wooden chairs placed in a semi-circle. Some requested tea or coffee from another servant, Edward McManus, an old short Irishman, who nodded then served them their drinks and biscuits with marmalade.

They sipped their drinks from fine china and Secretary of War Cameron began the meeting with a few broad comments then gave the floor to General Scott. The old general stood with some effort, steadied his heavy, frail body with the side of the chair then made his way to the front and gave a long sweeping bow with the yellow feather of his hat touching the floor. General Scott spoke with a raspy, tired voice, "The condition of the Secessionist Army is nothing more than a rag-tag collection of ruffians. They are passionate but undisciplined soldiers. Their commander, ah, General Pierre Beauregard, is a fine officer. In truth, even though their army is a loose collection of men, they do have many fine officers. Many of these men were also trained at West Point and other fine military schools such as, ah, the Virginia Military Institute. They are savvy military leaders willing to fight for their cause. Good men, ah, such as Joseph Johnston and Robert Lee, whom we all know and esteem, Thomas Jackson of said Virginia Military Institute, and, ah, James Longstreet, among others, many of whom served with me in the Mexican War. Indeed, it may well be that their leadership is equal to that of the Federal government."

Several of the men pooh-poohed while others sipped their drinks. General Scott then described his plan of how best to deal with the Secessionist uprising by first giving a lesson in geography. Scott explained the Shenandoah Valley ran from northeast to southwest, from the Potomac River to deep into the Virginia heartland. The Valley was bounded on the west by the Allegheny Mountains and on the east by the less imposing Blue Ridge Mountains. “This corridor is a natural pathway that we can use to march into the South and take their capital of Richmond.”

Scott went on to explain there were few passes through the mountains and the most northern passage was a gap where the railroad also went through at a place called Manassas Junction. This small railroad center was an east–west link through the Blue Ridge Mountains, 25 miles southwest of Washington. Scott again cleared his throat of phlegm, wiped his wintry, dark-toothed mouth with a fine linen kerchief then continued. “It may hold the key to the entire war. If we can strike at Manassas Gap and defeat the Rebels a crushing blow, we may then follow the Shenandoah Valley and march all the way to Richmond.”

Scott then went into some detail, offered plans for an attack on Richmond and a plan of separating the Southeastern states with an outline of using the Mississippi River to divide the Secessionist forces. When he was done, Scott tottered back to his chair and eased himself down, which opened the discussion to the other men, who each offered an opinion on how to attack the Rebels. Gideon Welles was adamant on using the U.S. Navy to divide the Southern states from the country and the world by means of a blockade. President

Lincoln quietly listened to each man's speech, twirling his spectacles in his hands.

The room became smoky from their cigars. Each speaker in turn took the center of the room, stood near the middle of a new Oriental carpet and gestured with great enthusiasm on what must be done with the Secessionists. Some smacked their fist into their hand, or raised one finger to make a point, or struck statuesque poses at the nearby mantel but each leader felt it was their opportunity to impress General Scott and win his favor. Their theatrics were performed in his direction.

General Scott then asked General McDowell what tactics he thought would be best. McDowell launched into a vivid description on how to put down the rebellion, point by point, complete with examples of European, or ancient Grecian battles, all of which would lead to a Union victory in the Secessionist's capital of Richmond. He went on for 45 minutes and when he finished the room was very quiet. McDowell had impressed everyone with his knowledge of military tactics.

Secretary of State Seward was then asked to speak but he declined with a simple statement, "Who would dare to follow such an expert presentation?"

There were no other speakers. General Scott turned to President Lincoln and for a moment it appeared they had forgotten he was in the room. Mr. Lincoln softly remarked, "If I were General Beauregard, I would take Washington."

This sent the discussion spinning in another direction because the military leaders had, for the most part, not considered the Confederates would take the initiative. All agreed Washington City must be defended at all costs and new demonstrations were made with great energy and enthusiasm. They must fortify the bridges, all roads leading to Washington, increase security and troops around key government buildings, and prepare gunboats in the harbor.

After a slight lull in the discussion, General Scott again asked General McDowell of how, specifically, they should deal with the Confederate army that was forming, in large numbers mind you, near Manassas, Virginia. McDowell stood, moved for the center of the oriental but before he reached the middle of the room, President Lincoln stood up and stretched. His dark suit accentuated his lanky stature, his sleeves were too short, and he said, "Gentlemen, your military expertise is much greater than mine. In Illinois, the greatest risk we faced were mosquitoes the size of your fist."

A few men chuckled then the President continued, "I will leave the fine details of planning to your wisdom, General McDowell, General Scott, but please proceed with utmost haste."

The meeting was over. The men shook hands all around. After three hours of debate, planning, and discussion on how to deal with the Secessionists, they had decided Washington City must first be fortified and defended, the volunteers trained for military fighting, then the Federal army must march to Manassas and attack the Confederates to scatter them. If they could rout the Rebels in one large battle then march on to Richmond and capture their capital, the rebellion may be stopped.

Brigadier General Irvin McDowell went to his headquarters on the Potomac and issued orders to have the Army of the Potomac divided into five brigades. McDowell ordered each brigade commander to begin drilling the volunteers on military maneuvers with every item of uniform, armament, and supply made ready for inspection. Every bridge, every road leading into Washington must be guarded with a company of soldiers with a reserve company of messengers ready to alert the main encampment if any attack should come. Gunboats were moored in the Potomac and the Navy Yard made ready for any necessary action.

Next General McDowell made his specific plans for an assault. He ordered his top staff aides to bring him maps of Virginia and of Manassas, complete with all the roads, rail lines, rivers and bridges. McDowell knew this was *his* moment in history and he would study texts of all the ancient commanders for wisdom. He was fiercely determined he would be intelligently prepared.

The Secretary of State, William Seward, who had been very quiet throughout the meeting at the Executive Mansion, held interviews with newspaper reporters from Boston, Philadelphia, Hartford, and New York, and local reporters from the *Star* and *National Intelligencer,* then spoke in the largest meeting room of the Willard Hotel. Mr. Seward was anxious to let everyone know the top Federal leaders had met and all agreed. Seward confidently declared the war would be over before the end of summer and concluded all his meetings with the rallying cry, "On to Richmond!"

The newspaper reporters fervently followed Mr. Seward and pounded a drumbeat of patriotic excitement. All the Northern newspapers proudly proclaimed an "exclusive" announcement of the Federal government's grand plans to swiftly put down the rebellion. Horace Greeley, the editor of the *New York Tribune*, quoted Mr. Seward and took up the rallying cry, "On to Richmond!" Every patriotic Northerner was certain they would win the war quickly and all cheered, "On to Richmond!"

~17 ~

He thought back to the beginning when so many enthusiastically joined the war cry, "On to Richmond!" A growing assembly of reporters and soldiers stood around the hospital cafeteria, a very large hall with two long rows of tables and chairs. Soldiers with various wounds hobbled about, or sat in a wheelchair and awaited help. Many were missing limbs or had a bandaged head or torso. Scores of young men were permanently scarred and *these* were the lucky ones. The Federal army had suffered over 200,000 dead with an equally horrible total of dead on the Confederate side. Here and there among the growing crowd, a female visitor or female nurse stood by a wounded soldier. He decided he would not change his descriptions because of the women present. Everyone needed to know everything. He thought of the first large battle of this terrible war and continued,

"After a very long ride to Washington City, the Vermont troops were assigned to the Army of the Potomac with General Irvin McDowell commanding. Overall, the volunteers were barely trained but their tenacity and enthusiasm were expected to make up for their lack of preparation. General McDowell had split the army of 30,000 men, and growing, into five brigades under the command of Daniel Tyler, Samuel Heintzelman, David Hunter, Theodore Runyan and Dixon Miles. General Tyler had a fine record from the Old Army; Heintzelman had served in the Mexican War and was noted for his bravery; even though Hunter had been in uniform for more than 40 years he had never been in a battle; Runyan, from New Jersey, had only commanded a small division; and Miles had more experience than the others but was rumored to enjoy drinking.

The Vermonters were placed under Colonel Heintzelman, although George did not receive a horse as promised by Colonel Whiting. Fine horses were in short supply. They began more training and during the first week small pox and bloody flux went through camp. George did his best to instruct the boys on what constituted proper sanitary water and provisions but 134 became ill with flux or dysentery and were placed under Doc Thayer's care in the hospital tent. Eight Vermonters died due to the flux, a terrible death with the bowels emptying out their life in bloody spasms.

After drilling for two more weeks the Vermonters received their orders and marched five miles into Virginia. Colonel Whiting led them on horseback, plump and proud on his skittish, gray and white-socked mare. After an awkward, confused beginning they covered the five miles in two hours. Most of these Vermonters were hardy, very fit and accustom to hiking in mountainous terrain.

When they arrived near Centreville, where General McDowell was massing his army, Colonel Whiting, George and the Vermonters were greeted by a host of various insects. Sergeant Bear Brisken flailed with his huge arms and yelped, "These gotta be the world's largest mosquitoes!"

"And the most resourceful!" Benedict added then slapped his exposed ankle, followed by another slap to his neck. The entire insect world thrived here with gnats, ticks, and horseflies but most prevalent were the large pesky swamp mosquitoes.

They set up camp and George was amazed at the thousands upon thousands of soldiers. They were busy setting up tents, attempting to march in maneuvers and all the while being harried by gnats, mosquitoes, and bugs. Individually the soldiers were a patchwork of differences. Many wore the navy blue wool uniforms the government issued in Washington City, some wore any variety of light blue to dark gray uniform from their state militia, or something their "Aunt Pearl" had made. They were a horde of companies, clad in different uniforms, diversely equipped, and ignorant of the principles of military obedience and concerted action. It was a troubling sight.

General McDowell sat in his tent and studied local maps and maps of ancient battles to further plan this large, decisive battle. McDowell flipped through them all but none of the maps of Virginia were detailed. He did not have a single good local map.

Bull Run River was a winding stream with steep, high banks surrounded by woods. Beyond the woods was a large meadow lined with more woods and further beyond were two hills. The main place to cross Bull Run was the stone bridge on the Warrenton Turnpike but there were also a few shallow fords.

McDowell examined the map of the meandering river, filled in the areas with a feather ink pen where scouts had located enemy troops, and recalled ancient battlefields. The obvious plan would be a direct attack on the Warrenton Turnpike, to cross the creek at the stone bridge, and attack the center of the Rebel line. That is what Alexander the Great or Napoleon would do.

After hours of study, General McDowell held a meeting with his five division commanders. His tent was littered with apple cores and his aide, Major Wadsworth, placed a large watermelon on a side table and used a tin bucket to gather the many apple cores.

Colonel Dixon Miles, an older officer with a white-and-black goatee said, "General, you're not taking any prisoners when it comes to apples, hey?"

The officers laughed but McDowell scoffed and noticed a faint smell of whiskey-and-mint on Miles's breath. McDowell had heard rumors of Miles's drinking and immediately decided where his division would be placed but did not reprimand him. It was an impromptu meeting after all. Instead he glared at Wadsworth until he left the tent.

McDowell wiped bits of cheese and apple from his mustache then went into the details of a coordinated attack. A small portion of the army under General Tyler was to cross at the southern ford, scout the strength of the Secessionist right flank but *not* engage them in battle. McDowell put his hand on Tyler's shoulder. "You understand, General? Do *not* bring on an engagement. You will determine their strength and no more."

Tyler said, "Yes, sir."

McDowell continued. Next the Federals would feint an attack on the center of the Rebel line, while swinging a large portion of their forces, including the Vermonters under Colonel Heintzelman, on a long march. They would cross at Sudley's ford north of the bridge then sweep down on the Southerners weak left flank with force. Colonel Miles's division would be held in reserve, near Centreville, to be ready to fill in any part of the Union line as needed. The officers all agreed it was a fine plan. Then McDowell nodded, unsheathed his saber, raised it dramatically and sliced the watermelon in half. He brought down the sword several more times, cutting one-inch pieces. Watermelon juice ran off the table and onto the straw floor. McDowell chuckled, picked up a slice of dripping red fruit, and gorged his mouth. "Mm, tasty. Help yourselves!"

~ ~

Confederate General Pierre G.T. Beauregard also noticed the strategic importance of Manassas Junction. General Beauregard had commanded the Rebel bombardment of Fort Sumter and was then assigned to command the Confederate army in the Shenandoah Valley. Beauregard was born near New Orleans, went to West Point and served admirably in the Mexican War where he advised Federal

Commander Winfield Scott on tactics at the battle of Chapultepec. Beauregard had an olive complexion, dark heavy-lidded eyes, and black hair. Women found him extremely handsome. He enjoyed his resemblance to Napoleon III and his dark mustache, which he had waxed daily by a slave.

General Beauregard had the advantage of being on Southern soil, had good information about the land and its particulars, and employed General Joseph E. Johnston to use the railroad to carry troops from one side of the mountains to the other if needed to defend an attack from either direction. When General Johnston observed the Union forces had settled into an encampment, he decided on his own to send most of his forces on the railroad back to Manassas. Johnston also sent the cavalry under James E.B. Stuart to aide General Beauregard in scouting the location of the main Federal advancement.

General Beauregard also took notice of the wooded banks of Bull Run River. The thick woods and steep incline were too great for marching infantry, horse-drawn artillery or supply trains. The water appeared too deep to cross at any point except the bridge. Beauregard concentrated his Rebel army into a defensive position with well-placed batteries and breastworks near the stone bridge and would counterattack when the time was right. The bridge was vital to the area but he also noted two hills beyond the bridge, Matthews Hill which was smaller, and the more substantial Henry Hill to the south which had an excellent view of the bridge and the Warrenton Turnpike. Beauregard placed some of his forces on Henry Hill to impede passage toward Manassas from Sudley Ford should the Federals try to circle around and flank them.

Then General Beauregard formed his own plan of attack. He would cross the bridge to strike at the enemy center with two brigades, drive straight for Centreville and would use the bulk of his army to sweep around the Federal left and take his flank. This would cut off any Union retreat to Washington City and would inflict a major, decisive blow to the entire Federal army. With a quick coordinated strike it may be possible to win the first big battle and perhaps ensure the birth of the Secessionist nation. Beauregard realized victory in this first, big battle may go to the commander who moved first. A priest was summoned, a devout Cajun whom Beauregard knew from New Orleans, who led a prayer for God's care and guidance in the coming battle.

~ ~

A cacophony of Federal buglers started reveille before dawn. George sat up in his cot, stared into the dark blackness and tried to focus. He stretched, reached his arms out wide, hit the canvas of his tent then found his uniform spread out on a small table next to the cot, fumbled with the brass buttons, pulled on his boots and moved outside. The soldiers made the stirring sounds of the slow hum and buzz of the camp awakening. Across a sea of tents, the young men, horses and wagons moved with growing energy. Once the Vermonters were assembled, Chaplain Lucius Dickinson of Cavendish said a prayer for God's care and guidance in the coming battle.

The sun rose clear and hot. Union General Daniel Tyler led his regiment south to Blackburn's Ford, where he gazed through binoculars across Bull Run River to view the enemy camp. There were a few pickets, a few canons, and the woods were well beyond the landing but it was not clear if anything was concealed there or if anyone moved behind them. Blackburn's Ford was shallow and easy to cross with a few Confederates on the other side, about 60 yards away, at the edge of the far woods. Tyler lowered the binoculars and made a valiant gesture with his gloved hand. "We'll cross here, men!"

The Northern troops waded through the shallow waters. Tyler wanted to embolden his men and shouted, "*We'll brush aside these few Rebels and march clear to Manassas!*"

When they reached the other side Tyler stopped his brigade then sent forward a company of young men from Massachusetts dressed in their clean gray militia uniforms. They were met by a line of Confederate soldiers also in gray uniforms. The two groups stared at each other's gray uniforms until a Rebel officer called out, "*Who are you?*"

A single soldier from Massachusetts called back, "Who are *you*?"

The Confederates wondered why their troops would be coming from the other side of Bull Run. The young Rebel with a clean-cut face called out again, "*Who* are you?"

The lieutenant answered proudly with a strong voice, "*Massachusetts men!*"

The Confederates responded with a volley of muskets, one shot struck the Northern lieutenant in the head and he fell dead on the spot. Other Union soldiers were also hit but most of the Massachusetts men returned fire.

It started with a few dozen muskets exchanging skirmishing fire but Tyler believed they could take these few troops and sent forward another company, who were shot at by Rebels concealed in the woods. The two companies of Union soldiers were now pinned down. A heated exchange of gunfire took place and the day grew warmer. The battle had begun.

Word was sent to Southern General Beauregard the Union forces had attacked at Blackburn's Ford but were being held down and were not advancing. Beauregard tweaked the right point of his dark waxed mustache. McDowell had gained the advantage of the first move but this was not their main force, not if one brigade could hold them. Beauregard knew he must remain patient and not be deceived at the first sign of a scrap. He still expected the Federals to advance *en mass* across the bridge to attack his center.

One of Beauregard's aides, Colonel Alexander Chisolm, asked if he should ride to General Johnston's last known position near Winchester on the other side of the Blue Ridge Mountains and request his services. Beauregard spoke with his Louisiana accent, "Yes, get General Johnston and his men. It's a fool's errand and it's probably too late, but yes, go. *Go!*"

Colonel Chisolm saluted with a smile, mounted his chestnut mare then whipped it on both sides and sped off for reinforcements. Beauregard smiled for his enthusiasm.

After an hour of skirmishing fire the Rebels still kept the Federal forces in check. Union General Tyler could not believe these few Rebels in the woods were able to stop his men. This was the right flank of the Confederates and they appeared concentrated in the middle near the bridge. Tyler ordered, "*Send in the brigade!*"

All of Tyler's Union forces moved into the clearing and were met with a strong volley from the woods. The Southerners were well-entrenched behind breastworks and their aim was very good. The Federals plodded forward then took cover behind large boulders in the field or the bodies of their fallen comrades and returned fire. The intensity of the battle increased.

In the afternoon General McDowell sent an aide with a message. The aide spurred his thoroughbred to Blackburn's Ford, splashed across the shallow water, found Tyler on horseback and yelled, "*Your orders were to survey the enemy and* not *engage them!*"

Tyler shouted back, "*We can win this now! Look! It's clear all the way to Manassas.*"

"*General McDowell orders you to Retreat! Now!*"

Tyler obeyed and hollered, "*Retreat!*" then waved his arm. A nearby bugler, a portly musician from Boston, trumpeted "Retreat" and the Federals ran back from the field. A great cheer rose from the Rebel side, then over 200 men ran out from the woods and shot at the fleeing Union soldiers. Here and there a Federal officer stopped to help a wounded comrade but dozens of dead bodies lay scattered across the open meadow.

Tyler ordered his regiment back to Centreville, where many officers gave him looks of disgust. He tethered the reins of his horse to a tent rope, went inside and wrote his report. He wanted to make it clear how close they were to winning the war. Then each company submitted a roll call for the regiment and the bad news was tallied. Eighty-three men had been killed or captured. Tyler then realized he had spent the better part of the day engaged in battle. He finished his report, handed it to General McDowell in his tent, and cursing rang out.

The entire day was lost with the greater battle plan sacrificed because Tyler thought he had seen something that was not truly there and he did not follow orders. Now the Federals must start their master plan again, tonight, before Southern General Beauregard counterattacked in the morning. General McDowell ordered Colonel Heintzelman to move his regiment, including the Vermonters, on a long sweeping march to the north to Sudley's Ford at 2 a.m. in order to attack at 5 a.m. A local railroad worker would be their guide.

Southern General Beauregard felt proud of his men when Federal forces retreated across Blackburn Ford. They had whipped the Northern advancement but this had been only one of their brigades. He considered a counterattack but decided this was not the time. Tomorrow the Federals would try again, most likely at the stone bridge.

At dusk Colonel Chisolm rode back into camp with his run-out horse trembling and panting. Chisolm dismounted, swiftly saluted the Creole commander and spoke excitedly, "Sir! General Johnston is coming! His boys are on the train and they should be here by mid-day!"

"Very good," Beauregard raised his eyebrows but spoke calmly. "And Stuart and the cavalry?"

"Not far behind, sir. I rode ahead as fast as I could."

Beauregard nodded and recalled his harsh remarks that Chisolm's ride would be a fool's errand. "For our cause to succeed, in spite of great odds against us, many fine efforts are needed," he clapped the colonel on the back. "You've done the South a great service, sir."

Then Lieutenant Bidwell reported the results of the afternoon skirmish at Blackburn's Ford. The Confederates had lost 70 men, mostly wounded, who were being cared for in a makeshift hospital tent in the rear.

Beauregard then called together his entire staff and an aide placed a kerosene lamp on the map table in his large tent. Beauregard studied the finely detailed, local map and took suggestions from his staff. They discussed troop placements, where commanders Bartow, Bee and Evans would be, considered where to place Johnston's brigade when it arrived and how to use the cavalry. Beauregard stated often they must remain calm through the battle and let reinforcements flow to where the battle was hottest. Reinforcements would raise the Confederates total forces to 35,000 men. Local informants and spies estimated McDowell's Federal army to be 37,000 men. Beauregard put one hand behind his back, appeared satisfied with their planning, raised a glass of brandy and smiled to his staff. "Now, gentlemen, we've got a fair fight."

After the skirmish at Blackburn's Ford rumor spread through the entire Federal Army tomorrow would be the "Big Battle." It was also conveyed to Washington City, where citizens decided it would be *the event* to attend. People searched for a carriage or wagon but most had already been hired. Only a few horses could be found, which were older or in poor condition. The officers, cavalry and sutlers had taken any quality horse weeks ago. Still curious onlookers, ambitious politicians and social climbers made their way to Manassas.

A flare of bugles awakened George from his light sleep at 1 a.m. Colonel Heintzelman issued the order to fall-in for an "easy march, less than two miles" to the north to Sudley Ford, where they would cross and begin their sweeping attack on the Rebel's left flank. In the pitch darkness, Colonel Whiting ordered George and the other officers to rouse the Vermont troops. They broke camp and assembled behind their flag bearer, Timothy Lauder, a very fast, athletic youth from Burlington. At 2:30 a.m. they began their march.

George noticed everyone appeared tired from being awakened this early but their adrenaline was running. Everyone knew they were headed for the "Big Battle."

The march through the night was miserable. The local guide was an ex-railroad worker who said he knew the shortest way to get anywhere but he led Heintzelman's brigade on a "short-cut" that took them three miles out of the way. The Vermonters hacked their way through underbrush and thickets in the dark. Their guide insisted a road was "just ahead."

Colonel Whiting and the Vermonters chopped their way through tangles of overgrown bushes and small trees. At 5 a.m. George heard rifle fire to the south and knew that would be General Tyler making his demonstration of force for the second day in a row, to feint an attack at the Confederate center near the stone bridge. He also realized they were now late in making their attack and glared at the railroad man with incredulity because, with the sun rising, anyone could tell they were headed more east than north. He then stared at Colonel Whiting, then up the chain of command to Colonel Heintzelman, and was astonished. Heintzelman continued to follow the Southerner's directions. The longer George stood still, the more mosquitoes, gnats, horseflies and insects of all kinds devoured his sweaty skin. He fanned them away and marched on.

They continued through the underbrush, the sun rose higher and the sky became lighter. He saw the Vermont 2nd infantry flag carried by Private Lauder, bouncing through the thick growth ahead, knew all the Confederates would have been awakened after the opening skirmishing fire and would now be ready for their attack. Their plan was ruined, again, before it had started. He swatted at the insects feeding on his face and neck and waved a path around his face then continued slogging through the swampy, heavy brush.

It was exhausting work cutting through the backwoods but the Vermonters arrived at the clearing called Sudley Ford and waded through the 50-yard wide, tea-colored creek. The water ran sluggish with a slow, thick swirl at every high rock or stuck log. Colonel Whiting managed to remain mounted while two majors whipped his mare into crossing the creek. In the distance further to the south, sporadic musket fire sounded, peppered with an occasional artillery shell. They crossed the ford without opposition, climbed the gentle slope and reformed in the sparse woods on the far bank around their color bearer Private Lauder, who gave a goofy smile like they had been on a pleasant hike.

George saw some Confederate troops near the edge of the far woods, about 200 hundred yards away and across a rough pasture. Further to the south was the formidable Henry Hill. Their map indicated beyond Henry Hill was a rolling meadow and to the north was the Warrenton Turnpike, which led back to the stone bridge. He looked at his pocket watch, already 8 a.m.

As General Tyler's Federal soldiers made their show of force near the bridge, the piecemeal rifle fire felt odd to Southern General Beauregard. Why weren't the Union soldiers firing in mass volleys and charging across the bridge with their entire army? Was McDowell afraid or had he planned something else?

A small lad of 15 rode up to General Beauregard on a dark horse. The boy was barefoot, shirtless and wore tattered pants. The boy slid off the saddle-less horse and ran straight to Beauregard.

"With Colonel Evans compliments, sir!" The boy spoke with a whistling lisp. "The Yanks are crossing at Sudley Ford. I seen 'em!"

The boy wiped his mouth with the back of his hand and pulled a wadded piece of paper from under the rope belt around his frayed pants then handed it to Beauregard. The hurriedly scribbled note from Colonel Evans read, "Look out on your left. You are turned."

Beauregard now understood McDowell attempted to swing around his left flank and sent an aide on horseback with orders to Colonel Bartow, General Bee, and General Jackson. "Advance without delay and reinforce the left flank!"

From the woods near Bull Run, George gazed out across the open field and it appeared too good to be true. There were only a few Confederates visible on the far edge of the woods but he also knew if he were defending this area, he would have had soldiers in the far woods with artillery, and more on nearby Matthew's Hill. He looked further west, saw the larger Henry Hill and wondered why Southern artillery had not fired. If there were artillery or troops on the larger hill, they would have seen them cross Sudley Ford and should have responded.

Colonel Whiting, on his nervous gray mare, ordered, "Take a brief rest but remain ready!" The Vermonters bright militia uniforms were muddy and wet from the knee down from wading Bull Run. The sun was well above the treetops and warming up.

Then a courier on horseback, a lieutenant in a crisp blue uniform, arrived from General McDowell and handed a note to

Colonel Heintzelman. McDowell ordered this brigade to remain where it was, in reserve, and *not* join in the battle.

George again looked with bewilderment to Whiting then Heintzelman, who had never been in battle. His face showed an expression of calmness and naiveté. They would wait.

In the soft loveliness of the summer morning an army of sightseers left Washington City, crossed the shiny Potomac River and drove through the wooded hills past ripening cornfields, deserted farmhouses and deep into the lush Virginia countryside. For such a great social event, all were dressed in their best finery. The gentlemen wore tuxedos or thin summer suits and the few women wore beautiful silk or dyed-cotton dresses with stripes, ribbons and large hats with feathers, bows or fresh-cut flowers. They carried opera glasses, expandable telescopes, bottles of wine, flasks of bourbon, or picnic baskets. When they reached the main body of the Federal lines they pulled up their carriages and spread their blankets in front of the Union position in order to have a good view of the grand, impending battle. A murmur went through the crowd. They would whip the Secessionists and be home before dinner. A few newspaper reporters and adventurous politicians crossed the stone bridge to be even closer to the action, at the very center of the Union plan of attack.

Another rider, a Union captain from New Jersey in full, dark-blue uniform with his kepi askew, rode hastily to Colonel Heintzelman, who was still on horseback. The captain did not bother to salute but thrust a note to Heintzelman. McDowell had now ordered the brigade to face left and march for Matthew's Hill.

Colonel Whiting turned in the saddle, ran his pink palm over his white mustache, and nodded at George, who walked to the front of the column and ordered, "*Forward!*"

Private Lauder held the regimental flag high, titled it forward, and the Vermonters headed away from the few trees lining Bull Run River and out over the stony pasture. Most gazed straight ahead with determination. Many appeared giddy and nervous. They were five hours late but Heintzelman's brigade finally came onto the battlefield.

As they marched forward in a column up the slope, they headed into the Confederate left flank. Then a barrage of artillery blasted at them but the Vermonters marched steadily onward, although many young men were skittish. Then a cannon ball split off the top of Captain Hitchcock's head and most of the soldiers stopped. A few turned back and fewer still continued onward. Hitchcock, a marine from Shoreham, lay on the ground with the lower half of his face intact but his nose, eyes and skull were gruesomely ripped off to leave a bloody mess. Some Vermonters stared in shock but more looked about nervously. A friend of Hitchcock, a portly youth also from Shoreham, collapsed onto his dead body and sobbed.

A thunderous volley of muskets and rifles came from the woods and several more young men went down. Fear passed through the Vermonters like a wave. Some trembled but most looked around excitedly, including flag bearer Lauder.

"*Steady, boys!*" George yelled.

Stocky Sergeant Brisken echoed with his deep, husky voice, "*Steady!*"

More of the officers yelled encouragement. The strong-willed soldiers resolved to move forward onto the battleground despite the horror.

Southern Colonel Nathan "Shanks" Evans was a tough, professional soldier who had been to West Point. Evans saw the Union soldiers coming at his front and hurriedly sent a note to General Beauregard that he had less than a full brigade to defend this position. His Louisiana Tigers were a loose collection of street brawlers from New Orleans including a few criminals, ruffians from a dozen different nationalities and impassioned Southern gentlemen fighting for "the cause." Feeling cornered and outnumbered Shanks Evans had one thought and hollered with all his strength, "*Attack!*"

The Louisiana battalion charged out of the woods, screaming down Matthew's Hill with large bowie knives flailing in the air and shooting their muskets and revolvers at random.

The Vermonters responded well and stood firm in one long line. George looked over his boys in their new blue uniforms and called out "*Ready!*" The volunteers leveled their muskets.

More Louisiana soldiers fired and a few Vermonters fell. The Rebels charged onward, wailing like demons.

"*Aim!*" The Federals raised their muskets. He hollered, "*Fire!*"

A single mass volley of bullets stopped the Rebel soldiers. A few went down awkwardly like a deer shot in full stride, crumpled over itself and sprawled out on the uneven ground. Then the Confederates turned slowly but all made their way back up the hill while Colonel Evans nodded with pride. They had achieved their purpose, which was to stop the Yankee attack. The boys in blue were scattered across the field and stood motionless.

Northern Colonel Ambrose Burnside sat on his sorrel horse next to Colonel Heintzelman on his well-groomed, black horse. Burnside pushed up his wide-brimmed blue hat and scanned the field with a collapsing monoglass, then remarked with great confidence, "We must be up against two full brigades. Send word back to McDowell."

General McDowell heard the battle beginning on his right near Sudley Ford and now ordered General Tyler to move his division forward to attack the center but the curious citizens from Washington were in front of the Federal line. People in carriages stood, cheered, waved and hollered, "*Hurrah!*" when a full division of Union soldiers marched around or over them to the front. A few newspaper reporters started a chant, "*On to Richmond! On to Richmond!*"

Federal Colonel William Tecumseh Sherman had found a new shallow ford a few hundred yards north of the bridge and moved his 3,400 soldiers across it. Colonel Hunter's division also took the field and forced the Confederates to retreat off Matthew's Hill. Sherman's men hooked up with Burnside and Heintzelman's division, a growing mass of men in blue, and stormed across the open field, charging for Henry Hill.

The battle raged louder, deafening artillery pounded the land and muskets fired. Men and boys yelled, fought, screamed out in pain and yelled again. McDowell, mounted on his horse, gazed through spyglasses but could vaguely see through the dust and smoke to the rolling meadow. The Union Army moved in unison and pushed the Southern army back. McDowell lowered the glasses, urged his horse forward across the shallow ford behind Sherman's troops and cheered his men, "*Victory! The day is ours!*"

The newspaper reporters in the crowd agreed and sent back dispatches to Washington City. The Secessionists retreated on all fronts. They had forced the Rebels off Matthew's Hill, on to Henry Hill and the Army of the Potomac would soon march on to Fairfax. "The day is ours!" they wrote. "On to Richmond!"

McDowell sent his aide Major Wadsworth to Centerville to telegraph General Winfield Scott, who was suffering a new bout of ill health in his home in Washington City. Despite all their planning and his faith in McDowell, General Scott still could not believe the good news in his hand. He shuffled around his home in full military uniform except for silk slippers and often re-read McDowell's telegram. "Victory is ours."

Confederate Colonel Evans had made a daring attack against far superior numbers. Even though the Rebels retreated to Henry Hill they had bought time for the Southern Army. Just then a train pulled into Manassas Junction. Onboard were thousands of Rebel reinforcements from General Johnston's brigade. Then hundreds of thundering cavalry led by Colonel J.E.B. Stuart pounded the earth, riding into Beauregard's main encampment. The reserve soldiers off the train, plus Stuart's cavalry, were ready to join the battle. Beauregard ordered them to reinforce General Bee and the left flank.

The day was hot but the fresh Confederate forces marched from the station out onto the open meadow and straight into the battle, roaring in full intensity. Artillery shells exploded from both sides into the field, musket fire snapped, soldiers yelled violently, smoke clouded the field, and screams of the wounded and dying rose into one loud, horrible cacophony.

General Thomas J. Jackson, the solemn professor from Virginia Military Institute, rode his fine quarter horse with quiet determination and led his young cadets and middle-aged volunteers onto Henry Hill then stopped them before engaging in battle. General Bee, alarmed at seeing Jackson withhold his troops, spurred his horse over to Jackson. "General! They are beating us back! Your men must join us!"

Jackson surveyed the field with the same resolute calmness of looking over a classroom. He ordered his troops, "*Kneel!*" then said to Bee, "We'll give them the bayonet."

Bee was shocked by the professor. Many of Jackson's troops were young students and wore the white pants and gray cadet coats of VMI. It appeared he would not send them into battle but preferred to keep them on the crest of the hill.

General Bee, who was from South Carolina, rode back to his brigade, most of whom were from Alabama. Bee knew another charge was needed *now!* Because he felt some distance from his men he decided *he* must lead their charge, ordered his men "*Affix bayonets!*" then looked back at Jackson once more. He sat high on his horse in relative safety behind their kneeling line. Bee dismounted and raised his voice with enthusiasm, "*Let* us *determine to die here and we will conquer! Follow me!*"

Bee led the screaming Alabamians down the slope of the hill into the swarming fray. The rushing soldiers fired a round each then charged with bayonets ready and slammed into the Union forces. Federal soldiers crumpled in violent spasms but some fired back. Then General Bee was hit by a bullet and fell to the ground wounded.

The Union forces were once again stopped and lacked direction. George yelled to Benedict and Sergeant Brisken, "*Reform into a column!*"

Many of the volunteers gazed at Benedict like he was a stranger then looked around with confusion. Which way should they go? Where did the column begin? Should they fall back to Colonel Whiting? Where was their flag?

Sergeant Brisken's dark brown eyes flashed with determination and he hollered angrily, trying to reform the Vermonters. Many of the soldiers had blackened cheeks from ripping open packets of powder cartridges with their teeth. Some brave but undisciplined soldiers held their ground and fired at the Southerners across the field, no more than 30 yards away but they did not follow the order to reform. The Vermonters were *not* coming together.

Still more Confederate regiments arrived onto the battlefield from the train. Beauregard had the new troops extend their flank and shored up their depleted ranks. More Confederates poured into the line around Henry Hill while George had some success in getting some of the Vermonters to regroup but the main body of Federals were falling back. Some of the Vermonters stood terrified and shocked.

Now Colonel Heintzelman, a hardy Rhode Islander, brought the rest of his brigade onto the battlefield. It appeared this time the Federals would break through the Confederate's lines. They went steadily up the slope of rough pasture then stopped, aimed and fired a fierce volley.

A bullet tore through Southern General Jackson's gloved right hand but Jackson didn't move. He simply held his wounded hand higher than his shoulder and the blood oozed through the torn glove and trickled down his wrist. Some young cadets and others new to battle wavered then withdrew to the rear. The Union forces moved *en mass* up the hill but Jackson remained steadfast in the saddle and ordered, "No matter how many Yankees come up this hill, do not move. You *will* hold. . . *this line!*"

General Bee lay wounded but saw the momentum swinging against the Southerners and knew they needed encouragement. He saw Jackson sitting high on his quarter horse, holding up his wounded and bleeding hand but looking firm and resolute. Bee yelled, "*Look! There stands Jackson like a stone wall. Rally behind the Virginians!*"

The Confederates stood their ground around Jackson and the fight for Henry Hill became more desperate. Screams of agony from piercing wounds shrieked on all sides and more canon shells blasted the smoke-filled field. Then even more reinforcements flooded into the Rebel lines and again bolstered their morale. They had survived yet another charge. The Union soldiers retreated under a thick fire of musketry and pistols.

Then the Rebels began their own counterattack, like a wave had pulled them by the tide of retreating Federals, and they followed them without any direct leadership. This huge wave of Southern soldiers now charged forward.

Federal General McDowell sensed the shift in the battle and thought of Colonel Miles's forces in reserve. He hurriedly wrote an order to Miles, "Bring yr brigade Immed. Cross th Bridge & Join Attack on Henry Hill." A courier grabbed the note and rode for the rear.

As the Confederates counterattacked, Union Colonel Heintzelman was shot off his black horse with a painful wound to his mid-section and Colonel Whiting's eyes widened. Whiting called out for help from a major, jumped off his mare then watched aides care for Heintzelman, who had to leave the field. He was carried past the Vermonters, many of whom stared after him. Private Lauder, the swift, dark-haired boy from Burlington who was their flag bearer, also gazed in astonishment but Lauder was not alone in his frightened and anxious state. George saw the nervousness on many Vermonters' worried faces: If Colonel Heintzelman went down, am I next?

"*Steady, boys!*" he called out, "*We have strength in numbers.*"

The Vermonters were still attempting to regroup in formation but Whiting approached him and spoke in a raspy, hushed voice, "Well, I guess if we have to do it, now's the time."

"*Ready!*" George hollered to the Vermonters. Then after a brief pause, with all the strength his deep voice could muster he yelled, "*Forward!*"

He marched with the Vermonters onto the battlefield and their group came together in a solid mass moving forward. Whiting stood still where he had dismounted. He looked around timidly then moved up and crouched behind the large back of Sergeant Brisken and followed him onto the open field, where wounded lay dotted across the rocky pasture and looked up in agony or desperation.

"Don't step on me, boys!" an older man called out, wounded in his midsection with the lower part of his new blue uniform stained dark maroon.

Another man wounded in the head leaned on one elbow. Blood ran down from his dark scalp and he cried out, "For God's sake! A drop of water!"

"*Keep marching!*" Brisken shouted and the Vermonters continued around the wounded.

George again looked over the ranks, saw Benedict marching nearby and wondered where was Veazey? Then he saw Veazey's tall frame, his dark hair under an officer's hat, in the middle-front of his company. Most of the Vermonters were downcast and thoughtful, including Whiting, who pulled out his sword. A few smiled nervously.

Then George felt the impending doom. They were *not* ready. He saw it earlier when they could not reform into a column, saw it again in their fearful faces staring after the wounded Colonel

Heintzelman, and now they moved into an area where courage and fierce fighting were needed. They lacked veteran leadership throughout the companies but they marched over the stony pasture through thick smoke and dust. Then he looked closer and saw the boys were uneven, undisciplined and searching for a reason to stop. He yelled, "*Forward!*"

Then Confederate General Early's brigade came onto the battlefield. They had marched all day, had arrived from over the mountains and met the Union advance head on. Early's Rebels fired a torrent of mini-balls that ripped through Heintzelman's brigade, followed by several canon blasts.

Union soldiers fell everywhere, left, right, ahead and behind. The Vermonters looked for leadership in the tumultuous confusion. Colonel Whiting had taken cover behind a large boulder. His sword lay on the ground near Sergeant Brisken, who fired his musket quickly and repeatedly. Brisken stood tall with privates and corporals a human river of roiling uncertainty swirling around him. Whiting peeked out from behind the boulder to see what was happening then returned to hiding and chewed at his nails.

Then another Confederate regiment arrived but this one came from the west, from *behind* the Vermonters' flank. They shot a volley of musket fire and more Union soldiers fell. Whiting reacted to this latest development with shocked terror, his mouth dropped open and he ran away, down the hill toward the bridge at Bull Run.

Benedict raised his sword upward and commanded the Vermonters to respond with a volley at the Confederates in front of them. When the few Vermonters raised their muskets and took aim, most of the Southerners dropped down or dashed to the far woods for cover. The Vermonters' late volley of bullets whistled through the air without effect and disappeared in the air or slammed into trees in the far woods.

Then more Rebel cannon shells blasted the Federal column. With each explosion more soldiers died and more men searched for answers to their unvoiced questions.

George hollered "*Reload!*" for another volley but some had already reloaded or had *not* fired with Benedict's order. Several Vermonters responded with scattered reports of musket fire, having misunderstood the command to reload with the command to fire and their bullets flew harmlessly into the far woods. The Confederate artillery continued to pound away, blast after blast, and with each lethal explosion came more confusion. A sense of urgency spread among the undisciplined volunteers.

Colonel Hunter, still on his roan horse in the woods near Bull Run, saw the attack had failed and ordered a retreat. The bugler's call rang out but it was clear the heavy-set trumpeter was scared and the pace of his call increased with his fear. More cannon shells blasted through the ranks then the Rebels emerged from the far woods, fired a thickening hail of mini-balls and the Federals ran faster down the hill. The Union bugler wailed with panic then joined the rush to the rear. The Vermont flag bearer Private Lauder, being a very fast runner, dodged around the soldiers and was soon ahead of them, swiftly heading for the rear.

Then the low thumping sound of Stuart's cavalry rumbled from around the backside of the hill and swarmed out across the open ground. The Southern cavalry, 400 strong, rode in fours and many of the front riders rode dark black horses. The sound grew into an earth-shaking tremor. Leaves on trees trembled and clods of dirt flew up behind the dark horse's hooves with each thundering stride. Each rider whistled, yelped, or slapped the hindquarters with leather reins to gather still more speed, followed by shrill sounds of swords unsheathed and pistol shots split the air.

The Union soldiers were filled with fear. They had heard of newspaper reports describing the devilish Confederate Black Horse Cavalry, a vicious, ruthless group who rode straight from Hell to kill any man in blue and now they charged at *them!* Many soldiers surrendered but most ran with wild abandon and screamed, "*The Black Horse Cavalry!*"

Great fear gripped most of the Federal army. Panic spread. One soldier after another turned and sprinted for the bridge. The Union retreat was underway.

General Beauregard saw the Union soldiers running and *now* ordered the Southerners to charge. The fleeing bluecoats dashed for the stone bridge and it became bottlenecked with soldiers pushing and shoving to get across. A Confederate shell exploded nearby and soldiers were knocked over and trampled. Horses reared up in fear. Everyone tried to squeeze over the bridge at once and sprinted through the crowd of curious citizens, who were horrified. The battle had been bloody and lost, and now the Union forces trampled through their picnic provisions and ran for their lives! Carriage horses were startled, frightened and ran in circles out of control, ran in every direction while their owners tried to calm them and steer them for the rear. More Union soldiers dashed for their original encampment of Centreville except now the Confederates chased them and were closing down on them, only 100 hundred yards behind!

The bridge was clogged with troops who jammed into each other in one tangled mass. Rebel canons fired down on them from the hills above and units became disorganized, mixed up, and everywhere soldiers in blue uniforms ran roughshod through the citizens for the rear.

Civilians whipped their horses frantically. Their carriages bounced over the uneven meadow with women and men clinging with fear of falling off. Once over the bridge, Federal soldiers ran with wild abandon down the Warrenton Turnpike.

On the battlefield George ran after the fleeing troops to stop them then slowed down to look for a horse. A wounded chestnut limped badly and several horses lay on their side, wounded or dead. Twenty yards away Colonel Whiting's rider-less horse ran a zigzagging route, its white-socked hooves trotting feverishly in a random course of nervous fear. Then, off to the side and 30 yards away, stood Colonel Heintzelman's aide, still holding his black horse.

"*Hey, boy!*" he shouted and sprinted in his direction. The aide stood petrified, frozen in fear as the Confederates were charging and closing fast, but George grabbed the reins from the boy, who said nothing but stared with his mouth agape. He swung up onto the well-groomed black horse, wheeled it around then dug his spur-less boots into its flanks and it responded with a jolt of sudden, miraculous speed. They swiftly passed many of the fleeing men in blue.

General McDowell scanned the smoky battlefield with a pair of binoculars and was horrified to see many soldiers and officers running. Then off to the side he saw an officer in a floppy hat mount a black horse but he rode ahead of the fleeing soldiers. "My God! Is there no discipline among these cowards?"

McDowell was sickened but felt duty-bound to send a messenger to telegraph General Scott the latest news. "Battle lost. Will regroup and hold at Centreville."

McDowell spurred his horse toward the rear and knew he must use the reserves to make a stand at Centreville but where were they? McDowell rode his horse hard for 20 minutes, passed hundreds of fleeing soldiers and arrived at the original encampment to find the reserve forces lounging around. Some played cards, checkers or ate a late lunch. McDowell steered his chestnut quarter horse through Colonel Miles's brigade and asked several officers where Miles was. Each shrugged until one private pointed to a large tent off to the side.

McDowell dismounted brusquely, threw his reins at the private and charged into the tent. Miles lay slumped back in a tufted velvet maroon chair with his boots off and stocking feet on a tufted maroon ottoman. A half-eaten plate of food was on a side table and Miles clutched an open bottle of liquor. McDowell screamed, "*Why didn't you follow my orders?*"

Miles smiled and offered a waded piece of paper that McDowell recognized, it was his note, then he said with slurred speech, "I cou'n't read ffss."

McDowell shouted, "*Colonel Miles! What in God's name are you doing?*"

"Mine doc'r prescrib'd ffss. Fa dysentric diar-r-rhea. Opium pills an' a li'l brandy. It's s'lovely."

"*You are relieved of your duty!*" McDowell stormed out of the tent. A lieutenant stood nearby and he ordered, "Lock-up Colonel Miles and order this brigade to fall in! *We need to make a stand!*"

On the battlefield George rode swiftly on Heintzelman's black horse and caught the fleeing Vermonters at the stone bridge, then shouted, "*Hold your ground!*"

They were scared and ignored him, running with the heavy flow of soldiers crowding for the bridge. Heintzelman's dark horse resisted the reins to turn around, perhaps in fear of stepping on someone's foot, so George tugged the reins sharply to the left. The thoroughbred wouldn't budge. He then patted its neck, whispered into its ear "it's okay, boy," picked up the reins, bending at the poll and shifted his weight back a little. The horse backed up in a diagonal pattern with a hind foot then the opposite front foot off the ground at the same time and a moment later they had backed into a much less crowded spot. He then eased his thighs forward, lay the reins to his left and the well-trained horse turned left amid the stream of panicked soldiers, squeezing to dash by.

On the battlefield hundreds of Union soldiers had surrendered with several hundred more rushing for the bridge. He galloped his mount 20 yards further away, pulled the reins to a sudden stop and jumped off the dark horse. He held out his arms to catch the sprinting young men. Benedict, red-faced and breathing hard, dressed in his new woolen uniform, arrived near the bridge and also tried to grab a soldier here and there. Then Sergeant Brisken, surprisingly fast for his burly size, dashed over and stopped the first man he blocked and grabbed. The cowering soldier flailed at him, frantically looking around, then stopped to meet Brisken's powerful stare. Brisken shook him, cursed and stood him up straight. A convert was made.

George put out his arms, grabbed another fleeing soldier amid a tide of terror-stricken animals and yelled angrily, "*Hey! You're Vermonters!*" That helped calm one, then another but most broke free and pushed their way through the crowd then ran away.

Brisken waved his thick, powerful arms and stopped one more, then another. After a few moments George, Benedict and Brisken had gathered a rough collection of Vermonters, with more from Maine and a dozen from Brooklyn. They made up almost two full squads, 23 soldiers stood ready and looked to him. He yelled, "*Form two lines!*"

Most of the Federals continued running, shoving their way through the stuffed mass of soldiers. Benedict and Brisken moved in opposite directions and organized those willing to fight into two lines. Brisken anchored the far end and Benedict stood next to him, awaiting George's next order.

Across the open meadow the charging Rebels had a wild pleasure in their faces. They screamed for blood and killed bluecoats with bayonets, swords and an occasional musket or pistol shot. They were 50 yards away and closing rapidly.

He shouted with an even voice, "*Steady your aim, boys! Keep it low!*"

Many of the soldiers glanced at him and nodded. He hollered, "*First line. . . Ready!*"

The mismatched squad leveled their muskets on their shoulders and took aim while the second line stood behind them. The wild panic of civilians, soldiers and screaming horses was behind them and up ahead, one late-running Union soldier, wild-eyed and without a weapon, sprinted hard through their lines. The Rebels were 30 yards away and approaching fast.

"*First line*," He ordered, paused to take a deep breath then yelled, "*Fire!*"

A blast of musket fire cut down some Rebels but a few more came running, screaming viciously and sprinting at them with violent, rabid determination.

"*Second line. Forward!*" he hollered. These few men executed the maneuver with the precision of a campground drill. The second line stepped up and the first line took a knee. Sergeant Brisken yelled, "*First line, reload!*"

He shouted, "*Second line. Aim!*" The Rebels came quickly, 20 yards away and closing fast. "*Fire!*"

Another vicious volley cut down more Confederates. Most of those still running stopped and gazed at their fallen comrades but a few charged on. He fired his pistol, picked off the closest two Rebels and yelled, "*First line! Forward!*"

This tight group responded instantly. The first line stepped up and took aim while the second line took a knee then began reloading at Brisken's command.

Most of the Confederates turned and ran but some were caught up in the heat of battle and charged individually, attacking with their bayonets that led to vicious hand-to-hand fighting. One Rebel screamed like a madman and ran straight for him, slashing the air with his sword back-and-forth erratically. Brisken saw him, ran out incredibly swift and swung the butt of his rifle, clubbing the Rebel on the side of his head. The screaming man was silenced, his skull split open and he fell hard. Then Brisken hustled back and rejoined the far end of their line.

"*First line. Aim!*" he ordered. There were a dozen Rebels in front of them but hundreds more stood back where their initial volley was fired, looking about or straggling back toward the main Confederate line. "*Fire!*"

A round of mini-balls filled the air and a few more Southerners hit the ground. Those not shot picked up their pace in retreat and tried to act calmly as if they had changed their mind and decided to jog back, then they ran, followed by a few Vermonters who ran forward, eager to take the fight to the Rebels. George knew this handful of mismatched but emboldened soldiers would not go far against the entire Confederate Army and he hollered, "*Stand here! Hold this line!*"

Those volunteers who had run out stopped, turned with dismay but all came back as ordered. Brisken cracked a gritty smile in his bearded face. He had a steadfast determination in his dark brown eyes and yelled, "*Re-load! Be ready for the next charge!*"

Many of the Confederates were spent from their mad dash across the battlefield and some were exhausted from their all night journey from beyond the Blue Ridge Mountains. The Rebel cavalry was also worn out from their journey, all day and the previous night, but gathered in the far distance. Very few noticed this Union double line of alternating fire but the worn-out Confederates stopped their pursuit. Most of the Federal Army and civilians were now over the bridge but most of the fleeing Union soldiers continued to run with fear and panic.

The smoke rose off the settling field, filled with the cries of the wounded, and he looked at the group of 23 soldiers around him, ready to do whatever he ordered. He wanted to take time to study each man's face. Who were these bold soldiers? Some were familiar Vermonters but most were not. They were hardened New Yorkers and outdoorsmen from Maine. They wanted to be led and, at last, even though the day had been shameful, they had performed their duty. No one else was around to notice.

Then he looked up to Henry Hill, felt awful about the wounded laying on the field but expected the Southerners would care for them then saw the Rebels aiding their fallen comrades. He again glanced back to see the Army of the Potomac, safely over the bridge and felt very disappointed but relieved.

He took a moment to look at the soldiers who stood with him. He wanted to memorize each and every man. There was Benedict, always at his side, wearing spectacles with sweat pouring from under his kepi and his thin blonde hair matted down. The huge Master Sergeant Bear Brisken with determined brown eyes, blonde-bearded face and musket in hand. Lieutenant Wheelock Veazey, tall with dark features and his handsome face smudged with black near his mouth from ripping open gunpowder cartridges with his teeth. Private Seymour Winston, a youth from Montpelier with peach-fuzz on his chin. Private Burt Cromartie, one of the first soldiers he had trained in camp with his smirk gone, now stern and keen for a fight. Private Cordon and the Burdett brothers from White River Junction, who he had also met in their Burlington camp were in line and set to respond. Most of these young men he didn't know and yet these few were ready for anything. Remarkable. Gritty. He looked over the battlefield to Henry Hill, where thousands of Confederates stood around, cheered and attended to the wounded. No, the Rebels were not coming again, not now.

"*Fall back to Centreville!*" he called out and these courageous, solitary few moved orderly over the bridge, then he followed them. On the other side of the bridge were more wounded and dead, littered picnic remains, and small craters from artillery shells. Screaming horses lay on their side with others dead. Somehow Heintzelman's frightened black horse had wandered across the bridge, circled and looked around with nervous fear and its ears pushed back in warning. He offered his left hand as a cue to relax, took its reins and coaxed it to stand still. Then he held its halter tightly, pulled it closer from its left side, stroked its black neck and whispered into its ear, "There, there. Okay. Good boy."

He reached into his coat pocket, offered a lump of sugar saved from morning coffee and the horse took it over its bit. The dark thoroughbred with a white flash on its nose bobbed its head and responded well but its shanks still shivered. He patted it and cooed, "It's alright, boy."

Sergeant Bear Brisken lifted a wounded man, carried him to a horseless wagon and eased the man down. Benedict holstered his pistol then helped another wounded boy limp to the wagon. Brisken picked up another young man, hoisted him over his broad back and carried him 10 yards then set him in the wagon next to the first wounded soldier. Benedict then helped a young man in civilian clothes, who bled from his left leg, step up into the wagon.

George moved his hand from the halter to the reins, walked Heintzelman's horse to the wagon, hitched it up and ordered them to move out. Lieutenant Veazey led the 23 soldiers plus the wagon along the Warrenton Turnpike. He looked back once more. No, they were not coming.

Brisken walked over to him and put his large, muscular arm on his shoulder then clapped him on the back with his thick, heavy hand. "That was a hell of scrap."

A thud slammed into Brisken's back. An instant later he recalled hearing the crack of a sharpshooter's rifle split the air. The bullet had hit Brisken square in the back and he fell face-first, grasping at his arm and pulling his coat, and landed heavily on the ground.

He knelt and rolled Brisken onto his back. The bullet had entered the middle of his large back, punctured an artery near his heart and made a gaping hole in his chest where it exited. Brisken's dark brown eyes still held a sparkle and a slight smile crossed his lips then his eyes went fixed and his breathing stopped. He was still.

He shook his head and remained kneeling. Benedict joined him. Veazey came running from the front along with a few other Vermonters and they huddled around Brisken. His chest had a jagged hole by his heart and it was a dark red, bloody mess.

After a brief moment he stood, enraged, and looked back for the sniper, searching the hazy dusk of twilight, past the bridge. He barely saw the woods around Bull Run River. At the far edge of the clearing appeared some vague movement in a tall oak tree but he wasn't sure. It was too dark. Still, he raised his pistol, took aim at a large limb and fired a shot at the oak. A distant faint smack thudded against something solid. Nothing moved. He aimed and fired again. Nothing.

He, Benedict and Veazey struggled to lift Sergeant Brisken's huge, lifeless body onto the wagon. From the wagon a wounded man pulled on Brisken's meaty arm, saw he was dead and fell back in horror but two others helped roll Brisken up and fully onto the wagon. Benedict crossed Brisken's arms on his chest then used his palm to close his staring milky-white eyes.

Veazey, his tall frame saddened and downtrodden, returned to the front of their assorted company. Benedict smacked the black horse's rear, the wagon lurched and again they moved out.

He walked along the darkening road and felt a strange chill on his sweaty neck. The sniper's last shot was meant for him. He examined that thought, turned it over and over again with various angles of reasoning on fate and God, then let it go and continued walking on the road. Yes, he thought bitterly. It had been "a hell of scrap."

The Rebels had won the day with the field now littered with wounded and dead. Southern General Beauregard considered a pursuing attack across Bull Run, on to Centreville and called together his staff to discuss their options. They must move to keep this momentum but were his men ready? After a long discussion, Beauregard decided to rest his army because they were exhausted from their journey and the battle, and they needed to care for the wounded.

The Federal reserve forces of Colonel Miles's brigade were assembling in Centreville but the frightened soldiers from the Battle of Bull Run ran through their encampment and streamed through the town. They jogged tiredly, stumbling, and dropped their haversacks, canteens, caps and shoes, and even dropped their guns to move faster. Sweat dripped down their heads, jogging and panting out of breath. Some were wounded and bleeding but they moved through the forming ranks of Miles's brigade. General McDowell and some officers tried to rally their forces and shouted words of bravado.

Miles's brigade, still disorganized, watched the wounded and fleeing soldiers and never assembled. They were confused and unsure of whether they should fall in or join the main force heading for the rear. They joined the fleeing Army of the Potomac.

George and this mismatched company caught up with the Vermonters and marched to Centreville, fatigued. It was now dark but several volunteers helped the wounded from the wagon and eased into their bedrolls, managed to find their tents and collapsed in exhaustion.

He removed his floppy hat, waved to a private with a fully lit candelabra to come over and stand with them, then asked Benedict to take a letter. Benedict took out a pencil and parchment then flattened it over the floorboards of the wagon next to Brisken's still body. He motioned for the private with the light to step closer and the private's eyes widened. His clean face showed he was untested by battle, a reserve.

"To Sergeant Brisken's family," George began. "I think you can find out where they live. Bennington, right?"

"Yes, sir," Benedict replied. "Go ahead. . . George."

"It was a terribly sad day for us, but Sergeant—" He was overwhelmed with grief and unable to speak. He stuttered, stopped, and tried to compose himself to somehow carry on. What good could be found here? He offered some humor, "Was his first name Bear?"

Benedict blurted out a brief laugh then burst into a sobbing cry. The private lowered his head with his shiny face contorted in pain, also about to cry. He continued solemnly, "Sergeant Thad Brisken."

"Yes, Thad," Benedict managed to say. "Short for Thaddeus."

"Thank you. Thad Brisken." He noticed his dried blood on his hands. The private took a knee. Brisken's chest was a large tangle of caked blood and mangled flesh yet his bearded face appeared calm. His eyes were closed but his lips were parted open in his blonde beard as if he was about to reinforce an order, or smile. "God. When we made camp at the Burlington Fairgrounds, you know, he was one of the first to volunteer."

"Yes, sir," Benedict said and moved his spectacles to wipe his eyes. A smudge of black powder smeared his cheek to his mouth. He continued, "I remember a story going around camp. The story was that one night Bear had taken an officer's horse for a joy ride. The next morning, story was, Veazey's dark thoroughbred, Justitia, a sleek and speedy horse, was missing. A very fine horse. They said Bear took it for a joy ride and refused to come in. I heard that and shook my head. Impossible. That would have meant Bear disobeyed an order. Hell, that would never happen. Duty, honor and country were not words to him. They *were* him. Of course later the truth came out—Veazey had given his permission to take Justitia for a ride and Bear had let the time get away from him. It had become too dark to make his way back and he didn't want to injure the horse so he camped out, just over the river and in the trees. No harm. Bear was a good man, a fine man and—"

His voice warbled with emotion and tears filled his eyes. "He was... Well, I'm not able to say it. You're better with words Benedict."

Benedict cried freely with tears streaming over his cheeks. The candelabra wavered and he saw the private crying, trembling with tears. He clapped his hand at the base of Benedict's neck. His face and new uniform were dirty. He squeezed Benedict's neck and said, "Will you let his family know how highly we thought of Bear and how brave he was? I'll sign it. A hell of a man, Bear Brisken. He will be missed."

More tears rolled off Benedict's cheeks and he held him, letting him cry into his side. After a moment Benedict somehow composed himself and set pencil to paper. He cleared his throat but spoke with a shaky voice, "Master Sergeant Thaddeus "Bear" Brisken was an adventurous young man, only twenty-four. He loved hunting, the outdoors and all things in nature with the bright enthusiastic sparkle of youth."

Benedict stopped writing to consider his deep-felt emotions. "He was not book smart but he was keen. He was a fighter and he had grit. He could be relied on. It doesn't sound like much but there aren't a lot of men that can Hell or high-water, god-damn-it be relied on. And with Bear, it was *guaranteed.*"

Then Benedict looked up, stared at him and they shared the same thought: If someone as brave and capable as Bear Brisken had been killed then what chance did either of them have?

A messenger rode up swiftly and dismounted awkwardly with a couple of quick steps then thrust out a note from General McDowell. He wiped his eyes and felt interrupted but there was no time for grief, not now, and opened the note then tipped it sideways to catch the light from the candelabra.

McDowell had ordered they retreat still further. He nodded to the messenger, who swung up on his horse and rode away quickly. He then asked the private to stand up, to take a single candle from the candelabra and go back to his unit. The private took out a candle, shuffled away but stopped, turned and said, "I wish I had met him. Bear Brisken."

The Vermonters had rested for 20 minutes. "Finish this up Benedict. Post it. I'll get Veazey to find a bugler and call assembly. Have you seen Colonel Whiting?"

Benedict snarled, "Last anyone saw, he was running hard for the rear."

He gave Benedict a shrill look. Benedict spat then responded more properly, "*No. Sir*. I have not. I have not seen the Colonel, not since the battle began in earnest. Sir."

When night fell, McDowell sent another telegram to General Scott in Washington City. He stated his intention was to retreat from Centreville and to hold at Fairfax.

General Scott, still in his full military uniform with gold epaulets and shiny medals, sat in his Washington City home. Scott had received a series of telegrams and was confused and appalled.

Where was their leadership? Scott coughed a few times, rubbed his aching feet then sipped whiskey and water from his cut-glass tumbler.

The demoralized and frightened Union soldiers kept moving. In the dark of night the officers and artillerymen slept on their horses and rode on, while common foot soldiers continued to jog, retreat, became tired, walked and stumbled along still further.

They retreated to Fairfax, where George assigned Veazey to choose six of their best soldiers to be outpost pickets while they set up camp in the dark. Most of the Vermonters didn't bother to set-up their tents and fell asleep when they hit the ground.

Most of the Federal Army continued their retreat beyond Fairfax. Officers and soldiers moved in one long blue column, hurrying in the dark. Then McDowell sent another telegram to General Scott, stating they were forced to fall back to the Potomac. Their routed troops would not reform.

Many Federal soldiers continued and did not listen to orders of any kind, and did not come to rest until they crossed the Potomac. They staggered through the cobblestone streets and fell down in exhaustion in the doorways of houses and apartments, crumpled on the curb, slumped against lampposts and stretched out in the gutters of Washington City. Many had covered 35 miles in 16 hours, and had run most of the way in great fear.

The survivors had fled to Washington in panic. The immense Confederate Army was said to be behind them and the Army of the Potomac was shattered and disorganized. Leadership from officers was missing. The Union Army was more a collection of young men in uniforms than an army ready to fight. They had brought panic with them from the Battle of Bull Run and rumors raced through Washington: The Rebels are coming! The fall of the capital is a certainty! *The Rebels are coming!*

No one from either side had prepared for the consequences of a large battle. Even though the Treasury Department had announced a great victory based on McDowell's first reports, a bulletin was issued for surgeons and male nurses to gather at five o'clock to care for the wounded still laying on the battlefield. Now at this late hour after dark, they left to attend to, and to transport back the wounded.

A squadron of 40 doctors and male nurses left Washington City to care for the wounded but there were thousands of wounded and dead, plus the Confederates held the field. Those Union soldiers who were well enough to walk were captured and sent to Southern prison camps. The Confederates had almost 2,000 wounded and dead, whom they cared for before General Beauregard reassembled his forces into one strong encampment.

The majority of the Federal injured lay in agony on the field through the night, into the next morning before medical attention arrived. Of the 20,000 Federal soldiers engaged in battle, McDowell had lost 2,900 dead, wounded, or captured. The Federals also lost cannons, firearms, supplies, dignity, and any hope of ending the rebellion quickly.

The war would not be over in one big battle. The plan of a quick strike then "On to Richmond!" would not be so easy. The

Secessionists had determined soldiers and they were ready to fight for their independence to start their own nation.

It was now clear gallant hearts and brash slogans were not enough. The Federal volunteers had been routed, shamefully whipped. They needed well-trained officers and disciplined soldiers. The politicians and newspapers blamed the officers because many of the officers were the first to run. Soldiers were left leaderless on the battlefield. The following Monday 200 officers submitted their resignations. The whole nation learned no summer excursion of volunteers would end this war.

General McDowell relieved Colonel Miles of duty and had him officially reprimanded. They removed Miles far from any future battle lines and placed him in the most out of the way outpost the military could find. Miles was assigned to a small arsenal in a quiet little town in the northern end of the Shenandoah Valley called Harpers Ferry. The Federal leaders hoped Miles would serve out the remainder of the war in desolate isolation without doing further damage to the Union.

Colonel Whiting went through a long process of legal maneuvering, testimony in court, and letters to the Burlington and Montpelier newspapers but he was relieved of command. Some of the soldiers said Whiting put up more of a legal fight than any fight he made on the battlefield. Others said Whiting did everything he could to save his name, which was all he had left.

The Vermont brigade would need a new leader. Governor Holbrook went to Washington City and visited the Vermonters' camp. The Governor wore his full-length black formal suit and addressed all of the soldiers in a long speech. Holbrook then turned to the officers of each regiment and asked them to write down one name, of who should lead them. They each wrote a name on a slip of paper, Lieutenant Benedict gathered the papers then handed the nominations to Governor Holbrook and saluted. When the Governor unfolded each paper, he read one name, then read the same name again and again. He smiled because it was unanimous and then it was only a matter of ceremony.

George Stannard was promoted to colonel and would lead the Vermont brigade.

~18 ~

Tuesday dawned clear and cool. The devastated Union Army had brought back with them from the battlefield a sense of panic and doom. Secretary of War Simon Cameron made plans for the inevitable fall of Washington City. Secretary Cameron's first priority was to ensure President Lincoln and his family could safely leave the city but how should he do that? Under heavy guard to New York? Escorted with federal troops perhaps further, to Boston? Cameron made various contingency plans. Next, to prevent any arms or ammunition from falling into Confederate hands, he issued orders to ship the arsenal stores to New York. Gunboats were anchored in the Potomac and *Wachusett* was made ready to take the President, his family and the Cabinet to safety. Finally, Cameron bundled important papers with instructions these documents were to be carried by plain-clothed men on foot then on horseback out of Washington.

President Lincoln did not flinch. In this crisis amid widespread panic he did not show any fear and ordered department clerks to be organized into companies. They were armed and made ready to fight. Lincoln faced his greatest critics, his Cabinet, along with a staff of generals who were military advisers and began the process of evaluating what had gone wrong. The Union Army, his generals said, needed more training and more soldiers to create an irresistible superior force. They issued a call for more men. Throughout the North volunteers responded with the rallying cry, "Preserve the Union!"

Next Lincoln relieved McDowell of command after the debacle of Bull Run and began the search for a leader who could mold the Union Army into a cohesive fighting force and defend Washington against a Rebel attack. With General Scott's advice, along with other generals trained at West Point, plus numerous discussions with Secretary of War Cameron and his advisors, Lincoln selected General George McClellan to be Commander of the Federal Army. McClellan, from Philadelphia, was a short, tough Irishman with dark hair, a long mustache and was known for his great organizational skills. He was a strict disciplinarian and would be the perfect person to instill a sense of confidence in the Union Army. The soldiers knew McClellan had their best interest in mind, loved him for it and called him by the nicknames "Little Mac" or "Our Mac."

In the late summer of 1861 the soldiers trained, marched, inspected their weapons, trained more, learned how to perform military maneuvers on the battlefield under simulated attack and trained more. One reporter wrote, "They did nothing but march and polish their buttons for the entire summer." When they did fight, although more confident, they lost at Cross Lanes then Balls Bluff, Virginia. In the west, the Union army suffered 400 men killed, missing or captured at Fort Fillmore, New Mexico then had over 1,000 casualties in battles at both Wilson's Creek then Lexington, Missouri.

The Federal generals were pressed by President Lincoln, his Cabinet and other politicians because they felt they must stop the flow of losses. General McClellan ordered new uniforms to be made of wool instead of shoddy, with light blue trousers and a tunic of dark blue. Most regiments wore the kepi, although some had hats of soft black felt. The soldiers looked like a new army.

The Vermonters felt the change and were proud of it, and served out the remainder of their nine-month time with more soldiers sick from disease, flux or dysentery than were casualties of war. Although they had been robust men of the wilderness, many had never been exposed to smallpox, typhus or cholera. If they survived the illnesses, they returned home to little fanfare, although the *Burlington Free Press* reported that they looked spiffy in their bright uniforms. The war had been much more difficult with a heavier cost than anyone in Vermont had imagined.

President Lincoln again met with his military advisors and with his Cabinet, including his new Secretary of War Edmund Stanton, who had replaced Simon Cameron. They had strengthened the total numbers of men in the Army, had trained then trained more and had lost. Everyone agreed it must be the leadership. In private, Lincoln expressed anger at the failed generalship and wept for the mounting losses of dead, wounded and captured, but he remained firm in his conviction along with the entire political body of the North. The Union must remain together.

In the South, they took the victory at Bull Run to be a confirmation of their superior leadership and better soldiers. Their victories in the west and in Virginia were God's will, ordaining their system of government and leadership. It was all guided by divine provenance. The reporters in Richmond and Atlanta wrote the North was filled with soft men who lived in cities and sat at desks while the South was a place of stout men who worked the land to earn their living. Of course they were better fighters.

The situation was clear to newspaper editors from Atlanta to New York. This would be a long war filled with many battles. Men of peace offered settlements and alternative solutions. Why not let the Southern states carry on with their way of life and let them form their own nation? Was it worth the lives of thousands of men? Talk in parlors and in Congress raged on. More editorials were printed, along with the names of the dead on the front pages of newspapers. Many had predicted the war would be over before Christmas but now all knew the horrible truth. This war would not be over any time soon.

~19~

The house was quiet. Decorations were hung for the Christmas season but when George asked about one or another, Helen could not remember who made them or where she had bought them. She didn't know who crafted this fine wooden angel with delicate wings or who painted the red flush on jolly Saint Nick's cheeks. Festive baubles were sprinkled throughout the entryway and receiving room yet it was foreign and puzzling. "What are these things?" he asked, and held up a small silver-painted toy horn. "Where is the glass ornament from Aunt Amelia?"

The fireplace crackled warmly. Helen sat on the red velvet sofa and played with the tassel drawstring of her white dress. "Which one?"

"The Christmas one," he said. "It's a snowy scene of Saint Albans. The village with a church steeple in falling snow."

"I don't know." Helen bit her lips, gazing at the pink rose print on her dress. "I didn't have time to look for it."

He noticed more decorations around the room. Cedar branches fringed the doorway and a white vase held holly with red berries on the mantle. Those must have come from Amelia, or perhaps a neighbor? "Where are the nutcrackers?"

"I wanted it to be cheerful and those remind me of the war." She dropped her dress tassel with a forced exasperation. "*What?*"

"They're toys. They remind me of Christmas." He thought back to one of the first Christmases he could remember. His mother lay in bed and everyone was very sad until his father pointed out a green velvet bag near the fireplace. He scurried over, picked it up and opened it excitedly. Inside he found a brightly painted red-and-green nutcracker. "Happy Christmas, son."

Helen broke the silence. "I don't look through your things! If you're upset with the way I've had the house decorated, why don't you say so?"

"No. It's beautiful. It's not what I expected, that's all." He walked to her and reached for her but Helen looked down with tears in her eyes. He took hold of her hands then said, "It's beautiful. Thank you."

"You can decorate the rest of the house!" She broke from him, raced for the stairway but called out, "I'll have nothing more to do with it!"

On Christmas morning she gave him a white silk ascot and he gave her a leather-bound edition of "Song of Hiawatha" by Longfellow. He did not wear ascots, which he considered pretentious ornaments of the nouveaux rich. She did not like poetry, or Native Americans. She said he could dress up with the ascot for the theatre like other men. He said she could start attending poetry recitals like other women. They stared at each other in silence.

He tried to make the gift exchange more pleasant by promising to attend a production of Wagner's *Das Rheingold* but Helen said she had seen it twice. The next week she offered they should each sit, individually, for new photographs to be made into carte de visites but he reminded her that his box of cartes remained unopened on the marble table near the front door. He had been busy with the war. She informed him that her box was empty, she was very popular, and she would need more for the New Year's Eve Ball to be held by the Akins. She would pose alone.

The remainder of his month-long leave was quiet without incident. He informed Helen he needed to see his horses and rented a dark gelding named Flint from Peck's Livery then went to his farm in Georgia. He gave each horse special attention, feeding them some dried sugar beets as a treat, and spent time talking with each and brushed their coats thoroughly. He did not find a single nick or sore spot on any horse and was very pleased with the care Tommy Lonegran had given them.

Then he walked through the pasture to the stone wall that ran up to the edge of the hill, where it met an old, rotting post with a wire fence. Sapling pines and small box elders dotted the side of the hill before the woods became heavy on the hilltop. The timber men had bypassed the great elms, thick maples and tall oaks atop the hill. It took too much effort to bring them down. Those trees had matured, formed a canopy and blocked most of the sunlight from reaching the forest floor, which was covered with leaves, small sticks, twigs and patches of snow. At last he came to the small clearing where his father had buried his mother. Her gravestone had somehow become tilted and he muscled it back up then used his boot to stomp down the edge on both sides to keep it straight. He took off his floppy hat, sat cross-legged on the cold forest floor and let the sunlight warm his face.

A red-headed woodpecker knocked on a large tree near the edge of the hill. The mature beech tree was magnificent with a thick stable trunk and two main branches extended out with many other branches lifting up and shooting off in every direction, creating a huge but now barren umbrella. He loved that beech tree. It was a reflection of who he was. It had withstood terrible storms and now thrived in the prime of adulthood.

He thought of his mother again and felt ashamed he could barely remember her facial features. Now when he tried to remember Rebecca's face he envisioned more of his Aunt Amelia's wrinkled and rouged face. He could see his mother's thin hands, the way her slender fingers wrapped around his hand and recalled her soft voice singing a sweet English lullaby, "Shoo shoo, shoo la-roo… Johnny's gone for a soldier."

He then thought of his father for a long time, saw Samuel's warm, shining brown eyes and his quick smile. Samuel had given him so much wisdom on working the farm, running the Trading Post, and dealing with people. He had given him a strong fabric of morals and ethics, woven into the tapestry of his life.

Now his family was gone. In its place was a horrible war with brutal killing and a disjointed, tense marriage with Helen. Tears fell easily. He thought of his peaceful childhood, mixed with flashes of the stark horrors he had seen and committed in this brutal war. He was a changed man. Flashes of atrocities from the horrors of war shred what remained of his inner peace and he sobbed for a long time.

~ ~

He walked Charger out of the stable into the frozen dirt ring. Flint, the dark gelding rented from Peck's Livery, looked over so Tommy went to it, took its reins, and promised to take it back to Burlington tomorrow. He mounted Charger in a single hop, thanked Tommy again and said goodbye. He nudged his spurs and Charger responded with a snort and a burst of speed as if to say, Where have you been and what took you so long? They were swiftly moving at amazing speed, in rhythm, as if no time had passed between them.

After 15 minutes of hard riding, Charger was lathered and he eased his grip on the reins. They were free, together and moved in unison. He took off his floppy hat, held it in his hand and felt the brisk, icy wind blowing through his dark hair. It was a beautiful, remarkable feeling.

Charger's breathing became heavy but he wanted to enjoy this sensation of their closeness, flexed his thigh muscles to hold on, and enjoyed the vigorous ride. Then he eased into a gallop, rubbed Charger's neck, and slowed him to a walk. Charger snorted again and bobbed his head as if to say, I missed you!

This felt wonderful. The air was crisp and clear, across Lake Champlain wispy white clouds floated over the mountains in New York and the mid-afternoon sun slid closer to the winter horizon. He thought, Perhaps this glorious moment is a harbinger of what would come with Helen and thought again, What should he say to her? He decided to speak from the heart and declare his undying love for her. Over time in a lengthy marriage they would remember this moment as an inconsequential distant memory because they loved each other very much. They would make it work.

He rode Charger back to Burlington, stabled him in the small barn behind their house and followed the sweet strains of a violin inside where he found Helen in the front room playing a piece of music that sounded like Chopin. She finished, looked up with a wry smile and licked her lips, then set down the violin on a small table. He took her hands and gazed at her. She was radiant with her dark curly hair accented against her cream-colored, French-silk gown with long sleeves. "I love you, my dear. Very much! I want our marriage to be better and I will do anything, anything to improve this. Our marriage is my strongest, my only desire."

Helen pulled back her hands, smoothed out her dress and smiled politely. "You smell like your horse Charger! I insist you take a bath *immediately!* Honestly, George! I know I told you this before and you act as if you don't care how bad you smell. Meanwhile I always wear perfume, dress as elegantly as I can and make my entire appearance beautiful for you. *Honestly!*"

During his month-long leave he often chatted with his Aunt Amelia, saw a few friends and neighbors, and went to Selzer's barbershop frequently, where he confided with Cranston and read the New York and Boston newspapers, and all the issues of the *Burlington Free Press*. At home he read "Song of Hiawatha," then bought a Charles Dickens novel called *A Tale of Two Cities* from Alvan Herndon, the bookbinder, who had opened a book shop of his own.

Bradford Dutton visited their house twice to play cards then Helen invited him to tea, along with Allysa and Cranston, and Mrs. Turner. She insisted on hiring a butler for their tea party, which was very pleasant. During the tea, George came to know Bradford Dutton better. Dutton was a brave, energetic firefighter, who had been severely burned on his feet and did not walk well, which prevented him from the war effort. He sported a well-trimmed mustache in the style now fashionable, after General McClellan.

On the eve of 1862, George and Helen attended the Akins's New Year's Ball, which he thought was much like the others, at the Akins' mansion. He did not feel like dancing but watched Helen, who danced every dance of the night. He spent most of the evening talking with men about the war, although he preferred to discuss the new businesses in Burlington. Each time he asked about a new building or how a certain business was doing, he was interrupted and asked to relate the events of the Battle of Bull Run again, the skirmishes at Yorktown, Golding's Farm, Lee's Mills or Williamsburg.

The one-month leave passed quickly. On the return train to Washington City he thought of his time at home. Over the holidays he often thought of the war and now on the train, he realized he should have spoken with Helen more about their marriage. What had Helen been doing? How often did she play the violin? How was she feeling? Was this distance he felt because *he* had changed? It seemed he was a very different person who could no longer relate to her. The flashes of this horrible war were overwhelming in contrast to the daily events in

Burlington. Was he quieter because of what he had seen and experienced?

When the train pulled into Washington, he felt even more separated, isolated and wished he could go back to Vermont and start over again. He longed to return to the days of courtship with Helen and tell her *all* his feelings. The train stopped with a sudden jerk and blew out a long blast of hot steam.

~20 ~

In January 1862 the war between the states continued much the same. The Union forces prepared with additional military training. The Confederate forces showed their knowledge of the terrain, their maneuverability and fighting ability, and often defeated the Federals in small skirmishes. Federal General McClellan settled into a hardened winter of training and waited for warmer weather to make the roads more passable to move troops and artillery easier.

President Lincoln again met with his military advisors, Secretary of War Stanton, and his Cabinet. Lincoln pleaded with General McClellan to attack the Rebels *now*. He wrote him letters, sent cables and gave firm instructions with couriers. In response McClellan mocked Lincoln, said he knew nothing of war and preferred to train his army and wait for the perfect opportunity to strike.

On February 22, the daily military meetings in the White House were stopped. Black crepe hung on the front door. In the Green Room the undertaker was busy. Willie Lincoln, the eleven-year-old boy who liked to play dress-up soldier, who had playfully jumped on General Scott's leg with abundant affection, died of typhoid fever. When they buried Willie, an immense wind blew and tore the roofs off houses and slashed the flags to ribbons. His father, the President, drove the hearse carriage blind with grief through the storm wreckage with his son Robert and two Illinois senators. Mrs. Lincoln, shut in her room with drawn, black curtains, was too overcome with grief to attend.

When the warming rays of spring finally came, the tulip trees around the Capitol bloomed and purple lilacs budded. Dry-goods stores cleared out their inventory of woolen blankets and boots to make way for straw bonnets and sun umbrellas. A new crop of volunteers joined the veteran soldiers who re-enlisted.

When the frozen mud had thawed and softened, General McClellan made plans to move the Army of the Potomac but they couldn't move yet. They had to wait for the mud to dry or risk being literally stuck in the mud. Warmer and drier weather came but McClellan continued to search for the right opportunity to engage the Confederates.

When the war had started in 1861 most of the Vermonters had volunteered for nine months of service. Many of those soldiers returned to civilian life, some re-enlisted but more volunteers joined and were trained. By 1862 the Vermont volunteers were very much a different group of soldiers.

In 1862 George led the Vermonters on Charger in hard fought battles at Williamsburg and Winchester, Virginia. Those battles were in the woods and valleys, across the rivers and over the hills of the South. Confederate General Lee and General Joseph Johnston used their knowledge of the land with experienced military maneuvers executed by hardened, seasoned soldiers to great effect. Those battles inflicted about 500 casualties to both the Union and Confederate armies. Because General McClellan was not ready to sacrifice his men for less than a decisive victory, it solidified a feeling that the Army of the Potomac was still not ready. Little Mac pulled back his army and ordered more training.

In April in the West, word came of a terrible, bloody battle at Pittsburgh Landing, also called Shiloh, Tennessee. Federal General Ulysses Grant led the Union army in two days of horrendous fighting with a total of over 23,000 men killed, wounded, or captured. The Federal casualties were 12,573, which staggered even the most-hardened politicians, reporters, and citizens. Newspaper editors wrote what every citizen now wondered: Was this amount of bloodshed to become routine and acceptable? At what cost should the Union prevail? Why shouldn't the Southerners be allowed to go their own way?

President Lincoln continued to meet with his Cabinet to better plan the war and was criticized by newspaper editors, politicians, and many of the generals. McClellan mocked him and frequently called him an "ignorant baboon." When a newspaper reporter asked if General Grant should be replaced because of the horrendous losses, Lincoln stood by him as the leader of the Western Army and said, "He fights."

After such heavy casualties the politicians in Washington and the people throughout the North needed reassurance the war would be worth the toll. Some just needed to know the war was winnable. Meanwhile Lincoln made still more requests to McClellan to engage General Lee and the Rebel army. McClellan refused. Instead, Our Mac trained his army through the warming spring months of 1862 and worked on a strategy of attacking Richmond from the south by going up the James River and the peninsula. Then, after more training, warmer weather allowed McClellan to move with some confidence. Much of the Army of the Potomac was transported away from Washington onto the Virginia peninsula and into a plan of attack.

Little Mac led the Federals in a series of battles in Virginia that began at Mechanicsville and concluded at Malvern Hill and was called the Seven Days Battle. Southern General Lee, the nation's foremost military leader, the man who had declined Francis Blair's offer of commanding the Federal Army, led the Rebels. From June 26 through July 1st the two armies twisted, turned and tried to outmaneuver and outflank the other. The fighting was fierce. When it was finished, over 51,000 casualties lay on the Virginia soil. Under McClellan's leadership, the Union had suffered another series of defeats and lost 25,903 more men.

For President Lincoln this was all he needed of McClellan's leadership and he replaced the popular general with General John Pope, a tough-minded leader from Illinois. Pope had trained at West Point, was politically connected, and was known as a fighter. He had a receding hairline high on his forehead, had let his long dark hair grow to his shoulders with a long goatee beard and quick light eyes.

General Pope and many others had analyzed what went wrong at the first major battle, the Battle of Bull Run. Pope was certain he could have led the Union Army to victory and he devised a new plan to fight and finish the entire Confederate army at the exact same site. He told newspaper reporters in Washington about his basic plan for a second battle at Bull Run, where he vowed to "bag the whole lot of 'em."

Pope moved the main body of forces, but not the Vermonters, toward the Second Battle of Bull Run. George and the Vermonters were stationed at Winchester and ordered to build a defensive post. They built Fort Sigel, maneuvered heavy siege cannons into position, and the orchards and timber around the fort were cleared with rifle pits and abatis constructed. It took five weeks in the hot August sun.

Doc Thayer treated 41 soldiers for heat exhaustion, sunstroke, dysentery, and disease. Captain George Beebe, a clerk George knew from Burlington, died of dysentery. Beebe had been a very popular officer, was genial, kind and his death sent a wave of remorse through the Vermonters. Doc Thayer, who had grown thin from the heat, expressed the remorse with his light gray eyes and spoke the words every Vermonter wondered, "If our boys are dying, why aren't we engaged in fighting the enemy?"

The Confederate Army now had even greater confidence, and also continued to train and re-supply. With fewer soldiers and materiel, General Lee had accomplished stunning results on the battlefield and was loved by his men. Southern President Jefferson Davis, also impressed with Lee's victories, placed him in command of the entire Confederate Army.

When Lee heard of Pope's boastful prediction "to bag the whole lot of 'em" at Bull Run, he prepared even more. Because Lee knew where Pope wanted to fight, knew the terrain and knew how to use his strengths to exploit the Union's weaknesses, the Confederates were waiting and ready.

On August 28th General Pope, much to his surprise, did not win his well-planned battle. The Union lost 15,039 more men. The Army of the Potomac's faith in Pope as a leader was shattered. One editor in a Northern newspaper summarized popular opinion and wrote, "General Pope should have waited until he had won the battle, won anything for that matter, until he opened his mouth."

President Lincoln promptly removed Pope from command and had him assigned to a post in Minnesota, where he would deal with a Sioux uprising. In Minnesota Pope continued to discuss his plans with local newspaper reporters. He became known as "a commentator" on frontier conditions and the conflict with the Indians. Because Native Americans did not read the newspapers, Pope had some success on the western frontier.

After the latest Federal defeat the Union Army needed a new commander. Again President Lincoln succumbed to his advisor's pleas, McClellan's popularity, and made him the commander of the Union forces. McClellan's appointment led to an immediate improvement in the morale of the Army of the Potomac. They loved

Little Mac and would do anything for him. McClellan knew the first thing he must do was to stop the Army of Virginia because Lee was not sitting on his latest victory at the Second Battle of Bull Run. Scouts reported seeing the Confederates moving toward Beaver Dam Creek and heading northward through the Shenandoah Valley. McClellan deployed his troops to head off Lee's advances and most of the Army of the Potomac headed north to engage the Rebels but McClellan also split off a very small group, including the Vermonters, to guard an arsenal.

Through the difficult summer months of 1862, the Vermonters had not done much to repair their poor reputation from the First Battle of Bull Run, where many had fled. Their hasty retreat had led in part to the full rout and humiliation of the Union Army, which became known as the "Great Skedaddle." More recently they had fought well but the entire Federal Army was unimpressive at Williamsburg. Now that McClellan was once again in command, Little Mac ordered Brigadier General Julius White's brigade, including the Vermonters, to remove their artillery or render it unserviceable, destroy Fort Sigel, and withdraw from Winchester. They were sent to even more remote post, far away from the front lines of any serious engagement.

The 748 Vermonters plus regiments from Ohio, Illinois, Indiana, Maryland, and New York were sent to guard a small Federal arsenal in a distant valley called Harpers Ferry. The arsenal was in a remote, idyllic outpost, immune from any fighting.

Because Southern General Lee knew McClellan was slow to move and hesitant to attack, he split up his army into three large groups that would move in two long, 25-mile marches to strike in a pincer attack on the small garrison at Harpers Ferry, while the third group moved on Antietam Creek to Sharpsburg. They would reunite in three days. Lee's plan of attack was called Special Orders 191. It was written down for each of the three division commanders but one copy of Lee's orders was found by two Union soldiers in a field wrapped around three cigars and was taken to General McClellan.

McClellan now knew Lee's army was divided into three groups, knew where they were going, and knew when they were scheduled to reunite. It was one of the most remarkable military blunders that had ever occurred. Now McClellan could strike a crushing blow to defeat the Southerners conclusively.

George and the 748 Vermonters had no idea General Lee had ordered two-thirds of his massive Confederate army, 25,000 men in one column and 30,000 soldiers in another column, to march in a closing pincer movement to attack the tiny garrison at Harpers Ferry.

~21 ~

The Federal arsenal at Harpers Ferry was located at the confluence of two rivers, the Shenandoah and the Potomac, and surrounded by three mountain ranges. The graceful beauty of this small town at the base of a mountainous valley where the two rivers met was charming. This peaceful setting was well known as the site of John Brown's raid three years ago in the autumn of 1859. At the time a Federal officer, Colonel Robert Lee arrived at the site and recaptured the arsenal with "swift and terrible justice." Lee's fine leadership squashed the rebellion but Brown's raid showed how far the abolitionists would go to free all the slaves. Brown's impassioned attack on a United States arsenal rocked the South and raised the cry that Republicans like John Brown were instigators of lawlessness and murder. A fearful dread of a Negro uprising spread through the slaveholding communities, which was fueled by Brown's fanatical speeches during his trial. A queasy uneasiness spread from New Orleans to Richmond. After Brown was hung for treason, and it was treason because he had attacked a federal arsenal, the quiet village of Harpers Ferry returned to its own idyllic business until the town found itself in the middle ground of a war. Almost all of the 3,000 citizens had left and only 104 people remained.

When George received their marching orders from General White, he was surprised to read he was to report to Colonel Dixon Miles, whom he remembered being censured for his conduct at the First Battle of Bull Run and was rumored unfit for command for being drunk. The Vermonters were ordered to withdraw to Harpers Ferry with their move hastened by a report from cavalry scouts, who witnessed a Confederate force of 25,000 men bearing down on Winchester. All stores that could not be carried in wagons were piled on extra tents and other combustibles with black powder spread around a few magazines of explosives. Captain Powell and five battery men were told to be ready to light a fuse if Rebels approached. At ten o'clock at night the dispirited Vermonters fell in with heavy packs and marched out of Winchester into the quiet, uncertain darkness.

They were 200 yards down the road when an incredible explosion thundered behind them. Captain Powell had done his duty, a brilliant fire blazed around the store houses until another, larger explosion blasted then burned brightly in the humid night.

The Vermonters, including Benedict and Captain Edward Ripley, continued their strenuous march through the long hours of the night. At daybreak they forded the Opequon River. The rushing water was breast-high and somewhat tricky for Charger. On the other side George was pleased to see Ripley rally the brigade, calling out, "*Move on, boys!*" and was even more encouraged to see them respond to Ripley's leadership.

He had known Captain Ripley for many years. Before the war the Ransom Guards had travelled to Rutland, where Ripley and the Rutland militia exchanged ideas and training methods and sometimes their militia came to St. Albans. He recalled one particular overnight expedition with the Rutland militia when they hiked up Killington Mountain. The next morning when he awoke, the sky was an intense blue, the air clear and fresh and the view was stunning. Edward Ripley, who rose before dawn to admire the incredible view, greeted him cheerfully. It was then he realized Edward loved nature even though he had come from a wealthy family near Rutland, where his father had made a fortune in marble. The Ripleys spent their summers at Saratoga Springs, where George had also traveled on occasion to see his friend Abner Doubleday so he had become very familiar with the entire Ripley family, who lived a life of luxury with servants. Edward's sister Julia was a well-known poet and their family entertained many literary celebrities at home. It was because of this literary atmosphere Edward loved letter writing and almost daily he wrote a letter to his parents, sister or brothers despite any difficult circumstances the Vermonters encountered. Also, even though the Ripleys were wealthy, Edward's father made certain his two sons were as tough and rugged as the marble quarries. At age 12 Edward became involved in the Rutland militia and he also took great care of his horses and became an accomplished rider.

The Vermonters continued their march through the early morning hours and followed their new flag bearer, Private Manning Hicks, 19, of Montpelier, a rail-thin boy who was known to be daring and steadfast. Hicks wore a new uniform with a kepi over his short, dark hair and carried the flag forward at an angle. At 8 a.m. they collapsed for a brief rest, then continued marching through the hot sun. They marched, took a short water break, marched for hours more, then took a brief late lunch, then marched until 4 p.m. when they came onto the ridge called Maryland Heights. It turned out to be a very difficult march.

He sat on Charger and looked down from the mountainous crest of Maryland Heights into the valley and the town of Harpers Ferry. It was beautiful but his first thought was as a military position this was an extremely bad decision and poor place to defend. Harpers Ferry was, in essence, located at the bottom of a broken bowl with the mountains looming above it. He was more amazed at what he did not see. Why were these mountaintops, across the valley at Maryland

Heights and below on Loudoun Heights, not heavily defended? What was to keep the enemy from taking these heights?

Down below, he saw the small desolate town. Captain Ripley sat motionless on Lightning, his fine chestnut quarter horse with brown points. Ripley wore a kepi over his shoulder-length dark hair and shook his head negatively. He assumed Ripley had recognized the same poor, defenseless situation. Further down river were the stone pilings of the destroyed railroad bridge, which was demolished by the Rebels at the start of the war to keep the Federals from using the railroad to advance into the South.

He eased Charger down the path and moved the Vermonters down from Maryland Heights into the once quaint village. Benedict and Ripley rode nearby while a few citizens poked through the rubble of abandoned buildings. Storefronts were dusty with wreckage and some had broken windows with their yards littered with heaps of shattered debris, old clothing, smashed bits of porcelain, tableware, busted furniture, broken clocks and pictures. Everywhere everything was broken beyond repair. A solitary dog barked from the boardwalk in front of an empty General Store with its contents long pillaged and left to rot. The dog's barking brought out a middle-aged woman who limped, held a shotgun and eyed the Vermonters with disdain.

The next lot was nothing more than a large pile of rocky rubble. In front of the next house lay a dead body in the doorway. Someone had placed an open newspaper over the face with a stone on it to keep the paper from blowing away. Flies buzzed up, circled around and landed on the corpse again. The person, a man, wore work jeans, a white, long-sleeved shirt and socks with several holes in the toes. Apparently the owner's boots were worth taking.

Another lot held the remains of a bombed-out building and at the next lot an old man stopped his meticulous sweeping of a storefront walkway to stare at him. On the walkway were assorted stacked bricks with stones piled at the far end. Behind the old man were the charred remains of a wooden structure with a stone chimney rising, naked and dead like so much of the town. The old man mumbled with confusion, then returned to sweeping the walkway despite the lack of a building behind him.

Benedict pointed out the infamous Federal Armory where John Brown had galvanized the abolitionist and freedom-loving people of the country. It had also been destroyed, burned, and lay in ruins, which is why Colonel Miles moved his headquarters west of town to an area called Camp Hill, where a row of ramshackle houses with rows of tents, a parapet, and a quickly constructed garrison stood. George had noticed there were no significant defenses to stop an approaching force from taking the mountains above Camp Hill, which was little more than an outpost on a small hill, so moving the headquarters there had gained no advantage.

In the late afternoon he sat upright on Charger and proudly led the Vermont regiment of 748 young men into Camp Hill through the rows of tents and small houses. He was struck by the soldiers' poor morale. They sat or lay on the grass near their tents and did nothing. Many of them did not bother to look up, much less salute an officer.

In the distance he heard men suffering in a big hospital tent, straining with the ill effects of flux and dysentery.

He made his way on Charger to a large stately house, last owned by Alfred Barbour, and dismounted then handed the reins to a private, who nodded instead of saluted and gathered the reins from all the officers then walked the horses to a barn in back. He went up the stone steps, past two guards who stood motionless, over the wooden porch with a few cracked boards, and entered the house.

Colonel Miles had converted the front parlor of the Barbour House into his headquarters. The office spilled over with maps, open books, letters and an old piano was piled over with sheet music. Miles stood in the center of the room, lost in thought with a wandering daze in his eyes. His pale skin was wrinkled around his eyes and mouth, and his tousled white hair went in various directions.

"Colonel Stannard and the Vermont Ninth reporting for duty, sir!" He saluted, stood at attention and felt a lack of military protocol in the parlor. Still, he stared at the United States flag in a corner behind Miles' desk, drowned in papers. Another moment passed then Miles made his way to the piano where he brushed papers off the keyboard to the floor with a large sweep of his arm. Another sweep revealed a maroon, velvet-tufted stool and Miles eased himself onto it then exhaled heavily. He rested his hands on the keys and then a cacophony of notes followed.

He relaxed his salute, stood at ease, and listened to the song among discordant notes followed by another recognizable phrase. At first he thought the song was "Dixieland" but it wasn't. It was a new song everyone talked about with lyrics from a recent poem called "Maryland, My Maryland." It was shocking and he stood bewildered.

Miles stopped, snapped a look at him, then picked up the melody with more missed notes. His face showed deep concentration but Miles spoke with relaxed pronunciation, "Yer lookin' a me as if a possum stole yer bre'kfas."

"No, sir." Music bounced off the thick white walls and Miles's pudgy body rolled back and forth while his fingers stumbled over the keys. "It's an inappropriate song, sir."

"Nonsense! It' s'about my state, *suh*, an' I'm very prou' o' *my* state."

"Oh. With all respect, why not a Union song? 'Hail Columbia'."

"Don't know it." Miles played on with more odd, acrimonious notes. "Are you saying I shoul' stop?"

"No, sir, but—"

"You thin' I shoul' stop?"

"No, *sir!*"

"Y' thin' I shoul' *stop!*" Miles banged the ivory keys with stiff fingers.

"No, I—"

"*I sho'l stop!*" Miles smashed his fists down on the keyboard and a loud discordant *bang!* echoed in the room, throughout the house and spilled out onto the parade ground where soldiers carried on with odd expressions. Miles spun on the stool and looked up at him, not quite focusing his eyes.

George looked around the room, searching for an open bottle or a liquor cabinet then sniffed the air. Miles yelled, "*An' now y' thin' I been drinkin'!* Well, I haven'. My sweet applejack's gone. So, I haven' a drip or a drop! *Ha!*"

"No, sir. It's, ah, your priority should be to reinforce the mountaintops around the fort and arsenal."

"Nah. Tha' woul' spread out ah meaguh forces."

He continued, "If we placed artillery on the surrounding mountains, cleared the woods around the artillery to see any approaching troops, and built redoubts to fortify those positions, we would have a much stronger defensive position."

"Oh, is tha' all?" Miles spat on the floor. "Th' position of our forces has been strage-gi-cally placed. I' studied th' maps. I'm no newcomer like you, *suh.* Wes' Point." Miles stood upright with a tired, awkward effort and made something like a salute.

He straightened and saluted back, which caused Miles to laugh. "You's a *got damn* volunteer! You asked for thi' shit."

"It's a poor defensive position that we—"

"Lookee, you and yo' Vermontuhs shoul' enjoy th' countryside. We ah quite fa' f'om any battle lines."

"Sir?"

"Do ya know who I am, *su-u-uh?*"

"Yes, sir! Colonel Miles commanding."

"Ya got damn right! You don't know, I se'ved with Gene'al Scott in the Mexican Campaign. Yessuh, ol' Fuss 'n' Featha's, the leadah of our en-tiah fo'ces. An' I was wi' Scott at Ve'a Cruz when a snotty young Cap'ain, one Robert *E-e-e-e* Lee, took all the valah for positionin' ou' guns. An', *An'!* I served with Zach Taylah at Fo't Brown. Mmm-hunh. Ol' 'Rough an' Ready' hisself. He hono'ed me with a promotion. Mmm-hunh, the *got damn* Presizen' of the U. S. of A. So, don't *you,*" he pointed stiffly, "tell *me* I don't know wha' I'm doin'!"

"That's very impressive, sir. Our defenses—"

"I can't believe I'm still listenin' to you! *Got damm!* I don't give a pinch of owl dung what you thin'. You're not even a pleb. Dismissed."

"But, sir."

"*Dismissed.* An' if I haff ta say it agin', you'll be court marshaled."

He saluted and left. His first impression was Miles would not do *anything* to fortify their defenses and he didn't know what to make of that. Later that night he met with his staff and all the officers in one of the Vermonters' barracks. Some of the young men sat on the bunk beds but most stood at ease two and three deep around the walls. He stood in the middle of the room, lit by a few candles on a small table and informed them of his meeting with their commander. He left out his assessment of Miles's physical condition. Several grumbled their opinion of Miles with choice words and cussing.

Then Colonel Trimble of the 60th Ohio regiment spoke with his lilting Midwestern accent, "It seems to me Colonel Miles shows incompetence by the very fact he did *not* act. I speak for all the men from Ohio and I say Colonel Stannard should take command. After all, you and Miles are both colonels."

Ripley stood and walked to the center of the room then placed his hand on his shoulder for support, stood up on a foot stool but kept his hand on his shoulder. A sudden blush filled Ripley's soft, round face but he spoke with confidence, "I do not hold rank here but I speak on behalf of *all* the Vermonters. I've met with *all* the lieutenants, majors, captains and a lot of the soldiers from every company. We feel, completely and to a man, if General White knew how inept Miles is, he would immediately appoint Colonel Stannard commander."

"Here, here!" the officers cheered a chorus of huzzahs. Ripley's cheeks glowed red and his dark brown eyes shone in admiration. "On behalf of the Vermonters, we ask you at least write to General White and let him know of our desperate situation."

He knew Trimble, Ripley and all the officers were right. The men would not follow incompetence. Many volunteers had signed up for the bonus pay so their fighting spirit was tenuous and they may leave this dire situation at the first opportunity. Also, morale throughout the entire camp was awful. He didn't want to break protocol and said, "Very good. I'll write to General White and I'll speak with Colonel Miles again."

"It's more than that, sir," Ripley gripped his shoulder. His kepi was tilted up and his strong voice conveyed the severity of his words. "Our *lives* are in your hands."

The room was packed with officers and each man looked to him. Then he stared into Ripley's fixed and determined eyes. The light from a hurricane lamp flickered. The message was clear: it was a bond of faith and trust. In all the years he had known Ripley, from their experience with the Rutland militia, even though Edward had come from a wealthy family, he had never, *ever* asked for any privilege for himself or for his men. Ripley did not blink or move away from his stare.

He knew he *must* act. Lives were at risk. He turned to Benedict, who had a piece of parchment, pen and ink ready. Did they plan this or was Benedict always ready? He used Benedict's back as a writing surface and composed a hasty note to General White. "Suffering from poor defense. Need yr. immed. help. Send men and guns."

He then went outside the barracks and gave the note to Major Gaines, a very short man who was a jockey in horse races around Vermont and New England. Gaines threw himself onto a sorrel mount and saluted but George grabbed the halter. He knew the note could be interpreted as mutinous, he could be court martialed, but the situation called for bold action. He felt his note may not be clear in its urgency and scribbled an additional line, pressing against the thin saddle for support. "P.S. Request perm. to command. Respond immed!"

He again thrust the note to Gaines, who snatched it and stuffed it inside his shirt. Then in a swift, expert motion Gaines wheeled the sorrel around, dug in his spurs and vanished into the black night.

The next morning he visited Colonel Miles again. Miles was slouched back on a small settee without his boots. Yesterday he hadn't noticed the settee piled over with maps and papers. He repeated his requests, offered more ideas for defense like stronger picket fronts established in each direction, a series of relay couriers set-up in case of attack, trees felled for fortifications on the hilltops with trenches for the men to defend their positions and more reserve forces requested to strengthen their lines.

Miles refused all these requests. He would not ask for help, no, no, no. Miles said they were perfectly capable of holding Camp Hill in a quiet valley and summed up his denial with a sarcastic snarl, "John Brown ain't comin' back."

He ignored Miles' comment about Brown, who was an abolitionist and would have given aid to their cause rather than *attack* them and, yes, John Brown was quite dead. "Colonel, it appears you do not intend to take any action."

"You's a got damn meddlin' *volunteer* who don't know *shit.* Dismissed."

"Sir, may I at least let my boys exercise in the mountains?"

Miles tilted his head to look at him sideways, but his eyes were glazed and he had difficulty focusing. "Mmm-hunh. Tha's tha firs' good idea you had. Let tha boys hike in th' woods. Dismissed."

He went to Benedict, who waited in the hallway and clapped him on his thin shoulder then walked outside the Barbour house and into the glaring sun. "Our boys are to do the following tasks under my orders. They need *vigorous* exercise *at once!*"

Benedict smiled and he returned a slight smile then moved away from the house across the parade ground to a row of cannons. "You'll need to write this down."

Benedict pulled out a piece of paper and a small, worn pencil and used a cannon barrel for support.

"First, meet with *all* the various companies from *each* regiment, especially any *volunteers,"* Benedict glanced up to exchange another smile, "anyone who wishes to exercise, every man from Ohio, Illinois, New York, *everyone*. We must clear the woods on the mountaintops *for exercise.* The Vermonters are familiar with timber operations. Our boys will take the lead. Colonel Wainwright, Charles I believe you know from the Ohio Artillery, will be in charge of Marye's Heights. Colonel Trimble will command Bolivar Heights. The men will also need to build a pontoon bridge across the Potomac River. Ripley will command that *exercise*."

Benedict stopped writing. Above his glasses on his forehead a confused crease formed and his dark brown eyes searched for an answer. "A pontoon bridge? The railroad bridge is destroyed but we have the main bridge to Maryland, the one we crossed."

George looked around then spoke quietly, "Altogether, all the regiments, we have what, fourteen thousand men? And we're stuck at the bottom of this bowl. We estimate General Lee has seventy-five thousand men in the area. We may need an escape pontoon bridge in case a defensive retreat is needed. We'll also build a second line of defense, in front of Camp Hill. I'll supervise that. I'll meet with Colonel Miles daily so he understands our boys are drilling. Who knows? He may come around to the idea of improving our defenses. But there's no harm in our *exercises.*"

Benedict said wryly, "Spoken like a West Pointer."

"Right," he chuckled. "Miles sure is odd for a graduate." He shook his head and considered how often he agreed with Benedict. He had known Benedict since the Canadian Expedition, then again on his visits and move to Burlington, and they had been side-by-side since their first encampment of volunteers at the Fairgrounds. They knew each other very well and had become more and more of the same military mind. "These are *my* orders and if anyone has a problem with them, you are to send them to me."

"Very good, sir!" Benedict said. "I know the Vermonters will appreciate their assignment in the woods, in the mountains. Very well done!"

Benedict saluted, turned and walked through the rows of tents with great energy. His orders, carried out with Benedict's enthusiasm, changed each volunteer. Each soldier responded with a sense of purpose. In an instant the morale of the entire camp changed for the better.

George again looked up and viewed the mountains surrounding them, surrounding the small town, the arsenal, and Camp Hill. He thought, Maybe Miles was right in thinking the Confederates would not bother this sleepy little village. He also knew his duty was to protect his boys to the best of his ability and continued to think of how they could defend this hopeless position. He prayed there would be enough time to make all the necessary changes and various preparations to give them a fighting chance.

A makeshift bridge was made of pontoons constructed of flat-bottomed boats, about 15 feet long, four feet wide and two feet deep. The boats were anchored 10 feet apart with planks and string tenders, then fastened by bolts and wooden pins, and then connected with wooden planks laid down as a bridge. The roadway over the pontoons was about 10 feet wide and could support the load of a six-mule team pulling artillery or supplies. Each end was anchored to the riverbank but the soldiers would need to break step when crossing to prevent the bridge from surging wildly.

The volunteers also cleared the woods on the mountaintops of Marye's Heights and Bolivar Heights. They laid the fallen trees in a semicircle 40 yards from the mountain top then cleared another area of 40 yards in front of their timber wall. Next they dug a shallow trench behind the logs to kneel in and give them more cover. Then, with great effort, they moved artillery onto the heights by using a six-mule team pulling from the front and two soldiers pushing on each wheel. They placed six guns on Marye's Heights and 10 more cannons on Bolivar Heights.

The volunteers had exercised for a few days when lookouts spotted a large Confederate force approaching from the Shenandoah Valley. Southern General Thomas "Stonewall" Jackson, hailed as the Confederate hero of the Battle of Bull Run, led an army of 30,000 men. They skirmished briefly with the Union pickets before sundown and camped on the foothills on the far side of Bolivar Heights.

At Camp Hill Colonel Miles said he would retire for the evening to think on their situation. George assembled then moved the Vermonters during the night to reinforce the Ohio brigade under Colonel Trimble. They had a short night's sleep but the next morning they were ready for Jackson's army of 30,000 Confederates.

Private Swardell of Maine, the lookout on another mountaintop, Marye's Heights, heard distant noises and scanned the horizon through his binoculars. In the graying dawn Swardell saw hundreds, now thousands more Confederate soldiers approaching from the east. This was another Rebel brigade led by General A.P. Hill. They had risen well before dawn to attack. It would be up to Colonel Wainwright and his few hundred soldiers from Maine to stop General Hill's force of 25,000 Rebels approaching Marye's Heights.

After a brief nap, George was awakened by bugler Randolph Derry, a boy of 15 from Danby, calling reveille on Bolivar Heights before dawn. He had slept on a single blanket, gathered his hat, pistol and sword then walked to the abatis the Vermonters had built. He placed his left boot on the timber then rested one hand on his left knee and his right hand on his pistol. He then went through his ritual for "good luck," although he knew there was no such thing, there was only preparation and discipline, but he used his fingertips to feel the etching his father had made on the Colt, "*Fight for Justice.*" He looked out over the gray-black mountains to the dismal overcast sunrise with the sky a pale gray and becoming lighter.

He heard a rustling and turned to see Captain Ripley approaching from the woods behind him with his uniform askew.

Ripley pushed down on his left boot to complete putting his foot into it, brushed his left hand over his long dark hair and put on his kepi. Ripley ambled over and said, "Isn't much of a sunrise, is it?"

Ripley's cheeks were paler than usual with two cherry-sized blushes on his prominent cheekbones. He had just awakened but there was a quickness in his dark brown eyes. Then he spoke fondly, "Nothing like the sunrises back home."

"Considering the alternative," he paused to let the old joke settle, "I'll take it."

They chuckled then both stopped suddenly, knowing today could be their last day alive. He knew Ripley missed his family and home life, wrote letters daily, then he recalled a joint militia expedition and the sunrise from Mount Killington, not far from Ripley's home near Rutland with its intense blue sky. It was such a deep, clear blue sky that it felt like a different world, one that was so beautiful, so entirely one in and of itself that it held all meaning. Then he realized that feeling was how he felt when staring into Helen's deep blue eyes. It filled him with purpose and the world had meaning. He was one with all.

He shook his head with pessimism, feeling the discordant uneasiness of the moment and the impending battle that was about to tear the world apart. He tried to stay detached from home and preferred to not think about returning. It was impossible and it distracted his focus from the situation at hand.

Ripley clapped his hand on his shoulder and grinned, "I heard you were courting a Countess. Did you marry her?"

“I’m afraid I did.” They both chuckled again, this time a bit longer but again each stopped abruptly.

“Well, she made out all right.” Ripley squeezed his shoulder, the same as a few nights before in the meeting of officers about Colonel Miles. “It’s an honor, sir.”

A bullet whistled through the woods and clipped a branch near their heads, followed by another and another. The Ohio men and Vermonters responded with a few random shots until he yelled, “*Hold your fire! Wait until you see them in the clearing!*”

An artillery shell blasted the top of a thick elm nearby and crashed down onto a group of soldiers. Private Ungermeyer was crushed under the large trunk and a whipping, nine-inch branch split open Private Yarborough’s skull. Both boys lay motionless. Another shell exploded on the front line and sent the redoubt, earth and the better part of a corporal’s torso flying. Then bullets ripped through the troops and more men fell.

Two swift jackrabbits dashed across the clearing followed by the graycoats marching out of the woods *en masse.* Hundreds and hundreds of Rebels moved into the small clearing 40 yards away. Before the full thought of thousands of charging men could have an impact on them, he hollered, “*Fire!*”

The instant the report cleared he yelled again, “*Reload!*”

Some Southerners fell and some crouched down but most marched forward, spirited on by an officer on a gray-and-white spotted horse that danced back-and-forth in front of the far woods. The Rebel officer’s voice was deep and clear, “*Fo-wahd!*”

The graycoats broke into a run and some fired their muskets. All gave the Rebel yell, loud, fierce, and filled with a blood-lust for killing.

Ripley turned to the artillery guns and slashed his sword downward. "*Fire!*"

Eight canons blasted, one after the other then two more in unison. The shots poured into the thick of the Rebels and dozens of charging Southerners fell with more looking about with panic and sudden fear. A few ducked low, dashed to the side then ran back to the woods. More followed in retreat but a few struggled against their fear and made their way toward the Union line.

"*Fire!*" he yelled. More graycoats fell, face-first or backward or slumped to the side. The rest of the Rebels stopped in their tracks, raised their guns and returned fire. Private Reed, just above the timber wall, was hit in the chest. Private Milne who had turned to reload, had a miniball enter one temple, pass through, and exit the other side of his skull. Most Vermonters took this moment to crouch behind the redoubt of stacked logs, clear the barrels of their muskets, and reload. Private Burt Cromartie, who he had fought in training camp, fired quickly. His youthful, patchy beard had grown in thick and his greasy dark hair was now long and gnarled. Next to him was his older brother Asa, also rough-looking but larger and heavier. They fired so rapidly it appeared to be a competition. Up and down the line, the Vermonters responded without faltering.

He stepped behind a sturdy oak tree and fired his pistol with deadly effect. A running middle-aged man fell belly-first then another stopped upright then slowly crumpled to the ground, and a third was knocked backwards with his legs flying up and the top of his forehead blown off. One shot missed then another young man buckled at his shoulder and dropped his rifle in shock, staggering back for the far woods.

The Vermonters rose above the redoubt individually, fired at will and picked off the Southerners in the clearing easily. Then a bullet thunked into the oak beside him, its white-splintered wood ripped open, followed by Corporal Angleton of Bennington being hit square in the forehead in front of him with his head snapping back and his blood spattered against the oak.

Then the Rebels ran back for the far woods. Ripley, with his sword raised, turned to him, ready to fire the artillery if given the signal. He hollered, "*Save it!*"

Ripley lowered his arm, hollered, "*Tend to the wounded and gather ammunition!*"

The Vermonters held their ground on Bolivar Heights and fought through two more attacks, each as vicious as the first. Their sharpshooters fired often at prodding attempts to circle around them to their right or left as the Southerners tried to flank them through the woods. At the end of the day the Federals had few artillery shells left and the soldiers were very close to running out of ammunition. Darkness fell very quickly in the mountains and it was suddenly quiet.

He assigned Ripley to command their troops and led a small squad of 10 young men, including Benedict through the woods, down the mountain and past the bombed out rubble of houses and craters to the fort at Camp Hill. They called out, "*We're Vermonters!*" and "*Green Mountain Boys!*" to the Union pickets.

When he arrived at headquarters in the Barbour house he was again stunned speechless. Colonel Miles lay relaxed in his office. He had expected to see Miles standing over maps, reading reports from officers who had counted the remaining stores of ammunition and reported casualties, but Miles lay stretched out on the sofa with his eyes closed and his bare feet showing with his boots off and crumpled socks nearby. A quarter-filled bottle of amber-colored liquid stood on the floor.

Captain Dodson, a messenger from Colonel Wainwright of Maine, entered a moment later but George remained motionless in the doorway. Dodson brushed past him and blurted out breathlessly, "Request reinforcements. . . and ammunition tonight, *sir!*"

Miles kept his eyes closed and waved his hand, shooing away a mild nuisance from his throne-like repose. Dodson, the winded messenger who he had met earlier in the week, was a lobster fisherman from Portland. Dodson had a look of bewilderment then spoke louder, "*Captain Dodson of Maine! Requesting reinforcements on Marye's Heights, Colonel!*"

George approached Miles and waited for his eyes to open but Miles waved his hand in a rhythmic motion like a metronome to some rhapsodic tune in his head. George added, "We also need reinforcements and ammunition on Bolivar Heights, *sir!*"

Then Miles opened his eyes. Again he rolled his wrist in a downward wave and spoke coolly, "Have tha men fall back to th' fort."

"You act as if you expected this," he replied and became aware he was caked with grimy sweat, smoke and gunpowder. His stomach growled.

"Any properly train' militury man could see this a-comin'."

"Precisely." It was all he could do to restrain himself from smacking the white-bearded smirk off Mile's face. "And your lack of action to prevent it, one might argue, would border on treason."

Miles reacted passively but showed the slightest hint of a smile. Was Miles amused because he was right? Or because he had accomplished what he secretly wanted, which was to give the fort and its arsenal to the Southern cause? Or perhaps Miles smiled at some unrelated applejack-induced fairy? "Wear yo' dress uniform tomorrah, boy. We ah surrende'ing."

"*Like hell we are!*" he shouted.

Miles reacted with sudden anger and tried to sit up but George kept the elderly man down with one hand on his chest. "Some of my boys died today and they will not have died in vain. We're defending our position as ordered. I'm sending a courier to General White for reinforcements!"

"You speak like yo' in charge. I'm commandah heah!" Miles tried to rise again and this time he let him up then glanced to Dodson, who stood with his mouth open. He was shocked at himself for restraining Miles—he could be court marshaled!—and straightened to attention. He could not bring himself to salute this scum.

Miles was enraged but his rhythmic motion was disordered, his brain clouded with applejack, his train of thought lost and he fumbled for words, "I'm. . . this uncalled-for action! I'm. . . *you!*"

"With all respect, sir, our orders are to defend Harpers Ferry to the last extremity."

Miles wiped his frothing mouth with a lacy kerchief and stood up with windmill-like arms, an unsteady, drugged old man. He straightened his disheveled coat and felt for his scabbard but he was not wearing his sword. Then he looked down at his bare feet and mumbled, then huffed, "How do *you* know *my* orders?"

"General White sent *us* here and ordered, If attacked, we were to defend this position until reinforcements arrived. *We* were ordered to fight until the last man."

"Tha's parlor tahk. Boys are dyin' up theah un'er yo' comman'. They're bein' slaughte'ed like pigs 'n more will die if they continue to fight. Gen'l Jackson and Gen'l Hill have close ta sixty thousan' men. There is no way, I say no way in *Hell*, our puny band of fo'teen thousan' can hol' 'em. I'm savin' lives by surrende'in'."

He considered what Miles said. Because no other couriers had come down, how did he know there were 60,000 Confederates? Maybe there were a few hundred if the main part of Lee's army had continued on? How did Miles know the Confederates' intention? Was he in contact with the Southerners or was he speaking with bravado? In either case, he knew not to challenge Miles again. He had shown mutinous behavior by forcing him down on the sofa and was at risk to be court-marshaled if he continued.

Outside a commotion of loud voices were heard. He peered out the window to see a company of New Yorkers coming through the western gate with a dozen prisoners. Torches illuminated the group walking toward the Barbour house and an occasional cheer went up from the soldiers. The captured Rebels had a glum look on their faces while the New Yorkers kept their muskets trained on them and received claps on the back and random cheers of huzzah!

Miles walked gingerly in his bare feet to the front door, opened it a crack and peered out. "Wha's all this?"

He followed Miles, past Dodson and opened the door then stepped by Miles out onto the porch. Hardened Union soldiers stood around the captured Rebels.

"Sergeant Kaplan, New York's Fighting Sixty-Ninth, sir!" The sergeant was a thin kid, about 19 with a crooked nose, curly black hair and a tough scowl on his face. "Eleven Reb prisoners for ya!"

The soldiers in blue again cheered raucously and he said, "Well done!"

"No, no, no!" Miles said. "We can't have this. We've no place for 'em. Esco't 'em back to our pickets an' le' 'em go."

"Sir! They've seen our defenses!"

"*You!*" Miles pointed at him with disgust from the doorway. "I alrea'y tol' *you* ou' plans fa tomorrow. *Dismissed!*"

He decided this was pointless, saluted out of habit and went down the steps. Dodson followed. He took Sergeant Kaplan by the shoulder, walked out of Miles's hearing range and said, "Take these prisoners up to Maryland Heights across the way. That may disorient them and give us a day until they report back to their commanders."

Kaplan glared up at Miles, nodded then used the stock of his musket to push a Confederate soldier toward the eastern gate. Kaplan paused to call out, "You mind if we get some food 'fore we head up?"

"Yes, that's fine," he said. "Also, gather as much ammunition as they can spare here. Rest for a few hours but head out well before dawn. Also, you and your boys are hereby reassigned to Colonel Wainwright of Ohio until this battle is over."

Kaplan's grimy face broke into a large grin. "Yes, sir!"

He then ordered Benedict to gather every third soldier from the fort and load five wagons with ammunition and supplies. Despite the newly widened road and with many young men helping, it was difficult hauling supplies up the mountain. It was very dark and the mules followed the path. Low tree branches smacked their faces and young saplings, once pulled back became thrust inside the wheel axels at every turn. They had to back up several times, which the mules resisted but they arrived at their encampment on Bolivar Heights moments before dawn.

Benedict, Ripley and the other officers distributed the ammunition while birds chirped with growing intensity. He put both hands on his lower back, stretched and sat down on the warm

Virginia earth to rest. He relaxed for a few minutes until Benedict returned, wiping sweat from his brow and offered his canteen.

He drank the cool, refreshing water. No sooner had he returned Benedict's canteen than a barrage of Rebel cannons sounded across the clearing. An instant later the trees and earth shook with violent spasms, and he and Benedict curled into the earth behind the timber redoubt. A few minutes of loud, thunderous hell were followed by the vicious Rebel yell as hundreds of men charged into the clearing.

He stood up and ordered all the Vermonters and the young men from Ohio and New York, "*Fire at will!*"

Again, the fighting was hot. After 30 minutes of intense gunfire, which felt much longer, the Southerners retreated down the mountain into the thicker woods below.

Four more attacks followed, each as intense and each felt near the point of breaking. In late-afternoon a cheer of thousands of Rebels echoed through the valley and he looked over to Maryland Heights where a white flag was being waved. Thirty minutes later the Southern artillery, now atop Maryland Heights, zeroed in on the fort and Camp Hill below. Trails of white smoke from Rebel guns rose as they blasted away from the mountaintop. Then blasts from Marye's Heights caught his attention and a Confederate signal flag waved. The Rebels had also taken Marye's Heights and, with Maryland Heights from the east, together sent a barrage of bombs into the valley below. They struck closer to the mark with each successive blast. The unease he had felt days earlier upon first arriving was realized in full as explosions smashed buildings into rubble in Harpers Ferry and zeroed in on Camp Hill with trails of smoke rising into the air.

George, the Vermonters, and the other Union soldiers on Bolivar Heights fought on with fierce determination. After two more hours of intense fighting the sun hit the far horizon, dusk came swiftly, and the battle ceased. They were out of artillery shells and each soldier had five rounds or less. Then small fires could be seen from the Southerner's campsites on both Marye's Heights and Maryland Heights, and he ordered everyone to fall back to the fort, as quietly as possible, with the canons.

They made their way down the mountain toward the fort but then George took a small detail of 10 men to the river's edge to check if they still held the bridges and their newly built pontoon bridge. Each was still in Federal control, although very few lookouts stood guard. Then they turned back, went through the deserted bombed-out ruins of the town and up into the fort on Camp Hill. One of the larger barracks had been converted into a hospital and many wounded also lay on the parade ground.

Colonel Miles, in full dress uniform, gazed out the window of his office. When their eyes met, Miles opened the window, somehow the glass panes had remained whole, and he screamed, "*Stan-da'd! Git in heah!*"

He marched up the Barbour house steps and past two guards, one of whom was fresh-faced except for boot black on his hands, which seemed odd. He went across the porch, stepped inside and was again surprised. The parlor was immaculate. No papers were in sight and the fireplace roared with flames from stacks of maps, books, and letters. The desk was clear. The piano stool was tucked underneath.

Miles wore his full dress uniform with polished boots, buttons and sword. He screamed, "*What in the name of Beazzlebub are you doin'?*"

"Sir! It was necessary to fall back to the fort. We're almost out of ammunition."

"I'm not talkin' 'bout now, confound it!" Miles paced around him with the veins on his neck and forehead bulging then yelled again, "*I'm talkin' 'bout all day long! What in the blazes ha' you been doin'?*"

"My duty, sir."

"*Your duty was to preserve life and fall back to the fort!*"

"Our duty, according to General White's orders—"

"*Don't contradict me, you son of a bitchin'* vol-un-teer!"

"General White's *orders, Sir!* were to 'hold out to the last extremity.' " He thought of the courier he had sent, Major Gaines, with his note requesting to take command but pressed on, "I have tried to preserve the lives of my boys to the very best of my ability. And with regard to falling back to the fort, here we are, sir!"

"Yeah, a got damn day late and a dollah sho't!" Miles hands shook, struggling to pull out his officer's sword from its sheath, then managed it. With a crazed, wild-eyed fury he slashed the shiny sword downward, sheared the air, and swung it back at him. He lunged away toward the door but Miles parried forward, pointing the sword inches from his throat and screamed, "*Tomorrah we shall—*"

Then Miles came to his senses, gazed at his raised sword, having drawn a weapon on a fellow officer. He breathed heavily, stepped back and wiped his sweaty brow with the back of his coat sleeve then lowered his sword. "I'm. . . I'm, um, Colonel, I. . . It's this medication my doctah prosc'ibed. That, an' I'm ve'y passionate about my men."

George wondered what he should say to this raving mad officer? That he was not thinking clearly due to his opium-and-applejack concoction? That he should resign immediately? Or that he was taking command? "Yes, sir. Of course. The men."

Miles slumped into his chair and dropped his sword, clanging against the desk and onto the wooden floor. Then his attitude swung back to arrogance, glaring at him with loathing and said with his thick drawl, "Tomorrah we surrendah at dawn, *suh!*"

He thought, Surrender at dawn? The enemy hasn't proposed that scenario and General White's orders were to fight to the last man. It was very confusing. He felt exhausted from the fight and frustrated in dealing with this drug-addled lunatic whose sympathies bordered on treason. Then he realized these words were Colonel Miles' *official resignation*. He considered Miles and thought, Good! *You* think that. He clicked his boots together, started a salute out of habit but stopped and stepped outside.

He examined the two sentries. "What are your names and units, soldiers?"

The first guard, a lanky youth with black hair and an eye tooth missing, said "Holcombe, Ohio First, sir."

The other guard, pudgy with blonde hair and boot black on his hands, saluted and smudged polish onto his forehead. “The same, sir.”

“The same? You’re Holcombe from Ohio, too?”

“Yes, sir. That’s my brother.” He examined the two soldiers but they were nothing alike. The second boy, about 16, was heavy-set with thin blonde hair, who explained, “My mother ain’t his mother. She died near fifteen year ago.”

“Oh. Both of you report to Lieutenant Benedict of the Vermonters. He’ll reassign you back to the Ohio regiment.”

“We’re guarding the Colonel’s office, sir.”

“What?”

“Colonel Miles said it was for General Decorum. Reckon he’s coming soon.”

He chuckled despite the horrible situation. “You are relieved of that duty. Report to Lieutenant Benedict!”

They both saluted and walked away but the chubby blonde had his knees buckle, he wavered a few shaky steps, then his legs collapsed and he fell to the ground. His brother kneeled and raised him off his back and George rushed to them. “What’s wrong?”

“We’re plum exhausted, sir,” the brother said. “We ain’t et in two days.”

“What?”

“I think the Colonel forgot, sir. Said it was *vital* to stand guard for General Decorum.”

“Right. Tell Benedict you need some food first. Then get a good night’s sleep. You’re going to need it in the morning.”

The blonde boy's eyes opened and he rolled his head lazily to look at his brother. "Where are we, Josh?"

"We're headed back to our unit, Jake. It's alright."

They helped Jake to his feet then he heard a loud crash inside Miles' office. Josh slipped under his brother's arm and supported him, then they walked toward the Vermont barracks where Benedict had set up a small portable desk with a kerosene lamp. Its dim light glinted across Benedict's glasses.

They ushered Jake inside then he returned to examine Benedict's quickly drawn map of the fort's interior. Benedict had marked down which regiments were on which walls, where the ammunition was and had started a list of units off to the side, in reserve, to be shuttled to any area of need. He stood over the desk, reviewed the map and tapped two fingers on the list of reserves. "Put the Ohio boys by the artillery and the Vermonters at the head of the reserves. I know they'll fight where it's hottest."

~ ~

At dawn a flare of bugles playing reveille awakened the remaining Union forces and they readied themselves for any attack but it was quiet. He stood on the parapet of the fort's front wall, faced Maryland Heights, and waited. Miles remained in the Barbour house. At exactly eight o'clock a Southern officer carrying a white flag rode his gray-and-white spotted horse down the road from Bolivar Heights, where they had fought for days. Across the parade ground Ripley stood by the 12 guns in the fort's battery and he called out, "*Shall we listen to what he has to say?*"

He shook his head no and waved his arm downward. All twelve guns responded with a well-aimed bombardment at the top of Maryland Heights and Marye's Heights. The Southern officer pulled up the reins, his horse reared up on its hind legs then stomped down on its white-spotted front legs, plowing from left to right before the Rebel wheeled about and rode back.

They lobbed more cannon shells upward, shells that seemed to lose steam floating upward, then blasted into the woods to little effect. He hollered, "*Hold your fire!*"

Confederate signal flags waved between the mountains. A moment later Southern shells rained down on Camp Hill. A few struck outside the fort with a few more blasting the walls.

"*Fire at their batteries!*" he yelled. The Maine artillery, under Colonel Trimble, had swiftly reloaded, aimed and fired their guns at Maryland Heights, one after the other, down the line in succession. The second grouping of cannons, on the other side of the fort, were aimed at Marye's Heights and they also fired again, one after the other. The Rebel guns shot back and their bombs probed closer. More hit the outer walls of the fort, two exploded inside including one on the bare, empty parade ground to no harm and the other shell smashed into the Illinois barracks but all those soldiers were now on the western wall.

Then thousands of graycoats poured out, marching down the road from Maryland's Heights and Benedict moved the Vermont and Ohio regiments to reinforce the eastern wall. He did not need to order it.

Colonel Miles stumbled out of the Barbour house. He wore his dress pants, a pristine white shirt and his beard was trimmed with his white hair greased and combed down. "*Got dammit! What in tha hell is going on!*"

He ignored Miles. Two hundred yards across the river, the road from Maryland Heights was filled with Confederate soldiers, piling up at the congested entrance to the main bridge. He hollered, "*Fire!*"

The boys on the wall responded with a volley of musket fire and many Southern soldiers fell. Hundreds more came down the roadway.

"*Damnation!*" Miles yelled with anger. He wore a white dress shirt but no coat or boots. When he stepped onto the parade ground dust kicked up and he became aware he did not have on his uniform coat, boots or hat. He shook his fists, did an infuriated two-step and stormed back into his office in his stockinged feet.

More Southern artillery shells fell into the fort, one after another and exploded with increasingly deadly effect inside the walls and buildings. The blasts hit them now, the ground heaved, rolled and dirt sprayed into his face. Then the hot air shoved him to one side and shrieking shrapnel ripped by, shredding the air and anything in its path.

The Union soldiers crouched down and hugged their muskets. He stood tall and bolstered the men with calls of encouragement, followed by Ripley, Benedict and Colonel Trimble. They reloaded, pulled up and returned fire from the western wall toward Bolivar

Heights, where thousands of graycoats poured down the mountain road. More soldiers fired from the eastern wall down the roadway to the main bridge, where thousands of Rebels crossed and charged for the fort.

"*Fire at will!*" Ripley hollered and shot his pistol with skill.

"*Benedict!*" he screamed from the rampart.

Benedict clambered off the northern wall and hustled to the ladder under him. "Yes, sir?"

"Assemble the Vermonters at the northern gate! Get our horses!"

Benedict dashed off to relay the order to their bugler, Wallace Derry, a heavily freckled, red-haired boy of 15 from Danby, who made the call on his trumpet then ran for the northern gate. Benedict sped to Ripley, gave him the order in detail, then sprinted for the stables. A moment later Benedict emerged with Folio, Charger, Lightning and three other officer's horses followed by Sergeant Cohl, a big timber man from north of St. Johnsbury, who also ran with three officer's horses in each hand. Benedict led them out of the barn and joined the Vermont regiment, spilling off the northern wall onto the parade ground, all rushing toward the sound of bugler Derry, including their color bearer, Private Hicks, who circled the flag above him and dashed toward the northern gate.

Colonel Miles stepped out of the Barbour house primped in his dress uniform with his shiny black boots and brass buttons polished, and he now carried a large white flag. His silver spurs jangled and a yellow feather curled off the top of his colonel's hat bobbed with his slow, stiff march onto the parade ground. The bouncing yellow feather and huge white flag marked Miles progress through and against the steady flow of Vermonters assembling at the northern gate, where bugler Derry, who had lost his cap to show his brick-red hair, trumpeted loudly.

Ripley sprinted to George then buckled over with his hands on his hips, out of breath and huffing, then asked, "What are we doing? . . . Sir?"

He hollered, "*Move out to the pontoon bridge!*" then swung up on Charger.

"Yes, sir!" Ripley grabbed the reins to his horse but it pranced sideways in the excitement, then he swung up on Lightning although he appeared confused, looking around the fort. Young men from Illinois and Ohio fired from the walls and the Maine artillerymen reloaded their cannons. "All of us?"

"I only command the Vermonters. Volunteers under my charge."

"Yes, sir!" Ripley swung Lightning around, clenching the reins and his pistol in his left fist, and signaled with his right hand to organize the men into groups of four. "*Line up! By squad!*"

"*No time!*" he hollered. "*Move out! Now! Doublequick!*"

"*Forward!*" Ripley hollered and waved his arm in a windmill motion. Sergeant Lloyd stuck bugler Derry's hat onto his head, who played the call to advance. The 700 Vermonters, led by the swift flag bearer Hicks, filed double-quick out the northern gate.

He rose up in the saddle and saw Colonel Trimble screaming orders followed by another round of cannon fire from the Ohio batteries, now pounding the eastern roadway filled with Southerners. Then he saw Miles amid the pandemonium, gazing around in shocked disbelief. Vermont officers were mounted and soldiers were rushing out of the fort. Then Miles turned with anger and stormed toward the line of cannons, being reloaded by the men from Maine.

"*Stop firing!*" Miles waved his white flag back-and-forth over his head. No one responded. He jumped up and down with his yellow-plumed hat bouncing, then again jerked the white flag back-and-forth overhead.

Rebel shells rained down inside the fort and demolished the barracks, slammed a house next to the Barbour house and exploded on the parade ground. Young men from Illinois and Ohio, protecting the eastern wall, were hit in growing numbers. Most fought on bravely. A cluster of Vermonters dashing across the parade ground were hit by a cannon blast and fell dead in their tracks.

"*Got dammit! Stop!*" Miles hollered and rushed toward the first gun in the line of cannons. "We are to *surrender!*"

The last blast from a Maine battery or an incoming shell from the Rebel barrage, exploded into Miles and tore apart his lower body, ripping his legs apart. Shreds flew from the spot where he once screamed. His bloody torso and arms, with his head still adorned with his hat and yellow plumage, rolled over twice and came to rest. His left leg and part of his lower body were missing. Bits of white flag, now reddened with his blood, were scattered in a wide circle around him. It was gruesome but it was not lost on anyone that Miles's last word was "surrender!"

In the sudden quietness Colonel Trimble said, "Good Lord!"

He flashed back to his fallen father and grimaced but turned, took a deep breath then hollered, "*Forward! Doublequick!*"

The remaining Vermonters and a few soldiers from Ohio and Illinois sprinted out the northern gate. He kept Charger firmly in place amid the rushing soldiers flowing around them and the last few officers mounted. Then he wheeled Charger around, dug in his spurs and led them out of the fort, through the town and down its cobblestone streets to the river road, past the quaint old mill and along the waterfront to the pontoon bridge. Rebels hollered and yipped 100 yards away, but they were streaming down the main street through town in the opposite direction, rushing toward the fort on Camp Hill.

The Green Mountain Boys followed flag bearer Hicks, who ran down the river road and scrambled to the river's edge then hustled around and under the heavy-hanging willow trees to an opening on the bank of the Shenandoah River, where the recently built pontoon bridge led to Maryland. He weaved Charger through the brush, around a very large willow tree and came to the outcropping and clearing where the pontoon bridge was secured. Some of the Vermont Ninth Regiment stopped to catch their breath but he yelled, "*Keep moving!*"

They ran onto the pontoons and sent it rocking back and forth, up and down. He wondered, Who and what was on the other side of the river? Because no one had fired at them, there may be no enemy soldiers there, or perhaps very few, but he knew they would encounter Rebel forces soon enough. His 700 soldiers would need to fight their way through any rear guard of Confederates before they could meet up with General McClellan's troops. He yelled again, "*Keep moving! Assemble on the other side!*"

From the mountains of Marye's Heights Rebel artillery flags signaled across the valley to the flagmen of the gunners on Maryland Heights, who responded with their own signal. In a moment they might turn their heavy guns to the pontoon bridge.

"*Ripley!*" he hollered. "*Get four men and cut the bridge in pieces after we cross! Every thirty feet!*"

Then a Southerner's voice screamed behind him. He turned in the saddle to see a Confederate officer on a dark thoroughbred riding swiftly, skillfully weaving his way around the willow tree and waving a small white towel. He screamed, "*Hey thar! Stop!*"

"*Ripley! Ready?*" he hollered. More of his boys began crossing but hundreds remained, clogging the entrance to the pontoon bridge.

"*Hey thar, Colonel!*" The gray-jacketed lieutenant almost ran his horse into Charger but expertly jerked the reins back at the last instant. His gloved hand thrust out a note. "Beg pardon and with respect, suh! A message from yo' Gene'al White, who at this ve'y moment is surrende'in' to Gene'al Jackson."

He wondered when General White had arrived, then wondered what had happened to Major Gaines, the courier with his note. His boys moved with difficulty over the bobbing bridge while hundreds more waited their turn. Then he grabbed the note from the Rebel lieutenant.

It *was* in General White's handwriting. "You must return. Surrender is complete. Our lives in peril should you proceed. Gen. Julius White."

"What the hell?" he said, patted Charger's neck to calm him, then stepped him away from the Southerner's dark thoroughbred.

"It's true, suh," the Rebel saluted now and his dark eyes pleaded with sincerity. "Yo' Gene'al White signed a surrendah of the *entire* Union fo'ces. If yo' men do not retu'n immediately, Gene'al Jackson will have them shot!"

"Bullshit!" Cromartie said. Sweat dribbled down each side of his grim face now stained black by his mouth from ripping open cartridge packs. He stood on the embankment and looked to his big brother Asa, who turned and hustled onto the bobbing pontoon bridge along with scores of Vermonters.

Benedict grunted from the saddle on Folio nearby, next to the first pontoon. Folio bobbed his head, a warm chestnut color with a splash of white on his nose, in anticipation of moving out.

Ripley appeared ready with his sword drawn and a squad nearby to cut the pontoons after they crossed the bridge, and adjusted himself on his horse Lightning. He gritted his teeth then slowly shook his head no. Ripley waited in silence then, realizing what would come, yelled in frustration, "*Son of a bitch!*"

He thought, In five minutes they would be in Maryland with the slashed sections of the bridge floating downriver. They *could* make it. He wondered, Would Jackson shoot *unarmed* prisoners?

"Please, suh!" the lieutenant begged. "Gene'al Jackson awaits yo' *immediate* retu'n!"

Again he thought of the thousands of young men at the fort. Would Jackson shoot all of them? Could he? Would he start with the officers? He grumbled, "Unbelievable," then in frustration shouted, "*Damn!*"

"Please, suh!" Then the Southern officer became very emotional with tears welling up in his eyes. "God knows he means it!"

"*Ripley! Get our boys back here!*"

"Sir?" said Sergeant Cohl, standing nearby.

"*Get 'em back!*" he yelled, his voice thick with anger. "*It's General White's orders!*"

Ripley's face flushed hot with anger and his eyes showed he disagreed, but he waved his gloved hand in a recall motion to bugler Derry, whose freckled cheeks puffed out and trumpeted the Recall and Reform order. The young men on the bridge stopped, piling into one another in confusion. The bridge bounced up and down and a few soldiers grabbed onto one another to keep from falling. Private Hicks jerked the 9th regimental flag overhead to keep it upright, lost his balance and the flag swung downward, almost touching the water, then his kepi fell off and floated swiftly downriver. Hicks regained his balance, stood upright and raised the flag high then circled it.

Bugler Derry sounded the order again and the men turned and started back to the riverbank.

Benedict spat then said, “The only choice, sir.”

“God damn it, Benedict, it wasn’t a choice! This is pure horseshit! It’s General White’s *order!* Get our boys back! *Now!*”

The Vermonters filed off the pontoon bridge back onto the landing. Burt Cromartie shook his head and snarled at him then tossed his gun in the river. More men threw their guns into the water to avoid surrendering them to the Rebels.

The Southern lieutenant yelled, “*Hey thar!* Y’all supposed to come back *with* your guns. All y’all!”

“Benedict!” he ordered, “Send a courier with this man. Inform General White, and their General Jackson, we’re coming back.”

“Yes, sir!” Benedict turned his thin body in the saddle on Folio. The Vermonters were stepping off the bridge, scampering up the muddy riverbank. He hollered, “*Norton!*”

Private Norton, a small man from Swinton, made his way through the Vermonters to Benedict on his horse. Norton, not over five feet tall, saluted. “Yeah?”

“Hop on the back of this Reb’s horse,” he pointed to the Southerner. “Tell General White we’re coming back.”

“Bull shit!” Norton spat. “I ain’t ridin’ with no Johnny.”

“*Get up there!*” Ripley screamed, letting out some frustration. Norton flinched then looked around the growing crowd staring at him. Norton cursed, grabbed the cantle of the saddle and swung up onto the horse’s backside.

Benedict reached over, slapped the horse's croup and yelled, "*Get!*"

The Rebel lieutenant and Norton sped off. A few soldiers watched in astonishment and most began marching for the fort. Several Vermonters stood around their flag, held by Private Hicks, who appeared unflinching in his resolve. They all thought the same thing and Sergeant Lloyd said it, "They won't get our colors!"

"I won't surrender our flag!" Hicks said. The flag had red-and-white horizontal stripes and a field of dark blue with a fierce golden eagle, defiantly proud, surrounded by a circle of 33 golden stars for all the states.

"Not the Vermont flag!" said another. "I'll do what you say, but our flag won't be captured!"

More men yelled in support, hooted and shuffled around Hicks, who was without his hat with his ruffled dark hair close-cropped to his head. He was a thin boy from Montpelier who had only recently become their standard bearer and he had performed admirably. Hicks swore defiantly, "*On my mother's grave, I'll die first!*"

A brief silence followed Hicks' outburst then Ripley spoke firmly, "We won't let our flag down, sir! Request permission to cut it up. Each officer can take a piece and hide it under his jacket."

Sergeant Cohl, a large lumberjack with an awkward gait, approached and bumped his broad body into Charger's flanks. "I can fit the whole of it under my shirt!"

He thought, Yes, the flag would fit there without notice. He turned in the saddle, pointed toward town and beyond it to Camp Hill then yelled, "*March to the fort!*"

The Vermonters marched and Ripley moved Lightning over and tugged on his right arm with anger. "What about our colors?"

He replied discretely, "Sergeant Cohl will handle it."

"Yes, sir!" Ripley saluted then leaned down from Lightning to whisper into Sergeant Cohl's ear, who received the message with a nod.

The Vermonters returned to the fort, where most of the Union soldiers had already stacked their guns into several huge piles along with one stand of regimental flags from Maine, Illinois, New York and Ohio, all on the ground. The area where Colonel Miles had fallen had been cleaned up and on the other side of the parade ground, near the rubble at the base of the barracks wall, lay corpses in a large, oddly-shaped jumbled mass with several blankets over them.

The Confederates milled about, watching over the Federal surrender. The Rebels smelled foul. Most wore butternut sackcloth and some had gray uniforms but all were well-armed. They were a rough cast of men with their clothing matted with dirt and filth, and they scratched themselves repeatedly, a sign of lice and parasites in abundance.

The surrendering Union soldiers stood in long lines near the eastern wall. Some of the Rebels, led by their officers, went through the lines and took pistols, swords and meal bags. Here and there a Confederate screamed with glee and held up a silver fork or spoon, then another whooped over fishing tackle and still another stood dumbfounded at his luck in snatching a gold-cased watch.

General White stood next to his fine black horse with white socks near the Barbour house. White stood motionless with his untarnished saber, immaculate gloves and polished boots. Standing nearby were his staff of morose officers, who were all in spotless new uniforms with white-collared shirts.

He marched over and saluted White, who gazed at the red Virginia earth with a look of despondent humiliation. White was speechless. No one moved.

He hollered, "*Benedict!*" and marched toward the Barbour house and Benedict hustled to catch up. He charged up the cement steps, where several Confederate officers, hardened with nothing but bone, muscle and bronzed skin, chatted on the wooden porch. He pushed past them in their gray coats and a few snarled then one said, "Git outa here, ya damn Yankee!"

A gritty Rebel colonel with a scar near his right ear and long, greasy blonde hair grabbed his right arm. He spun away, knocked on then slammed his fist on the closed door repeatedly and called out, "*General Jackson!*"

The Rebel colonel pulled his pistol, cocked the hammer and continued to grab at him then yelled, "*Git back with yo' men!*"

He twisted away from his pawing hand and pounded again. The door opened and the Southerners stopped cursing him and stood straight. General Jackson seemed annoyed and was dressed in citizen's clothes in a dingy, faded gray suit. He was tall, hatless and his long dark beard was speckled with food particles. Jackson chewed more, swallowed then brushed his beard downward and looked into his eyes. "Yes, sir?"

He was thrown off by Jackson's terrible appearance but composed himself and pressed his point, "Did you agree to protect us under the terms of surrender?"

"Yes, sir," Jackson's light blue eyes examined him up-and-down, twice.

"Then by God drive away those lousy thieves of yours and stop them from robbing my men!"

"What?" Jackson snapped, and his cool eyes widened in amazement.

"Your men are stealing *personal* effects," he said with disgust. "You are responsible for this unjustified behavior and *you* must put a stop to it. *Immediately!*"

Jackson looked over the parade ground, saw the mayhem and without hesitation barked for his aide inside the house, "*Pendleton!*" Then, realizing he wasn't coming, glared at the long-haired colonel standing nearby. "Jeffers! *You* are responsible for our men behaving like gentlemen!"

"*And* have them return any personal effects," George demanded.

Jackson's light eyes glared at him, then he nodded and said, "Of course."

Colonel Jeffers had a look of bewilderment. Perhaps he had never seen anyone demand anything from Jackson. Then Jeffers raised his eyebrows, holstered his pistol and saluted formally and rushed off the porch to the long lines of Union soldiers.

Jackson studied him in his dark blue uniform and floppy hat. "You the Vermonter? Ah, Colonel Standuhd?"

"Stannard," he pronounced clearly. "Yes, sir. Vermont volunteers."

"Right. Yo' Ve'montahs were the only good unit at Bull Run. I saw it. Then I read who you were in the Richmond newspaper. They printed a letter from a Captain, ah, Eaton, I believe. Now I know this situation must be difficult for you and yo' men, but you did the hono'able thing, suh. There is no shame in this."

He looked into Jackson's light blue eyes and had not realized they had come close to meeting at Bull Run. He wanted to know the truth of the moment but avoided that question for now. "Almost all of the horses are personal possessions also."

"Oh? Oh, of cou'se, as voluntee's," Jackson said with mild reluctance. Good horses were a rare commodity and needed by Southern officers. "Yo' men may keep any ho'se *without* the U.S. Army brand."

He continued to examine Jackson to size him up. He could return to his meal at any moment so he asked, "Would you have shot these men?"

He watched Jackson and saw a hardened soldier who would do his duty but underneath was a continuous tossing-and-turning current. It reminded him of a hermit that lived in the woods east of St. Albans, who sometimes wandered into town and spoke weird, outlandish thoughts unconnected to anything. It appeared that some other force outside this world drove Jackson deep inside. It would not have surprised him if Jackson began spouting crazy salad phrases of foreign languages, or curses, or "Hallelujahs!"

Jackson brushed at his beard again, knocked off a few morsels of food and gazed heavenward then placed his pale hands together in prayer. "As God is my witness, I shall do whatevah *He* commandeth. I am *His* inst'ument. May *God's* will be done."

Jackson relaxed his praying hands, returned from his revelry to a more easeful posture, and with his gaze no longer heavenward, glared at him again.

He continued to watch Jackson. Beyond his frenetic blue eyes, the tall general *was* a crazed fanatic who seemed capable of *any* horror, who would justify it by saying it was *God's* will.

Jackson broke the silence, "All y'all are prisoners of war, and as we are in tha North shall be sent ta one of y'all camps until exchanged for Southe'n pris'na's. Dismissed."

"No, sir," he said firmly. "You will record the name and rank of each man individually, so each man may be exchanged as *individuals* become available." He knew this was the proper procedure, for a lieutenant may be exchanged for a lieutenant later but more importantly it would occupy Jackson and his men for hours, perhaps the remainder of the day to record each soldier's name and rank. He added for emphasis, "Sir, you insisted upon proper protocol in our return to the fort and now *I insist* on proper procedure in this matter. It is the *honorable* thing to do."

Jackson spat upon the wooden porch. He motioned to a standing officer, a sunburned colonel with a blue jay's feather in his cap, and nodded. "Colonel Mitchell will honah this procedu'e. *Dismissed.*"

He saluted and hoped the extra time would delay the Confederates in their movement toward the main body of the Federal Army and General McClellan's men. He thought, perhaps this extra time will somehow make a difference. Little Mac will use this time to his advantage and will strike Lee's divided forces for an important victory.

~22 ~

Federal commander George McClellan was given an extraordinary gift before the battle of Antietam. McClellan knew exactly where, when, and what the Rebels intended to do. Southern General Lee had somehow lost Order 191, wrapped around three cigars, which was found by a Union corporal and given to McClellan. Lee's plan was to split his forces for a few days before their rendezvous later at Sharpsburg, also called Antietam. Rather than strike with a force almost five times greater than his opponent, McClellan waited, planned and waited longer.

Two days later McClellan sent General Hooker to cross the northernmost bridge to attack Lee, while General Burnside was to move to another bridge two miles further south, cross it and strike at Lee's exposed left flank. While Burnside did move his men, he did not attack. A small force of Rebels kept Burnside's division from crossing the bridge on their first two attempts then when they did cross, rather than attack immediately, they waited for more orders from McClellan. They waited several hours while Hooker met heavy resistance to the north in an area that became known as Bloody Lane, and in a wheat field, and in the woods north of Antietam. The fighting was intense and hundreds died in minutes. One soldier said they fell "like tall grass under the scythe." General Hooker was wounded and General George Meade took over his command. The two forces fell into a bloody stalemate and it halted the Union advance.

Then Burnside at last received additional orders to advance but by this time Lee had pulled units from his reserves and other companies that had not seen action and moved them into the line of combat with Burnside's soldiers. Then, in an incredible stroke of fortuitous timing, Southern General A.P. Hill arrived from Harper's Ferry with General Jackson and his men, and marched into the exact location to stop Burnside's forces. They shored up the Southern line but also had enough troops with fine leadership to attack Burnside's left flank to great effect. When the day of fighting drew to a close both sides remained on the battlefield exhausted with heavy losses.

The battle of Antietam was another large, gruesome affair with both sides taking thousands of casualties. It produced the single bloodiest day of fighting in the war. The Union lost 2,108 men killed, 9,549 wounded, and 753 missing. It appeared the Southerners had won the day when the Federal forces withdrew but McClellan considered it a tactical withdrawal to avoid losing more men over unfavorable ground.

The Southern invasion of the North was stopped. After a day to care for the wounded and replenish their supplies, the Rebels retreated south.

The mood of the Union Army was bitter and grim. The battle demonstrated another occasion of inept leadership at the highest levels, where they were placed in a bad situation and lost another battle over poor ground followed by another bad decision to attack a well-defended area. In two years of fighting this war it seemed that not a single general had learned anything about attacking a well-defended position or of the ineptitude of sending forces into battle piecemeal, rather than in a coordinated attack from various directions to leverage superior force.

As the Federal forces withdrew the mood in Washington City became desperate and gloomy. President Lincoln once again had to consider what to do with an ineffective and belligerent General McClellan. Lincoln also saw the tactical stalemate at Antietam for an opportunity to give a speech called the Emancipation Proclamation, which stated any slaves in the rebellious South were now free. Of course no Southerner would free their slaves due to this Proclamation, for it was against the essence of their States' Rights, but it gave a moral overtone to the war. Now the war was seen as a rebellious movement of States fighting over political separation and it defined slavery as the root of this cause. No foreign nation could support the South without also crossing this line of ethics. Lincoln's speech kept France and Britain, who had strong economic ties to the South, out of the war. It was a savvy political move and it gave the Federal Army more time to win this bloody war.

~23 ~

George rode in a train of 22 passenger cars as a prisoner of war to Camp Douglas, near Chicago. A single boxcar was crammed with all their horses including Charger. The Union prisoners gave their word they would not fight and proceeded to the Federal camp named after the Illinois senator.

On the train he read a Washington City newspaper account of the battle of Antietam and other newspapers with their false stories about Harpers Ferry. The *Rutland Courier* gave a poor report and the Montpelier newspaper, *Green Mountain Freeman*, stated that after the Harpers Ferry campaign nothing more could be said of the Vermonters than “disaster, slaughter, defeat, and skedaddle.”

He had a lot of time to think about what he read and experienced first-hand. Would Southern General Jackson have slaughtered Union prisoners? Jackson seemed crazy enough to do anything but he probably would not. Would his Green Mountain Boys have made a difference if they had escaped? Continuing this thought, what would have happened to the Confederates’ divisions of McLaws and Anderson if they were trapped by General Franklin at Brownsville Pass? Thinking further back in time, upon their arrival at Harpers Ferry, what would have happened if they had been able to prepare a better defense at Harpers Ferry? What would have happened at Antietam if the other Confederates were engaged for even one more day in fighting a determined force of Federals at Harpers Ferry? He thought of all those scenarios and more until the train chugged into Camp Douglas. His sole conclusion was this was another occasion when his direct superior officer, this time Colonel Miles, had compromised the lives of *his* boys through incompetent leadership, bordering on treason. In that moment, he vowed he would never allow that to happen again.

The Vermonters were prisoners and had taken an oath to not fight until they were exchanged for an equal number of Confederate soldiers with an equal number of officers. Until such an exchange they were under their own guard and bound by honor not to fight.

Federal reserve soldiers from Chicago ran Camp Douglas. They had never fought, not even a light skirmish against the Rebels, but they had read many newspaper accounts with the same wrong story of what had happened at Harpers Ferry. There were so few guards at Camp Douglas that the 11,000 captives from Harpers Ferry were essentially watching themselves. Also, there were no obstacles to prevent outraged citizens or the local Chicago militia from coming to the camp to gawk at this "band of cowards," which all the newspapers called them. The common feeling among the reserve soldiers was anyone captured must be afraid to fight. In every newspaper report of any other battle, hundreds to thousands of men fought bravely and many died for their country. These Vermonters had laid down their guns to surrender at Harpers Ferry. The reserve guards resented them being here and most did not want to be near them in case their situation was contagious.

On the second day in camp George received a note from Doc Thayer to come see him at once. He walked through the hospital tent, shook hands with various boys and called them by their first name when he remembered or asked for their name when he didn't. At the far end of the tent he saw Doc Thayer, who had grown thinner while his dark mustache grew longer. Doc changed a bandage on a private's severed right arm.

He continued to shake hands, to pat a boy's shoulder, and chat amiably with the wounded. "William, be sure to get some steak. We just received provisions including fresh beef. Thomas, thank you son. That was a difficult fight. I'm sorry, I don't know your name—"

"Knowles, Corporal Regis Knowles, sir." The soldier was missing both legs from the knee down and struggled in his cot to sit up to attention.

"Regis. Rest well, rest. Steak is on the way!" He winked and patted the boy's arm. Then he saw Sergeant Lloyd with a pristine-white gauze bandage wrapped around his head. "Orley? What happened? Were you hit?"

"No, no. I had a back tooth pulled. It was bothering me mightily."

"Ah," he exhaled with relief. "Well, don't let that slow you down from getting some steak!"

"Yes, sir!" Lloyd winked and laughed good-naturedly. "I've got two sides to my jaw. I can still put up a good fight on the other side!"

He chuckled and arrived at the back of the tent. Doc Thayer finished his work with the gauze bandage on the wounded soldier, a peachy-cheeked, beardless boy who looked up from his cot.

"What's your name, son?" he asked.

"Clarke, sir," the boy gave a broadening smile. "DeWitt C. Clarke, sir."

"Relax, DeWitt." DeWitt was very thin but had a rounded, boyish face.

"I know the Clarks. Are you related to Worthington Curtis Clark, of St. Albans?"

"No sir, but I know them. My family is Clarke with an 'e.' I'm from a village outside Montpelier."

"Oh. Farmer?"

"My father is. Hay and sugar beets." His eyes shined with pride and he shifted his weight and again struggled to sit upright on the cot. "But I'm thinking differently."

"Are you, now?"

"Sugar beets are sweet, but they don't inspire me." DeWitt had quick dark eyes and raised his left hand with one finger pointed upward, as if stating a theory. "I'm thinking it's time to start practicing law. DeWitt C. Clarke, esquire."

"Yes. That does have a nice ring to it," he nodded and DeWitt smiled. Doc Thayer gave a serious look to him, which made him more concerned for the boy. "DeWitt will be fine, won't he? He'll be able to get an education and be a lawyer, won't he Doc?"

“I’ve already got my law degree,” DeWitt said, “from Dartmouth.”

“There ya go,” Doc said, brushing his long dark mustache downward but still solemn-faced. “Now you can open a practice. Where would you start? Montpelier?”

“Yep, that’s where the business is, near as I can tell. There or Wash City.”

“Lieutenant Veazey’s a lawyer, a judge now. He’s from Montpelier,” George squeezed DeWitt’s neck near his back then let his hand stay there like a father would and gave him a proud smile. “I’d be happy to recommend you, son.”

Doc stood waiting, then nodded toward the large tent’s entrance with a sad look on his face. “I’ve got news for you, Colonel. George. From back home.”

Doc’s weary gray eyes were filled with watery tears and he recalled first meeting him at one of Mrs. Turner’s soirees, then realized he also knew Helen. “Is she alright?”

“Who?” Doc asked.

“Helen.”

“What? Yes. Near as I can tell.” A tear rolled out of Doc Thayer’s eyes. “No, this is about our friend. Doctor Côté.”

“Oh. What? Is he okay?”

“He’s passed.”

“No.” He blinked several times and thought he had misheard. “What?”

He was confused. The tent was full of ailing men and boys. Some were severely wounded, some dying, some sick with disease or dysentery, and some dazed by medication. All lay in their cots, staring at him, asking with their pleading eyes to come over and visit. Dr. Côté dead? "He wasn't involved in this."

"He was old," Doc said, trying to add some logic to the news.

"He survived Napoleon's retreat from Moscow. He was part of the French revolution. Survived the counter-revolution."

"He was seventy-three when I met him, years ago," Doc's attention had been drawn away by a loud moan of pain from a nearby soldier but returned his focus to George and placed his thin hand, caked with dried blood, on his shoulder. He swallowed hard but remained silent, sharing his pain, then offered in a warbled voice, "I'm sorry."

He leaned on a tent pole and the ceiling billowed under his push. His stomach quivered, began lurching up, and he felt uneasy. A thick lump formed in his throat. How could this be?

Doc's eyes glistened with tears. "This is never easy. I thought you'd want to know."

"Yes. Yes, of course. Thank you for telling me." He staggered down the aisle and stepped outside the tent. A tear rolled over his cheek. The fresh air filled his lungs but he felt numb and could not understand it. Dr. Côté dead? His gut wrenched, convulsed again and he doubled over then deposited his chewed breakfast on the ground which smelled awful. He heard soldiers in the hospital tent heaving from flux and a thought crossed his mind: he didn't want to become ill. He heaved again but mostly spittle came out. No, he thought. It was the horrible news, not some disease. Still, he feared becoming ill. They had lost hundreds of good men to disease and dysentery.

Then he remembered Dr. Côté's perpetual "Who's back?" gag, his corny jokes, and his adventurous stories of fighting with Napoleon. How could he be gone?

A single wire nailed to posts every ten feet ran around the camp and he leaned on one of the posts. Soldiers milled about, scurried to and from the 20 barracks, the hospital tent and the dining hall.

He again thought of Dr. Côté, his many visits and recalled many stories of how Dr. Côté had attended to and treated officers on Napoleon's staff, from minor to severe sword wounds and bullet wounds, for cholera, dysentery, syphilis and food poisoning. He then remembered what Dr. Côté had said about surrender. They had stood in the Trading Post by the counter and he adjusted his spectacles with his short, round fingers, sipped cognac from his flask then said, "Oh no, surrender iz not a choice. Zee commanding officer of zee surrendering unit does not survive."

"Why? What happens to the officer?" he asked.

"Off weef heez head! Klack!" Dr. Côté made a chopping motion with his forearm to imitate the guillotine. "Zar are no cowardz in zee French Armee!"

Samuel cleared his throat then lifted his glass of amber liquor while Dr. Côté, the plump Frenchman continued, "No, no! Tactical retreats *mais oui, but of course.* Even in zee French Army. But surrender? *Jamais.* Never. To put zee arms down and zay, I will not fight. No."

As a boy he sensed some other meaning in the doctor's words and now he was beginning to understand what it was. It seemed to be a deep sadness, perhaps for those comrades lost, or for some mystical sense of valor. What was that valor? Was it a post-mortem sense of bravado despite inept leadership? Or the valor of doing one's duty under impossible odds, a sense of "into the valley of death rode the six hundred"?

He wanted to speak with Dr. Côté *now.* Where was the valor in surrendering at Harpers Ferry to save others' lives? What philosophy would Dr. Côté offer for having fought bravely at Bull Run and Harpers Ferry, only to receive no commendation but rather humiliation? What was the point? In the grand scheme of life, what was he doing? What would Dr. Côté say of his awkward marriage with Helen?

He kicked dirt over his vomit and looked out over the campground. Five officers filed out of the dining hall including Captain Ripley, who looked thinner and somehow shorter. Ripley said something to the four officers who stood watching him as he came over. His gait was agitated with something on his mind. His dark hair was well past his shoulders and he had let a dark mustache grow. A few breadcrumbs hung on his mustache, perhaps he felt them and brushed them away, then saluted. "Afternoon, sir!"

“At ease, captain.” Ripley’s dark eyes looked troubled, perhaps he had his own bad news weighing him down, and he said, “You’ve heard of Dr. Côté?”

“Yes. I’m sorry for your loss.” Ripley spoke with a clipped harshness, showing something else bothered him. He realized they had not spoken since their surrender.

“Edward, what’s on your mind?”

“Me and the boys were talking, sir,” Ripley flexed his hands in agitation. “We’re still hungry, if you catch my meaning.”

“We’re a strong lot. But there’s a pain gnawing in my gut, too.” He saw Ripley was very uneasy and tried to make a joke with him. “Maybe it was the steak?”

“No, it ain’t the steak. I heard some’s coming but today it’s Monday’s beef stew. Again.”

“Don’t you need beef to call it beef stew?”

“Yes, sir. Near as I can tell,” Ripley’s red cheeks flushed but he was still irritated, restrained a smile, and snarled, “I can’t say I’m strong enough, or hungry enough to eat it again. I’m holding out for real steak.”

“I know the feeling.” He also felt too worn down from the surrender to chuckle at this tired joke. Ripley, who was always very emotional, grunted some curse words and his cheeks turned dark crimson then he lunged at him with a right-fisted haymaker that landed square on his jaw and made him stagger backwards, stung his teeth and nose, and the pain was intense. Tears formed in his eyes but he saw Ripley bull-rushing him so he leaned in, grabbed him and held on.

Ripley shouted, "*You son of a bitch!*"

He wrestled Ripley sideways, pinning down his arms as he struggled to free himself. Ripley squirmed for several moments, grappling, and they both breathed heavily. Then Ripley stomped his boots and bent over in frustration, then burst out in a sudden blast of crying but he held on to George's waist. He continued to hold Ripley, to let him writhe in anger and frustration. Then Ripley stood upright, hugged him, and sobbed. "I, I don't know how I'll face my folks! My wife. *You did this!*"

"It's alright. You're a good man. I've seen you fight with the best of 'em."

He held onto Ripley, feeling his own humiliation of the surrender and absorbed it all. Ripley continued to cry for a moment, wobbling, then stood upright and leaned back, looking at him with his watery dark brown eyes. He held onto Ripley's shoulders at arms' length. "I'd be *honored* to serve with you. Anytime."

"Thank you, sir. That means a lot coming from you."

"The fact is we had no choice. We had orders from General White and I had to consider the lives of those at the fort."

"Of course, sir," Ripley swallowed hard, appearing to take some comfort in this thought, and said, "*We* were the ones in the fight. *They're* the ones who surrendered!"

"*Captain!* We'll have none of that," He let loose of him and continued, "We're *all* in this together. First, we're Vermonters and *we follow orders!* And our orders were to go back to the fort. Second, how many times has any one of our men fought at your side? Perhaps saved your life?"

Ripley nodded yes but he was still angry with clenched teeth and wiped away his tears with maddened strokes. "Absolutely."

"Very good. We *are* brave. Don't let *anyone* tell you otherwise, or make it sound like our fight was less than what we did. *We* did our duty. It was *my* decision to return and I stand by it."

"Thank you, Colonel." Ripley hugged him strongly and the pure emotion of it made him think of what it must feel like to have a child of his own, someone to protect and nurture their every interest, to lift them up when they've fallen, brush off their wounds, and send them on their way with renewed hope.

Then Ripley parted and rolled his neck to relieve his tension. "How much longer will it be?"

"Not soon enough, Edward. Not soon enough." With his left hand he clapped Ripley's shoulder, shook him, and watched him buck-up to attention.

Ripley cleared his throat. "I appreciate your kind words and I'm sorry I lost—"

"In your honorable service." He gave a quick, formal salute. "Sir!"

"I can't wait to get back at them Rebs, sir." Ripley saluted back.

"Yep. We'll have our chance again." The four officers watching by the mess hall said something to each other, then two walked away, across the yellowing fields of Camp Douglas. "It doesn't seem like this war will end anytime soon. We'll get our orders and hopefully they'll put us in a position to fight."

"Yes, sir." A more normal, less reddened color had returned Ripley's cheeks and his eyes glistened with hope.

"Be careful of what you wish for, son."

"Yes, sir." Ripley nodded, saluted again, and walked away then turned back with a sly grin on his face. "Speaking of being careful, that 'beef stew' is awfully green."

He grunted. "Based on your scouting report, I'll fight that battle another day!"

"A wise choice, sir!" Ripley chuckled, tugged at his kepi, and marched back to the two waiting officers with his stature taller now. Once again, Ripley had pride and confidence in his step.

~24 ~

A message came that a colonel in the Confederate Army had been captured along with several hundred other soldiers. They were signed over, exchanged as prisoners of war for Colonel Stannard and the remainder of the Vermont troops. They were not told who the Confederates were or where they were from but the Vermonters term in Camp Douglas was over. Although no guard had stood over them, they now had the freedom to go where they wanted. George informed Benedict and gave the order to pack up and report to Union Station for the six p.m. train to New York City.

As he gathered his personal items he felt an odd sense of release mixed with growing discomfort of returning to Burlington and Helen. It had been six months and he felt even more distant from her. What had she being doing during this time? She had only sent two letters, describing the cold winter weather, the latest theatre plays and opera, and had requested in each letter a demand to his superior officer he be given a promotion so he could receive more money from the government. Somehow Helen did not understand from his letters being captured was not a good thing and would not lead to promotion. In his letters he tried to convey he had served his country with honor, fought with determination and bravery at the cost of many personal wounds, and yet he was subjected to degradation despite his unyielding courage. It was a great frustration and humiliation. Why couldn't Helen understand his feelings? Foremost on his mind was the question of whether she would love him after all the changes he had endured. He had killed and killed often for his country.

He, Benedict, Ripley, Veazey, Lloyd and the officers supervised the men, who assembled to board a train at Union Station. Charger and the other officers' horses were loaded into four separate cars. Most of the Vermonters were very happy to be returning home. Many had volunteered in January of the previous year and their term of enlistment had expired. Their being held prisoner was also a hardship on their families. They would return home in time for spring planting but those who had worked in factories or ran their own business had imposed hardship on their children and wives, who had to take over their role in business or at the factory. Cousins and older uncles chipped in to help the families of the boys in service and now, at last, they would return home to a more normal life. All carried an invisible scar of their service, seared into them months ago in the bucolic setting of the Shenandoah Valley, where they fought the Confederates and killed men by the score. Would anyone at home understand?

He watched the Vermonters assemble in long lines then board the train of 34 cars. Sergeant Cohl stood near the lead train car steps and pulled out the Vermont 9th infantry flag from under his coat as if it had been there the entire time. Cohl presented it to a grim-faced Private Hicks, who had somehow received a new kepi to cover his longer, dark hair. Hicks also had a new pole and attached the flag with its red-and-white stripes and a field of blue where a golden eagle screamed amid a ring of 33 gold stars. Hicks then turned and dipped the flag in salute to him and the officers. The boys filed onboard led by Sergeant Cohl.

Captain Ripley watched each soldier from each of his companies, red-cheeked and proud, board the train. Then Ripley jerked to attention, saluted him and climbed the steps into the second car. Lieutenant Veazey, his dark hair and attractive features now tinged with gray, was grim with seriousness but snapped to attention and saluted him. Veazey placed his leather-gloved hand on the shoulder of Corporal Van Damme, a wizened older man of near 50, who had let his white beard grow long during the imprisonment. Van Damme spat on the ground and Veazey shook his head with disgust then climbed the steps into the third train car. Lieutenant Franklin, who had been waiting and watching, saluted then entered the fourth car just behind the Cromartie brothers. The staff of adjutants boarded the last car. Then Private Hicks saluted, turned and marched with their flag to the front of the train and up the steps into the lead of 34 cars. Lieutenant Benedict, who had put on some weight during their inactive imprisonment, turned to him, saluted crisply and said, "Vermont's finest all aboard, sir!"

He appreciated Benedict's enthusiasm, nodded solemnly and stepped onto the bottom stair. The engineer leaned from the engine with his head and one arm out the window, looked back and waited for his signal. He waved his hand, a casual motion one would use to greet a casual friend, and the engineer turned and released some steam. The immense power of the black engine lurched forward, he grabbed the handrail from the bottom step and each car jerked in succession then in unison. The steel wheels slid then moved on the rails and rolled away from the platform. He mounted the last few steps, looked back over the receding tracks to the large building of Union Station, growing smaller in the distance and then the horizon with many houses and buildings of Chicago gathered on Lake Michigan. Their time in Camp Douglas was finally over.

He thought of where he was headed, toward the clear waters of Lake Champlain, freedom and home. He thought of Helen's pretty blue eyes and the deep laughter she could give so easily. Through all the hardship he had been through, he was determined to also rise through these difficult times with Helen. Wasn't it better to confront their problems with bravery, he thought, than surrender? In his heart he knew he wanted to love her forever. Yes, they had had some hard times, misunderstandings, but together they could grow a more beautiful relationship. Their marriage and their life together were much more important than single events. They had taken a vow to God, before all their friends and relatives, but what would she say?

~25 ~

President Lincoln stood over his desk covered with maps, military plans and traced two fingers to a large block representing General McClellan's army against a smaller block of Confederate forces led by General Lee. Lincoln had an old man's face, haggard, worried, wrinkled and pale with a tightness around his mouth. The only relic of youth was a dark brilliance in his eyes but now he glared at Secretary of War Stanton. His tired, weak voice cracked with emotion, "Why won't he attack?"

The Federal Army had stopped Lee's forces in the Shenandoah Valley, the Southerners had withdrawn from Antietam, but why didn't McClellan pursue them? Was he waiting for another Special Orders plan from General Lee to fall into his lap?

Secretary Stanton, his long dark beard grown streaked with gray, unhooked his wire rim glasses, stood up straight and slapped the top map with his hand angrily, "Mac's fully supplied and outnumbers the traitors. It's madness!"

For months various meetings were held with Stanton and his staff. President Lincoln wrote telegrams, wrote letters, sent messengers and pleaded for McClellan to attack. After much exasperation Lincoln relieved McClellan then named General Ambrose Burnside to be Commander-in-Chief of the Union forces. Burnside was a good friend of McClellan and they had attended school together at West Point and shared many of the same thoughts about training the Army with more discipline, of fighting a tactical engagement against the Confederates including choosing a fortified, defensive position, and only attacking with superior forces. President Lincoln had hoped that a change in leadership would provide a more aggressive commander who would take the initiative and attack the Secessionists.

Burnside was tall, portly, known for his long hair that grew from his cheeks up to the sides of his temples and his men called the excessive hair "sideburns," a play of words on his name. He was well-liked and had a good-natured smile ready for all. Although Burnside oozed a plump joviality, he was more admired for his temperament than respected by his men for any military brilliance. He also inherited McClellan's plan for attacking the Confederates at Fredericksburg and waited for his entire Army before crossing the Rappahannock over pontoon bridges, which President Lincoln approved in spite of his urgent request for immediate action.

On Burnside's staff was General Winfield Hancock, a short, fiery leader from Pennsylvania. Hancock had dark hair, a receding hairline with a dark mustache and he used his military knowledge to try to persuade Burnside, pleaded with him, to cross the Rappahannock River at a bridge three miles south of Fredericksburg, sweep around and attack the exposed flank of Lee's army. Burnside preferred to wait for the entire Army of the Potomac to be called up, to build a pontoon bridge, to cross the river together and to attack en masse. This was how it was done in military engagements.

While Burnside and the Army of the Potomac waited 17 days for the engineers to receive material and build a pontoon bridge, Confederate General Lee used the time to amass his army, which swelled to 78,000 men, and to maneuver his forces into an extraordinary defensive position. They left the town of Fredericksburg and moved to the top of the Marye's Heights, behind a stone wall, with an open field of 200 yards beneath them. Lee's right flank, General Jackson's corps, was reinforced with the forces of A.P. Hill's brigade and more reinforcements were brought up from General Longstreet's corps to solidify the main line. General Lee stood with Longstreet and reviewed their forces and the terrain from behind the stone wall. They agreed. It was a tremendous defensive position. An artillerist, Edward Alexander, rail thin with a wide grin, patted a cannon and said, "A chicken couldn't live on that field when we open on it."

The Army of the Potomac grew to a colossal, immense force of 110,000 men. They encamped across from the small town of Fredericksburg on the banks of the Rappahannock River. A handful of Rebel pickets remained in Fredericksburg. On the morning of December 10th, the Union shelled the mostly abandoned town but the bombs destroyed houses and killed civilians. For the first time in the war, a large population of citizens was exposed to the atrocities of war, including the horror of being wounded, maimed or killed. Men, women and children were ripped apart in mid-stride with indiscriminate wrath with their lives destroyed in mid-breath.

The few Rebel pickets and snipers offered little resistance and gave up the town, which the Union soldiers took quickly. General Hancock, who had trained at West Point, recognized the Southerners' well-fortified position, across an open field, entrenched above them in the hills, and knew the outcome of any battle here was predictable. Hancock stopped his men, made another request to Burnside to move their forces downriver, march around the hillside and attack the Rebel's backside flank. Burnside felt confident their far superior numbers would be unstoppable. The Federal soldiers were headstrong, rowdy over their victory in taking the town, and looted and destroyed property. The Confederates, some of whom lived in the area, looked down from the hills with horror and growing anger. They wanted vengeance *now*.

At dawn on December 13th the men in blue attacked over the open ground, up the hill. They fired in vain at the stone wall and the graycoats shot back and killed or wounded hundreds of unprotected men. The Union forces attacked again, fell in the bloody killing field and retreated. Led by the Irish brigade, they attacked again. In spite of their courageous efforts, they also fell on the bloodied field. Men who were not wounded dropped to the ground to seek shelter behind the corpses of their comrades. Again the Union forces attacked and again they were easily rebuffed. Confederate General Lee tipped back his gray hat and turned to Longstreet, tall, stiff and watching the slaughter below, "It is a good thing war is so horrible or we would come to like it."

After a full day of attacking up the hill, the Union soldiers dug deeper under bodies of their fallen comrades and awaited the descending night. When darkness fell a strange storm of mysterious dimension occurred, an expression in the natural world of a supernatural phenomenon that many men, on both sides, thought was the language of God. Brilliant flashes of blue, green, and white light raced across the sky in immense, wild swirls. It was magnificent, beautiful and an undeniable expression of an awesome supreme power. All who saw it felt it was an omnipotent force of loveliness. The Southerners felt this was a sign from God that their victorious struggle was blessed. The Northerners felt it was an ironic display of beauty, of God's love amid the ugliness of maiming and killing moments earlier. Men who had never prayed in their life saw the light of God. One day there would be peace and when that day came, *their* righteousness would be testament to His greater glory.

The next morning at first light, the Confederates took their blessing to begin killing again and the Federals fought back with equal intensity fortified with renewed faith. The horrible battle continued through another day. With insane devotion to a terrible plan the Union Army attacked 16 times. They were easily repulsed with cannons fired from the hills above Fredericksburg and Rebel muskets poured into them. The Union batteries responded with lethal blasts aimed at the Confederates and the soldiers in blue fired their muskets into the stone wall above them.

After two days and 17 failed attempts to take the fortified hillside, Commander Burnside conceded to the wisdom of his fellow officers and the battle of Fredericksburg was over. Lee had won another decisive victory for the South. Over 12,000 Union men had been killed, wounded or captured.

President Lincoln sent a congratulatory telegram to the General Burnside, stating the number of wounded and dead was "comparatively so small" and gave him "the thanks of the nation." He also considered replacing Burnside because it was clear his leadership had failed miserably but he decided to wait. The most prominent person on his list of generals under consideration was "Fighting Joe" Hooker.

The Rebels lost 4,500 men along with hundreds of citizens of the town killed or wounded. Lee led his Southerners away from the battle with a renewed sense of superiority glorified under the confirmation of the "Northern" lights.

The momentum of the Rebel forces carried on through the winter and into the spring of 1863 with more Confederate victories. The Southern leaders considered their next move and it was clear the Federal position was dire. Confederate President Jefferson Davis took this opportunity to meet with his political advisors and military leaders, including General Lee. President Davis asked them one question, "Is now the time to move north and deal a convincing blow to determine our nationhood?"

~26 ~

In the spring of 1863 the Vermonters returned from Camp Douglas, from Chicago to New York to Burlington, by train. When the locomotive pulled into the Burlington station there was no brass band and no cheering masses to exalt the soldiers as when they left over one year earlier, which was much longer than their nine-month term of enlistment. Wives, mothers, younger brothers or other family members of the soldiers greeted their loved ones with great hugs and kisses. Private Hicks, their flag bearer, said something to Lieutenant Benedict who nodded affirmatively, and marched out of the station with their colors. Bugler Derry, now 16, played "Tenting on the Old Campground Tonight" and as his last note was resonating in the cavernous hall, Derry left for home.

George looked around, looked everywhere. Helen was not at the depot. He thought perhaps she did not receive his letters announcing when they would return, then noticed Mrs. Orley Lloyd and Mrs. Theodore Farnsworth, both avid fans of the theater. Surely each of them had discussed the Vermonters return with Helen. He walked through the arched entrance of the station and saw a stack of newspapers and the headline read:

Vermont Brigade Returns To-Day

3pm Arrival

The Captured Prisoners Released

Some of the Vermonters gave him a hardy handshake and several more, including Captain Ripley and Private Burt Cromartie, gave him a bear hug as a final farewell. Their term of service was done. Most of the young men made their way for home alone.

He went to the first of two boxcars for the horses, nodded thanks to the farrier and led Charger, already saddled with his gear, down the ramp. He thought it would be good to walk with Charger and led him from the station then found himself thinking over the past two years. He thought of everything he had seen in the war, from the cowardice at the opening Battle of Bull Run, to disturbing losses of men killed or wounded, including the terrible, unexpected loss of Sergeant Brisken, collapsing by his side, to the incompetence of Colonel Miles at Harpers Ferry and their imprisonment at Camp Douglas. The Vermonters had left as raw volunteers, young boys with an eagerness to do good, some of whom once fled in the face of fire, and all returned as hardened veterans, including young men who were bold, fought bravely and witnessed the terror of war with the horrifying random deaths of innocent civilians. The experiences of the Vermont brigade, filled with awful events, were a sea of bitter experiences. Now there were no thanks and no comfort from the citizens of Vermont. There were only a few families of fine young men. Worst of all, Helen was absent.

He walked next to Charger, nodding and neighing often, and noticed new cobblestone streets and a few new buildings and businesses. He smelled stewed tomatoes, onions cooking then noticed a new restaurant on the corner across from the village green called Glen's Eatery. Then he saw another new shop with a large plate-glass window with a swirling red, white and blue sign of Linton's Flowers followed by a refurbished storefront with a wooden Indian out front with a simple sign of "Cigars" then on the corner, a dual office space for two lawyers called Brogan & Nyerson. Not only was Burlington untouched by the war, there had been growth. It was heartening to see. Some good was still happening, in total contrast to his experience in the war with destruction at every turn. He felt discordant with the tranquil beauty of Lake Champlain and tall elms around the village green.

Then he noticed the scarred civilians. One ex-private in uniform limped badly and another citizen slumped with a downcast gaze, perhaps holding onto the dishonor of Bull Run. Then he saw Private Lowe, hobbling on one leg and a crutch toward the waterfront and a waiting ferry. Lowe would be aware of his service forever. He also saw a deep pain in the friends and relatives of those who did not return. Their permanent loss and sadness could not be touched.

Here and there a familiar friend said Hello! and asked how he was, and still more friends saw the creased disturbance on his face and, after a kind greeting, let him be. He walked quietly to the solitary clopping of Charger's hooves on the brick streets, made his way to Elm Street, rounded the corner and started up the small hill. Somehow his home appeared foreign. In one year the weathered boards now needed painting and the rainspout above the porch had detached from the roof. A gust from a damp, northwestern wind almost blew off his floppy hat but he held it down. Heavy spring storms would be coming soon, then he figured he had better fix the drainage gutter before a sudden downpour would cost the entire porch.

He walked Charger around back to the small barn, removed his saddle, bags, blanket, and halter and gave him some fresh water and oats in a wooden bucket then went around to the front and stepped inside the quiet house. The furniture was still in the same places but the walls were covered with bright new wallpaper of a tiny floral rose with a green vine. Two champagne flutes with a bit of fizzing golden liquid stood on the table by the Victorian sofa and a playbill lay on the floor. A gray cat rubbed itself against his legs. He walked further into the front room, looked up the staircase and called, "*Helen?*"

He listened for any movement then thought of the stillness in the moment before battle at Harpers Ferry when he listened for twigs breaking in the forest before the Southerners attacked. It was quiet. Then the cat meowed and strutted for the kitchen. He followed the cat to the back of the house and found a loaf of bread becoming moldy on a cutting board. A bowl of fruit was on the oak dining table with a few apple cores in a bucket by the sink. He picked out a whole pear, bit into it then spat it into the bucket where it made a hollow tinny sound. It was rotten on the underside. He took out a large bread knife, cut away the mold from the loaf of grain-and-wheat bread and sliced off a fair portion from the middle section. He saw a jar of preserves with a familiar bow and a swirling **A** on the label, from his Aunt Amelia, and took it down from the shelf. It was still sealed with beeswax, opened it, dipped the bread knife into the blackberry preserves, slathered it over the bread and tasted its mouthwatering deliciousness. The preserves had been made with the right touch of sweetening to keep the fruit fresh and flavorful. He ripped off a small bit of bread, dipped it in jam and gave it to the cat which sniffed it, let it drop to the floor, sniffed again then ate voraciously. He slathered more jam on the bread, took another bite, then heard laughter and footsteps crossing the front porch. He heard Helen's voice faintly, growing louder as she approached, then the front door creaked open and she giggled like a girl about to meet her first beau. She was home and anxious to see him!

"You got in the last word!" a man's voice said. "You're a corker, Helen! You're—" the man's voice stopped.

He strained to listen closely. Faint smacking noises sounded through the wooden kitchen door, perhaps someone was eating something? He set down the bread, stepped out of the kitchen and saw Bradford Dutton, the fireman with one disabled foot moving slowly, waltzing with Helen. He looked more closely and was shocked. Helen kissed Dutton on the mouth, neck and frantically unbuttoned his shirt.

He tightened his fist around the handle of the bread knife, coated with blood-black preserves and cleared his throat. Dutton broke away, eyed him up and down then noticed his colonel's uniform. He had not taken off his floppy hat, which he now removed in Helen's presence.

Dutton nudged Helen away and spoke haltingly, "I'm sorry. George. We went for a walk and—. When did you get in?"

The cat meowed in the heavy silence and rubbed itself on his inner left calf against his blue uniform trousers. "I've been here ten minutes."

Helen's face flushed. She dabbed her lips with the side of her thumb and spoke with authority, "You should have announced yourself! This is most improper of *you!*"

"This is *my* home," he said. Blood pounded in his temples and he found himself flexing his fist around the knife then set it on the polished end table but his movement was deliberate and loud like a challenge. Then he noticed his unopened letter on the mantel on top of his poetry book by Whitman and he felt more anger.

Helen was extremely nervous, her face flushed again and her eyes darted this way, that way, and she appeared to search for some answer. Her tongue repeatedly moistened her dry lips then she pushed Dutton toward the front door. "Leave, uh, *sir!*"

Helen turned dramatically to him. "Why didn't you tell me you were coming? The last I heard you were out west. Chicago or some place! This is *most* improper!"

Dutton stood dazed in the doorway, patted down his vest then pulled at his pockets, searching for his carte de visite. He stepped back-and-forth like a horse around a sidling rattlesnake then spoke anxiously, "Helen, I—"

"Braddy! *Leave!*" she cried.

"But what of—"

"Leave *at once!*" she scolded him like the Countess she was, then stepped to Dutton, grabbed his coat sleeves and whispered, although her voice was still audible in the quiet house, "I'll send you a note."

He had no idea of what to say to Helen or what to do. His impulse was to beat the living hell out of Dutton and continued with that thought while Dutton hurried down the steps, dragging his right foot. His eyes followed Dutton, blood pounded in his temples and he heard Helen cooing but brushed past her, not looking at her, knowing her beauty would influence him and hurt him. He shoved the front door while she mumbled something about "impropriety" then the door slammed open against the outside wall.

"Where are you going?' she demanded. "Where are you going?"

He followed Dutton down the walkway and Dutton glanced back, gathered speed, and moved faster onto the brick street and waved at a passing coach. The driver pulled back the reins, Dutton hustled then with effort pulled himself onto it and they sped off.

He followed the carriage with his eyes. Anger bubbled over and he spat on the roadway. Sweat dripped from his forehead and he popped his right fist into his left palm. Helen screamed something from the porch but he ignored her and ran with determination, heading for the town center where he thought Dutton lived.

The coach turned onto another avenue, which confused then relieved him. He stopped and thought, What good would it do to beat Dutton? How would *Helen* change from that? She wouldn't. Her unbridled passion was not Dutton's fault, although Dutton knew they were married and deserved a vicious beating. If he didn't beat Dutton, what would people say? That he had been cuckolded and did nothing, and thus leaving an opening for more cuckolding? No, something must be done but what?

~27 ~

It was a dismal spring, the worst he could recall. There was no joy in the warming weather and the blooming season. Helen moved out of their house to live in the luxurious Wilson Hotel for reasons, she said, "she would explain later." He tried to forbid her from leaving but she wrestled away and said, "We can discuss this later but it's pointless!"

He spoke many times with his Aunt Amelia, with some friends, and with neighbors. He discovered Mrs. Turner had travelled to London then to places unknown to her staff, and also Obadiah had gone to Boston and enlisted in the Army as Massachusetts had formed a regiment of Colored Troops. Throughout Burlington and Vermont, people treated him like he had an infectious plague. After a few pleasantries they said, "Good day." He knew people judged him, surmised his marriage with Helen was a disaster, and his service in the war was disgraced by the humiliation at Harpers Ferry that no one understood. All of it made him miserable.

One week later he happened to encounter Bradford Dutton, carrying a brown-paper wrapped package while he walked on the boardwalk past some of the new storefronts in downtown Burlington. He crossed the brick street to confront Dutton but said nothing, thrust his hands around Dutton's warm throat, and slammed him against the glass storefront of Linton's Flowers, which made a loud noise but the thick glass held. He squeezed tighter around Dutton's pulsing throat and saw his green eyes widen with increasing panic and fear. He thought of screaming, "*Stay away from my wife!*" then somehow he flashed on the memory of the hefty Canadian redcoat soldier who he had gut-shot. The soldier's stunned eyes had the same expression of shock and fear of death. Dutton dropped his brown package and scratched at his wrists.

He thought of screaming, "*You bastard!*" then thought of the Rebel lieutenant he had shot at ten yards, popped him in the forehead and took his life effortlessly. Like an enemy soldier, Dutton deserved to die. Wait. Did Dutton deserve to *die?*

Dutton slid down, his writhing legs buckling under him, but he held on to his hot, sweating neck as he slumped against the beam supporting the storefront window at the corner. Mrs. Linton hollered something from inside then rapped on the plate glass window and it pulled him back into the moment. He released Dutton, who collapsed onto the boardwalk and massaged his throat, breathing in deep, rasping gulps.

He became acutely aware of everything. He was breathing heavily and his hands were shaking. He removed his floppy hat, wiped his brow with right palm, replaced his hat, and cleared his throat. He thought of saying something definitive, some final words to Dutton, but decided he had received his message. He also wondered, Were there others Helen had encouraged? What good did this do?

Mrs. Linton rushed out of her store onto the boardwalk, calling out something about "Amelia" but he ignored her, walked away, and realized he was even angrier and more miserable than five minutes earlier.

~ ~

It was a very wet spring and seemed to rain without pause. He did not relish the prospect of spending any time in the remote woods, now swamps, of Georgia, Vermont in this damp spring, although he missed his neighbors, the Lonegrans and the Thirods, but he wanted to check on his horses. He went through the motions of daily life in Burlington and paid another polite, quiet visit with his aunt and with a few friends.

He attended various spring celebrations but through it all he was not in a festive mood. All the soirees and afternoon teas were filled with stories about who was with whom and which person had made which event an affair to remember. He did not care.

He went to see Helen at the Wilson Hotel and was told she was not in. He left her a note explaining he was going to his house in Georgia for a few days, then considered to write that he hoped to find some comfort in being at his childhood home, in caring for his horses and the farm, and hoped to find some peace in walking in the woods. Then he felt it was not appropriate to write those feelings on a card, which was followed by an odd sensation. Perhaps those feelings were not to be shared with *her*. If not Helen, with whom could he share his life?

He rode Charger to his home in Georgia, dismounted and took Charger in the barn, then went to the stables. He moved from stall to stall, and stroked and patted each individual one by one. Tommy Lonegran had done a good job feeding and grooming them while he was gone, stopping by twice a day, and had exercised them regularly. Tommy had also patched a few weathered shingles in places where a gap had developed in the barn then he noticed a nail stuck out about one-eighth of an inch and made a mental note to tell Tommy the importance of hammering a nail flush so a horse would not cut itself on it.

A wolf howled from the hills above the farm then paused for a very long moment, waiting for a response. There was none. Then it howled again, a solitary hunter.

When he returned to Charger, tethered just inside the barn, the white stallion whinnied and stomped his right forefoot. He poured fresh oats into Charger's wooden bucket, pulled a carrot from his pocket and fed him from his palm. He patted Charger's front quarters, rubbed his neck, and his head bobbed down then up and he whinnied again. "It's good to be home, hey?"

He cradled Charger's neck against his body. He and Charger were one and the ease of their comfort made him realize how discordant he and Helen were. While he groomed Charger he thought, What was the worst part of Helen and his marriage? Her infidelity. And what was the best of Helen? What could be the best of any wife? That she loved him so much she could not stand to be away from him? And wanted to be the mother of their children? Both of these thoughts were untrue. The more he thought about it, the more it gave him a headache. He knew deep down, she did not love him with all her heart. She was *not* overwhelmed to be apart from him.

He considered walking up to the clearing to visit his mother's grave but decided he wanted to be away from the farm. He wanted to go where people would *not* know him, or know of his father, or his Aunt, where he could be anonymous with lots of distractions and crowds of unfamiliar people.

Tommy Lonegran arrived and he pointed out the protruding nail, gave Tommy 20 dollars, and arranged for him to continue caring for the horses and to exercise them regularly. Then he rode Charger back to Burlington, lodged Charger in Peck's Livery, gathered a few belongings from their house on Elm Street and took the overnight train for New York City.

The following morning, he awoke with the train approaching New York City with its many buildings and stately homes of red or white brick with high, peaked roofs. The train arrived at the huge depot and lurched to a stop. The passengers stretched then emptied out into a fever of activity in the city. He lit the stump of a cigar, picked up his one leather bag and melded into the vibrant energy of the people, each moving with purpose. Through the teeming crowd he spotted a line of horse-drawn taxis but decided to walk and moved out of the depot into the turmoil, alone and unrecognized.

The streets were filled with people. They hustled about, vendors hawked their goods of colorful fruit or vegetables, or services of shoe repair or knife sharpening. There was a vast variety of people of all colors who spoke assorted languages and went about their business with little regard for him. Wagons bustled by. On Broadway avenue a line of fishermen hawked their fresh catch on beds of crushed ice, which gave a pungent smell of the salty sea. A seller sang, “Here’s your fine clams/As white as snow/On Rockaway these clams do grow!”

He puffed the short cigar, continued walking then realized no one had said anything to him, not even “Good day!” A moment later he bumped into a rough-looking man, whose coat swung open. He saw both a knife and a knobbed stick in his belt. A recent, terrible scar ran across the man’s forehead and he scowled. Neither of them spoke but his adrenalin ran hot and he was ready to fight. Then the other man walked away. How did that happen? he thought. Why would he instantly be mixed into a fight with a complete stranger? He shook his head then continued down Broadway avenue.

Flocks of geese waddled on the broad street along with cows and pigs, all making their muddy wallows on the avenue. Saloons and brothels were abundant with several on every block. A well-dressed gentleman invited him to enter a building to play faro, behind curtained windows, or any game of chance he wished to wager playing.

Pairs of policemen walked through the rowdiness, taking coins from merchants as payment for protection. They appeared more interested in receiving money than stopping crime and some of the grizzled policemen appeared as shifty as the hoodlums. Cranston, his barber friend, had told him he had read an article that stated 14 uniformed policemen worked in the city. The article also said companies of firemen were controlled by gangs of thugs so fires often raged out of control, accompanied by brawls, confusion, and mayhem.

He recalled the Vermonters' chaplain, Father Lucius Dickinson had said every winter a bevy of pretty girls came for the festivities of the season and although New York had its share of churches, orphanages, and an active Young Men's Christian Association, it was known as a dark place where weak-minded bachelors were exposed to the temptation of saloons, gambling halls, and "light" women. Father Dickinson said, "The very existence of hotel life is proof of the city's immorality!"

He followed the recommendation of his friend Cranston and checked into Molly's Moon Star Inn, where a middle-aged woman with very broad hips mopped the entry room. "Watch where you step!"

"Oh," he moved to the dry side of the room. "I'd like a room."

"Sure. Take any one you like upstairs. How long will you be staying?"

"Um-m," he thought of how much time he had and when he might see Helen again, and regretted the thought. "I don't know. Three nights, maybe more."

"That's fine," she gave the same broad smile Cranston had with a dimple in her chin and a crooked eye tooth. "Let me know which room ya like. Make yer self comfortable."

"Thanks. By the way, Cranston Selzer sent me."

"Cranston who?"

There was an awkward moment of silence. "I'm joshing ya! I'm Molly. Cranston's my nephew. He's a good lad. Too bad about his eyesight tho', otherwise he'd be helping our boys."

"What's wrong with his eyes?"

Molly made a sad, clucking sound. "Cranston was kicked by a horse when he was a lad. Sometimes his eyesight is fuzzy, that's what he says, but I think it's always bad."

"I didn't know," he said. "Why doesn't he get glasses?"

"Oh, he's been to every eye doctor in New England," Molly said with a downward wave of her hand. "They can't fix his kind of fuzzy. Yep. If a bear was charging 'im, he couldn't shoot straight to save his life!"

"Hunh." He thought of how bad Cranston's eyesight must be but recalled many fine haircuts and shaves, and reasoned his eyesight must be poor at distance, which explained why Cranston hadn't enlisted. "I'll take a room in the back. I don't want to be disturbed."

"Suit yer self. Make yer self at home. After I finish mopping, I'll make you some lunch if you like."

"No, I'm fine, thanks."

"There's apple pie on the dining table, back this a-way."

"No, thank you, although I appreciate your kindness." He headed for the staircase but Molly called out, "Can you sign the book, sir? It's not that I don't trust you, it's the city. It's a big place. Even for friends of me Uncle Cranston's."

He felt embarrassed for forgetting his manners. "I'm George Stannard," he said, reached out over the wet floor and shook her hand. "It's a real pleasure to meet you."

"Molly Selzer." She had a firm grip, damp from mopping, and her thin brown hair was pulled back into a braid. "Sorry 'bout the wet hand."

"It's okay." He turned, signed the book on a small desk by the front door then went upstairs to a room in the back. It had a single bed, a small stove in the corner and a porcelain tub against the opposite wall. Although small, the room was very clean as Cranston promised. He eased off his boots, sat on the bed and wondered when he would see Helen again.

In the late morning after chatting with Molly, he decided to see some of the sites she suggested. He visited St. Paul's, the docks at the South Street Seaport and Cooper Union where Mr. Lincoln had given a rousing speech to begin his campaign for president.

Molly also gave him the address of a "meeting house" where he should visit a friend of hers, John Jacob. The address was a three-story building with four large pillars in front, a pyramid-shaped roof and a compass frieze above the doorway he recognized as the Free Mason's symbol. Two businessmen in top hats went inside. He watched for a moment then went up to the doorway but before he knocked the door opened and a short butler in full, formal attire bowed and said stiffly, "Yes?"

"Miss Molly Selzer suggested I visit her friend John Jacob. Is he in?"

"Yes, he's in the parlor to the right." The short butler waved him in but raised his hand to stop then spoke with an annoyed tone, "Would you like a tie, sir?"

He felt embarrassed of his clothes. Because he was still on leave, he wore a comfortable white shirt, dark pants and black coat, all underneath his heavy woolen Army coat. His floppy felt hat was comfortable but he was not dressed for a business-type meeting. "I'm sorry, I didn't expect I would need a tie. I'm walking about."

"You didn't expect it?" The butler harrumphed in a condescending tone. "What sort of people do you suppose come here?"

He did not respond but wondered, How in the hell should I know? The butler reached his smallish hand into his front pocket, produced a black bow tie, and pointed to a mirror in the hallway. "*You*. . . may tie it over there."

He took off his hat and coat, hung them on a rack near the door then stood in front of the mirror. He shook his head in mild agitation and thought, Who are these people?

As he made a tie knot he thought of dressing for the theatre with Helen and wondered, Where is she at this very moment? He patted down his hair, wet his hand, patted it down again and proceeded into parlor on the right.

The room was thick with cigar smoke, men lounged in chairs, sat at a card table conversing, stood in groups around marble-topped tables near the windows and peered out at the bustling avenue. Their conversations were not about the war, which surprised him but about business companies, new inventions, and ships sailing into port with various cargoes of goods. This had surprised him because the Masons hc knew were businessmen but they discussed freedom and liberty. This room was filled with discussions of commerce and in every conversation a profit was a wink away.

Two servants with dark black skin wiped tables, ran silver trays of food from the back kitchen, stoked the snapping fireplace, emptied shiny brass spittoons, and wiped the tables again. Unlike the immaculate butler, they wore simple but well-worn dark pants and white shirts. Their discomfort and downcast gaze made him feel uneasy and he wanted to leave. Then a tall man with a very large, bulbous nose grabbed him by the forearm. “I’m John Jacob. I understand you’re looking for me.”

He nodded and tried to free his arm but Jacob held on, shaking his hand limply and searching for some hidden meaning. After their handshake, somehow he had failed at something already, Jacob asked, “Who sent you?”

“Molly Selzer. I’m George Stannard.”

“Oh,” Jacob renewed his handshake. “Pleasure to meet you.” He took a step back and studied him. “Are you the Stannard who was at Harpers Ferry? The Vermonter?”

“Yes. We had more fight than what was written in the papers.”

“Yes, I know,” Jacob said. “A friend, Josh Logan, gave me a full account.”

“Logan. From Middlebury?”

"Yes, that's the one. My nephew married his sister. Good lad."

"One of the best," he said and thought of Logan, quick, nimble, a sharpshooter.

"You deserve a medal, not the scourge the newspapers so wrongly encourage!" Jacob had a look of disgust on his face.

He thought of Colonel Miles and his drug-filled idleness. "The whole encampment was a difficult situation, from the start."

"Difficult *hell!* You were about to cross over the bridge when that coward General Miles called you back. And what happened to him, anyway? Dead. Good riddance, the traitorous bastard!"

He recalled the very moment they stood at the pontoon bridge and received General Jackson's threat, still vivid in his memory. He said, "It was General White's order. Miles was dead by then. I couldn't disobey an order or leave in good conscience if something were to happen to our boys at the fort."

Jacob's black suit was neatly pressed and he stroked his right hand over his vest. "Jackson wouldn't have harmed those men. If you would have continued on to Antietam, why, that would have made all the difference!"

"I couldn't take that chance. I met General Jackson later, God rest his soul. He was crazier than a tick. He may—"

"We know whose side Miles was on!" Jacob interrupted. "Miles was the Benedict Arnold of modern times. The traitorous bastard!"

He found himself surrounded by a dozen men in suits, listening and agreeing with every word Jacob said and bobbing their heads like pigeons in the city square. The blue smoke from their cigars hung about the room and here and there a man puffed more. They reminded him of the ignorant generals who had their theories of who did what and why but were unwilling to listen or amend their "facts."

"So, now what?" Jacob said. His dark eyes searched for an answer.

He was lost by the question and replied, "Now what. . . what?"

Jacob plumped the underside of a white carnation in his lapel. "Your business. What will you invest yourself in *now?*"

"I'm in the service. I'm committed to seeing this war end."

Some said, "Here! Here!" but many of the men harrumphed, shrugged and shuffled away, disappointed the ending of the story held no moral or no pot of gold to be had. What did all those deaths mean?

Jacob continued, "You're not investing in, what, maple syrup or whatever it is you have in Vermont?"

"No."

"Timber?"

"No."

Jacob nodded slowly then turned to the few men standing around the mahogany-paneled room, noticed a stout man with a pocked face nearby and said, "Let me introduce you to Mayor Opdyke."

They shook hands. The Mayor of New York was very enthusiastic and said, “Please! Call me George.”

“My name’s George, too.”

“How ‘bout that! Always good to meet a war hero, um, veteran. War veteran! We’ll finish them off this spring, don’t you agree?”

“We’ll do our best.”

“On to Richmond!” the Mayor chirped.

He could see the benefit of this Masons group, bringing together men of commerce and politics, but he thought there would be more discussion of freedom and liberty. He was tired of war talk with those who had never been in battle and the heavy cigar smoke bothered his eyes. He shook hands with Jacob again and excused himself, undid his tie in the hallway and handed it to the butler without a word, swung on his coat, grabbed his felt hat and went out into the bright daylight.

He walked down the cobblestone street, enjoyed the sharp, cool air and thought of those businessmen who searched for an inside track to profit despite the war. Then he saw a grizzled, heavy-set man approaching him with two dark-skinned men in chains and leg irons pulled behind him. It reminded him slaves were still traded in New York and in Washington City. It was still a thriving business. The tall grizzled man stopped with his cargo near the steps of the Mason’s building, waiting for someone to come out and complete this transaction. Then he was startled by someone grabbing his shoulders from behind and shaking him vigorously, shouting, "*Hey there! George Stannard!*"

He turned to see Billy Caldwell! His dark eyes glistened and his white teeth shined in his broad smile. Despite the mild spring air he wore a thick, black bear fur coat and beaver skin hat. He reached out to shake hands but Billy gave him a big bear hug. Billy's skin normally had a reddish-bronze glow but now he appeared sallow, lighter from the gray of winter, so he asked, "Are you okay? You look a little pale."

"Not as pale as you, my friend!"

He laughed then tried to explain himself. "No you look, um, paler."

Billy laughed again. "Oh no! I'm turning into a white man!" He laughed heartily and hugged him again. "How are you? I read you were at Harpers Ferry."

"The epitome of incompetence," he shook his head. "It's a long story. I'm sorry but have you heard about Dr. Côté?"

Billy's happy face fell sad. "Yes. I'm very sorry, my friend. Come let's talk."

They walked to the nearest pub, a place called Helmut's Tavern. He opened the plank door, smelled a rush of fragrant food and heard a roar of cheerful voices. The tavern was one large room with two blazing fireplaces, to the left and right with a bar across the back. The smell of smoked goose, sauerkraut and fresh ale hung in the air. They sat at a long table with eight other men, ordered shepherd's pie from the very heavy, pug-faced bartender with ale for George and hot tea for Billy.

Because they were good friends, they fell into an easy conversation and it seemed no time had passed since they last met. He spoke at length of the wonderful spirit of Dr. Côté and Billy shared several long stories of his own. Then he shifted the conversation to his horrible experiences in the war. His voice was filled with bitterness, describing the awful leadership he had witnessed from the opening battle at Bull Run to the ineptitude of various commanders of the Union Army the past two years, to the recent debacle at Harpers Ferry. Several of the tavern patrons listened and nodded in agreement while a few others at the far end of the table laughed at their own tales. He finished his rant and said, "Colonel Miles was the worst, most incompetent leader I have ever known."

Billy nodded with pursed lips and reflected while nearby patrons watched and listened as the fireplace crackled warmly. Then Billy spoke solemnly, "It is clear the Union Army is losing. Men who have never been in battle are running the war. Many officers are political appointments. Everyone wants to be a hero but many of these generals do not know the first thing about how to shape a boy into a soldier, or how to move troops in the heat of battle, which, as you know my friend, is what war is about. Their ignorance has cost *thousands* of young men's lives!"

Just then the hefty bartender chased a small pig across the sawdust floor. It squealed to the amusement of the patrons and many laughed and watched the squeaking piglet cut left then scoot right and evade the bartender's short reach. Then the bartender dove to the floor and rose with one leg of the shrieking piglet in his triumphant grasp and the patrons responded with applause and sarcastic huzzahs.

Billy continued in a solemn tone, "Yes, I too have had enough of this war. I am going West to Min-ne-so-ta, where my people are fighting for their land. I can help unite them. Do you understand? I can help *my* people there."

He nodded. To Billy, this Civil War was yet another foreign war led by butcherous incompetents. Billy made it clear he still believed in the principles of freedom and equality but he also believed he must help his *own* people. Then Billy asked about Helen and her health, "Why aren't you home with her now?"

He used his fork to push aside what was left of his shepherd's pie and shrugged. "It's been difficult. My marriage is not what I expected."

Billy nodded seriously and again weighed his words before he spoke, "A good woman is not easy. You want her to be a good worker, smart, beautiful, agreeable. I thought you did well, so this news is disappointing. Do you want to talk more, or do you know what to do?"

"She ain't exactly a good worker!" He chuckled and shrugged again. "I've thought about it. I've thought about it so much my head hurts!"

Billy grinned. "I know you always give your best. Let me tell you what my father told me, which is the way of our ancestors. When in doubt, do the loving thing. Take loving action."

He reflected. "I wish I had met your father. He was a wise man. Tell me, why aren't you married yet?"

Billy burst into laughter. "What? Can't you see the hog's ring in my nose?" He laughed again and slapped the table, which made their mugs jump. "The fact is I *am* married, my friend!"

"What! Why, that's wonderful!" he shouted then held up his mug of ale and toasted, "To a long and healthy marriage! Hurrah!"

"Thank you," Billy smiled, drank his tea and smiled again. "Her name is Two Blackbirds. She is Chippewa and that is part of why I am going to Min-ne-so-ta. Her family is there."

"That's perfect!" He chuckled then said, "You've found your 'Bluebird of Happiness' in Two Blackbirds!" Billy laughed warmly with him.

They talked for hours, long into the night, about Helen and marriage, more about Two Blackbirds, about home life, more about the war, and about Dr. Côté and his cheerful, courageous spirit. When it came time to part, they walked outside the tavern into the brisk cool air of dawn. He wished Billy well on his trip to Minnesota, congratulated him again on his marriage to Two Blackbirds and asked him to please be in touch with a letter from Minnesota and, if possible, to visit him after the war. He said, "You're always welcome in my home."

"You and I," Billy hugged him strongly, then parted but held him at arms' length and stared hard with his dark, raven-like eyes. "We are brothers for life! I *will* see you again. Together we will laugh and tell the old stories. I *will* see you later!"

~28 ~

New York City was the most fantastic place he had ever been. The streets came alive with vendors at dawn's first light and people milled about from diverse places like Spain, Cuba, China, Greece and India, with large groups of Irish, Africans, English and Dutch. Very rich people rode in finely painted carriages, lived in mansions on Fifth Avenue with servants but it also held poor immigrants where three families, a dozen or more people, crammed into a one-room shack.

Walking down a cobblestone street he smelled food cooking with lots of curry, seafood with potatoes boiling, leeks and rice, and saw men in tall hats or bowlers with Hasidic hair curls and bald Buddhist monks. Because he wore his colonel's uniform, he was sometimes saluted by other soldiers, boys, young men and was offered plum pie, rice pudding from an innkeeper, a fresh one-sheet of news from a paperboy and a tall beer from a bar wench standing in a doorway. So many things were offered that he had a unique sensation. He wanted to give back. He thought, What have I done in my life for the elderly? The sick or wounded? He had taught school children in his county but he also received some pay. What else had he given?

Then he rounded the corner to the Colored Children's Orphanage on Fifth Avenue, a tall stone-and-brick building of three stories with a black-painted iron fence around it. A number of African American children played in the courtyard and a middle-aged white priest with a big belly and a walrus-shaped mustache watched over them. He was the only white person in sight. Two African American nuns stood near the entry gate.

"Hello!" he called out.

The two African American nuns looked over then the large white priest shuffled to the gate and spoke with a raspy Irish brogue, "G' day! May I help you?"

He smiled but noticed one nun observed his uniform then crossed herself. He pressed on, "I'd like to help you. Is there some work you need done?"

"We cannot pay fer odd jobs, sir." The priest wore a traditional black robe with a white collar and pointed to a hand-painted sign near the gate that read, No Work !

"I am not asking for pay."

"Food neither. It's been a difficult month. We don't have 'nough for three squares for th' childrens. Got two more this week, one's a babe."

"No, no, sir. I'm here to help you. Do you need any horse grooming or any help with the children?"

The Father squinted, patted his side, and spoke directly, "We don't have any horses but these kids all need adopting. D'ya have a good home?"

"I do but I live in Vermont. And I'm not looking to adopt a child. I simply want to help. Maybe do some odd jobs or help take care of the children for a day?"

One of the nuns glanced upward and said, "Thank heaven. May I speak, Father?"

"Ycs, of ca'rse Sister Margar't."

This nun had a long scar twisting across her face near her right pale-gray eyes. The scar ran over her cheek and creased by her mouth, perhaps the result of some dreadful accident or fire. "May I suggest tha colonel help feed tha babies in tha kitchen, so's Sister Catherine can watch tha older childrens, or t'other way 'round?"

The Father stroked his long walrus-like mustache and nodded, "Sounds parf'ct! I'm Father Kelly. What da ya think, Colonel—?"

"George Stannard," he shook Father Kelly's hand. "I've seen a few Negroes before but I've wanted to ask. . . "

Father Kelly took out his pocket watch, checked the time, and said, "Yes?"

"Do they do anything differently from you or me?" The far nun spat on the ground, causing the one with the scarred face to walk over, shove her then cross herself.

"Why yes!" Father Kelly said with a wry grin. "Each one's a person, just like you or me. Some eat with thar left hand or thar right, or both! Or use a fark! Each is different and complex, just like any other person."

"No, I meant, well, their functions. Their hearts and minds, their desires. Or do they simply sing and dance, or act as servants?"

Father Kelly assumed a stern face, which reminded him of Pastor Keyes about to launch into a sermon. "Ay. Some folks say the hand of the Almighty has carsed 'em and put them in thar place. No, I say. This is man's doing, not God's. Shakespeare wrote, 'If you prack me, do I not bleed? If you slight me, do I not carse?' Ay, they're human. God gave 'em dark skin but the rest be the same. These kiddies is baptized by me right off. Then thar taught scripture until we find homes for 'em. Problem is, who wants a little black child? Once in a while a colared fam'ly will take one or some rich man on Fifth Avenue gives 'em a home and once in a blue moon by the grace of God an average white family takes two or more. Most of 'em stays here. It's not an easy life but I've made certain they'll get into heaven. Thar's no doubt in me mind on that score."

He was embarrassed. "I'll stay as long as I can today. I'll do what I can."

They had just finished feeding the babies so he started by taking a warm, wet cloth with mild soap and tenderly washed the larger children's faces and hands. He cleaned each in the long line then noticed a bright-eyed girl with pigtails smiling, showing a missing front tooth, who rejoined the end of the line. When she came to the front again, he acted surprised and confused then gave her a hug. She hugged him back and wouldn't let go. Then she took him by the hand, he dropped the washcloth, and she led him to a playroom where eight more girls sat on the floor.

Sister Margaret, the nun with a scar from her light gray eyes to her mouth, followed a moment later and watched over them. He sat on the wooden floor, the children played jacks and the cute girl with braided pigtails said, "Sir, my name is Dorothy. Everyone calls me Dottie. You needs to play wit' us."

He grinned and took the ball from her small hand. Dottie sat down, gave a broadening smile and waited for him to begin. He noticed this, made a serious face of concentration then bounced the ball and scooped up a single jack. "*One!*"

He looked around, pretending everything in the world depended on his next move, to each of the nine girls, then up at Sister Margaret. He bounced the ball and scooped up two metal jacks. "*Two!*" he said solemnly and again looked around. The girls giggled so he stared at them sternly, raised one eyebrow then the other, then raised each eyebrow back-and-forth and all the girls laughed and laughed, and Sister Margaret chuckled. He waited until they settled then bounced the ball higher and tried scooping the jacks only to send them flying in assorted directions. "Three-e-e ha-ha-*ha!*"

They all laughed, including Sister Margaret. Dottie demanded he try again and all the girls joined in screams of delight. He again played with grave seriousness and scattered the jacks on three then laughed with them for a long time and rolled over on the floor in a fit of laughter. Dottie leaped onto his chest and all the girls piled onto him playfully. They laughed together for a very, very long time, much longer than called for. It was unexpected but he felt very, very happy.

~29 ~

For two weeks he helped at the Colored Children's Orphanage and developed a growing realization he wanted children of his own. He loved each of them for their own unique qualities. Each was delightful and wonderful in their own manner, even if some were very quiet, or a bit ornery. It became clear to him he wanted to start a family with Helen. Although he was in New York to avoid being with her, he had a growing, overwhelming feeling he must return to her. He wondered, How could he charge into a hailstorm of Rebel bullets but he preferred to avoid her now? It was because he knew it would be disappointing and painful. He also knew it would be better to work things out as soon as possible. He said his goodbyes to Father Kelly, Sisters Margaret and Catherine, the children and especially Dottie then to Molly Selzer at the Inn, and made his way back to Burlington.

It was early March and now he felt pressured by time, knowing the Army would call him back soon. He had thought about their marriage for a long time and decided he had taken a vow of marriage and he would do his best to live up to his vow despite any and all problems. He would also take Billy Caldwell's advice to "do the loving thing," and would start by romancing Helen again.

In Burlington he called on Helen at the Wilson Hotel. A bellhop was sent up to fetch Helen and this time she came down the narrow staircase in a bright yellow dress, showing off her curly dark hair. Descending the staircase her dazzling blue eyes looked about the lobby anxiously with a joyful smile across her full lips. Then when she saw him her smile faded. He noticed her disappointment but pressed on and said, "You look lovely," and reached out to hold her hands but she kept them by her side.

They spoke awkwardly about each other's health then the weather, which caused him to chuckle, recalling his comments to

Hazel about the cows when he had first seen Helen. Then he asked, "May I take you for an early dinner and a night out on the town?"

Helen looked down, then away and paused a long moment. She said softly, "Yes."

Although Helen was reserved and their conversation brief and filled with awkward silences, he was thrilled. His heart raced with anticipation and renewed hope.

She asked, "Should I wear a gown for dancing or formal attire for an event, such as a night at the opera?"

"The latter, more formal attire," he said.

"Should I wear something appropriate to be seen in public such as at a fine inn for dinner, or something more comfortable for a carriage ride about town?"

"Formal dinner attire." He felt she had read his mind and thought perhaps the events they enjoyed together had become routine and predictable.

At 5 p.m. he hitched Charger to his carriage then picked up Helen at her hotel, where she had changed into a beautiful silk dress the color of robin's egg blue, accentuating her stunning, glistening eyes. She also wore a white fur cape and white fur muffler. She was so incredibly beautiful that he caught his breath. Somehow he had forgotten how beautiful she was! He was startled, jumped into action and took them to McSorley's Inn, a richly decorated restaurant with the finest English china and the best chef in the area, a man who had once been chef to the Duke of Saxony before he came to Vermont. Although it was late afternoon, the inn was romantically lit by dozens of candles and a staff of attendants saw to their every need for wine or fresh-baked bread and served them a delicious meal of oysters, lake trout, potatoes in cream sauce with onions and a chenin blanc wine from Loire.

They had a pleasant conversation although Helen remained aloof to his efforts. At the end of the meal, after another long silence, she said, "McSorley's is charming but I was here last month with Magnus Loblolly. He's a tycoon. He made his fortune from textiles. We dined on precisely this same meal with these exact same servants."

He reflected on this unfortunate repetition then spoke bluntly, "I'm different. I'm also your husband."

It was unusually warm for March. After dinner he drove their carriage for a leisurely ride over the broad brick avenues of Burlington, from the university to the lake shore then eased back on Charger and stopped the carriage on a windswept, sunny hill, shimmering in the late afternoon sunlight with beech, poplar and pine trees overlooking Lake Champlain. The sun was just setting over the lake, a rising crescent moon glowed and bright-white Venus shone brilliantly. It was stunningly beautiful.

"We're alone," he said softly, turned and gazed into her bright blue eyes. Then he spoke from his heart, "We're in this beautiful, incredible world together, you and I. No matter what, I am devoted to you and I intend to make our marriage work despite our differences in taste, despite our distance apart due to the war."

She reacted to his quiet speech with a display of her fan, fluttered it over her full bosom then licked her lips. Then she raised the fan over most of her face, showing only her captivating blue eyes, and said, “As your wife, I am of course available to you.”

He moved slowly and she closed the fan, then he tenderly embraced her. After a moment she eased away and pointed the fan at him then added, “*Of course,* you must also realize the Countess Bokowski *must* attend certain functions as required of someone of my station.”

He was stunned and furious. Her reaction was for her social position rather than their marriage. Then he realized it would not benefit them to be angry and he let this fade. He knew at her core, she would always be who she was. He could not change her desire for the social spotlight and he did not want to do this, knowing this was for the best. He thought, Perhaps they were making progress in resolving their differences, then offered, “I will do my best to enable you to be the star of social functions and I will attend as many as possible together.”

Venus, the evening star, rose higher and shone brighter. Other stars appeared, twinkling in the purplish dark-blue sky then a gorgeous blaze illuminated the darkness as a falling star streaked across the horizon. Helen cried, “Oh! Make a wish!”

He smiled softly, stared into her beautiful eyes, and said, “It’s already been made. To love you forever and raise a family together.”

She rapped her fan on his upper arm. “That’s two things! And you’re not supposed to say them *aloud!*” She closed her eyes and prayed, and he moved very close to her so when she opened her bright blue eyes he was very close to her face. She looked into his soft blue eyes, put her hand behind his neck and drew him closer then kissed him passionately but then broke away.

He was deeply in love with her again. He tenderly touched her dark hair, caressed it around her temples and whispered, "Tell me your wish."

She again playfully smacked his shoulder with her fan. Then she reached out and smacked Charger's hindquarters and said, "Drive!" and Charger lurched, the carriage took off with a start, and he gathered the reins.

He had bought tickets with a plan to go to the opera but now thought perhaps they should return home, at this moment, to make romance together. Helen used her fan to stroke his jaw line then teased his lips. She raised her eyebrows and said coyly, "I know what you want."

They rode on in silence. He decided, yes, now is the moment! Then he spoke passionately, "Let's go home."

"Oh, no! That's it?" she said. "Why did I wear one of my best gowns?"

She hoisted the robin's egg blue silk of the dress and fluffed it out with a huff. "I thought we were going out tonight! Don't tell me you planned dinner and a quick retreat to our house?"

"No, I have tickets to the opera."

"Oh, wonderful!" she cried. "I've been anxious to attend and I prayed that's where we were going!" She bounced on the seat, tugged at his arm and pulled him closer, and whispered, "We'll go to the opera and we'll have a very romantic night *later.*"

His eyes became teary with the thought. This was the beginning of their beautiful new life together and he wanted everything to go perfectly.

He drove Charger to the opera house and arrived to a growing crowd gathering around the front doors. Helen received many compliments of how beautiful "the Countess" was and he also overheard someone in a lowered voice say, "the Great Skedaddle," and "Surrendered!" It filled him with anger but he couldn't determine who had spoken. No one dared speak to his face. With all of the attention Helen received and people motioning at him, they were the most talked-about couple of the evening. It reminded him of their wedding day with elite society's foregone conclusion: She was much too beautiful, too important, to be with this dubious officer. They took their seats in a balcony box.

At intermission several men ignored him and gave their compliments to Helen. Others tipped their hat to him then said something to their colleague that again sounded like "surrendered," or "skedaddle." Women fluttered around Helen, admired her gown and pearl necklace, and gave glowing remarks about her diamond ring, her emerald rings, her dark curly hair or her oriental fan. Helen excused herself and took a moment to freshen up and Alyssa, Hazel and Beatrice followed her. Then Cranston approached him with an outstretched hand and spoke with enthusiasm, "George!"

Cranston's dark hair was slicked down but it had turned gray on the side. For the first time he noticed his slightly-off right eye, his eyes searching back and forth to find his bearings. George grasped Cranston's hand and shook it warmly, then heard another voice behind him say, "Quitter."

"Whatja say?" Cranston asked, smiling broadly with his eyes focusing on him.

"Good to see you, Cranston!" he said, then heard another lowered voice, again behind him and laced with disgust.

"Who in the hell is it? Speak to my face!" He turned to challenge everyone and each man looked away. Then a short, pudgy man in a tuxedo with a close-cropped beard said, "Seems you's taught 'em good."

Cranston grabbed George by the arm. "Calm down! These are the village idiots. They don't know anything about war, or what you've been through."

"I'm sorry. I'm a bit touchy on the subject."

"I've met calmer mountain lions!" Cranston chuckled then put his long arm around him and patted his back. "We know you done your best. You're a good man."

Cranston drew him closer and whispered, "I visioned it. I don't tell no one but sometimes I get visions. I seen you on the battlefield. You stood tall when others ran."

Cranston's eyes were slightly bloodshot. He was much taller and had a faint trace of rum on his breath. Then Cranston spoke in a normal voice, "Please don't tell no one 'bout my visions. I, I don't want to be known as a loony."

"No," he said. "What you said was pretty much spot on."

Cranston added, "I did read a lot of newspapers and my vision was later, after the battle. But my vision was diff'ernt than the papers. I don't tell no one 'bout my visions. Not even Allysa."

"I understand."

"The point being," Cranston squeezed his shoulder again and his dark eyes watered with intensity. "I know you're a good man. You wouldn't run."

"I saw plenty of good men running."

The short man said in a drunken voice, "Ya taugh' 'em how to run *goo-o-od.*"

He felt like flattening him with one punch but focused on Cranston's friendship, took his hand and shook it again. "Thank you for that, Cranston. I appreciate your kind words and faith in me."

"Ain't just me. Lookit all the soldiers who voted for you to lead them. I think they know a thing or two. Not these idiots 'round here."

"Thank you." He felt very good to have such a close friend.

The theater manager called out "End of intermission!" He thanked Cranston again and returned to his balcony seat. The lights dimmed. He sat alone in the box, looking over the crowd then noticed Alyssa cheerfully leading her husband Cranston to their box. They appeared to be very, very happy after two years of marriage. He saw Hazel with her new beau, Captain Baxter Isherwood of Shelburne in a spiffy new uniform, easing into their seats. Then he viewed Beatrice, floating into her box with her mother and aunt, and all wore the same color yellow dress made from the same bolt of cloth but adorned differently with red flowers or white feathers. The lights were extinguished and the opera began again. Helen had not returned.

It was some before Helen arrived to her seat and she was flushed. He did not know what to say although he felt hurt and curious. What had she been doing? Then he thought if he challenged her, it may compromise their plans for romance later. She raised her opera glasses, gazed down at the stage and was silent.

Then he noticed Helen glanced at him then returned to looking through the opera glasses. He could not watch the opera but observed Helen. After a moment a slight wrinkle of mischievousness accented her lips and she licked them. Then she raised her white-gloved hand and sniffed her gloves at some vague hint of cologne on leather. A thin smile came to her.

~30 ~

As warmer weather allowed the wheels of canons to become unstuck in the thawing mud, the generals leading the war effort planned their next offensive. He saddled Charger and returned to duty, and was promoted to brigadier general in the Army of the Potomac outside Washington City. A few key officers, Benedict, Ripley, and Veazey, re-enlisted along with recently promoted Corporal Hicks, who would be the flag bearer of the new 13th infantry regiment. This group of Vermonters, along with the 12th, 14th, 15th, and 16th regiments, was mainly composed of nine-month recruits. Because they were new and thought to be unable to maneuver or engage in a full-scale battle against the Rebels, along with the Vermonters' poor reputation, they were held in reserve. After two months in reserve duty with continuous military drilling ad nauseam, the Vermonters called their encampment Camp Boredom.

Despite the boredom the rites of spring were celebrated every payday with a continual flood of show people, comedians, singers, dancers, prizefighters, gamblers, vendors of obscene literature, and proprietors of rum-jug shops. They leached onto the outskirts of camp and sucked every available dollar from the soldiers. Also, a not so secret invasion of women arrived, gay light-o'-loves who swished in the impromptu music hall and on officers' arms, whores who beckoned soldiers to makeshift shanties in the muck on the edge of camp.

One Sunday morning George received an anonymous note, claiming dozens of Vermonters were seen at Martha's Inn, a pub near the center of Washington City. The actual wording was vague but implied officers and soldiers spent all their leisure time in this particular pub and returned to camp without their pay. They risked "the possibility of loss of men available for duty due to disease." He recalled Madame Turner's house in Burlington. Such establishments were often on the "other side" of the railroad tracks but in Washington they were on Pennsylvania Avenue and Second Street, and Louisiana Avenue and Sixteenth Street, mixed in with true hotels and inns.

At 4 a.m. a heated skirmish shattered the night. A band of 15 Confederate raiders dressed in plain clothes attacked the 3rd Pennsylvania Battery guarding eight cannons. In the darkness the Confederates walked a dozen draft horses, stealthily approached from behind the pickets through the sparse woods and tried to steal the cannons. The sentries faced the western approach with their backs to the big guns but the raiders came in the night on their right, the northern approach, through the sparse trees where the Potomac River curved around the battery to the eastern and southern approaches. Richard Ewing, a sentry from Harrisburg, was knocked unconscious with a heavy blow to the back of his head. Eldridge Faneuil, also from Harrisburg, was mortally wounded with a slashed jugular vein. As Corporal Faneuil collapsed and died he fired a warning shot, winging a raider and alerting the entire camp. In the ensuing firefight three Confederates were killed, including the leader of this ragtag band, and another eight Union soldiers were wounded before the raiders fled in the night, leaving behind two of their big horses that had reared up and escaped in fright.

The next morning a fine mist hung over the campground. After breakfast Captain Philip Parker of White River Junction asked to speak with George in his tent. Parker was 23 and educated at Dartmouth, with a shaven mustache waxed into curls at the end. He blushed often and fidgeted his hands but otherwise stood at attention.

"What is it?" he asked, turning over the note warning about Martha's Inn and loss due to disease.

"I'm concerned, well, it's about last night," Parker began.

"Yes, our boys need to be more alert." He set down his pen and rested his hands on the small folding desk. "We're at war."

"Yes. There's more to it, sir," Parker mumbled, unsure where to begin.

"Spill it, captain," he said, wondering what Parker might know about the raid on the Pennsylvania batteries. He was inclined to call in Benedict, who had announced Parker and left, or to call guards in case something dangerous escalated. Parker's demeanor was more his embarrassment than threatening.

"You see, I um, I spent an evening of leisure with Miss Duvall last Saturday night. After payday."

"Yes," he said and thought, Maybe this is unrelated. He had a regular stream of shy, backwoods boys who had lost their virginity followed by the consequential guilt over a girl back home, which resulted in the young man's "confessing" to him. Something was very different about Parker. He wasn't naïve despite his constant blushing and reluctance to talk. "What is it?"

"The fight last night, it was precisely at the spot where, um, well, it seems too much of a coincidence, doesn't it, sir?"

He sat upright in his chair, ran his hands over the folding table then smacked the top with his open right hand and rumpled a few pay requests. The morning sun baked the canvas tent, making the air stuffy. He wanted to open the flap, let in some fresh air, but knew this discussion required some fortitude for Parker to come forward and also should remain private. "*What spot?*"

"The Third Penn-sy. I mentioned it was next to us, um, to Miss Duvall."

He stood and approached Captain Parker. They were about the same height but Parker was soft around the edges, flushed again, and a single bead of sweat trickled from his left temple. "You mentioned it?"

"I should start at the beginning," Parker said, "to explain."

"It better be a goddamn good explanation."

Parker shifted his weight back and forth, slowly swinging his arms then interlocked his fingers together. "Miss Duvall, I'd heard of her from some of the other boys so I was curious. It was after payday on Saturday night. I went to Delilah's Swing and she was everything as described and more. She has pale white skin and a beautiful face with dark curly hair and the most gorgeous, bright green eyes. She looked exactly like a beautiful, beautiful doll."

He mumbled out of exasperation and tried not to say anything derogatory.

Parker continued, "For some reason, I had to show her how important I was. You see just before I went to her room I saw a politician. I'd seen his engraving picture in the paper, he's a senator or something. So I felt I had to impress her."

"Go on."

"So I went to her room. It stank of semen and smoke and sweat, old carpet and cheap French perfume. I was getting nauseous and I didn't know it was timed, you know. Sometimes I can talk for a spell. But I wanted to know her first, you understand, because it's only right. I realize now Miss Duvall did not say a word until she said, 'Time's up!' and she already had my money! I was still in uniform and while I chatted she done this little dance. She was nearly naked but then she said, 'Time's up!' and she turned on the edge of the bed and began rolling up her stockings. She has the most beautiful, long legs. She buttoned one stocking to a garter with a clip then rolled up the other. It was mesmerizing. She ran her hands up her stockings, showing off her slender legs. Then she stood and turned to me, I was seated in a tufted chair, so her sweet-smelling. . . flesh was no more than inches from my face."

The captain stopped then looked around the tent. All was still. George went to the closed flap, listened for the guard outside and said, "What did you do? What else?"

"This next part is difficult, sir."

The captain was reluctant so he raised his voice, "Corporal Faneuil is *dead* and eight more wounded! Three Confederate men were killed and I need to know *why* you're standing here, *goddamnit!*"

A tear slipped from Parker's left eye and he continued, "She said, 'Don't you care about me, Phil?' She had such pretty green eyes and her skin was very white and soft, and then she lay back on several pillows on the bed. I think I would have done just about anything to be with her, sir. She said, 'Honestly, Phil, I have other affairs, you know that.' I thought about that politician fella and I wanted to be more important than him. She asked me to show her, show her how important I was in the Army by drawing a map. And I did. I drew a map of us and the Pennsy batteries and, and all."

He scratched the back of his neck. "Good Lord."

"Miss Duvall kissed my cheek and said *I* was special. Then she kissed my ear and twirled my mustache. Then with her other hand she stroked my manhood. Well, I grabbed her by the waist and had my way with her. She made these lovely purring moans. Then she swung up and rocked steadily, um, in the saddle, in even galloping strokes with her bright, sweet smile and she moaned right next to my face, into my ear, and I had the most incredible, wonderful feeling I've ever felt."

He felt frustrated by the betrayal of Captain Parker and saddened for his deteriorated relationship with Helen. Growing anger filled him, fueled by the raid that resulted in four deaths with many wounded. How would *he* account for all that?

"At that glorious moment," Parker said, "Miss Duvall *laughed* like somethin' was funny. She said it was my conviction in the words 'I love you,' you know, right at that specific moment what caused her to laugh so hard. She slowed down, then stayed there and let me feel her warmth. She hugged me and it felt like *I* was the only man in the world. After a moment she slid off me and got dressed. She said, 'Philip, I'm so proud of you,' and she clasped the final button over her breasts. Then she sat at her dressing table and patted her cheeks with rouge. Miss Duvall smiled at me in the mirror, put on long white gloves and, and that was that."

He wanted to slap Parker but instead punched his right fist into his left hand, then said, “You drew a map of the exact location of our cannons? Where our men were?”

Parker flushed again and nodded. Another tear spilled over his reddened cheek.

He recalled the new group of security people who had been formed under the command of Allan Pinkerton. The initial purpose of this squad of agents was to protect the President in Washington, a Southern city, but they had evolved into investigating the passing of information from Union generals to Southern sympathizers. “I’m confident Mister Pinkerton and his detectives will want to speak with you and Miss Duvall. Return here at six p.m. Dismissed. *Benedict!*”

Parker stood still, staring at his polished boots then kicked at the straw on the ground. He said, “What is it?”

“Well. I believe such unions are sinful. Any man who engages in such will be damned to eternal Hell and—”

“You’ve done that.”

“Yes, I’m going to Hell. I do repent. But there are, ah, complications, sir.” The captain’s nervous hands fiddled with his gold wedding band.

“Yes, sir?” Benedict ducked into the stuffy tent, saluted then saw Parker fidgeting and somehow comprehended the privacy of the situation and stared straight ahead.

He paced, rolling his own band of gold around his finger and thought of Helen. What was she doing now and with whom? Then he focused his thoughts on this female spy, knowing Pinkerton and his agents would have great interest in this information and in locating Miss Duvall. "You're not the first person in this situation. But you betrayed the safety of your fellow soldiers. *That* is a sin! So now you'll do everything you can to help us. Is that understood? You'll find her and do whatever is needed to make her our prisoner. Do I make myself clear?"

"Sir, I, I still can't believe she's a spy. I—"

"*What!*"

"I think she's in love with me," Parker chuckled, an admission the situation was beyond his understanding. "Or maybe I, maybe I want to believe she loves me." He chuckled again then crouched into a squat and pounded his fists against his forehead, then succumbed to crying. "I'm a married man! I've ruined my life!"

Benedict looked down at the captain and George pulled up Parker by his armpits out of his squatting position. "You've made a mistake, Phillip. You'll take this lesson to heart, not repeat it, and be a better man for it."

Parker hugged him, crying in heaves into his shoulder. After a moment, he slowed down, sniffled, then drew a handkerchief from his pocket and dabbed his eyes. George looked into his wet, dark eyes. "You'll live, Parker. Some days you'll wish you had died, but you'll live."

"Will I be court marshaled?"

"Yes. First you'll help us catch this spy. Report back here at six! Dismissed."

At six o'clock that evening Captain Parker led George, Benedict, four privates, Sergeant Lloyd, and Detective Allan Pinkerton and six of his agents to Delilah's Swing. The pub was locked with a small note nailed to the red door:

CLOSED by ORDER of the MEDICAL BUREAU

Parker turned to Benedict and said, "Does this mean what I think it means?"

"Yes," Benedict stared hard at Parker from underneath his lieutenant's kepi and rested his thin hand on his shoulder. "You need a full physical examination."

George added, "By one of *our* medical doctors. See Doc Thayer." He had clarified this because even though the soldiers knew the self-acclaimed "doctors" hanging around the outskirts of camp were charlatans, who followed in the wake of loose women, they still went to them out of embarrassment. Those "doctors" were blatant liars, promising to deliver a permanent cure for gonorrhea in three days, syphilis in all its forms, and offered expensive vials of a cocaine-laced drinks or bottles of miraculous pills. Those quacks were gone the following morning with their pockets stuffed with greenbacks, leaving the fleeced boys praying for relief.

"Where else did you meet her?" Pinkerton said and caught everyone's attention. Pinkerton was tall with a bowler hat and wore a full dark suit and vest. "Miss Duvall. Where could she be?"

"I, I don't know," Parker stammered. "I only met her here once."

"Bullshit," Pinkerton said and spat a stream of tobacco juice from his puffy right cheek that splattered Parker's polished boots. "Dunston showed me a report. You've been with her, what is it?"

Dunston, a burly man about 30 years old with a thick brown beard, said, "Other soldiers reported Parker met her four times. Once here, twice at Carmen's House, and once at The Peach Inn. We believe she also works at The Wild Rose."

"So," Pinkerton said, then shoved Parker, "Should we hang you as a spy?"

"I'm sorry!" Parker blurted out. "I said I met her *here* once. It's embarrassing."

"*Shit!*" George spoke angrily, "You'll get the full wrath of the Army now. Tell us everything! Take us to her. *Now!*"

Parker walked down the avenue to another pub two blocks away. The Peach Inn was a rowdy tavern with soldiers and prostitutes spilling out onto the walkway. The outside walls were covered with penny sheets of playbills and three women leaned against the building with one or both breasts exposed, which was enough to have a group of soldiers, including a few Vermonters, gawk at them. One boy bragged of how the Vermonters were single-handedly going to win the war. Benedict recognized him and jerked him away by the sleeve. Sergeant Lloyd lashed into the group with loud, voracious fury. His pale Irish face reddened and he yelled, "*Private van der Hoff! What in God's name are you doing?!*"

Pinkerton shook his head with disgust then pushed Parker through the doorway and past a rough-looking doorman with a broken nose angled to the side and a Bowie knife in his belt. George and the other agents followed him inside. It smelled of spilled beer, vomit and unbridled sex. An older, toothless man sat in the corner and played a bouncy schottische on the accordion while a dog at his feet gnawed a ham hock bone. A dozen women in various states of undress paraded through the room while soldiers, from privates to generals, gaped in amazement. A few recognizable politicians wore suits and gazed at the women lasciviously.

Pinkerton grabbed Parker by his left elbow. “Which one? Where is she?”

Parker scanned the crowd of partiers. Some women were seated at tables, others stood around the room then he pointed to the end of the bar where Miss Duvall clung to an older gentleman in a dark gray suit and black tie. George recognized the man, who was a prominent Southern senator. Parker said, “That’s her but, but may I have a word with her first?”

“No, you may not!” Dunston said and shoved him out of the way. “Bullshit!”

Dunston and Pinkerton advanced to Miss Duvall, who was stunningly beautiful with dark hair, porcelain skin, and bright green eyes. Her hair showed her age, threaded with gray streaks. She saw Pinkerton in his bowler and gave him a large smile.

Pinkerton announced, “You are under arrest for treason and sedition, for aiding a hostile power with secret information during a time of war and—” Pinkerton turned to Dunston, “—what else?”

Dunston grimaced but spoke through clenched teeth under his brown beard, "We've got a list at the office. Who owns this smelly, pigshit place?"

Miss Duvall shifted her expression and spoke with wide-eyed innocence, "I don't believe I understand your remarks, suh. Secret information? Now I ask you, where would I get such information?"

"Huzzah!" said another well-dressed gentleman, who also wore a gray three-piece suit. He slumped over the bar with one eye swollen shut, smirked, swirled his cut-crystal tumbler of amber liquid and called out, "She spurns Northern scum!"

Pinkerton grabbed her wrist roughly and Duvall shrieked, causing a little girl to rush forward from behind the end of the bar. The little girl had dark brunette ringlets and pale skin, a small replica of Miss Duvall but the girl's white dress was torn and tattered.

Pinkerton spat tobacco juice on the floor, landing near spilled beer and vomit chunks. "We've got you in bed with half the generals of the Army of the Potomac!"

"Surely that's more of a he'p. I'm not *harmin'* anyone!" she cooed. Her cheap perfume could be smelled above the rank stench of the pub. She glanced over at her child then said, "Mommy's off to talk with these men fo' a spell."

George stepped between them and offered the girl a piece of hard candy.

"At your peril, suh, if you even *touch* my child!" Miss Duvall cursed then turned away. Her high cheekbones raised into a charming smile and she spoke with a grand flourish of her outstretched arm,

"God knows how many very, *very* important politicians have graced my table, enjoyed a drink, and relaxed under my care."

Pinkerton remained steadfast. "Your threats are no good. We have the blessing of the President himself *and* the leadership of the Army to arrest you. Take her away!"

Miss Duvall continued her righteous rant, "In these times of war, you ought to have more *important* business than to consult a lady on her affairs!"

Dunston pushed her caboose and she snaked around, faced him with venomous wrath then swung her fists and cursed, "Let me *be,* you damned Yankee!"

"You're off to jail," Dunston said with an even voice and used his pudgy hands to block her blows. "*If* you're lucky, for a very long time. But more 'n likely you'll hang."

"How dare you speak like this in front of my *child!*" She reached back for the youngster but Pinkerton shoved her toward the door and said, "You ain't the first spy to hang and you won't be the last."

Miss Duvall made her way to the door but casually removed a hairpin and several dark curls flowed out onto her shoulders along with a small, black velvet pouch that fell to the floorboards. George called out to Pinkerton, picked up the black pouch, loosened the drawstrings and took out a wadded parchment. He unraveled the paper while Pinkerton looked on. It was folded several times, a very large, detailed map of the Army of the Potomac and held the names of generals in charge of each corps, their regiments, and the placement of Union batteries. On the side was a listing of officers' names and ranks with notes beside them, "Loves A" or "Needs M first."

Pinkerton shook his head, refolded the map and tucked it inside his vest pocket.

Dunston hollered, "*Hey! Who owns this shitty place?*"

No one responded. A few men chuckled, drank, spat tobacco juice on the floor or continued their conversation with rowdy women.

George went outside and breathed in the fresh air. Benedict had bound the wrists of several Vermonters and Sergeant Lloyd held the rope in his large right hand like the reins of a six-team coach. He nodded to Benedict then motioned to Lloyd, who led the arrested soldiers, including Parker, back to camp.

Detective Pinkerton later thanked him for his assistance, described the additional evidence they found in Miss Duvall's room at Delilah's Swing including Captain Parker's map, a general's missing spurs, a quantity of opium, and a detailed drawing of a secret new weapon which was an ironclad ship being developed by the War Department. They also recovered several dispatches from Southern leaders to Miss Duvall in an easily deciphered code, thanking her on various dates for relaying the latest Federal Army's plans. The dates showed this had been going on since the beginning of the war.

Parker was court martialed and sent to prison in Montpelier, where his wife reconciled and visited him regularly. Parker was sentenced to serve time in jail for the duration of the war plus five years.

The Washington *Evening Star* newspaper had an article on Miss Duvall, calling her the "beautiful Rebel of Sixteenth Street." Matthew Brady took her photograph, which showed her resolute, handsome face with pursed lips of defiance. The article described the ample evidence the government had collected and claimed she was a "dangerous, skilled spy." It also romanticized her as a "fascinating female Rebel" with "almost irresistible seductive powers."

From her jail cell Miss Duvall ranted from morning to well past midnight, playing the role of an aristocratic lady persecuted by rabble. She used foul language unsuitable for the general public although reporters were mesmerized by her every action and every invective spouted. She shrieked at the sight of contrabands, cursed at every soldier in a blue uniform, and spat at anyone she deemed an "occupying enemy of Southern pride," including women, children, and the reporters themselves. Her behavior was deemed unfit for anyone to witness other than the most hardened and callus soldier. Still the reporters documented her every move during the trial and were stunned but pleased with her conviction as a spy. They continued to follow her, admiringly detailing her every move: "A squad of eight Federal soldiers in crisp blue uniforms led her into the prison courtyard, escorted her up the freshly built platform, slipped a black hood over her head that almost matched her new black dress, and hung her until her body was still."

~31 ~

Senator Randolph Kenndy was a smooth-talking politician from Maryland. Kenndy did not have a fiery reputation like Senator Sumner of South Carolina, who had caned the right-senator from Massachusetts over his speech against slavery, but Confederate President Jefferson Davis knew Kenndy was adept at negotiation behind closed doors, where a deal was quietly made to approve one item in exchange for concession on another item. Kenndy's skillful negotiation had made his reputation, which is why Davis selected him to deliver his secret plan for a peace settlement to President Lincoln.

Kenndy was six feet six inches tall and was not shy in using his height to stand over his counterpart or use forceful words to coerce a settlement. He wore fine clothes and polished spats.

It was a bitterly cold morning in early 1863 when Senator Kenndy was announced to President Lincoln. Kenndy had made the appointment two weeks in advance, so Lincoln knew it was of some importance to the senator. Kenndy arrived 15 minutes early for his 11 a.m. appointment and was somewhat surprised to see Lincoln's little boy, Tad, running through the White House on his stick horse. Kenndy stood and watched Tad racing around in circles, and with each pass he came closer to hitting a table with a tall oriental vase, which trembled on its narrow base. Tad looked up, noticed he was being watched, and made an even more spirited wild loop, bumped the table, and sent the vase flying for the floor. Kenndy leaped over and caught the vase in mid-air while President Lincoln entered with his calm, gangly walk.

"That's from China," the President said in his deep, raspy voice. "Ming or Ching Dynasty," he laughed. "I get them confused."

Kenndy grinned, "Your boy almost made it the Broken Dynasty! He ought to be kept on a leash!"

Lincoln smiled, affectionately rubbed Tad's dark hair and gave him a hug. Tad huffed then squirmed in anticipation of returning to play. Lincoln said, "He's just a boy. He can play all he wants—outdoors! Bundle up. It's cold!"

Tad galloped off, then Lincoln led Kenndy into a small, private receiving room and they sat on large tufted chairs with a round white marble-topped table between them. Lincoln was quiet but examined the immaculately dressed senator, noticing his slicked-back dark hair and his well-groomed fingernails.

"I'm here to discuss very important matters." Kenndy squeezed a small satchel. "The Southern states have—"

"Would you like some coffee or tea?" Lincoln smiled and nodded to the butler, Peter Brown, who stood in the doorway. Brown was African American, much shorter than each of them and held his trained gaze with downcast eyes. "Maybe some fresh orange juice?"

"I beg your pardon, sir," Kenndy said. "No, I decline."

"You 'decline.' An interesting decision, sir," Lincoln smiled to himself. "Peter, I'll have a glass of orange juice. Are you sure, Senator? It's fresh from Georgia. I reckon oranges ripen sooner down South. A kind little lady brought oranges as a gift yesterday."

"No, thank you."

"Sweet little lady named Constance. Appropriate name, don't you think?" he chuckled amiably. "She was barely taller than my boy Tad, but she has a heart as big as all outdoors. You see, the thing is, she told me her father was killed at Manassas and her brother fell at Antietam. She has a beau, Horace I believe was the fella's name, and she wasn't sure where he was. The last she heard Horace had been captured and headed for a prison somewhere in the South. Maybe even Georgia. Anyway, I digress. Constance said, with true greatness and spirit in her speech, she wanted me to know her family felt strongly in *defending* the Union. She gave me these oranges and asked me to take them as it was the only thing left she had to give. Bless her heart."

The President gazed down at the worn green carpet, reflected and smiled faintly. Peter returned with a silver tray and two glasses of freshly-squeezed orange juice, set them eloquently on the marble table with his white-gloved hands, bowed and left with the silver tray.

Lincoln raised a glass then smiled jovially to Kenndy. "It's quite good. You may have some if you change your mind." Lincoln took a drink, noticed Kenndy watched him, and smiled again. "Now, Senator, what would you like to discuss?"

Kenndy ran a hand over his hair, opened the satchel and took out a few documents. He stood to make a presentation of his prepared speech, tucked his thumbs under his vest coat, and spoke clearly, "The Southern states—"

"Senator before you go further I'm not one for speechifying. Yes, I can stand in front of a large crowd and debate, or talk until the sun comes up about various issues. But it's only you and me here. Talk to me. Like father and son."

Kenndy gave Lincoln a wry look then and offered a compromise, "Brother to brother?"

"Of course. I have family who consider themselves Southerners first. I, however, consider us *family* first. We're all together in this. We just have squabbles that need to be worked out. Unfortunately, as Constance can testify, it's gone beyond words to a great deal of bloodshed. It's gone far beyond what anyone had ever imagined." His voice trailed off with genuine pain. "You see, Randolph, is it okay that I call you Randolph?"

Kenndy nodded and his eyes watered, touched by Lincoln's heartfelt emotion.

"Randolph, it's not just Constance. *Every* day I see people who have lost loved ones. *Every* day I receive mail from fathers, brothers, wives, loved ones, telling me of the terrible loss they have suffered. *Our* entire nation is suffering."

Kenndy was off his mark, tears welled up in his eyes and he rubbed at them angrily, paced and tried to find a new starting point. "Yes, we are suffering. And that is why I have come to you today, with the authority of the Confederate States of America, President Jefferson Davis, to offer a settlement of peace. Um, as you can see, here—" he held out a formal proclamation to examine but Lincoln held his glass of juice with both hands. "I, ahem. It states, uh, that peace can be had, immediately, by negotiated settlement. We are willing to stop fighting, should you also cease, on April first. Then we can then discuss the settlement and the separation of our nation from the United States."

Kenndy had misspoken and Lincoln pounced on his words, "Yes, the *United* States. Our forefathers fought dearly to have us *united*. And thus it shall remain, under my *elected* watch by the people Randolph."

"I regret to hear that, sir, but please hear me out."

"Randy, what could you possible say that would sway my mind, could wrench the memory of Constance's suffering and thousands of others before her, that we should depart from this course? Shall I trample the memory of her loved ones and of my forefathers, your forefathers, to make their bloodshed in vain?"

Perspiration formed on Kenndy's forehead. He used his coat sleeve to dab it away. "I, um, the *Confederate* States, President Davis has issued me to state unequivocally that unless a settlement of peace is begun we shall be forced to take the fighting North. Unless you commit to peace now, our soldiers, led by our superior generals shall invade *your* land. We will move this unnecessary bloodshed to *your* soil."

Lincoln drank, folded his long fingers around the glass, but remained silent.

"We implore you to stop the bloodshed now," Kenndy continued. "General Lee has shown time and again that we will whip you. Except now it will be on your soil. It will be your Northern farms and houses destroyed. Why, everyone knows our generals can outmaneuver and win the battlefield. Time and time again, they have proven this. General Lee can whip any Northern general. We will continue our struggle until our freedom is won! But at what cost to *your* people, sir?"

Kenndy stopped and stood above Lincoln, who stared straight ahead, deep in thought. "You have a choice, Mister Lincoln. It does not need to continue. It is on *your* conscious. *Now,* sir. Peace may be had."

"It has been my charge since I was elected, Randy." Lincoln looked up with his large, sad eyes. His wrinkled face was calm as if nothing of any consequence had been said and he spoke with resolve, "I do not intend to give up my duty."

Kenndy looked around the room for a formal writing desk to place the peace proposal but there was none. Kenndy offered the documents again, was ignored again, and dropped them into Lincoln's lap but the President stood up and they fell to the floor. They stood inches apart and stared into each other's eyes with determination.

"Won't you have some juice, Randy? It's quite good and it's so hard to come by this time of year."

Kenndy ground his teeth in frustration and snarled, "It's on your head," then exited angrily, leaving the papers littered on the green carpet.

~32 ~

Helen wrote him a letter stating if he could come to Burlington she would meet him at 4 p.m., without tea, at their house this Saturday. The last time he was home he was quite miserable but he filed for and was granted a one-week leave.

On his journey from Washington City he thought of Helen, their home life and the many events they had shared. He recalled the time a circus came to Burlington on its way through New England to Boston. He enjoyed the dancing white stallions from Austria, was awestruck by a big brown bear walking on its hind legs led by a trainer then remembered beginning to tell Helen the story of hunting a black bear that was upsetting farmers in Franklin County but she wasn't listening. She sat enraptured by the antics of a clown with a flower so he watched every delicate nuance of delight on her face. The way her eyes crinkled when she laughed, the slight backward tilt of her head, the way she tucked the brown curls of her shiny hair around her ears, and the childlike way she bounced up-and-down in her seat. When the clown had finished and a gave an exaggerated bow she clapped enthusiastically and when the clown exited then tripped and fell in a sprawling heap, she laughed heartily and applauded louder. Why couldn't he and Helen enjoy the good times of their life together? How could he make this happen?

The train chugged away from New York City and he recalled a winter sleigh ride with Helen on a December late afternoon. They had stopped to admire a beautiful copse of woods, the sloping field of tall grass poked through the first layer of snow, and snow fell in the dimming twilight. A low, slate sky hugged the horizon. She pulled back their fur blanket and had, under the blanket, raised her dress and unhitched her corset so when she exposed herself he saw her lacy blue garter and the shiny black curls of her soft mound. A gentle snow fell, almost too shy to alight on such a precious sight, then a single flake rested on her dark bed of hair. He kneeled down to kiss it and the precious crystal melted on his warm lips. Her radiant blue eyes flashed with excitement and a knowing smile caused her cheeks to show their dimples.

Even now, with the rattling hum of the train's wheels rocking over the tracks, he smiled fondly. He remembered the long moments after, of how the threatening sky turned ominous and the snow fell heavier, obscuring the trees on the hills. His immediate thought was, Which way is home? There were no stars, no moon in the evening sky, and the town of Burlington was not visible. He loosely shook the reins, hoping Charger would instinctively head back but he was so well-trained he merely bobbed his head, stomped his right forefoot and shifted his weight, causing a strap of bells to jingle.

Helen became alarmed and said, "Can't you find the road?"

"The snow has drifted over." The road and meadow was a field of glossy white. "Which way do you think it is?"

"Oh for heaven's sake!" She buttoned up her corset with haste. "You're lost!"

"We're not lost. We're southeast of town. It's only, I'm not sure which way to go around this hill."

He again shook the reins evenly and Charger pulled their sleigh up the slight rise to the right. Beneath them was another small hill with an outcropping of craggy boulders leading up, but up to what? The dark sky dropped thick clumps of snow and a sharp icy wind blew the snow drifts higher, impeding their progress.

"That's it! You're lost!" Her knees bounced up and down with aggravation.

Rather than go back to the copse of woods then around the other way, which he suspected was correct, he pressed Charger on and followed a narrow clearing into a darkened grove of pines and evergreens. It was clearly *not* the way, but now he understood that and allowed Charger to make their way through the trees. Helen complained bitterly, went on after they slid onto the road leading to Burlington, chided him past the Unitarian Church, and cursed him still when they moved into the long drive of Mrs. Turner's courtyard to the Italianate mansion.

Obadiah, the servant, waded out from the front door into the shin-deep snow, took Charger's reins in one hand and helped down the Countess with the other. She lifted her dress to run through the snow into the mansion, not looking back to say goodbye.

At that moment he thought their relationship had ended. He glanced down and saw a single crimson drop of blood stained one of Helen's tracks in the pure white snow. Obadiah did not notice but steadied Charger's back and said, "You should go home befo' it gets wo'se."

At first he thought Obadiah meant Helen's temper and his relationship with her, then understood he meant the storm. He nodded and pulled to the left to ease Charger around, away from the huge mansion.

As he rode on the train and recalled the memory of that stormy night he shook his head with dismay. He decided he should focus on how to handle their relationship *now.* In her letter Helen wrote she would meet him at 4 p.m., without tea, in their house. Without tea, he thought, what a strange phrase.

It was a few minutes after 8 a.m. when the locomotive pulled into Burlington station. Other soldiers were met by loved ones, he knew Helen would not be there, but he was still disappointed. Then it struck him he was accustomed to disappointment with her.

He was also concerned for his horses and the farm, and decided to check on them before going home. Across from the train depot was Kingston's Livery, which was easier and more convenient than Peck's Livery, which he preferred, but time was of the essence so he stabled Charger there and rented a chestnut-colored gelding named Cinnamon for the day. He paid Aaron Kingston one dollar in advance and rode out of Burlington, past all the businesses, past well-kept homes, and made the two-hour ride to Franklin County, where the land was familiar and untouched by war.

As he rode by a few farmhouses he thought of his neighbors. When would the oldest Thirod boy, Ronan, now 18, join the cause? Did Lenore Bengston get over her chicken pox? When would the farmers plant hay, oats or a garden?

It was 11 a.m. when he rode past the weathered Trading Post, by the old house his father had built and went to the stables. He dismounted, let the rented horse feed on the budding grass shoots and entered the stables where he was pleased to find Tommy Lonegran brushing the horses. Tommy was now 15, filling into a hefty young man with broad shoulders but he still moved with an awkward gait. Then Timmy came out from the grain storage area and said, "Hey there, Mister Stannard!"

Tommy had cared for his horses very well and he shook his hand firmly then young Timmy's hand, and thanked them both again. Then he went to the dark quarter horse named Jupiter. It neighed and bobbed his head when he patted Jupiter's neck, gave him a carrot, and felt his well-groomed dark coat. Again he was very pleased with Tommy's meticulous care and smiled to him.

Tommy then began to chat away in a streak, informed him of his family and neighbors, while he took out a gray blanket and swung a fine saddle over Jupiter. Tommy explained Mr. and Mrs. Waite were both doing well, considering their old age, Lenore Bengston got over her chicken pox just fine, livestock prospered and local farmers' were planting soon in hope of a bountiful yield. The entire county had done well and the war was like a history lesson in a land far, far away.

He knew if he continued to converse with Tommy, or stopped to speak with those neighbors, he would not make it back to Helen until after dark. He shook Timmy's hand again, then Tommy's hand firmly and gave him an extra silver dollar and asked him if would let the gelding rest here tonight then return it to Kingston's Livery in Burlington tomorrow, where he could then fetch Jupiter and ride him back here?

Tommy gawped at the silver dollar and gushed a broadening smile. "You got it!"

He walked Jupiter, now a fully mature black quarter horse, out of the stable and into the grassy ring. Cinnamon, the rented horse, barely looked up from eating. He mounted Jupiter gently, nudged him with his star-shaped spurs and Jupiter responded with a jolt and a quick snort, as if surprised to be asked something. After 15 minutes of hard riding, the quarter horse became lathered and he eased his grip on the reins, slowed him into a steady gallop, and Jupiter responded with a comfortable rhythm in his breathing.

He arrived back in Burlington in mid-afternoon, 3:15 p.m., and his heart raced in anticipation of seeing Helen. Rather than put Jupiter in the shed in back, to save time he led him to the hitching post in front of their house, dismounted, slid the reins through the iron ring and hustled over the hard ground to the porch. The house was in good shape, having survived the spring without much wear on the paint. The shingles and eaves appeared sturdy and the shutters were in place.

Inside the house it was immaculate and bright, and he thought Helen must have had a servant come by to clean the house for his arrival. It looked splendid. The furniture was polished and candles glowed in every corner of the room. The long rays of the setting sun poured through the fine sheer curtains. He sensed a presence over his shoulder and turned to see Helen at the top of the stairs. She wore her best navy blue silk dress with a low-cut, white lace cleavage. His heart pounded hard in his chest and he admired her beauty, smiling up to her. She looked down to him and descended the staircase with ease, with her white-gloved hand gliding over the polished cherry wood railing.

He thrust out his arms to embrace her but when she reached the landing she clasped his hands with her gloved hands then shook them. "How are you. . . dear?"

He broke his hands from Helen's gloved hands and again reached to put his arms around her waist but she stopped him and stepped back. "My dress is silk, dear. You'll wrinkle it."

She wore powder on her face and sniffed the air, smelled his damp clothes and the strong scent of Jupiter, leather, tack, and spoke with disdain, "You smell like Charger!"

"I rode Jupiter from Georgia. I can take a bath and, ah, I'll be ready by four."

"Yes. Please do." She turned abruptly, floated out the front door to the porch, eased down on the swing and fanned herself even though it was cool.

He took a very quick bath in cold water, washed himself briskly and wrapped a towel around his waist but did not want to wear the same smelly clothes. He went to his closet in their bedroom to put on an appropriate suit but stood still. All of his suits were gone! The armoire was empty except for a few ties and suspenders hanging. What had happened to his good black suit? His fashionable navy blue suit? He checked the dresser but it held undergarments and heavy winter sweaters.

He then went into her room, thinking perhaps the suits had been cleaned and mistakenly returned by a servant to the wrong closet but no, Helen's room had been newly decorated with bright ivory wallpaper with tiny pink roses. One could not mistake this for a man's room. Nevertheless he looked in her armoire and saw many huge puffy dresses, including a new pink gown and a few bright blue dresses he did not remember seeing before. In her closet were more dresses then he looked in the highboy dresser where she kept many undergarments and he felt he shouldn't be snooping around. In the hallway he opened a closet and poked through a few towels and linens then returned to his room and put on the same clothes he had worn before, which smelled like Jupiter's lather, which he tried to cover with a healthy splash of cologne. He sniffed again, smelled it again and clapped more cologne onto the inside area of his thighs.

The late afternoon sun was dimming with darkness coming when he went back downstairs. Helen was still on the porch swing with a tight, dry smile creased on her face. Her smile faded when he stepped onto the porch. Then she pulled over the folds of her navy blue silk dress, which he avoided, and eased into the swing next to her. He said, "I wasn't able to find any of my suits."

"No?"

"No. You don't know where they are?"

She blinked her bright blue eyes, stared at him doll-like then fanned herself again. "Well, yes, I guess I did let Mr. Timmons have one. He worked so hard on the upkeep of the house last week, the shutters and eves. It seemed a shame to have him go home empty-handed."

"What do you mean?"

"You haven't sent me any money in spite of my *several* letters and I had to give him something. It was quite humiliating honestly."

"Oh," he said and scratched his beard, still damp with bathwater. A single drop dripped from his dark beard onto his white shirt. He did not want to become upset and tried to think of something pleasant. "Tell me about the upcoming theater season. What shows are planned?"

"Oh!" she huffed and snapped shut her fan. "I know you don't care for that."

"Yes, I do. I'd like to know." He wanted to hold her but observed her gazing distantly down the darkening street while she bit her lower lip. He continued, "I want to attend with you. It's something we can share."

She looked at him sideways then returned to fanning herself. In the street a tall thin man limped by with a small torch and a little red-haired boy held his hand. The man stopped, dropped the boy's grasp then lit the gas street lamp. A pocket of light glowed. The tall man noticed them, waved and called out, "*Countess! General! How are ya?*"

He started to speak but Helen shouted over him, "*I'm fine!* It's a lovely evening but I didn't get any fresh flowers today and the market is such a long way! Are you coming back this way when you're done?"

"Yes, ma'am," he used his free hand to shield his eyes from the streetlamp. "Would you like me to bring you some?"

"That would be marvelous!" she cooed. "Perhaps some lilies if they're fresh? Otherwise a few roses."

"It'd be my pleasure, Countess." He extended his arm to wave goodbye and the little boy waved energetically.

He waved back and said, "I could have done that."

"Yes. But you didn't."

"And lilies won't be in."

"You have no idea what flowers the market has." She returned to fanning herself, blinked several times then pointed at Jupiter tied to the hitching post. "You went to your horses."

"I needed to check on them."

"*They* were more important than *me!*"

"You weren't at the depot and I figured you weren't waiting for me."

"And I *was!* Here, in my house for hours! It's, it's humiliating is what it is!"

They sat in silence. A brisk breeze blew from the north. He smoothed down his wet hair on top, wiped his wet hands on the sides of his shirt and changed the subject, "Has there been any news from our neighbors?"

"No. Besides you know more about the war than our neighbors, don't you?"

He nodded, "I meant personally. If any of our neighbors became ill. What is happening in Burlington?"

"Ha! We both know you could care less about the latest gossip!"

He had already decided he didn't want to engage on topics of "gossip," instead had meant social activities, balls, theater and so on, but decided to let it go. Still, he was curious to know about Cranston and Alyssa, Hazel, and other good friends. "Did we have any interesting letters? Anything like that?"

"Nothing for you. Of course not."

"There hasn't been any word from Billy Caldwell, my Mohawk friend?"

"Oh good Lord! I can't possibly be held accountable for every little Indian boy that comes around."

"What?" He was confused. "An Indian boy came by?"

She collapsed her fan and parried it at him with her blue eyes glaring and said, "I told you. Some Indian boy came by and I sent him away. There was no possible way he could have anything to say to me."

"He probably had a message from my friend."

"I very seriously doubt that. And you should know I don't engage in conversation with ignorant Indians! Ha!" She snapped her wrist, opening her fan with a pop, and fluttered it.

He reflected on her response. A young Indian boy stopped by the house, perhaps asked to speak with him, and she had sent him away. Further discussion of this topic would anger her more but he had to speak up. "Billy Caldwell is a good friend of mine. He is Mohawk. I had been hoping to hear from him for quite some time.

Now, apparently, I'll never know his whereabouts. Or if he is alive or dead."

"Then good riddance! Indians are below our station."

The dampness of his wet, smelly shirt began to chafe him and he could no longer hold back. "What happened to my good black suit? All the others?"

Helen made a clicking noise like he was stupid. "I told you! I gave it to Mister Timmons for his work. Must you bring up *that* humiliation again?"

"You gave Joe Timmons my best suit?"

"Yes."

"What of the dark blue suit? The one I wear to the opera."

"That one fit Roy Gunderson so well I let him have it."

"Roy Gunderson? What'd he do?"

She snapped her fan shut then jerked around to face him. "If this is the way it's to be, so be it. He's done *everything* in your place since you've been gone. I let him have it *all!* I want a divorce."

Helen pushed back hard with her feet and set the swing rocking awkwardly. He put his boots down, stopped the rocking but could not believe what he had heard. His pulse pounded hard in his temples. "Did I hear you correctly?"

"You did." She pushed off again but he stopped them again and flexed his legs to keep the swing in a pushed back position.

"I, I can't believe this," he said. Then he took a deep breath to relax, a reflex of habit in aiming his pistol, and said, "I want everything to work out fine."

"There's nothing to work out. You've been gone. I have needs. I have had needs from the beginning, needs *you* cannot meet. There's not much to say. Why, look how long it took us to get into an argument! Five minutes. It's ridiculous!"

He was angry and did not know what to say or where to begin. This was incredible. She *has* been unfaithful! Of course they argued in minutes because this was the first time she had spoken to him! He had not even told her of the war and the horrors he had endured. He rubbed his forehead, tried to remain calm, then attempted to speak in a loving tone but his voice cracked with emotion, "Were you unfaithful?"

"How *dare* you ask such a question!" she fumed. "I told you but perhaps you need it spelled out. I have *needs*. Many different types of needs and you have not met *any* of them! I spoke with a lawyer on Front Street. He drew up divorce papers. You are to sign them and the sooner, the better. That way we can carry on with our lives."

"*You've* decided. That's it?"

"It's self-evident. Why carry on with this charade?"

He stood. His head hurt and his pulse pounded throughout his body, which made his war wounds ache in his thigh and left hand. He flexed both hands into fists, realized he was doing this then shook them to relax. So this was what she wanted it. What the hell happened? He was incredibly upset and said, "I can't. I took a vow to God."

He shuffled off the porch and Jupiter made a neighing sound. He needed to take Jupiter to Kingston's Livery so Tommy Lonegran could ride him back tomorrow. At the hitching post he looked back to Helen but she had left. The empty porch swing swung oddly at an angle, unevenly.

~33 ~

In spring 1863 Confederate President Jefferson Davis received Senator Kenndy's report on their peace initiative. It had failed miserably. President Davis had bitter contempt for Lincoln and all the self-righteous Northerners. He realized how stubborn Lincoln was and knew if the Southerners were to be successful, they must do something more persuasive to Lincoln and all the Northerners.

At the Confederate Executive Mansion, an impressive white building of two stories with a flat slate roof, President Davis met with his Cabinet, advisors and military leaders to formulate a plan. To accommodate them, they met in the formal State dining room, which had a high ceiling, tall windows with elegant drapery and opulent cream-colored wallpaper. Richly attired slaves served them Madeira wine. President Davis, in his best gray three-piece suit, discussed their situation with his advisors, who all cried for blood. Judah Benjamin, a rotund man with a cherub face, was first appointed Attorney General then shifted to the War Department. Benjamin pounded the large oval table with his fist when he spoke, "Let those *destructive*, *vicious*, invading *Northerners* see the horrors of *war* in *their* towns and in *their* houses!"

Another Cabinet member, Secretary of the Navy Stephen Mallory, who was from Key West, Florida stood and bowed to each of the advisors. Mallory had made his reputation by clearing out the Seminole Indians and from his position to allow sea captains to use flogging to retain order. Mallory spoke passionately, "Yes! We must make the Yankees see atrocities and then, *then!* they will let us go our own way. There ain't nothin' like a good *thrashin'* to make a stubborn child think!"

Many of Davis's advisors felt their goal should be to strike terror in the souls of those pompous Northerners. To a person they believed after one more convincing victory, on *their* soil, England would no longer remain idle but must give support to the South to renew their economic ties and re-start the flow of cotton and other goods from Southern ports. After one more major victory, on Northern soil, they would force Yankee politicians to embrace a peace settlement.

Davis agreed. He turned to General Lee, who sat on his right and said, "We must take the fight to the North."

Lee, in his immaculate dress uniform, stood and gave a full, formal bow. His white beard was trimmed and his light eyes held a proud gaze. "With honor, sir."

The next day President Davis gave a speech on the steps of the Richmond capitol, a speech he had made often, to affirm the Southerners wanted to be a free, independent country. They had no aspiration to attack "another country" in the north but had been forced to fight for their freedom, just the same as the founding fathers did.

Lee developed a strategy to invade the North. He was now very familiar with the terrain of the Shenandoah Valley and knew he could always return to its safety. He was also very familiar with the fighting ability of the Northern soldiers and generals. His plan was to move his forces through the Shenandoah Valley then strike in Pennsylvania. After a convincing victory there, with a defeated, demoralized Union Army, they would then be free to march on Washington or New York City. President Davis approved Lee's plan.

Lee led the Confederate soldiers northward. Citizens of Washington, New York, Philadelphia and Boston became alarmed. Newspapers throughout the North detailed their movements with large headlines:

INVASION!

SOUTHERN REBELS ATTACK OUR CITIES!

Lee and his Army appeared ready and able to strike at any Northern city they felt inclined to attack. The citizens of the North felt, for the first time, this war *could* come into their homes. After the horrors of Fredericksburg, where *civilians* had been killed and their homes destroyed, Northerners worried the war *could* destroy their homes, take their livestock or goods, and injure or kill their family members. Common citizens from Portsmouth to Plymouth, from Harrisburg to Hartford, braced for the coming of General Lee and his Rebel Army.

Federal President Lincoln continued his search for a competent commander to lead the Union forces to victory and end the rising tide of bloodshed. Throughout the warming spring months the

Union Army was in a confounded situation. Although the soldiers were not afraid to fight, they wanted to prove themselves, they often performed poorly under stress. They took horrible losses and the generals were blamed for their inept leadership. Then Federal generals became timid to attack because they were often outmaneuvered on unfamiliar terrain. More awful losses followed. Next the generals feared any battle for their own reputation, avoided any confrontation, and often found themselves once again fighting on poor ground and more horrific losses ensued. It was a terrible situation. The Union Army, and thus the nation itself, was in grave danger.

~34 ~

After their bitter fight, George took Jupiter to Kingston's Livery and the next day retrieved Charger and headed for Georgia. For some reason Charger broke into a canter, without being asked, several times. Each time he reined Charger back into a walk.

He thought of his father and wished he was alive to talk with him about Helen, his feelings and the horror of this awful war. Then he thought again of the incompetence and near treason of Colonel Miles. It was one grand *humiliation,* to use Helen's word, but in the end it was beyond his control in spite of all he did. Helen had managed to take his personal life and humiliate him further. He sank into depression. What did he do wrong? Didn't he confront their problems head on and offer to do everything in his power to make their marriage work? Or was his reaction too much? Was he wrong in taking leave and coming home with great expectations?

He needed a peaceful place to think. Perhaps Helen was right. Perhaps they should part amicably but then what would become of his life? Would he ever meet another woman with such beauty, enthusiasm, and inspiration? What of his plans to have a family? It was all very troubling. He took a long, slow ride home.

Again Charger again skipped into a canter so this time he urged him into a gallop and it felt good to be in rhythm with him. They rode by farmhouses north of Burlington and rode easily across the Vermont countryside. Charger bobbed his head in agreement and continued on a steady, galloping pace. He enjoyed this, too! George rubbed and patted his strong white shoulders and said cheerfully, "Atta boy!"

The day was warm and clear, and the beauty of Lake Champlain drew his attention. The water was dark blue with white caps far off shore, kicked up by a steady breeze from the west. He focused on the calming blue water and eased Charger into a walk. Immediately his thoughts returned to Helen, their disastrous marriage, and he considered it for a long time.

The road of turns and straight shots through the woods, always following the beautiful lake, was very familiar but passed slowly. He eased Charger past his father's Trading Post and past the riding ring. He dismounted very distracted and when his boots hit the ground his first thought was to return to Burlington to be near Helen. He walked Charger into the stable where the air glistened with tiny specks of dust, illuminated by rays of sunshine slanting through an open window. Timmy Lonegran brushed the last of his 14 horses, after he had sold eight to the Federal Army which was in dire need of good mounts. He felt a sense of symmetry and comfort to see Timmy following his older brother's lead, taking fine care of his horses.

Although he wanted to return to Burlington immediately, he kept up a conversation with Timmy for about an hour until the boy asked pointed questions about the war, probing for details about the death of their neighbor Vincent Caravaggio. He would not explain the details of Caravaggio's death to Timmy, or to anyone. How could he explain to anyone not familiar with war that Vincent, who was very much a capable and steady soldier, ran into a burly Rebel private in front of their redoubt, was turned and impaled onto a sharpened timber pole, then hacked to death by a Confederate lieutenant with a short sword until Benedict swiftly shot both Rebels? He was quiet then later shook Timmy's hand in thanks, nodded goodbye, and started back.

Then he impulsively decided to visit friends in St. Albans, where he had spent much of his time with the Ransom Guards and had made friends through teaching and from working at the foundry. He circled Charger then headed north for St. Albans and continued to think of his horrible marriage. Along the way he dismounted to ease the load on Charger and walked with him. When he was in view of St. Albans he mounted Charger, walked him past the re-built foundry on the left where he had worked, then up Main past the banks, hotel, and Brownell's General Store. Further ahead, across the village green, was the old schoolhouse, where he had taught in winter for years. He again dismounted then led Charger into Agnello's Livery, where he personally watered and washed him. He ran his palm over every square inch to inspect for any nicks or cuts. He took out a small bottle of ointment from his saddlebag then tenderly rubbed the salve over a small scratch on his underside where a branch must have caught him. He ran his hand down Charger's front left leg until he got near the hoof then squeezed, lifted his foot, and used a pick to clean out the shoe, inspected it for any issues, then set down his hoof. He repeated it for all Charger's legs and hooves then patted him several times on the neck and forequarters, and gave him a large carrot.

The blacksmith, Uno Agnello, noticed his typical, meticulous care and grinned, "If I didn't know you better, I'd say you should marry that horse!"

Agnello was quick to smile. He had moved from Ogdensburg to St. Albans after the failed Canadian rebellion of 1838 because he felt more aligned with these free-thinking Vermonters. Agnello was now over 50 and too old to fight in the Federal Army, although he was still in good shape. He was short, very muscular with enormous biceps and forearms, and smiled through his soot-smudged face.

"God knows I love him!" George replied while Charger happily munched at the carrot from his palm. Then he again thought of Helen and wondered if another person could see how much he doted on her? If anyone saw him with Helen, would they say that he should have married her? Did he truly love her? Where was she now?

He wondered if he should have been more demonstrative with Helen. Perhaps he needed to get her a gift of reconciliation? He decided to let Charger rest and went to Brownell's General Store, where he smelled various perfumes and felt bolts of imported French silk fabric. They were all very nice and each was very expensive. He decided on a small bottle of French perfume called "Cote d'Azure." When he paid for the bottle he asked the owner, Hank Brownell, "What's it mean?"

"Cote d'Azure?" Brownell wore spectacles, coarse overalls and a flannel shirt. He scratched the back of his balding head with his left hand and it was then he noticed Brownell's missing right arm, which had been amputated at the elbow. Brownell laughed then winked, "Beats the heck out of me but it sure smells purty!"

He laughed but stared at his missing arm. He had heard Brownell had been wounded at the battle of Antietam but he did not recall the details. Yet here was Brownell in good spirits. "Heard you gave 'em hell at Antietam."

"Yep," Brownell said. "It was hot and damn quick, too. Some Johnny Reb bullshit concoction of ten-penny nails and buckshot got me. I woulda been fine if it didn't hit me right on the bone."

"I'm sorry," he replied, then added, "But it's good to know we have fine men at home to look after things."

"Darn tootin'," Brownell smiled again. "Course nothin' happens 'round here except ol' man Wisner gets drunk ev'ry Saturday night and tries to shoot some phantom bird or beast. Hey, I heard you was in jail somewheres for raising too much hell."

“Jail? I was a prisoner of war. They made us—”

“I know, George! Everybody knows!” They both laughed. Brownell leaned over and took hold of his shoulder with his left hand then his dark eyes welled up with tears. “Damn it’s good to see you again, George.”

Brownell looked around to confirm the store was empty then confessed, “I ne’er told anyone ‘cause it was my first battle. I didn’t get a shot off. Not one!”

“ ’S’okay, Hank. You’re not the first to go down at the start. It’s happened to plenty of good men.”

“I know, I know. But I feel untested.” Brownell’s dark eyes watered.

He had seen plenty of soldiers, from hardened Saturday night brawlers to timid backwoods farmers, and there was no way to predict how a soldier would react in battle. Each was different. The best he could do was to train each man until it became a gut reaction to follow orders, to fire your weapon calmly, and to be strong despite every fiber in your body screaming to run for your life. He had no idea how Hank Brownell would react in the heat of battle.

“Give the Johnnies hell for me, will ya?” Brownell said.

“You bet.” He gave Brownell a formal salute, took his package and walked out.

There were more, similar encounters of well wishers. He began to wonder how many young men from St. Albans, or from all of Vermont, had been wounded or killed? A moment later he realized it must be worse in the South and included civilians.

At Agnello's Livery, he put the perfume bottle in his saddle bag, mounted Charger and walked him down Main Street, past the village green and out of St. Albans. South of town he spurred Charger into a gallop and rode easily for 20 minutes. Charger was very strong and the long days of standing about Camp Boredom by the Potomac seemed to have had little effect on Charger's stamina. They bypassed Georgia and the Trading Post, where he needed to rein in Charger to keep him on the Post Road, and continued on at an easy gallop. After a while he let Charger walk and continued to think about Helen, his gift and reconciling their differences. What else could he do? He would not divorce her. He had taken a vow.

Then Charger noticed a very large house close to the road and edged over closer to the building without being reined toward it. A very pretty young woman in a white cotton dress stood on the porch and smiled warmly.

He found himself easing back on the reins but Charger stopped abruptly, which was strange. The woman, who had long, curly brown hair, stood by a vined post and held a bunch of white myrtle flowers in her hand. She smiled brightly.

He was stunned by her warmth and felt himself being shy but preferred not to speak with her and nudged his boots into Charger. Oddly, Charger did not respond. He bobbed his head twice and the young woman burst into a hearty laugh.

He took off his hat, bowed slightly in the saddle and again urged Charger on. This time they walked past the porch. The young woman had deep, dark brown eyes and he stared transfixed, turning in the saddle and looking over his shoulder to gaze at her lovely, smiling face and into her warm, kind eyes.

Now Charger was sensitive to the reins and when he leaned back to his left, Charger wandered off the road to the left, into knee-deep grass and again the woman laughed with gusto. He turned forward in the saddle, noticed they were in tall grass and heard the woman laughing good naturedly. He replaced his hat, tugged it down, and eased Charger back onto the Post Road. He mumbled, "What are you doing boy?"

He was not certain but he thought that large house was owned by the St. Albans foundry co-owner, Mr. Clark. He eased his grip on the reins, looked back once more and examined the white house with dark green trim around the windows. It was an impressive three-story home with a large wrap-around porch.

He again nodded to the woman, who watched him and stepped down off the porch into the road to stand next to a blooming myrtle bush where she waved with enthusiasm. He made a clicking noise, jangled the reins and Charger moved into a trot. Now, instead of continuing to mull over his failing marriage, he found himself thinking about the woman on the porch. Who was she? Why hadn't he noticed her before?

Approaching Burlington, he felt perplexed because he was no further in his plan of making peace with Helen. He had a fancy bottle of French perfume and little else. He eased Charger past a few new buildings on the northern edge of the growing city, past the town center and the village green, which bustled with soldiers and citizens pouring out of the train station after the arrival of the afternoon train. Many of the women held bouquets of flowers then he saw Mrs. Abigail Linton, the heavy-set florist who was friends with his Aunt Amelia.

Mrs. Linton stood at a table in front of her newly opened shop on the village green and he impulsively decided to get Helen flowers, dismounted and asked Mrs. Linton for some red roses. She replied, "If Mrs. Stannard knew ya spent half yer pay on Dutch roses, she'd be after ya with a switch!"

He kidded her back, "It'll be our military secret!" but then thought, No, Helen wouldn't care how much something costs. Then he recalled choking Bradford Dutton to within a moment of his life on the boardwalk behind her. "I apologize for the commotion I made here. It wasn't right."

Mrs. Linton's laughter faded and she grasped his forearm. "It's understandable. George. I'm very sorry to tell ya this but I *must* mention what people are saying. They say Helen has taken a room at the Wilson Hotel."

"Yes." He cleared his throat, "We're having some problems."

"Well, I never heard of such a thing! Never in me life." Mrs. Linton used the back of her soiled hand and rubbed the end of her nose. "It's one thing to have problems but to leave yer husband an' move into a hotel, why I never!"

Mrs. Linton was a good friend of his Aunt Amelia and he considered discussing his marriage but she continued, "Well, if that don't beat all. It's unheard of!"

"Right. Well, now you've heard it. I'm sorry this is upsetting you Mrs. Linton and I wish I knew what to do. Helen. . ." his voice trailed off.

Mrs. Linton again clutched his arm and tears welled up in her eyes. "I have to tell ya something else. Prepare yourself. I heard she's been seen with Lucious Redfield. And he bought flowers this morning!"

He nodded. It was another blow and prepared or not, it hurt. He did not know how to respond to such an accusation, the type of which he had heard more often than he cared. He noticed tall elms growing at the edge of the village green and Mrs. Linton continued her barrage, "You know Lucious Redfield. The carpenter fella what does all the fancy carvings in the churches."

"Yes. I know him." He scratched the back of his neck, wanted this conversation over but said, "His father moved here from Carolina. Made his money in tobacco, right?"

Mrs. Linton nodded. A tear fell from her reddened eyes and ran down her cheek. Then she busied herself, making a bouquet of white daisies and black-eyed susans. "Flowers is a good place to start, George. She knows ya have a good heart."

"Yes, but it's more." He wanted to explain the situation and decided, Why not? It felt like everyone already knew his personal business. He clutched the beautiful bouquet of roses with its layered petals, opening in all their splendor. "I could hope by giving her these flowers, and another gift I have, that it would all be settled. But I know that won't do. Not with Helen."

“Maybe you should think, what does she *need?*” Mrs. Linton said, holding a spray of baby’s breath but again wiped tears off her cheek with the back of her soiled hand.

“Oh, I’ve thought for a very long time,” he looked into Mrs. Linton’s sorrowful, gray eyes. “You see, I’m afraid what Helen needs is *no* husband.”

Mrs. Linton took a deep, shocked breath. “Hush! You shouldn’t say such things.”

“Maybe I shouldn’t, but it may be the truth.”

“Why, that’s unheard of!” Mrs. Linton dropped the spray of baby’s breath and used her soiled hands to fan herself dramatically. “I mean, I can’t, I can’t fathom this!”

He bowed, walked out then led Charger by the reins to the Wilson Hotel across the green and tethered him to a hitching post. He decided to leave the perfume bottle in his saddle bag for another occasion, held the flowers and smelled their bounty one last time, and went through the lobby of the Wilson Hotel. No clerk was on duty so he went up to Helen’s room, knocked on the door but she did not answer. He returned to the lobby and waited in front of a counter, where after a moment Thaddeus Jenkins, the proprietor, entered from a room in the back. Jenkins was a thin man with short red-and-gray hair and knotty hands deformed by arthritis.

“Have you seen Helen?” he asked.

Jenkins leaned over the counter, cupping his knotty hand to his right ear. “Wa-wa-what’s that gah-gah-general?”

He raised his voice but was still not understood. Jenkins needed him to shout but he did not want the world to hear he had no idea where his wife was. Instead he set the bouquet on the counter and said, “These are for Helen.”

“I’ll pa-pa-put them with the others.” Jenkins carried them over to a back shelf and set them in a vase that contained two other bouquets of red roses. They were now mixed in with the others, inconsequential to the group of more than 40 roses.

“*God damn it! What are you doing?*” he hollered.

“You said to pa-pa-put them with the others. For Miss Helen.”

“I did not! God.” He kicked the base of the counter. “Who are the others from?”

Jenkins gazed at the flowers. Had he not heard him? What was he doing? Then he turned back and spoke with a quiver in his voice, “Well, sa-some are from Pah-Pah-Paulson, sa-some are from Lucious Redfield, and sa-some are from you, Ga-Ga-George.”

“Why’d you do that?”

“Ca-Ca-Countess Helen told me to pa-pa-put them ta-ta-together. Each day.” Jenkins smiled, showing deep creases in his freckled face. “She pa-pa-prefers them that way.”

He gritted his teeth and left enraged. He was so furious he could not focus on where he was going but with whom should he be angry? Jenkins? Paulson? Redfield? Helen? Yes, it was *Helen.* She was her own breed. He had known that but now what?

~35 ~

He tried to think through his anger and walked Charger through Burlington to their house and stabled him in the small barn in back. He walked around to the front of the house, the sun was sliding through the trees near the horizon over the lake below, walked up the steps, past the still swing and into the house, which felt empty, foreign. He didn't recognize any decoration. Its quietness made him uneasy. Apparently the cat had been moved elsewhere. He endured a restless night where every sound echoed in the emptiness. The next morning, still without word from Helen, he decided to send another note to the Wilson Hotel. He wrote he would return to Georgia to live in his father's house until they resolved their problems and, to save money, she could stay in their house. He gave the note to Jenkins and waited a day. No response came.

The following morning he felt compelled to take off his wedding ring and put it in his pocket. He walked Charger out of Burlington, headed north on the Post Road to Georgia and realized he was depressed. He didn't care about anything and let Charger ease along at a languorous pace. After a few miles he again saw the large house near the side of the road with the same pretty woman on the porch, rode closer and saw her rocking gently in a wooden chair while doing embroidery. He nudged Charger closer, tipped his hat and said, "Good day, ma'am."

The young woman looked up with her beautiful brown eyes, said nothing, and returned to her embroidery of green stitching on a white kerchief. Again, oddly, Charger stopped without being reined in. The woman wore a very nice yellow dress that showed off her curly brown hair. After her small, thin fingers tied down an imperceptible, tiny knot, she looked up again. “General, would you like some lemonade for your long ride?”

He rested his hands on the saddle horn. “That’d be nice, ma’am but I’m only going to Georgia.”

“Why, Georgia’s thataway and nearly fifteen hundred miles,” she said with a serious face and pointed south. Then she gave a broadening smile and said warmly, “You better have somethin’.”

“No. Thank you, ma’am, just the same.”

An old man with a cane came around the house from the barn in back, skirted the edge of a small watermelon patch, squinted up at him and called out, “Who’s there? Is that Thomas Ainsley?”

“No, grandpa. It’s a general heading *north* for Georgia.”

“Well Georgia’s south and fifteen hundred miles!” The man grinned a tight smile, slapped his knee then spoke to his pretty granddaughter. “Did you ask him in for pie?”

“No, grandpa. He says he’s fine.”

The old man said, “Emily makes the best cherry pie.”

“I’m fine, really,” he said. “I only stopped to say hello. A few days ago I rode by and noticed you.”

“You don’t say,” the old man said then after a pause he added, “What’s the matter with you—don’t you like cherry pie?”

“I think he’s in a hurry,” Emily said loudly. “After all he’s heading *north* to get to Georgia.”

“No disrespect general, but ya ain’t crazy, is ya?” the old man said.

He laughed easily then so did Emily. He dismounted, put his floppy hat on the saddle horn, bowed and introduced himself.

She smiled again and said warmly, “My name’s Emily.” She pointed over her shoulder to a small table. “I can get the pie and serve it here on the porch, if you like.”

“That’d be very nice,” he said. He was surprised at how easy it was to be relaxed and feel good with her. She brought out two wooden chairs for them and served two dishes of cherry pie and two glasses of sweetened lemonade on a small table. After they spoke for a few minutes he learned, as he had suspected, she was Emily Clark, daughter of Mr. Worthington Curtis Clark, who co-owned the iron foundry in St. Albans, where he had worked. He recalled the horrible fire at the foundry then remembered he had heard Mr. Clark had died of pneumonia a few years ago. He said, “I knew your father. He was a good man.”

“Thank you, that was some time ago,” Emily nodded and continued, “I don’t have any brothers or sisters. It’s just me and Grandpa Joe. Oh, and a pet rabbit named Helen.”

He burst into laughter. “That’s an appropriate name for a rabbit!”

“How’s that?”

“I know a Helen and she has rabbit-like behavior!”

Despite his laughter Emily noticed his discomfort and it touched her. She gazed into his eyes with concern, reached out and caressed his upper arm, then spoke from her heart, "I can tell you're in pain but at least you can still laugh. Maybe you're due to, well, I'm sorry. It's not my place."

"No, go ahead. Say what's on your mind." For some reason he winked to her, it just happened reflexively, along with his next words, "Be bold."

Emily's brown eyes glistened with hope and she spoke with genuine warmth, "I know it seems like everybody knows everybody else's business these days, and it's none of mine, but maybe you're due to meet someone nicer."

"I think I already have."

She smiled and they were distracted by a light snoring sound. It came from Grandpa Clark, who had fallen asleep in the rocker. They both burst out in laughter then she put her hand to his mouth to quiet him.

The afternoon passed with long violet shadows stretching across the lawn until the sun kissed the mountaintops on the far western shore of Lake Champlain. He and Emily continued to sit on the porch, over a second slice of pie, and sipped a small glass of sherry. They watched the first fireflies glow then disappear in the shrubbery amid the dim fading light, then beam again somewhere new. He gently held her soft, warm hands. In its own way, the moment was perfect.

He waited still longer, knowing he must go, then announced, "I should move along and get Charger back home. Sometimes he gets antsy riding in the dark."

"We wouldn't want that," Emily said with a warm smile, underscoring her bright eyes. "Feel free to stop by next time you're around. I bake bread—fresh every day."

The low golden light of dusk illuminated her beautiful face and she tucked her dark hair around her ears. Her rosy cheeks and face glowed radiantly. Then she finished the embroidery of bright white myrtle flowers with green stems on a white kerchief by stitching her initials ECC with green thread in the corner and presented it to him. "It was a real pleasure chatting with you, George."

"Thank you, Emily." He stared into her eyes. Charger whinnied but he did not want to leave. Why hadn't he noticed this beautiful, wonderful and kind woman before? "It's been a genuine pleasure for me, too."

Grandpa Clark awoke on the porch. "What? Why, yes, indeedy! A real pleasure. Come back anytime, George! Feel free to bring the missus."

He swallowed hard, thought of Helen and the wedding band in his pocket, and felt guilty. He knew he may never have another social engagement with Helen and knew he would not bring her here. "Thank you very much, Mister Clark. Emily. Good day."

He folded Emily's present of her kerchief and tucked it in his pocket over the ring, put on his hat, swung up on Charger and rode slowly up the road, heading for Georgia and home.

He again found himself thinking of Helen and felt deeply troubled. He felt drawn apart from her and more hurt than ever before. It was a wound that would not heal. He had given her everything, all his worldly goods, his heartfelt emotions, and all that was left was a great emptiness that resounded and pained him. In the enveloping darkness tears welled up and spilled over his cheeks. He did not think it was right to use Emily's pristine kerchief, so he let his tears run like a cleansing salve all the way home.

~36 ~

He thought often of Helen's request for a divorce. It was so upsetting he wondered if it was real. Day after day he awoke wondering, How could it be? Is this a test from God? Didn't they get married and vow to live together forever? How was it he lived in Georgia, attended to the farm and his horses, while Helen lived in Burlington?

He wished his mother was alive to discuss this. She would know how to deal with this woman and would have sage advice about their marriage. What would she have said? He thought and prayed for an answer but it was a baffling mystery.

He poured hay then alfalfa in the long trough for the horses, stirred them about with his hand, and each of the 14 horses came to eat except Charger, standing asleep in his stall. "Hey! Sleepy head! Wake up!"

The white horse stomped the ground once, then turned at the neck to look at him with its large dark eyes. He poured oats into Charger's bucket and sauntered over. He had not ridden Charger in several days and recalled the feeling of riding together, a feeling of close unity. It might be good to ride again, he thought. It was a very nice day with high puffy clouds floating on a warm, light breeze from the west.

After a breakfast of fresh eggs and bacon, he saddled up Charger, walked him out of the stable and swung up into the saddle. Then someone came running toward him on the road. It was the post carrier from Burlington, Eliot Landsdale, who waved then rushed up onto the grassy yard, scaring a few blackbirds out of the large oak tree.

He turned Charger to meet Eliot, who was very thin with spectacles and carried a leather mail pouch. Perspiration ran down his temples from under his dark curly hair and he smiled jovially, showing two teeth missing on his right side, and said, "Howdy do. Got a letter for you. It's from that attorney feller, Ben Reivers."

"Thanks." He reached down and took the parchment envelope.

"It looked important so I came out right away." Eliot stood near the porch of the Trading Post, removed his postman's cap and wiped sweat off his forehead.

"Thank you, you did right." He adjusted in the saddle and held up the letter. Eliot appeared to be waiting for him to open it.

"Sometimes people like to reply right away," Eliot said then strolled away a few steps, turned his back and sighed, pretending he had never seen this view of the rolling, grassy hills of Georgia. He added, "I'll give you a moment."

George squeezed his eyes shut because he knew what this was, then opened his eyes again. Why did this small envelope feel so heavy? He used his forefinger and ripped it open. Inside was a brief, four-line letter:

To: *Gen. George J. Standard,* of *Georgia,* Vermont March *24*, 186*3*

Your presence is requested at the office of Judge Yarborough Whalen on the *2nd* day of *April,* 186*3.* A discussion and settlement of marriage to *Countess Helene Marie Bokowski* has been filed. Failure to respond to this notice will be held in contempt.

Sinc. yrs.
Benjamin Quincy Reivers, Esq.

A settlement of marriage? What an odd phrase. He felt his marriage was settled. He read it again. April second was next Monday.

"It sure is lovely here, general," Eliot cleared his throat then adjusted his leather pouch. Another moment passed while blackbirds circled about then settled in the oak. He read the note again and tears formed in his eyes.

"Will there be a reply?" Eliot asked with his back still turned.

He started to respond but his throat was thick. He cleared it and said, "No."

Eliot turned around, smiled graciously, walked over and stroked Charger along his nose. "Fine lookin' horse. What's his name?"

“Charger. Thank you. We’ve been together. . . a long time.” He thought the same could be said of him and Helen. He had known her four years and they been through many difficulties together. A tear rolled down his cheek, which he ignored. He rubbed Charger’s white mane and neck. “Charger was born not too long after my father died.”

“I remember Samuel. Good man. Honest, cheerful.”

He thought of his father behind the counter of the Trading Post, beaming at him with a smile of pride and confidence. Then he thought of Samuel laying outside the fort in Canada with his life easing out into the frozen snow. His last moment alive was etched in his mind, with his teeth clenched in a grimace of pain.

“You can’t ever replace a good man,” Eliot said, coughed a little then spoke with emotion, “You know, I wish I was serving with you now, sir.”

“Eliot. Please call me George, you always have.”

“You know I was too young for the Canadian Rebellion and now my eyes are too poor for this fight. If’n anything happened to my spectacles, I’d be a goner in no time.”

“ ‘S okay, Eliot. There’s plenty to do here and I’m sure you’re doing your share.”

“I wish I was doing more, don’t you know? I wish I could serve.”

“Right.” He felt Charger move to the side impatiently, implying, Are we going to stand and talk all day? Can’t we *go* somewhere?

“Would you like a ride back to Burlington? We can talk along the way.”

“That’d be right nice of you, George. My feet are killing me. I gave my good boots to my nephew, he signed up last month, and now I’m wearing these old clod busters and they’re too small!”

He offered his hand and pulled Eliot up onto Charger’s back behind the saddle, then folded the letter in half and stuck it in his waist. They rode for Burlington, admired the rolling hills and meadows full of cows, and enjoyed a light, warm breeze. Eliot gave him all the news about his neighbors and repeated some of what he already knew from talking with Tommy Lonegran, Aunt Amelia and Mrs. Turner, who had complained there was not enough cotton to make a nice dress. He let Eliot talk but thought about the parchment letter and the meeting at the Judge’s office next Monday. What should he do?

The city of Burlington was busy although there were fewer young men around. People were going in and out of several banks, or a new barber shop, a new general store and even a new lawyer’s office. He considered hiring an attorney to represent him but felt there was no point to it. When they arrived at the Post Office, he noticed across the avenue the staid, old law office of Benjamin Reivers. He steadied Eliot by his arm as he slid off Charger, said “Good day!” lay the reins to the left, clucked twice in his cheek and rode off with Charger.

The following Monday he hitched Charger to a post outside the office of Benjamin Quincy Reivers, Esq., went inside and met Mr.

Reivers, the lawyer, then Judge Whalen, and signed a few papers. Reivers was an officious, older man with a gaunt complexion and horrible breath. Judge Whalen, who was an elder colleague of Judge Veazey, ushered him into a new world of divorce and explained the entire record of their marriage would be expunged, then felt obligated to explain expunged meant "it was as if it never happened."

He said nothing, roiling with rage, depression, anger, and a deeper humiliation than the surrender at Harper's Ferry. He thought, Something as monumental as years of marriage could not be "expunged" but he was spent fighting this and wanted it over.

A few minutes later he stepped outside. His ears were ringing and he was dazed and did not know where to go. He loosened the reins from the hitching post, held onto Charger's neck, leaned in and cried. Charger remained steadfast then bobbed his head at the sound of his sobbing. Mr. Reivers called out from the door, "Need some help?"

He did not bother to wipe his eyes, he knew more tears were coming, swung up onto the saddle with effort, jerked the reins to the side and dug his heels into Charger's ribs harder than intended. They sped off for the Post Road and Georgia, the farm and home. He had to get home.

When he turned Charger into the yard, the postman Eliot was waiting for him, sitting on the grass. Before he dismounted Eliot gawked at his teary face, then with a business-like posture stood and held out a wax-sealed note.

He thought, Now what? broke the seal, unfolded the note and read the message. He had been ordered back to Washington to the Army of the Potomac.

~37 ~

General Lee, instructed by Confederate President Jefferson Davis, marched his soldiers north. They no longer fought a defensive war to protect their capital of Richmond but instead invaded the North, moving toward Pennsylvania. President Davis had coordinated this northern attack with another courier to hand President Lincoln a secret plan with a new offer of peace, immediately following the next Confederate victory. After a great, decisive battle it would be clear to Yankee politicians the Southern states should be allowed to remain free and independent. When threatened with the plundering of Northern cities, how could Lincoln refuse a peace settlement?

Over the past few months of the war Lincoln had been worn to his breaking point, again, with General McClellan and was alarmed by the invasion. Lincoln could take no more delays and no more excuses from the Commander of the Union Army. Lincoln had tried week after week and sometimes wrote every day imploring McClellan to move the huge Federal forces into position to stop Lee and the Confederates *now*. Then he relieved McClellan of command. Next came a series of appointments where Lincoln tried one inept general after another in an effort to find a leader who could win a battle against the astounding maneuvers of Lee.

The momentum for the Southern forces carried on through the spring of 1863 with more Confederate victories, culminating in the battle of Chancellorsville. On May 1st, the first day of battle, General Lee and his Rebel soldiers met the new Union Commander, "Fighting Joe" Hooker. Even though the Confederates were outnumbered by 40,000 men, every attack and every flanking movement by the Union forces was met with fierce resistance.

On May 2nd Lee used his forces to strike at the Union. In the morning, in a daring maneuver of speed and ingenuity, General Thomas "Stonewall" Jackson swept around the Union flank through the woods and surprised them. By mid-afternoon General "Fighting Joe" Hooker was so demoralized he stood in the doorway of the house that was his headquarters overwhelmed, some say frozen in fear, for hours while the Federal Army was pounded. Despite months of training the soldiers in blue once again ran for their lives. They ran for two miles in a speedy retreat and the rout was on. General Lee now threatened to finish off the entire Army of the Potomac. Only the setting sun saved the Union forces from total annihilation.

The Confederates had whipped the Union again. In the closing darkness, General Jackson sensed an opportunity because the fleeing Army of the Potomac was in shambles and disorder. If the Southerners pursued them, they had a chance to capture the entire chaotic army in retreat. At dusk Jackson went out with his scouts and a few officers to obtain first-hand information on the position and strength of the Union forces. When they returned to the Confederate line after dark, Rebel pickets fired at them. It was mayhem for a few moments with the pickets firing and the officers screaming to stop but in the confusion one officer was killed and another bullet struck Jackson in the arm. He was rushed to a nearby house, operated on by their best doctor, and his arm was amputated. The entire Confederacy was relieved Jackson was not wounded more severely.

That night the Federals regrouped. Over the next two days of battle, General Hancock pulled together regiments to form some resistance and it was Hancock's stubborn, proud fighting ability that saved the Union Army from being destroyed. The Federals had lost another battle and 14,000 more men.

Southern General Jackson's recovery was slow, then worsened. He fell in-and-out of consciousness and pneumonia set in. Jackson was fervently religious but now his wife, staff officers, and all the soldiers around him prayed for his recovery. His situation was desperate, then miraculously Jackson managed to open his eyes and said, "Let us cross over the river, and rest under the shade of the trees."

The room went quiet. A moment later Jackson died.

Jackson, who had been shot in the arm, had been one of the Confederate's most savvy and tenacious leaders. When the news reached General Lee, he was distraught and secluded himself in his tent for hours where he was heard sobbing. When Lee emerged, with his puffy light eyes reddened from crying, his voice warbled with emotion, "This is the most devastating blow to the Southern cause ever."

Despite their success at Chancellorsville the Federal army had slipped away and General Lee and Southern President Davis felt they still needed a major victory to show the Northerners, Great Britain and the whole world, these independent-minded Confederate states should be given their own nationhood. Lee maneuvered his army around the Shenandoah Mountains and under his direction General J.E.B. Stuart and his cavalry struck a swift victory at Brandy Station. Then General Richard Ewell followed with a decisive blow at Winchester, for the second time in the war.

As the summer heated up the temper of civilians of the North became short. Southern agitators living in northern cities increased their sabotage and inflicted chaos at the core of daily life. A coach traveling from Hartford to Boston carrying the mail and bank deposits was robbed at gunpoint and six guards were killed. Several suspicious fires burned government offices in various small cities in Pennsylvania and New York. A cargo ship containing supplies for the Northern Army was ripped apart by an explosion in the hull and sank off Cape Cod. Disaster and chaos appeared everywhere, dissolving the Union foundation.

Lee marched his men further north and crossed the border from Maryland into Pennsylvania. The people of the North felt vulnerable. If Lee had won so many battles, and with the Army of the Potomac being used to defend Washington City, what force would stop the Rebels from continuing further north to New York City, Hartford, or Boston? Who would save the common folks of these northern cities from the tens of thousands of ravishing, plundering soldiers of the Confederacy? Panic spread among the Northerners along with fervent prayers to preserve the Union.

President Lincoln prayed and he also took action. The Union had 100,000 soldiers in the Army of the Potomac, which had been defending Washington but now hurried in pursuit of General Lee; 70,000 men fought in the Western Campaign at Vicksburg under General Grant; and 60,000 men marched under General Sherman's orders in the Southern Campaign. Lincoln knew more soldiers were needed and instituted the first Draft for an additional 100,000 men to be selected. The Draft would be for all men aged 18-45 who were fit for service, or a person could pay $300 to hire a replacement for himself.

News traveled by telegraph throughout the nation, by horse and rider to every village and every citizen. People all across the Union wondered where it would all end. Over 125,000 men had been killed and now the war was coming north, possibly to their home state and their home town. More men were being drafted into the Army, for the first time against their will, and thousands more would be killed for a cause some could not support. Newspaper editors wrote, If they were fighting for freedom, then why shouldn't the Southerners have freedom to be their own nation?

The Confederate forces led by Lee's skillful maneuvers had won victories throughout the Shenandoah Valley. The battles of Chancellorsville, Brandy Station, and Winchester had given even more momentum to the Southerners. The Union losses of 14,000 men at Chancellorsville, 500 at Brandy Station, followed by 3,000 at the second Winchester battle made people believe Lee could advance and win at will. Not one of the many generals Lincoln had appointed as Commander had been able to stop him. During the war they had lost major battles under Generals McDowell, McClellan, Burnside, McClellan again, Pope and now Hooker. The Federal Army, despite endless training, despite delaying tactics by McClellan and other generals, maneuvered cautiously and failed miserably.

The mood in Washington was gloomy and desperate. Was there no one in the Federal Army who could lead the Union to victory? Was Lee such a brilliant tactician he could outmaneuver any Union general and win any engagement over whatever ground was chosen? In this desperate situation President Lincoln, along with his advisers, selected George Gordon Meade to command the Army of the Potomac.

General Meade had a worn, tired-looking face with drooping black bags under his eyes and a wiry gray beard on his chin. Behind his back some soldiers called Meade "the old goat" because of his appearance but it also fit his often irritable mood.

Meade's first task was to take stock of the 100,000 men under his command. They were in good shape, although weary from training day after day after day. They were demoralized from their recent losses and there was also an air of resentment. Many felt they had lost because of poor leadership and if they were given a chance to fight on open ground, or God forbid on favorable ground, they would put up a good fight. Meade's first orders were to consolidate his forces into one large mass and for General Buford and General Reynolds to *not* engage in a fight until they were all together.

Meanwhile General Lee marched his forces further north, where he sought a decisive victory to enable a peace settlement. Lee's massive army of 70,000 men converged on a little town in the rolling hills of Pennsylvania where several roads met. It was a small town of no strategic importance, although many of his soldiers needed shoes and it was rumored a shoe factory was in this town called Gettysburg.

As Lee moved his Rebel Army into Pennsylvania, General Buford's bluecoats were surprised. The Union soldiers instinctively fired at the Confederates to keep them from taking this small town despite Meade's orders to *not* engage the enemy until the entire Federal Army was united. After a day of increasingly intense fighting, the Federals withdrew through town to the heights of Seminary Ridge and Cemetery Ridge, with two small mountains, Little Round Top and Big Round Top, just to the south. It was good high ground with a large open field in front of them. The decision to take and hold this high ground would set the stage for the two huge armies, totaling 150,000 men, to face-off in one great, decisive battle. The outcome had the potential to destroy the Army of the Potomac and determine the fate of the Southern states.

~38 ~

At 4 a.m. George received an order from the new Federal Commander of the Army of the Potomac General Meade. The Vermont 12th, 13th, 14th, 15th, and 16th Regiments were needed in

Pennsylvania *post haste*. A battle was imminent. Meade did not mince words and did not panic but these were new, nine-month volunteers from Vermont and their term of service would be completed in a few days, on July 1st.

He ordered Benedict to have the troops fall-in and the brassy sound of several buglers called out. They had spent most of their nine-months drilling, making reinforcements of timber and earth, drilling, eating bland to bad food, playing cards, digging trenches and marching, also known as drilling. Most of the Vermonters called their encampment Camp Boredom. Sometimes very light skirmishes with the Rebels gave them something to talk about but mostly they drilled.

Moments before 5 a.m. the sun was beginning to rise and split through the woods. Campfires smoldering from the previous night were extinguished. The Vermonters were unshaven and grouchy at being awakened so early, and they were hungry. They stood in long, almost straight lines behind their five color bearers including Corporal Hicks, the thin, swift veteran who had performed well at Harpers Ferry.

George sat high on Charger and walked him in front of the soldiers, who were in good order although here and there a shirt stuck out or a hat was cocked off to the side. Their firearms were clean and ready, and their ammunition haversacks stuffed. Despite all the drilling they had performed George knew they were an unknown, untested group. They were green volunteers who had not been in a fight.

He steered Charger to the front of the regiment, wheeled him around and sat for a moment. He was uncomfortable addressing all 2,000 soldiers and hated giving speeches. He preferred to talk face-to-face but there was no time for that. Many of these boys would have their nine-month enlistment expire in a few days and they needed to be told their options.

"Boys, we've been called to serve our country," he began in a serious tone. "General Meade has ordered us to march to Pennsylvania and he wouldn't have called us unless there's going to be a fight."

Many of the Vermonters appeared sleepy. "It's my duty to get us there and damn quick. It will not be an easy march but thank goodness we've been practicing our marching!" Some laughed but most showed an anxious expression of fear.

"It is also my duty to remind you, officially, your term of service has ended. Anyone who wants to go home can." A few of them shouted, "No!" but again far more said nothing, perhaps contemplating the terrible battle to come.

"Many of you know when Fort Sumter was fired on two years ago, I was the first Vermonter to throw my hat in the ring. I love my country. Some of you have families back home and some of you joined for the pay. So there's no hard feelings if any of you want to head back. Lieutenant Benedict will arrange your passage. But we need every one of you who can fight to come with us. I'm counting on you. Vermont looks to you. General Meade and the entire Army of the Potomac need us. Our country needs us. I hope you will join us, but there's no hard feelings if you feel obliged to go home. That's about all I've got to say. It's been my privilege to serve you and I sure do appreciate any of you honorable men who care to join Vermont's finest. May God bless us as we move into this battle."

Colonel Ripley, red-cheeked with his bright brown eyes burning with passion, raised himself high on his horse Lightning and shouted, "*Vermont's Fighting Ninth is with you!*"

"*So is the Twelfth!*" Colonel Veazey hollered and pumped his fist in the air from atop Justita, his dark thoroughbred. His bright smile shined amid his tanned skin.

He knew it was fortunate he had solid, reliable leaders to command each regiment, then realized he had trained them this way. They had grown into hardened, experienced leaders. Now all the Vermonters were shouting and cheering.

He took off his floppy hat and wiped the sweat from his brow. It was ungodly hot already. He turned and faced Benedict, who sat on his mount, Folio. Benedict had been with him since the beginning of the war and understood what lay ahead. His face was stern, contrary to his bookish spectacles, and he spoke grimly, "God help us."

Each of the 2,000 Vermonters were eligible but only three boys requested passage to go home, which George knew was a very good sign. They meant to fight. They gathered their gear and broke camp within an hour after dawn. The boys were in good spirits and did not complain much, even when the temperature rose to 98 degrees.

A few minutes after noon, after they had marched for 12 miles, he ordered a 30-minute break for lunch and water, and called his staff of officers together under the shade of a huge elm tree. Those who had been marching sat or lay down but the officers who had been riding horses, as he had on Charger, dismounted, stretched and watered their mounts then stood at ease. He stroked Charger's white muzzle and poured water from his canteen into his palm. Charger drank eagerly then a water boy came over with two buckets in each hand for the horses. Charger and Folio, Benedict's horse, drank the wooden buckets dry and licked at the bottom. The water boy watched with astonishment then dashed off to the creek to refill the buckets.

He stretched again, walked around the soldiers, sometimes patted a young man on the back or shook hands and offered his canteen. Then he went back to the shade of the large elm where the officers had gathered and waited. Three crows stood perched on an overhanging limb. "So far the boys are doing well but we have a difficult march ahead of us. It's very important to get there as soon as possible. That means *absolutely* no one can break ranks from the march. Absolutely *no one* and not for *any* reason. Is that clear?"

"Yes, sir!" Ripley said.

"Yes" and "Yes, sir" the other officers echoed. Ripley took off his kepi then wiped the sweat from his brow with a large white kerchief embroidered with his initials EHR in red in the corner, passed the kerchief over his face, over his trimmed dark hair and placed his kepi on the pommel of his saddle. His face was flushed from the heat but his dark eyes appeared eager for the challenge.

He continued, "Before any stop, canteen runners will be appointed to fill canteens."

"Yes, sir!" Ripley, Benedict, Veazey, and all the officers said.

"Very good. Make sure the boys understand. It's important."

"Yes, sir," said Veazey, who had also taken off his hat and used it to fan his red-hot face. Beads of sweat ran from under his dark hair and ran in rivulets over his tanned skin, gathered around his white collar and added to his wet shirt. Justitia, his dark thoroughbred, sweat profusely. "We'll march to Hell for you, sir."

He appreciated the confidence and nodded. "Before we reach this town, it will feel like we've been *through* Hell."

Veazey replied with his deep, smooth voice, "We will do this easily."

"A walk in the park," Ripley said with a grin.

A smile came to him. These were good soldiers. He saluted with pride and those who were on the ground stood and all saluted, then the officers moved through the troops to pass along his order to *not* break ranks, not for *any* reason. The soldiers sat on the ground eating hardtack or jerky and some stretched out in the shade of the trees that lined the road.

One of the three crows fell off the limb and hit the dirt road with a small puff of dust. Its beak was open with its grey tongue in the dry, powdered earth.

After 20 minutes of rest, the order was given and the Vermonters fell in. Ripley put on his kepi, mounted his fine chestnut horse Lightning, and called out "*Forward!*"

They marched for 17 more miles.

That night they rested for six hours. Benedict had their new bugler, Gregory Sutpin, an eager boy of 16 from Montpelier, sound reveille to awaken the Vermonters before dawn. They rose, broke camp, and began their march again.

He saw the Vermonters' spirit dwindling, tiring under their heavy load, under long woolen coats, under the hot broiling sun. The temperature rose to over 100 degrees. The boys drank their canteens dry and the dusty road parched their throats.

In the early afternoon an entire company of canteen runners were sent ahead and filled hundreds of canteens from the nearby creek. When the Vermonters' column reached them he ordered a ten-minute rest. The soldiers fell out and the runners distributed full canteens. The young men drank then collapsed in the shade.

Lieutenant Stephen F. Brown was part of a company that was somehow overlooked and not supplied by the canteen runners. Brown, a barrel-chested policeman from Swanton, grabbed several canteens, ran down to the creek that winded its way along the dusty road, and filled a dozen canteens with cool creek water. He did not hear the order to fall in or see the long blue line marching again. Brown was surprised to see the 13th Regiment marching without him, ran clumsily with the canteens swinging around his neck, and received a great cheer when he distributed them, then returned to his place.

George heard the cheer, saw what had happened, and turned to Ripley. "Halt the brigade."

Ripley wheeled Lightning around, yelled "*Halt!*" several times and buglers sounded the order. Ripley then spurred his horse back along the very long line of boys in blue, who stopped in confusion.

He felt disheartened but knew he had no choice. All the Vermonters had to keep moving. Any order could not be disobeyed. "Benedict, assign two corporals to arrest Lieutenant Brown. Put him in the rear wagon under guard."

"Yes, sir! Corporals Fisher, Sullivan, come with me!" Benedict and two corporals hustled back, past the long blue column to the 13th Regiment. He rode Charger at a slow gallop behind them until they reached Brown, who still had water dripping from his short brown beard and his sleeves were wet from the elbows down. Sweat poured from under Brown's cap and ran down his temples.

Benedict ordered, "Sullivan, relieve Lieutenant Brown of his sword and musket!"

The corporal obeyed and Brown stood still with amazement and confusion. Benedict took Brown's sword and saluted him. Sitting high on Charger, George said, "An order is an order, lieutenant."

"But sir! The men were thirsty."

He tipped back his floppy hat and wiped his brow. "I appreciate your concern for your fellow men but no soldier can disobey and break rank under any circumstances. Put him under arrest in the last wagon."

At the rear of the long train were the ammunition and supply wagons, where Brown hopped into the back of an empty wagon, alone. The two corporals, Sullivan and Fisher, followed then stood at attention behind the wagon.

He nodded to Benedict, who circled his horse Folio then used a signal flag to notify Veazey at the front of the column. Veazey's deep, booming voice could be heard faintly over the mile-long train when he hollered, "*For-ward!*"

The long blue column began to move again. He nudged Charger with his boots and they galloped, and in a few minutes took their place with Veazey at the front.

As the Vermonters marched for hours, the intense heat bore down on them and the load they carried felt heavier. Corporal Deters, a tall thin boy of 17 from Barre said, "After Sunday, I'm goin' home. I won't need any of this stuff."

Deters shed his heavy pack then his coat and a few more soldiers took off their long woolen coats and tossed them to the side of the road. Here and there a young man dropped his bedroll, tent, or took off his boots. They even discarded bulky food rations.

When word of these actions spread through the long blue line to the front George turned to Veazey, Ripley and Nichols. "Veazey! Inform those boys who dropped their gear they must fetch their packs."

Veazey, who had become an expert rider on Justitia during the war despite being a large man, turned his dark thoroughbred and rode back alongside the column. On the way Veazey turned to curse every Vermonter without gear. Some of the young men refused to go back for their equipment, even after his order, so Veazey threatened them with court martial, which persuaded them to retrieve their gear.

Several exhausted young men from Ripley's regiment sat motionless, dazed and disoriented, until Ripley approached them and ordered, "Fletcher! Harris! Round up any discarded pack and put them in the rear wagons!"

There were several near-empty wagons designated to carry the future wounded but now soldiers tossed in gear, including next to Lieutenant Brown. Of the 2,000 Vermonters, three young men with bleeding blisters eased themselves into the last wagon, where Brown gave them a sulking glare.

On the second day of their march they covered 29 miles. Two of the three soldiers with sore feet later rejoined the column. It was a brutal, exhausting march, in blazing hot weather, over sometimes rough country. They had many more miles to go before they would reach General Meade's encampment.

George prayed they would not be too late and that these raw soldiers would not be too exhausted to fight. He had to drive them very hard on their march and feared for their condition and temperament. He wondered, after this hellish march to the battlefield, would these fatigued, inexperienced boys fight?

~39 ~

The Vermonters were drained and needed rest after their second grueling day of marching. They made camp moments before nightfall and some set-up tents but most collapsed on blankets by the roadside. It had been another very long, very hard day and he worried for his boys. If he pushed them too hard, what good would they be in battle?

He tethered Charger to a stake, watered, fed, then watered him again then set-up his tent and helped Benedict and then Ripley with their tents. He did not eat. He lit a single candle and went inside his tent. It was ten feet wide, ten feet long, with a pole in the center to raise the ceiling to almost eight feet and he set the candle on the ground, not bothering to unpack his small writing table or gear. He took off his uniform and boots, sat on the edge of his cot, untied then used his neckerchief to dab sweat from his face, neck, and brow. He smelled Emily's faint perfume on the cloth and paused to gaze at the embroidered bright white myrtle petals then the green thread with Emily's initials "ECC." He sniffed the kerchief, thought of seeing her again, and knew it was impossible to survive this war.

He lay the wet kerchief on top of his uniform coat, stretched and tried to relax but did not sleep well. He heard several soft, distant booms and hoped it was heat lightning and not Confederate canons shelling Meade's encampment and the Union lines. He tossed, turned, and agonized over the thought the battle had started. He sat up in a heavy sweat, itched his back, arms, and head. He smelled freshly ground coffee, rose from his cot, pulled on his boots and went outside his tent. Snoring filled the air, a few soldiers stood on guard, and a pot of coffee bubbled over a small fire. Stars twinkled in the wavy heat of the night sky then heat lightning boomed in the distance again.

"Have some coffee, general?" a thin private called out. His cap was low on his brow and the light of the campfire flickered across his bony face. There was an odd familiarity about him but the boy turned away shyly, perhaps intimidated by seeing a general walking about in his sleeping britches.

He walked over in his long johns then itched his backside again. His piles were acting up from spending so much time in the hot saddle. He poured hot coffee into a tip cup then said, "Thank you, private. I can't quite see your face, son. What's your name?"

"It's me. Jim Freehan." The bill of his cap covered his forehead but he had bright blue eyes and a hurt, confused look on his face. "Sir."

"Ah, Jim. What in the world?"

"I had to sign up." He tasted the watery coffee and Jim pushed back his cap, showing his short-cropped blonde hair. He seemed eager and determined but he appeared young, perhaps not more than 13. "I asked to serve under your command."

"You're with Colonel Nichols?"

"Yes, sir, the Fighting Sixteenth. Huzzah!"

"Shh. We don't want to wake the boys." He examined Jim's puffy eyes from a lack of sleep. His musket was almost as tall as he was.

"Jim, son. You should be in school. How old are you? And don't tell me whatever it was you told the enlistment officer."

"I'm fifteen, sir," a big smile came over him. "I got my pa's permission."

"Ah, Gordon. A good man, fine man." He recalled when he was 18, pleading with his father to join with the "Sons of Liberty" in the fight for the Canadian Rebellion of 1838, then recalled the gruesome image of his bloodied father, lying in the snow. He took another swallow of hot, watery coffee and paused to think. He rested his hand on Jim's bony, boy-like shoulders and said, "I'm proud to have you with us, Jim. The Fighting Sixteenth, hm? We haven't actually been in a fight, have we?"

"No and—"

"I think I would have heard about that."

"—and my nine months is done. I was real happy you had us come along." He appeared fit but was scrawny for his age. "Just the one skirmish. Once I saw a Reb high-tailin' it through the bushes. Just marchin' and sittin' on my ass in Camp Boredom. Nothin' to talk about back home. Shit, this Army life don't even compare to the foundry fire."

Jim spat then added, " 'Scuse my language."

He wasn't upset with Jim's language but wanted to tell the boy to be careful what he wished for but he was distracted by his memory of the foundry fire. He hadn't thought about the fire in detail for a long time. Painful, horrible visions shot through him and he spoke through the distracting memories, "You remember that day?"

"I was there!" Jim creased his forehead and again appeared hurt. "Remember, I got Dan Andrews and the whole fire brigade? Place woulda burned down completely if it weren't for me."

He remembered him as a small boy, little Jimmy Freehan running up the dirt avenue, followed by a group of firemen close behind. "Yes, of course, Jim. All true."

He nodded then squeezed Jim's thin shoulder, lacking any manly muscle. "I'm glad you're with us, son. I know you'll make your pa and all of St. Albans proud. I feel fortunate to have this cup of coffee with you. Thank you."

He finished the hot water flavored with coffee, hung the tin cup on a hooked rod by the fire, nodded, and headed back to his tent. He lifted the tent flap but looked back to study little Jimmy Freehan shuffling to the picket line with his long baggy pant cuffs dragging in the dirt, a thin, exuberant youth. He then thought of Jim's father, Gordon, who would need to work his farm alone if anything happened to his son, and he felt the shiver of an eerie premonition of death.

He entered his tent and sat on the edge of the cot, recalled the foundry fire, and stretched out. A bullfrog croaked then another bullfrog answered. The single lit candle, two-thirds its original height, dropped wax on the green, grassy ground. He remembered the day of that horrible fire, a clear August morning, and the god-awful way it turned uncontrollable very quickly. The fire was intense with little he could do against its raging flames. He rolled over, away from the single candle's light, and tried to sleep. His recurring nightmare returned:

He was stunned by the frozen panic evident in the face of Elijah Moore, the foundry co-owner, who stood trembling. Why didn't

Mr. Moore move or say something? The entire building was engulfed in flames, shooting through the roof, the front door, and threatened to destroy the entire foundry. Then Mr. Moore moved his trembling body into a vigorous gyration, almost like a dance, jumping up and down, and screamed, "Put out the fire! Put out the fire! My God, put it out! Put it out!"

He supervised men loading slag into the furnace, which was a fiery forge glowing hot with molten iron. Everything was fine until a great explosion ripped apart the furnace. Two men loading the pit with long iron rods were knocked off their feet but another man, Vernon Johnson, huge at six feet ten inches, was closest when he pushed a cart of coal toward the furnace and was flipped over backwards.

The blast slammed George against a nearby brick wall and the impact forced the wind out of his lungs. The sudden blow reminded him of when he was 14 and Thomas O'Sullivan caught him by surprise with a haymaker to the chest and sent him backwards into the brick wall of Brownell's General Store. Now he had that same uncomfortable feeling and tried to breathe but couldn't, couldn't inhale, couldn't pull his chest upward. He had no breath. His nostrils flared out with his mouth wide open and he tried in vain to breathe in. Then he relaxed, pushed downward, exhaled a brief grunt and drew in a deep searing hot breath of acrid smoke and burning air.

The two slag loaders, Richard Lomas and David Ardent, scrambled to their feet and hustled for the front entrance. Then the furnace collapsed outward and flames shot out of the pit, roaring out of control and licking the walls of the large room. The fiery forge glowed hot with molten iron and flames.

Vernon Johnson lay face-down unconscious. Flames snaked across the floor, followed a greasy trail, licked onto the wooden slag cart, and danced across Vernon's oil-stained pants and shirt. The fire caught on his flannel shirt, on his right sleeve, and his pants burned into the thickening black air. Flames fed on his back and his dark hair then his head was afire with flames. The defiant, raging fire claimed this victim.

He scrambled low to Vernon, ripped open his shirt, then wrapped it around his right forearm and patted out the flames on Vernon's burning scalp, then clapped out the flames burning his back and felt his sticky wet flesh. He strongly shook Vernon but he didn't respond. He kicked the burning wooden cart away but it rolled toward the hollow that had been the furnace. Then he tried to rouse Vernon again, his back smoldering, and rolled him over onto his back then swatted down the flames dancing across his pants to his boots. Vernon was big, heavy, well over 275 pounds and he struggled to lift him. He thought he heard Vernon groan.

"Get up!" *he yelled. Vernon rolled his head to the side.*

He pushed his hands under Vernon's damp armpits, tugged frantically, pulled again, and Vernon's weight moved an inch but a ball of flame shot across the ceiling in a fast warning. The fire had started near the coal bin and another fireball of reddish-orange flame burst across the room in search of fuel and found his head, wrapping its stifling, oven-hot presence around his face, and singed his eyebrows, nose, and mouth. His face felt tight with his head woozy like it was caught in a scalding vice. He needed to go down, rest, and he took a knee.

His face was one large searing pain. He turned away, turned back, rose then pulled on Vernon's armpits, lifting his shoulders off the cement floor. He recalled Vernon's impressive strength, of how two men struggled to lift a 12-foot iron beam but Vernon picked it up one with one hand and toted it anywhere easily. He wished he had Vernon's strength now and pulled, pulled again, and felt exhausted and dizzy. Sweat dried instantly, caked on his scalp, and scalding heat tightened its grip around his face and head. He had to stop to rest and knelt again.

Then Howard Kline, a short man, ran in to the foundry from outside, covering his face with his small hands then folded arms, then jerked on his arm. "Come on! Get out!"

"Help me with Vernon!" *he screamed. They each tugged under a damp armpit, pulled hard and Vernon budged, maybe a few inches, then he rolled his head to the side.*

Howard screamed, "We can't! He's too heavy!"

"We have to!" *he yelled. They pulled again and again, and moved this giant man inch by inch then he slipped and fell on his rump on the hard cement floor, feeling spent with no more energy. Howard was right. He had to save himself but felt the scorching heat when another fireball raced overhead, shot out the front of the building then caught on the overhanging beams and licked its way onto the ceiling. The smoke grew thicker, darker, and filled the large room.*

Howard yelled, "I'm getting out!"

He had heard him but he felt more peaceful on the floor. It was cooler. He wanted to lay down, rest. It would be easier to lay back, relax a moment, and then something deep inside him hollered with a piercing shrill scream, No!

Howard yelled again, "I'm leav—" *but before he finished he grabbed the back of Howard's pants, pulled himself up in one staggering stand and looked into his tearing, bloodshot eyes and screamed,* "No!"

He shoved his left hand under Vernon's armpit and used his strong right hand to grab Vernon's belt. Howard mimicked him on the other side, took him by the belt, and they lifted with all their might, dug in with their boots, and kicked their way across the cement floor. They made progress toward the filtering clear light of the doorway across the room and through the thickening black smoke.

He pushed his legs, pumped harder, moving across the uneven cement toward the light then something happened, some great energy came to them, and somehow they were able to go faster. They stumbled out the front door, a box-like rectangle of flames, and thick black smoke poured out with them into the clear air.

Outside they fell then rose and pulled Vernon further and lay him on the dirt avenue by the hitching posts. He breathed with difficulty still, coughed several times, and then he saw Chapman Bascom, the assistant foreman, run up and kneel over Vernon, listening for a heartbeat or a faint breath. Chapman's eyes widened then he massaged Vernon's chest and tried to make him breathe.

"Someone fetch Doc Kendrick!" *Chapman screamed.*

He coughed a few more times, bent over and felt out of breath like he had run a very long distance. He couldn't quite breathe enough, couldn't breathe any fresh air, and he tasted smoke. His lungs ached.

Mr. Moore stood rigid next to him with an agitated panic in his face, his lips trembled, drool spilled out of his mouth, and tears formed in his eyes. Then Mr. Moore screamed with clenched fists while he stomped the ground. "Put out the fire!"

He coughed again then spat out a glob of black soot. Black cinders and debris covered his pants and had burned holes in his shirt, still wrapped around his right arm, which he pulled off. His face felt very hot and he touched it but it felt foreign, smooth, hairless and searing. Heat radiated with pulsing intensity from the building. He noticed how close Vernon lay to the flames, now leaping out of the four, street-front windows and doorway. Thick black smoke gushed under the ceiling, seeped through the roof, and massive orange flames raged out of the chimney stack, eating away at the roof and then the area around the chimney caved into the foundry pit and an immense fountain of flames burst through the roof and rolled into a huge cloud of black smoke, billowing into the sky.

"Somebody do something!" *Mr. Moore screamed.* "My foundry's on fire! Oh my Lord!"

"Everyone out?" he asked weakly.

Mr. Moore's face was filled with panic and twitched in different directions. Sweat poured over his forehead and down his temples. He tugged at his uncomfortable bow tie but continued his gyrating dance of panic. "My foundry's on fire! Do something!"

Then Worthington Clark, the other foundry co-owner, rode up on a fine chestnut thoroughbred and dismounted quickly. People mobbed around Clark, pointed with excitement to the fire, or at him then Howard, or to Vernon on the ground. The crowd had grown to over 30 people and stood transfixed with some staggering about but going nowhere. Off to the side Mrs. Simpson fainted and her yellow cotton dress collapsed around her with her black shoes sticking out from under her white petticoats. Jimmy Freehan, who he knew from teaching at the schoolhouse, stood nearby and watched while sucking his forefinger.

"Jimmy!" *he hollered. The boy ran over and wore knee-length britches, a tattered shirt, and no shoes.*

"Run to the hotel and get the fire brigade!" He coughed. "If Dan Andrews isn't there, run to the barbershop," he coughed again, "Bring all the men there!"

Jimmy gazed at him with wide eyes and swallowed.

"Go! Run quick!" he ordered. The boy darted away and his bare feet kicked up puffs of dirt.

"Chappy!" *he yelled but the young assistant foreman kept massaging Vernon's chest then lightly slapped his cheeks. He felt nervous with an awful anxiety but spoke deliberately, "Is anyone inside?"*

"I don't know!" Chapman pumped at Vernon's chest without looking up. "I didn't see anyone."

Then a wagon with two horses raced down the street while the driver, Mary Yonkins, tugged the reins downward and back but the horses were spooked and ran with wild-eyed panic, jerking this way then that way with terror due the bright flames, roaring sound, and commotion. The wagon bounced over a pit in the street and a small barrel flew off the back end, smashed on the roadway and broke open, spilling its thick brown liquid.

*Erastus Jewett dashed from the crowd, grabbed the sideboard of the bouncing wagon and lifted himself onto it in one swoop, jumping over the bench seat and took the reins from Mary's hands and jerked down. The horses responded by running straight ahead at full speed. Erastus stood, leaned back and hauled the reins back and hollered, "*Whoa! Whoa!*" The horses skittered, slowed, then stopped.*

He turned back to Chapman. "We had ten men working today, right?"

Chapman massaged Vernon's still chest rhythmically but Vernon's huge body was motionless and appeared lifeless.

He pointed out foundry workers among the growing crowed and counted aloud. "Ten total. Terrence, Mark, John, Donald, Tad," he paused at the sight of people huddling over Mrs. Simpson, reviving her with her parasol by her white-gloved hand while several men tapped her cheeks or rubbed her arms. "Richard and David. You and me. How many's that? Nine, right? And Vernon. That's ten. Plus Mister Moore."

"Where's Orson?"

"Who's that?" He had worked at the foundry for over a year and knew everyone. He thought of the new hire, Mark Turnbow but the name Orson drew a blank.

"Leeds," Chapman said. "He's the new delivery man for the coal company. I signed for his delivery this morning."

He gasped with recognition and ran to Turnbow, the new hire with a pock-marked face. "Did you see Orson Leeds get out?"

"No. Who's that?"

Red-hot flames consumed the building with its wooden front only the suggestion of the foundry it once was with its brick sides and back walls crumbling down and most of what was the roof now a blaze of fire. A terrible feeling of dread overcame him. Leeds was trapped inside!

He hustled to Donald Goshen, a short, heavyset worker and shook his arm but Donald stared transfixed by the fire. "Did you see Orson Leeds get out?"

"What?" *Donald yelled to be heard above the fierce noise of the crumbling building. Sweat ran down his temples and dripped onto his plaid shirt that was too small for his thick waist.* "Orson?"

"Yes! Did you see him get out?"

Donald grabbed his shoulder and shouted, "No, no. He was already gone. He left for Burlington fifteen, twenty minutes ago."

"You're sure?"

"Yes. I waved to him as he drove down Front Street."

"You're positive?"

Donald appeared puzzled but nodded. "Yes, I told him to give my regards to Virginia Hall, she's my cousin in Burlington. He said he would and left."

He blinked with relief, gave a heavy sigh and coughed again. The back brick wall collapsed into the foundry pit and another huge ball of orange flames shot upward, darkening the massive cloud of smoke in the sky.

Jimmy Freehan ran up the middle of the street and dashed straight to him. He pointed up the street to where Dan Andrews ran with a small white towel in his hand and shaving cream still on his face. A group of four men rode on a red pumping wagon and barreled down the street after him. Dan waved to an area in front of the foundry, where the wagon's horses screamed to a shuddering stop and he yelled, "Point the hoses at the base of the fire!"

Two men hopped off and directed their dry hoses at the ground while two more men pumped up-and-down on the handles by the enormous barrels of water. A moment later a slow stream of water trickled onto the ground but it grew into a solid line of water they poured at the base of the burned-out frame then directed by Dan into the windows.

Jimmy Freehan backed away, off to the side. He nodded his appreciation to the boy, who smiled and showed one front tooth missing. A bead of sweat trickled from under his thin blonde hair.

He went to Doc Kendrick and huddled over Vernon's still body, where Mr. Clark looked on with concern. Doc Kendrick opened his black bag swiftly, tossed his black tall hat to the ground and placed a horn next to his ear and the cup over Vernon's chest. Doc Kendrick motioned to Chapman to stop pressing and he listened intently with his eyes searching the darkening sky. After a long, still moment he shook his head no.

"Oh God!" *Mr. Clark cried. Chapman covered his face with his hands and burst into tears. He hugged Chapman, who turned and sobbed into his shoulder.*

He awoke. The vivid events and emotions of the fire were palpable. It was a horrible tragedy of losing Vernon but he also felt the urgency of Orson Leeds's life *possibly* in danger, which was echoed by 80,000 soldiers in the Army of the Potomac but those soldiers were not *possibly* in danger. They were *definitely* in danger.

He sat up and glanced at the flame of the single candle. He recalled from the fire his feeling of complete exhaustion but how after a brief pause, given the will, incredible strength came. One had to try, try again, and if needed *try again.* When someone's life was in danger you *had* to give it your all again and again. Right now thousands of lives *were* in grave danger.

He stood, put Emily's kerchief around his neck, lifted his uniform off the end of the cot, and dressed in the quietness. Some soldiers snored and campfires crackled. He lifted his timepiece from his vest pocket and opened the case, 4:35 a.m. He replaced the timepiece then ran his hands over his sweating head and stepped outside. It was still very warm. He drank from his canteen then poured some of the warm water over his head, refreshing, corked the canteen and rubbed his wet beard and face, thinking again of that feeling of someone being trapped inside an uncontrollable, raging fire. He thought of Vernon again, of the simple jokes he had told, of how he bellowed with great laughter after he told the punch line even before others could laugh. He used a hand towel to dry his face, walked to Ripley's tent nearby and spoke firmly, "Colonel Ripley!"

Ripley mumbled then awoke with a sleepy voice, "Y-yes?"

"Colonel! Have the boys fall-in," he ordered. "We're moving out!"

No birds chirped in the blackened skies. The buglers called reveille and most of the soldiers rose but more than a few had to be shaken awake. They relieved themselves, prepared rapidly, put out fires, and some ate swiftly. The star-studded sky was beginning to lighten to a dark purple-orange glow in the east.

He packed up his gear and tent, then saddled up Charger. His piles were sore and he mounted him gingerly. The first rays of dawn broke over the horizon through the trees. He stood in the saddle, examining the long blue column of weary young men. They had marched 70 miles in two days through ungodly heat. He was proud of what they had done but knew there would be a more brutal test and very soon, perhaps at the moment they arrived. He waved his arm forward and the immense mass of 2,000 soldiers moved out.

They had 28 more miles to go.

Veazey, still wiping sleepiness from his dark eyes, nudged Justitia next to Charger. "What's the name of this little town in Hell?"

This caught Ripley's attention, his soft brown eyes perked up, and he rode his chestnut quarter horse, Lightning, closer. Benedict on his mount, Folio, leaned over to listen as the horses' hooves pummeled the dusty road. He spoke clearly so he would not have to repeat himself, yet softly so he would not be overheard, "Gettysburg."

~40 ~

On the third day of the Vermonters' march the temperature rose to 100 degrees again. They traveled 28 more miles in hot, humid weather with their packs, totaling 89 miles in 60 hours since they left Camp Boredom.

At their last planned stop for water and rest George noticed tiny drops of blood oozing from Charger's back. He unhitched then removed the saddle and saw Charger's back bleeding from the long, exhausting ride. One of the canteen runners set down a bucket of water but Charger didn't drink. He removed his gear and saddle then took out a dry cloth from his saddlebag, damped it with salve and gently rubbed the affected area. Charger's eyes rolled back and looked at him then he lowered his head and drank a little water. He would walk Charger for the duration of their march.

Every Vermonter knew that upon their arrival in Gettysburg they may be placed into battle and because this was their last stop, Father Dickinson walked up a slight ridge, raised his arms over the entire mass of soldiers and said a prayer, short and to the point. Then they broke camp and continued their march through the blazing hot day.

A few miles from Gettysburg he heard the booming cannons and sporadic gunfire but then it stopped. They drew closer, marching up the Emmitsburg Road with the sun setting, and found themselves in front of the Union picket line. The pickets were startled by soldiers in front of them and shouted, "*Who goes there?*" and "*Who?*"

Several men at the front yelled, "*Vermonters!*" and the pickets responded happily, "*Green Mountain Boys!*" lowered their muskets and let them inside their line.

Dusk descended and George climbed up on the bench of an ammunition wagon to view the terrain and Meade's placement of his troops. For once they held good, high ground with two small mountains forming a base at the southern end, and a very long blue line of soldiers with some behind a short stone wall, and a large open field in front of them. It was a very good defensive position.

He ordered his officers and the Vermonters to rest and remain here, asked Benedict to care for Charger's bleeding back, and went to Meade's headquarters but General Meade had retired to a late dinner. Instead he reported to General Winfield Hancock, a short man with a trimmed dark mustache. After a lengthy discussion, Hancock ordered him to be the field officer for the night. He was grateful for the honor but thought, So much for resting after a three-day, 90-mile march in the blistering sun. Hancock said there had been difficult fighting but, yes, they were not too late to be of service tomorrow. They *had* made it in time.

Hancock ordered him to move the Vermonters into a position of reinforcement, in the middle of the long Federal line along Cemetery Ridge. George saluted, returned to his staff of officers and ordered them to move out. The boys, although tired, marched another mile to the middle of the line. It was not long after they had settled that General Meade heard of their arrival and ordered them to march two miles back to the far southern end of the "fish hook" portion of their line, which was perhaps the weakest point of the entire front where it curled around Little Round Top mountain. The Green Mountain Boys marched in the dark, arrived in their new position and greeted the young men from Maine when a courier arrived with a note, stating that Meade had changed his mind. The Vermonters then marched back, another two miles and became reinforcements to the left of the very center of the long Federal line. One company was to guard the ammunition train two miles behind their line but the majority of the Vermont regiments would reinforce the center of the line, where an attack appeared eminent. Off to the right in the blackened night sky, he could see the vague outline of a few trees.

"Colonel Veazey, close-up the line and position the Thirteenth and Sixteenth to the left of that copse of trees."

At last Corporal Hicks and all the other color bearers planted the U.S. and Vermont regimental flags in the earth. The Vermonters set-up tents and campfires flickered in the darkness. From all over the open field in front of them, moans and cries of the wounded rose. No one had gone to their aid. He called, "*Colonel Nichols!*"

Nichols hurried over in his stockinged feet with his riding boots off to the side of his tent. He stepped over the uneven ground and gave a quick salute. "Yes, sir?"

"Pick eight men. Do *not* tell him but one is to be James Freehan of St. Albans. Transfer those eight to the Fifteenth Regiment, specifically to the company guarding the ammunition train in the rear. Those eight boys will first bear the wounded off the field. If needed, take more from the Fifteenth to help with the wounded."

"Yes, sir!"

"This single company from the Fifteenth," he repeated, "will be stationed in *reserve* to guard the ammunition train but the majority of the Fifteenth will support the Thirteenth and Sixteenth. Is this clear?"

"Yes, sir!" Nichols saluted then went off in the dark without putting on his boots.

As field officer for the night, he did not rest. Most field officers preferred to stay in one central place to gather regular reports but rather than sit in Meade's headquarters he wanted to be among the soldiers, gauge their morale, and survey the terrain. He knew Charger was fatigued and let him feed and rest. He noticed Benedict and Ripley helping Corporals Branch and Hughes care for the officers' horses.

He stood on the stone wall and gazed out over the open field. The eight stretcher bearers made many trips, returned with many wounded, then began to stumble and drop their load in the dark. Colonel Nichols, still in his stockings, found him, then saluted and announced, "Sir! I'm sorry, it's too dark. We can't see a thing an' we're liable to have some cranky Reb shoot us. I'm sorry, sir. We shouldn't continue."

He knew more lay out there, said "Damn" but nodded reluctantly. He stepped down off the wall and again told Nichols to reassign those boys to the reserves to guard the rear ammunition train. He rubbed the strain off his face, stretched, and walked behind their lines, attempting to study the terrain in the dark. He spoke with a few soldiers who were still awake, on their right from Pennsylvania, then made his way through the Vermonters' position to meet young men from New York and Minnesota on their left, ready for battle. He moved back and forth, stopping to gaze out over the darkened field to examine the terrain. To their right was a small knee-high wall built at an angle with a small copse of trees. To their left was a low ravine and further left was a fruit orchard of some kind with another orchard further out in front. It was too dark to see what kind of trees. Straight ahead the low ravine rose then leveled out into a great, open field.

The Vermont boys on picket duty were in good spirits despite their grueling march. He could also see they were frightened, which they should be. They had witnessed the remains of a hard day of fighting with wounded and dead littered about the battlefield in the uncomfortable and odd positions in which they had fallen. Although it was the first day of battle, everyone knew more intense fighting would come. Here and there an animal barked or hooted. A soldier still on the battlefield gave one last, rasping breath before expiring, or cried out insanely loud with a blood-chilling, shrieking cry against death. No one awake was unmoved. The boys on picket duty were jumpy, nervous, and were startled at every awkward sound for seven long hours.

Just before dawn on July 2nd Brigadier General Abner Doubleday approached him from behind the Vermonters position on the left-center of the line. Abner had become a large, heavy-set man, much different from how he had remembered him at the Hunter's Camp near Ogdensburg. Even in the dark he noticed a sour look on Doubleday's face and warmly shook his hand, grasping his forearm. "Abner, how are you?"

Doubleday shook his hand strongly then took off his large wide-brimmed hat. He perspired profusely and dabbed the back of his neck with a large blue kerchief then spoke in a deep, tired voice, "It was a hell of a day, for the record."

"So I heard," he said. "We got here as fast as we could. Pulled in at sundown just in time to see the god-awful wounded and dead. A real eye-opener for most of my boys. Got jockeyed around, center, left and back here again."

"A superb march," Doubleday said but his distant gaze showed his thoughts were elsewhere. The dark grayish light of dawn was beginning and Doubleday stared out over the open field to the Rebel position in the far woods, where tens of thousands of graycoats camped beyond the tree line. "God help us."

George thought of the horrors to come and imagined where the Southerners might attack. Neither spoke for a long, difficult moment. The sound of soldiers writhing in pain crept through the heavy shadows of the dark, gray-and-black field. Doubleday spoke in a raspy, soft voice, "There will be more."

In the eerie, pre-dawn light he sensed a horrible feeling then felt a huge swarm of swirling, haunting ghosts hung over the battlefield. From many restless places littered across this uneven field, the chilling vast emptiness of death lingered and rose from the dead. Spirits left corpses, were joined by floating dead from nearby Culp's Hill, from Cemetery Ridge, from all points in between, and around them. The dead were present.

He had felt this sensation before, with his father at the Windmill, with Bear Brisken at Bull Run, and he tried to ignore the spirits now. A chill raced over his damp neck and he spoke to drum away the feeling, "Hotter 'n Hades and it's only July. What will August bring?"

Doubleday kicked at the earth, reflected for a long moment, perhaps he felt the same eerie sensation, and spat on the ground. "More of the same, I'm sure. Except now we've got a new butcher leading us into Hell."

"Meade? He's a fighter, is what I heard. Have some faith, he may be good."

"The hell he is."

He nodded, thought of their bitter surrender at Harpers Ferry, where defensive positions were ignored and the Confederates were allowed to dictate the battle. "Well, I won't be put in a position like Harpers Ferry again. Our boys mean to fight."

"I don't blame you," Doubleday said. "I read about it and the surrender by that traitor, Miles. I knew in my heart you had nothing to do with it."

"You don't know the half of it," he said. "We were in position to cross the river. We could have fought through their reserves and we would have been part of Antietam. The Rebs wouldn't have had our guns and—" he paused. "Well, Antietam would have been one hell of a lot different."

"Who knows? Idiot bastards were *leading* us there, too."

"I'm not saying it wouldn't have been bloody but we may have prevailed. I've seen how a few good men, in the right spot at the crucial time, can make all the difference."

Doubleday nodded with conviction, knowing what could happen in a hot battle. "Yeah, I was with Major Anderson at Fort Sumter." He mocked Anderson in a high voice, "We *held out* for thirty-six hours!" then his voice returned to its naturally deep tone but raspy from a long day of yelling orders in battle. "Do you know how many casualties we had at Fort Sumter? Zero. 'Held out' my ass. Where do they find these guys?"

"God knows. Although I don't blame them for choosing the West Pointers," he said, "after all, I'm nothing but a *got damn volunteer!*"

"Right." Doubleday said. "A volunteer with wisdom and a lion's heart."

Doubleday clamped his hand down on his shoulder and squeezed it. "Maybe when this war's over, we'll play a game of base ball together. What do you say? Your Vermont Green Mountain Boys against my New York Yankees?"

"I'd like that," he grinned. Tears came to his eyes with thought of surviving this hellacious war, which he rarely allowed himself to think. It was too beautiful to consider. He shook off the idea of home, refocused his thoughts and looked out over the open field where the first clear light of dawn illuminated yesterday's field of battle. He noticed how the fog remained in the low areas, particularly in front and to the left side of their line. It was this unique definition in the terrain, this low-lying ravine, he had hoped to discover by walking the line. The mist continued to clear over the battlefield and he now saw the field littered with corpses in grotesque, odd positions. With the growing light, the wounded men moaned more and cried out for water. One weakened man screamed a hoarse, rattling wail then yelled, "*Someone! Please shoot me!*"

Another dry voice echoed from the middle of the field, "*Shoot me!*"

"*For the love of God, please, shoot me!*" this time from the right.

Doubleday said, "Let's get a squad of *volunteers* to fetch those boys. Union or Reb."

"*Benedict!*" he called out. Benedict emerged from his tent in the soft gray light, still in his britches. "Send a detail of twelve men with stretchers to bear off any wounded. Quick! Before it becomes light enough for any Reb to take a pot shot at us."

"Yes, sir! I'll have Colonel Biddle assemble several squads."

He firmly shook Doubleday's hand again. Neither man spoke but deep friendship and utmost respect was exchanged. He marched off, heard Charger knicker when he went past a dozen horses, but made his way for Meade's headquarters down the road. He passed by the makeshift field hospital, a large tent where doctors had operated all night. He saw a huge mound the size of a very large haystack and moved closer. It was an immense stack of bloody limbs, a massive pile of arms and legs, and a dark red trail of blood led from the mound to the operating tent, where kerosene lamps flickered. A surgeon's aide came out carrying more limbs like cord wood stacked in his arms.

He turned his head and tried not to see it. His stomach was queasy, he picked up his pace but was overwhelmed and stopped by a small box elder, doubled over, and puked. There was nothing in his stomach. He wretched again, wiped his mouth with the back of his sleeve, straightened up and continued on his way.

At the small house Meade called Headquarters he reported to Hancock, who was already up drinking coffee and examining a map. He saluted. "General Hancock."

" 'Ease, general." Hancock looked up with his quick eyes, his dark hair greased and combed, and his uniform pressed. "Care for some coffee?"

"Yes, sir. That'd be good."

"Made it myself. I didn't want to disturb Major, um…" he pointed to a major asleep in a wooden chair in the corner. "Hm. Don't remember his name. He's General Howard's aide. Anyway, it's strong, the way I like it."

He poured a cup from the porcelain china service. It was bitter but very strong. "Thanks. This is good."

Hancock offered him to look at the map. It was very detailed with contours shown for hills and troop positions drawn in pencil. He recognized the topography and noted the two hills overlooking the main field. “This hill,” he looked closer for the name, “Little Round Top is critical.”

“Yes. A hell of a fight there yesterday. Boys from Maine did a splendid job, quite remarkable really.” Hancock touched his mustache then threw back his shoulders. “It was a good thing I sent them there.”

He felt Hancock’s boasting was out of place but said nothing, instead drank more coffee and gazed at the map then recalled the huge pile of limbs near the hospital and swallowed hard. “No activity overnight, sir. A detail is bearing off the wounded. That’s it, sir.”

“Very good. They’ll come again today. Lee’s got his blood up. He’s an old West Point grad like me and when he’s angry like this, well, the fighting will be hot today. Fortunately there’s only a few things he can do. He could—”

“If it’s all the same, sir, I’ll return to my men.” He didn’t mean to be short with Hancock but he was very, very tired. At this moment he had no patience for war stories or speculation.

“Of course.” Hancock noticed his blood-shot eyes. “Get some rest.”

Outside it was becoming very hot again with the sun over the horizon. Colonel Biddle and his squad toted stretchers of wounded to the hospital tent. He spoke in detail with Colonels Veazey, Randall and Nichols, and officers Ripley, Benedict, Lloyd, Brown and all the others, gave them his impression of the terrain, the strength and position of the enemy, and ordered, “Remain calm. The fighting will be fierce.”

He then walked off to the side and sat down at the edge of an orchard with his back to an old plum tree. A dull pounding hummed in his ears, an echo of thousands of young men and horses trampling from yesterday's march. He felt some satisfaction: he had done his duty in getting the Vermonters into position. The plum trees' leaves were famished by the brutal July heat but a light breeze gave him pause to wonder of its majesty in spring with the smell of ripening plums in the air. He closed his eyes and imagined his father's apple orchard back home with the faint fragrance of blossoms dancing delicately in the early morning air from thousands of tiny white petals flowering, freeing, floating like gentle snowflakes in the breeze.

Benedict roused him from dozing by shaking his shoulder more and more vigorously. "General! General! *George!*" He opened his eyes and saw Benedict's anxious face. "The Rebs are moving on our front."

He rubbed his face. His floppy hat lay by his side, he put it on snugly, stood up and went to the line of horses where he moved his saddle to examine Charger's back. It was much better and healing. He nodded to Benedict then mounted Charger in one easy motion. Benedict mounted Folio, a fine chestnut quarter horse with a spray of white on its nose. They galloped to the front, 40 yards away, where they pulled up behind the several long lines of Vermonters.

He asked for and took the field glasses from Benedict, scanned the open field in front of them, then turned to the activity on their left. The Confederates were attacking the hill to the south, Little Round Top but their entire force was so large other regiments were splitting off and coming their way. He handed the glasses back to Benedict.

"*Hold this line!*" he yelled. The 2,000 Vermonters were ready, just to the left of the stone wall. They had dug in, found timber, rocks, fence railings, whatever cover they could carry, and formed a defensive line. They had been ready since daybreak.

General Dan Sickles, wearing his round hat and uniform with flair, circled behind the New Yorkers on his gray horse. Sickles was pudgy for his short size and was a gruff, fiery politician with a wild temper. It was well known he had shot and killed his wife's lover. Sickles used his leather gloves to wipe sweat off his face then brought his hand over his dark mustache before ordering, "Alright, boys. *Attack!*"

The New Yorkers moved out from their long line, over the field and straight into the peach orchard. George hollered, "*Vermonters! Hold your position! Stand here!*"

Several Vermont soldiers stumbled out in confusion but some of the officers, Veazey, Nichols, and Ripley repeated his order, "*Stay here!*" or "*Stand firm!*" then watched Sickles' New Yorkers advancing on their own, wheeling two canons for support. They were about one-half mile in front and to the left of the Vermonters, flowing through the peach orchard toward a farmhouse on the Emmitsburg Pike. They set up their canons but before they could fire the advancing Rebels turned and swarmed for them.

General Hancock raced up on his fine, brown quarter horse with his aide, a bright-eyed lieutenant on a dark mare, to watch the events unfolding. A few hundred Rebels were in front of them but Sickles and his men were out in the open, exposed.

Hancock's aide, Lieutenant Hooker, a wiry young man from Pittsburgh, spoke with a clipped, city quickness, "He sticks out like a sore thumb."

Hancock smirked. "Wait a while. You'll see him come tumbling back."

The Confederates moved quickly, exchanged musket fire, then charged the New Yorkers and vicious fighting ensued. The Rebels swarmed the soldiers in blue, who collapsed at a heavy rate. Some New Yorkers fought well but they were no match for several hundred graycoats. They abandoned their canons and dashed back for the main Union line.

George had witnessed this before and he was not about to let *their* fear infect *his* boys. He yelled fiercely, "*Hold your position! Steady boys!*"

He saw the panic coming, moved Charger up and down the line behind his Vermonters, and hollered every few seconds, "*Steady boys!*"

The Rebels remained back on the open field and rejoiced at their capture of the two canons. Most of the Confederates had continued their advance on Little Round Top. Hancock saw an opportunity, rode over to Colonel Randall of the 13th Regiment and asked, "Do you think your boys can take back those canons?"

"Yes, sir!" Randall saluted to Hancock, drew his sword, dug his spurs into his chestnut-colored horse and hollered, "*Company B, follow me!*"

Randall led Company B on a quick charge, away from their lines, through the peach orchard and out into the open field. Lieutenant Hooker, Hancock's aide, was astonished at how quickly Randall had acted upon Hancock's question without being ordered and spoke with surprise in his voice, "My, look at the Vermonters go at it!"

The Rebels were shocked by this sudden charge and many turned and ran with a few stopping to return fire. Some had forgotten to reload since Sickles's initial attack, soon realized their mistake and raised their hands to surrender. Randall and two captains rode their horses around the Rebels and his company disarmed them, then herded them into one large mass. Then the two captains pointed and issued orders while two sergeants used ropes to hitch the cannons to the captains' horses with astonishing ease and swiftness, then wheeled the canons back into the Federal line. Company B and Colonel Randall followed, escorting the captured Rebels while sometimes checking their rear for a counterattack but none came. The Confederate officers were focused on attacking Little Round Top with their forces concentrated and flowing toward the small mountain to their left. Hancock's foresight had paid off.

When Randall and his company returned, George smiled with pride but noticed there were more prisoners than there were boys in Company B and ordered Company C to help escort the prisoners to the rear. Then he turned in his saddle to Hancock to show his satisfaction. The Vermonters were well-trained and had executed this maneuver with precision, bravery, and efficiency.

"Good thing I recognized an opportunity for a counterattack," Hancock said smugly. "We don't need *our* guns firing on us!"

Hancock's aide laughed and clapped his gloved hands. "Yes, sir!"

The remainder of the afternoon was uneventful for the Vermonters although they heard the battle raging for Little Round Top to their left. Also, about a mile to their right, another fierce engagement roared on Culp's Hill. Some of the Vermonters spoke their fear of a Rebel breakthrough, leaving them exposed to an attack from behind, but Benedict heard them and said firmly, "If they break through, we'll know! In the meantime keep your eyes forward and your nerves steady!"

The fighting on each side of them sometimes slowed and fell silent, only to pick up again minutes later. It continued throughout the long afternoon and at times great screams of horror pierced the dim roar of the battle. Then the sun lowered to the horizon and the Vermonters were still in position, waiting. The sky grew bluish purple-black and Venus and stars appeared, wavering in the rising heat. The second day of the battle of Gettysburg was over and they retired the field to the pickets then ate voraciously.

He rode Charger back to Meade's headquarters, reported on what had occurred on his front, what his troop strengths were, and stood ready to receive any orders Meade may have. Hancock and a few other generals conferred with Meade, who listened, nodded often and bit the first knuckle of his forefinger. More generals arrived and offered various theories and opinions of what would happen tomorrow.

He found an empty chair in the corner, sat and waited patiently, knowing they would not listen to a volunteer or anyone who had not graduated from West Point. He was exhausted and pulled his floppy hat down over his face.

A moment later Benedict shook his shoulder and said, "Let's head back. I'll send a courier back for any orders."

He pushed up his hat. The room was very crowded with a dozen generals including Doubleday, offering their opinion with another dozen aides nodding their approval when their particular general spoke. One general stated how weak they were at the southern end of their line while another general worried Stuart's cavalry would encircle them and attack from behind. Then Hancock spoke and the other generals quieted down and listened. "Lee has attacked this hill twice and twice more to the north. Surely he must feel our center is weak and surely he will attack there tomorrow."

Meade, bugged-eyed and appearing elderly with his skin drooping off his neck, bobbed his head in agreement. "He'd be a fool to charge over that open ground but I follow your point. We'll reinforce the center, with Sedgwick's Sixth Corps in reserve."

He stood, stretched, saluted Meade, then saluted again to no one in particular and left the stuffy room. In the darkness he and Benedict walked Charger and Folio behind the Federal lines. Benedict spoke of how impressed he was of Colonel Randall and Company B, added he would write about their heroism for the Burlington *Free Press* and said he could not wait to get back to his tent to write.

He smiled for Benedict's enthusiasm, thought of the article appearing in the newspaper and the long-overdue pride the people of Vermont would have for their soldiers. Perhaps this would help make up for what had happened at Harpers Ferry. Then he wondered what the citizens of Burlington were doing right now, of where Helen may be. He shook his head sadly then thought of Emily Clark, sitting on the porch with Grandpa Joe. In the dark, star-speckled sky Venus shone on the horizon radiantly and he thought, Perhaps Emily is gazing at Venus and these same stars now.

They tethered their horses to a line staked in the rocky soil and again Benedict mumbled something about the newspaper. He opened his tent flap but he was so tired he replied, "Okay" without clarifying what Benedict had said, tossed his floppy hat to the writing table, watched it fall off to the ground, pulled off his boots and collapsed face-first onto his cot. He had been awake 45 hours and fell asleep instantly.

~41 ~

A vague pounding sounded behind him then a louder boom then another blast. He awoke to another explosion behind them, yanked on his boots, put on his hat and left his stifling hot tent. Outside the air was hotter still. His boys hugged the rich Pennsylvania earth and another shell screamed overhead and exploded on the hillside of Little Round Top to their left, then another shell blasted well behind their lines, not far from the ammunition train. Charger stood steadfast tethered to a line, the first of 16 horses, while some skittered from side to side, pulling at their lines.

He jerked down his coat and thought of young Jim Freehan guarding the ammunition train. He lifted his floppy hat, used the crook in his arm to wipe the sweat dripping off his face and forehead then tugged down his hat. He was groggy from his odd sleep, focused his hearing on how close another canon blast pounded the earth, it was well behind their line, then another and another. Instead of blasting away at the ammunition train, two miles to the rear, these opening salvos were poor shots, intended to hit the main Union line but the Confederates were well off their mark. Or perhaps the Rebels figured the main body of troops had been pulled back, encamped well behind their picket lines and they aimed their cannons there?

The barrage started at 1 p.m. with over 170 Confederate guns firing at the Union center. It became clear their intention was to pound the middle of their line to reduce resistance to a full frontal attack in an effort to split their forces in two.

The Union guns, over 100 artillery pieces, fired in response. They aimed for the Confederate batteries and some found their mark. The heavy guns pounded back and forth, and some Union men were killed near their batteries when three Rebel bombs landed on the Federal line. Then suddenly shells rained down on the Vermonters. Blast after blast smashed down on them, ripped them into parts, leaving fragments of flesh, broken bones and a bloodied mess.

Overwhelming fear pushed the Vermonters further into the earth and many pawed at the dirt while the Rebel batteries pounded them.

"*Nichols! Veazey! Ripley!*" he hollered. "*Advance one hundred yards!*"

Their new bugler, Gregory Sutpin, a spry blonde boy of 16 from Montpelier, sounded the advance. Colonels Nichols, Veazey and Ripley rushed the Vermonters forward behind Corporal Hicks, first of the color bearers, carrying the Vermont 13th infantry flag. Trumpeter Sutpin had not seen any action but he played the advance call flawlessly. The Vermonters scrambled low to the ground then the officers motioned for them to stop and cover. They slid into the shallow ravine just in front and to the left of the Union line. The bombs exploded behind them, where they had been, and more fell even further behind the main line, missing everyone. The shelling continued for a long time but there was nothing else the Vermonters could do. Some accepted their fate and fell into an almost hypnotic sleep.

Smoke rose over the battlefield, clouding the Confederate's sight of the Union line. Now most of the Rebel shells fell well beyond the main line, smashing into the empty sloping field and woods behind them on Seminary Ridge. The Confederates were very long in their aim or perhaps they thought the Federals had retreated to escape their barrage. Then their aim became even worse. Now their shells landed still further behind the Federals. Some shots landed in the supply area over one mile behind the main line, where the blasts killed horses, mules and smashed wagons into shreds. Jim Freehan unhitched one of the panicked horses from a wagon, mounted it and rode it deeper into the woods. He calmed the horse, found a large oak tree, dismounted and tethered it to a sturdy box elder. He stroked its neck a few times, sprinted back for another horse, then another, then led them two at a time with a firm grip on their reins and ran beside them, followed by four more. The incessant Southern artillery blasted the area.

Because more and more shells peppered the reserve ammunition train, George wondered if part of the Confederate plan was to have their cavalry circle around and attack the main Federal line from the rear. He considered sending a note to General Meade then thought better of his speculation and recalled the scene of dozens of officers crowded in Meade's headquarters with each general offering their own speculation. He knew Meade must be under a barrage of speculation now.

For over an hour the Union cannons responded then Meade ordered them to stop, to save their ammunition for the inevitable charge that was coming. The Federal artillery remained silent while the incredible firepower of 170 Confederate guns pounded away for another hour.

The Vermonters' horses, including Charger, were tethered near a stand of pine trees just behind their original line. George slid down into a small hole where Corporal Bertram Aggard huddled against the earth but looked to him. He had known Aggard's father from the Trading Post, a dairy farmer from near Georgia and his son Bertram was a copy of Mr. Aggard except much younger, perhaps only 14. Sticking out from his cap and around Bertram's youthful face were short blonde curls like a cherub and he had a tiny pug-like nose, rosy cheeks and a slight mischievous grin. Aggard spoke in a boyish voice, "Welcome to purgatory, general!"

"Like hell! I'm not dead yet." He slouched down while the shells blasted away further behind them. "Bertram, how's your father?"

"Call me Buster. He's dead. Got the typhus last fall. Tha's why I'm here. No sense watchin' the cows while this is goin' on. Anyone can watch the cows."

"I'm sorry," he said, thought of how young Buster was and saw the youthful naiveté in his light blue eyes. He knew there was nothing to be done about it now. "Your father was a good man."

Buster said, "He thought highly of you, too. And your pa."

He thought of his father and smiled. Another shell came screaming down, this one would be close and he pursed his lips with fear, braced for the inevitable blast until it exploded 30 feet away. The force rocked the side of their hole and he reacted instinctively, curling up into a fetal position and covering his head with his arms. He recalled his father's sudden, bloody death and wondered if he would die the same way—killed by a cannon shell. He recalled the gruesome image of his father's crushed skull, then of Colonel Kent ripped in two with his grisly stump of a body in the snow and his mangled legs pointing skyward. Another shell screamed above then came down for them, whistling loudly. He squeezed himself harder, tucked his knees higher into his gut, closer and closer now until the bomb blasted in the woods behind them, splintering off the top of a big pine tree 20 feet away.

He rose. The last blast had been close to Charger, had frightened him, and he reared up, screaming but his reins held firm. He saw panic in Charger's eyes and couldn't stand it, slapped Buster on the shoulder and shouted, "*Your pa would be proud!*"

He scrambled out of the hole, sprinted to Charger, untied his line and took the reins in one hand then patted his front quarters with the other. "Easy, boy! It's alright."

Charger reacted to him, relaxing under his care. More shells exploded in the area but now he stomped his hooves with confidence, an easy challenge. He felt very connected to Charger and stroked his chest then one shell screamed down even closer and blasted a hole in the ground 15 feet away. Dirt volcanoed into the air and Charger's eyes rolled back, widened, and stared at him while he skittered left but did not rear up, then pranced sideways a few more steps. He stayed with him, kept his reins firm, moved with him sideways then tugged the reins down and spoke with calm confidence while stroking his neck, "It's gonna be fine, boy. Easy, Charger. Easy. Easy, boy."

Then the shelling seemed to slow down. The Confederates had fired 170 artillery guns at the main Federal line for two hours, blasting away with everything they had then stopped. It was the longest sustained artillery barrage on the North American continent in history.

Thick smoke hung over the field in the hot, humid air. It was difficult to see the enemy lines but all the Confederate leaders believed the two-hour bombardment must have reduced the Union center to rubble. Instead the Rebel shelling was ineffective and the bulk of the Federal line was intact.

In the sudden silence he stroked Charger's neck and forequarters then mounted and eased himself down, once again patted Charger's neck and wished he had a carrot to give. Then he stood tall in the saddle. Some of his boys were still asleep but they awakened each other, got their bearings and stood up. It was oddly silent. After making it through two hours of terrible, tremendous fear over 1,500 Vermonters let loose their tension in one great loud cheer. They shouted and whooped with joy. They had survived.

"*Nichols, Veazey, Ripley, Benedict!*" he yelled. "Have the boys fall into position *on the line!*"

Trumpeter Sutpin called on his bugle and Corporal Hicks carried the Vermont 13th Regiment flag high and swiftly led the boys, hustling out of the shallow ravine and back to the main line. Here and there a few good friends and fellow soldiers lay killed or wounded and they rushed to attend to them. They had 38 casualties.

He walked Charger among the Vermonters and the overall effect of the shelling was clear. Each soldier was now steeled with resolve. Here and there a young man beamed with pride, and admiration for him, sitting confidently on his white horse, and he shared the same feeling with each of them. It was a bond of unity. They were in this together. They were ready for the hell that was sure to come. Everyone knew it was time for the massive Confederate charge.

The Southern soldiers filed out of the far woods, 15,000 strong then assembled in massive, long lines and stood ready. They waited for General George Pickett, a West Point graduate with long, curly brown hair under his kepi, to give the signal. They had been ordered not to give the Rebel yell until they were within 100 yards of the Union line but first they had to cross over a great open field, almost one mile across, without firing and without yelling.

Union General Hancock spurred his brown quarter horse with dark points behind the long blue line, cursing and shouting words of encouragement. George, Benedict, and the Vermont officers remained mounted in position but watched Hancock ride up and down, behind the middle of the Federal line. One of Hancock's aides called out, "General, you make a fine target up there. Please stay down!"

"*Sometimes the life of a commander does not matter!*" Hancock yelled and dug in his pointed spurs, causing his horse to jerk sideways yet it remained under his tight control. Again he shouted to the soldiers in blue, crouching behind the stone wall, "Steady, men of Pennsylvania! *Steady!*"

Then it began. Southern General Pickett gave the order and the Rebels in gray or butternut uniforms marched forward out over the open field. Compared with every other Confederate charge, it was eerily quiet save the trampling sound of 15,000 men crossing the field.

Most of the Vermonters were nine-month soldiers and their tour of duty had expired without having been in a serious battle and yet they noticed the eerie stillness. The veterans who had heard the

Rebel yell wondered why it was quiet now. The bayonets of 15,000 Rebels gleamed in the bristling hot July sun and they crossed the Taneytown road then climbed over and broke through a wooden fence. Then the Federal artillery, having saved their ammunition, opened fire. Each shell took a handful of Southern lives. Over 100 Union cannons fired down on them and blasted gaping holes in the mass of Rebel soldiers, who were now reforming on this side of the fence.

General Armistead of Mississippi saw the damage the Union guns was having, raised his hat upon his sword, and encouraged his men. Because they were heading in a southerly direction, he hollered, "*Double time! Beyond that line is home!*"

The Confederates charged faster over the open ground. They ran hard for the blue line ahead of them, now one-half mile away and closing fast. Federal soldiers fired their muskets from the stone wall and all along the blue line and some of the Rebels fired back. More and more Union soldiers fired their muskets and pistols then the noise grew to a loud continuous roar of cannons, muskets, pistols, and screams of horror and pain.

Then several Confederate colonels hollered something, pointed their swords toward the copse of trees behind the angled wall, the Rebels changed direction, and they ran over the open field. They had turned away from the Vermonters toward the clump of trees at the very middle of the Union line. At 100 yards they began their Rebel yell, loud and vicious, fired their muskets and many Federal soldiers fell while others crouched behind the stone wall and timber fencing, and fired back.

They continued their charge and it was clear the Confederates had changed their advancement away from the Vermonters and moved straight for the stone wall and clump of trees 100 yards to the right of them. George also recalled the way the fog hung in the shallow ravine just in front of their line and hollered, "*Veazey, Nichols! Fourteenth and Sixteenth, Forward one hundred yards then Pivot to Right Face!*"

He knew this was a risky move but knew it *must* be done. The battle may be lost if the Confederates broke through the Union line.

Veazey and Nichols rode behind their boys, shouted his orders and had the Vermonters marching out into the field, behind swift Corporal Hicks carrying the flag, through the low ravine, and up the small rise for 100 yards. Then Veazey stood high on Justitia and boomed his order loudly, "*Pivot to Right Face!*" and the colors high above Hicks's head spun in a quick motion, jerked right and all the boys followed, the entire regiment pivoted right, swung into position and flanked the charging Rebels. It also exposed a huge hole in the Union line where they had left.

George kept a keen eye on the field to see how the Confederates would respond and was ready to react. Benedict and Major Andross were next to him on horseback and Sutpin, the bugler, wide-eyed and skittish, stood nearby, ready to signal the boys to fall back if needed.

General Doubleday saw them move out, rode over with speed then reined in his roan horse next to Charger. He shouted, "*Glory to God! See the Vermonters go at it!*"

Then Hancock rode over, slapping the reins on his horse's flanks with fury, along with his aide Lieutenant Hooker. Benedict and Andross saw the rage in Hancock's face and exchanged worried looks like they had been caught doing something wrong.

Hancock rode hard and yelled then reined in his horse to an abrupt stop. Blood veins popped from his neck and forehead, and he screamed, "*What in the hell are you doing? You've opened a hole in our line!*"

"*We've flanked their right side!*" George yelled.

The Vermonters had completed the pivot flawlessly then formed two lines. Veazey's strong, practiced voice cut through the raging din, "*First line. Present arms!*"

"*You've gone to Hell!*" Hancock shouted furiously.

"*To Hell it is then!*" he yelled back, "*It's the only thing that can save the day.*"

Out in the field Veazey's deep voice boomed, "*Fire!*"

The 13th and 16th Regiments, 1,500 Vermonters, opened a lethal crossfire into Pickett's flank and hundreds of Southerners fell as almost every bullet found a mark. The incredible noise raged louder with gunfire blasting, cannon shells exploding, and screams of pain and horror piercing the air.

He watched the second line move forward like clockwork and Veazey's deep voice cut through the din again, "*Second line. Fire!*"

The effect was withering. Again almost every bullet found a Rebel soldier and hundreds more fell in the middle of the field then chaos spread through the Confederates. Some Rebels turned anxiously toward the Vermonters, others fired their muskets and pistols but the main Federal line also fired on them with lethal effect. A great roar of canons firing, men yelling, muskets shooting, swords and bayonets clashing, pistols firing, young men and boys hollering in pain, horses screaming as they reared up and fell, and smoke and dust rose over the huge battlefield.

"By God, George!" Doubleday said, impressed by the Vermonters fighting skill. "By God, *by God!*"

Then Lieutenant Stephen Brown, who had been reprimanded for filling the canteens with water on their long march, picked up an axe and charged into the Rebel lines, followed by dozens more Vermonters with nothing more than bayonets. Brown unleashed a violent, slashing whirlwind, killing and maiming Southerners with every step and his comrades also fought fiercely. Then one Confederate after another saw they were due next for Brown's lethal blows and dropped their musket and surrendered. Another volley from the Vermonters first line shred most of the standing Rebels but a few fought on and moved over the stone wall.

Then a Confederate shell screamed down and exploded into Hancock's horse and saddle. The explosion killed his horse and sent Hancock flying. Lieutenant Hooker's and Benedict's horses reared up, screamed, and both officers were thrown off. Hancock hit the ground hard at an awkward angle and he bled heavily from his lower torso. Benedict scrambled to his feet, picked up and adjusted his spectacles then calmed Folio but its chestnut forequarters quivered violently and his eyes were wide with panic. Benedict grabbed Folio's halter, pulled his head to him, held his neck, and patted his front quarters.

George jumped off Charger and rushed to help Hancock. A piece of shrapnel had ripped through his pommel and sent a nail clean through Hancock's leg very high near his groin. Blood poured profusely from his wound and he writhed in agony with blood gushing out in pulsing heaves from his artery. He was in danger of bleeding to death.

Then Benedict was by his side and screamed, "*Get a stretcher!*" to Private Johnson, who ran for the rear.

Lieutenant Hooker, Hancock's smart aide from the city, screamed, "*My God, the general's hurt.* My god! *My god! What do we do?*"

A growing puddle of dark blood oozed beneath Hancock into the grass. He knew he must apply a tourniquet to his leg or the ruptured artery would cause him to bleed to death in seconds. He glanced at Benedict and knew he shared the same thought. Already Hancock's eyes were circling unfocused, his face grew very pale then his eyes closed. Hooker screamed again, "*My god! Oh my god!*"

He took off his neckerchief from Emily, Benedict pressed both his hands on top of Hancock's wound, while he used the kerchief to tie a tourniquet above the wound, and pulled it down hard and taut. Benedict placed two fingers on the kerchief and he knotted it tightly. The bleeding stopped.

Private Johnson returned with a stretcher and another private. They lifted and slid Hancock onto it and when he jostled onto the cot, he opened his blue eyes.

"Thank God!" Hooker said.

"I'll stay here with my men," Hancock said with bravado.

"You've lost a lot of blood general," Benedict said. "You need immediate attention!" Benedict pointed to the rear and the privates hoisted the cot then raced Hancock toward the field hospital.

George's hands were wet with Hancock's blood and he thought of Emily's kerchief of white myrtle, now bloodstained, gone. He wiped his hands on his pants, mounted Charger and once again scanned the battlefield.

Some Vermonters fought fiercely at the front and most fired in syncopated rhythm, and they had a tremendous effect on the Confederates. Very few Southerners were still fighting. Some limped back away from the stone wall while many, many more surrendered. The wave of Confederates no longer moved forward. Thousands lay wounded or killed, hundreds surrendered, and scores retreated.

Now the Vermonters were taking more prisoners than they could handle and the incredible roar of the battle diminished. Some vicious hand-to-hand fighting continued but as more Confederates were killed or wounded, more and more surrendered. After another moment it was over.

The Vermont 13th and 16th Regiments had captured hundreds of prisoners. They suffered some casualties but had inflicted a devastating blow on Pickett's charge. Their flanking maneuver made it impossible for the Confederates to advance further when their destructive crossfire cut them down in their tracks.

General Lee did his best to withdraw his forces from the battlefield in a somewhat reserved, dignified manner. He positioned veteran soldiers under General Longstreet to form a reserve guard to stop any Union counterattack but none came. Then the Southerners maneuvered back through the woods, back toward the Shenandoah Valley to regroup. They treated their wounded and took food from the locals. A supply train made its way to them and brought more ammunition and more food.

The Confederates had lost entire regiments. Pickett's whole brigade was devastated, almost wiped out with only a few wounded or depressed stragglers making a hasty retreat across the field to the far woods. Tens of thousands of Confederates died in the battle and many senior officers were killed. Their invasion of the North had been stopped. Instead of a decisive victory, it was a colossal defeat. There would be no offer of a negotiated peace. Unlike any other commander, General Lee was not vilified for his frontal attack against an entrenched enemy but he would take note of the battle's great failure and would never repeat this mistake again. Now his forces were greatly reduced and he must follow Longstreet's constant advice to fight a defensive style of engagement by picking his spots to fight, then retreat and use the hills and rivers of his native state as protection from the vast numbers of the Union Army. The Rebels made their way south from Gettysburg, endured to fight another day, but now they fought for survival.

Union General Meade did not know how devastated the Confederates were or he may have pursued Lee to hasten the end of the war. Instead Meade was satisfied with winning the day. The invasion was stopped and Lee moved his very reduced army south. It was a clear victory for the Union after countless defeats and "strategic withdrawals."

As Hancock recovered from his wound a newspaper reporter asked him how he came up with such a brilliant maneuver to win the battle. Rather than explain what had happened, he said nothing. Over time Hancock abandoned his silence and took credit for ordering the flanking movement on Pickett's charge. He explained it was his decision but he was so gravely wounded he could not remember when he ordered it. "The battle was so hot, you understand. There was confusion everywhere but I saw the opportunity for a flanking attack."

Later General Meade set the record straight. Meade wrote, "General Stannard made the most critical decision in the most critical battle in our nation's history."

George was very proud of his boys. They had kept ranks over a long, exhausting march of 89 miles in 60 hours and had arrived ready to fight. They showed incredible courage over two days of vicious fighting. No one could ever again say these Vermonters would not fight, and never again would he have to hear the vicious lies that echoed after their surrender at Harpers Ferry.

For their role in the battle of Gettysburg several Vermonters were awarded the highest honor for valor and bravery, the Medal of Honor. Colonel Wheelock Veazey was awarded the Medal of Honor because he "rapidly assembled his regiment and charged the enemy's flank; changed front under heavy fire, and charged and destroyed a Confederate brigade, all this with new troops in their first battle." Lieutenant George Benedict was awarded the Medal of Honor because he "passed through a murderous fire of grape and canister in delivering orders and re-formed the crowded lines."

Although George was responsible for these activities, and also for saving Hancock's life, he said nothing to promote himself. His overwhelming pride in his young men, his brothers in arms, far outweighed any official citation or medal.

The small town of Gettysburg, with 2,400 civilians, began the thankless job of cleaning up the horror. The Union and Confederates had 51,000 total casualties and over 5,000 dead horses. While the Union Army had repulsed the invasion, many Northern generals, newspapers, and President Lincoln called on Meade to follow Lee and strike one last crushing blow. Instead the Federal Army and local civilians cared for the wounded and buried the dead, who gave off an unbearable stench in the hot July sun. It took several days.

~42 ~

Newspapers ran articles on General Lee's invasion of the North culminating in a terrible battle in a small town called Gettysburg. The reporters had learned their lesson years earlier that the war would not be over quickly and it was irresponsible to claim victory. Tens of thousands had lost their lives at Gettysburg and a heavy anxiety of an impending attack remained. Many were still worried Lee would continue his invasion and there were no other troops to stop him.

Wild rumors spread of what Lee's Rebel army would do to the people in the North. One rumor had Lee moving toward the Chain Bridge in Washington with 150,000 men but that would be a stop of relief where he would gain support from the many thousands of Southern sympathizers who lived there. Once refreshed and resupplied Lee and his Confederate army would move to attack defenseless New York City or maybe he had already decided to bypass Washington for the easier target of New York.

President Lincoln knew more troops were needed and issued a call for men by conducting the first Draft. The frenzied citizenry of New York, already suffering with another day of stifling heat and mugginess, reacted to Lincoln's call for more soldiers with disgust. A few days earlier newspapers had described the horrors of tens of thousands of Union soldiers killed at Gettysburg and now Lincoln issued a Draft for more men, who would be headed for certain death.

The city of New York was home to many laborers and immigrants but there were also many rich people who lived on Fifth

Avenue in grand mansions. Thousands of poor Irish, some of whom remembered the Irish famine of 1840, and poor African American freedmen, all hustled to get any job they could. When it became known there was a provision in the Draft for a person to have another man serve as a replacement, that one could pay $300 to avoid the Draft, it was clear this was a poor man's war and the rich would not serve. It infuriated the poor.

Lincoln had also described a new cause for the Civil War in the Emancipation Proclamation, stating the war was to preserve the Union but also to abolish slavery. A heated reaction brewed in New York City where the poor and Irish competed with African Americans for menial jobs and now they must also fight and die for them. Outraged by the Draft to serve in a war they did not believe in, fear of losing the menial jobs they had, and seeing rich people buy their way out of the whole affair, created an angry mob of Irish and poor whites.

A growing crowd of workers from the shipyards, machine shops, railroads and iron foundries marched up Eighth Avenue despite the very hot, humid weather. The protesters carried signs that read "No Draft," and rallied in Central Park, where a few people spoke in fiery language about the injustice of the Draft. The crowd became angrier by the minute then marched over to the Draft Office on 46th Street but it was closed. This made them even more frustrated and angrier. They set fire to the building. Then someone shouted they should march on to Horace Greely's newspaper office, where they printed the names of those drafted. Along the way they picked up rocks and ripped boards off shanty houses.

At the newspaper office another rousing speech was made. A red-faced Irishman screamed about the lost opportunities in America, the fat rich people who were paying their way out of the war, and the shifty Coloreds who weren't being drafted but were ready to take their jobs! A newspaper clerk came out of the doorway and raised his hands to quiet the crowd. The clerk had ink on his hands and protective sleeves on his forearms to keep his white shirt spotless. He stuttered but explained Mr. Greeley would not be coming in today. One protester smashed her "No Draft" sign across the iron fence and ripped off the sign. Another man saw this, did the same, and waved his stick in the air then shouted, "*Let's get the niggers!*"

The angry mob cheered with wild zeal and marched uptown, chasing every African American they saw. Joseph Jackson, a quiet young man of 19, tended a small herd of cows and watched them graze near 34th Street at the East River. The angry crowd descended on him, beat him unconscious, and threw his lifeless body into the river.

The mob moved further uptown and arrived at 43rd Street and the Colored Orphans Home, where 109 children lived. The vicious crowd threw rocks at the windows and the frightened children ran to their caretakers, who were two middle-aged African American nuns, Sisters Margaret and Catherine, and a white priest, Father Kelly. Sister Catherine led the children down the back stairs and out onto the playground behind the building while Sister Margaret and Father Kelly went to the front entrance to deal with the screaming horde.

Father Kelly was heavy with a long walrus-like mustache that touched his vestment. The rage of the crowd was palpable with its violence coiled and ready to strike. Father Kelly, despite being a man of devout faith, stammered for something to say to this wild mob. They smashed windows with their sticks then someone deep in the crowd threw a rock that struck Sister Margaret on the chest. Her light gray eyes widened in shocked horror. Then another rock flew past, narrowly missing her head. She lifted her habit to run and dashed around the side of the building toward the playground.

"*Hey! Stop it!*" Father Kelly yelled and raised his arms. A rock flew from the back, hit his forehead and opened a gash, and blood flowed down into his left eye. Father Kelly took out a handkerchief from his pocket and dabbed at the blood on his forehead then held it to his wound. He screamed, "*People! T'ink of what yer doin'!*"

Then the crowd surged for the wide front doors but Father Kelly extended his arms to block their way. Another woman ripped off her "No Draft" sign and used the stick to beat Father Kelly's thick waist. He doubled over in pain then a young man shoved him out of the way and yelled, "*Don't help tha niggers or you'll get the same!*"

Someone from the mob tossed a torch into a broken front window and the building was soon on fire. Another torch was thrown into the corner window and flames raced up the side. The front doors were kicked open and more torches tossed inside, which caught fire on pews, side tables, and chairs, and grew into a raging inferno.

The crowd backed away from the intense heat then hooted and screamed with glee at the rising flames. They swung their sticks in crazy, air-slashing motions, beat the cobblestones on the road, picked up rocks, doubled their hands into fists and stormed away from the burning wreckage in search of prey.

Nearby Henrietta and Abraham Franklin, a middle-aged African American couple, lived in a room in a boarding house. Abraham stuck his head out of the first floor window to see what the commotion was and the crowd focused its fury on this black man, pulling him out of the window. He wore plain pants and a white long-sleeve shirt but did not have on shoes. Henrietta, in her cotton nightgown, ran out the front door and screamed for his defense. Abraham was a coachman by trade but had a deformed left hand from a childhood accident at a blacksmith's forge and he tried to block the fists that pummeled him but there were too many.

Henrietta threw herself into one tall man's side and fought him. Another man ripped open the back of her nightgown while another man kicked Abraham in the face. Henrietta screamed again.

The boarding house owner, a pudgy white woman, stood in the doorway. She was middle-aged with pale skin and had come from Ireland when she was a child. She made a disgusted face then went back inside. Henrietta saw her closing the door behind her and she screamed again and again. No one came to help.

Henrietta screamed until a boy of 13 swung a blackjack and smashed the back of her head. She crumpled in a heap. Then a large rock hit Abraham in the temple and he collapsed onto the cobblestone roadway. A big, thick-boned Irishman kicked Abraham in the face and split open one eyelid then his nose. Abraham tried to stand but couldn't find his balance, grabbing for the ground with his deformed left hand and feeling around with his good hand. He clutched one man's leg and tried to lift himself but more punches and kicks struck his body. The angry mob beat both of them savagely until they could not move and then they continued to beat them until they were dead.

A short, middle-aged man made a loop in a rope and tied it around Abraham's neck. Two more men joined in and they dragged Abraham's battered and bloodied body across the cobblestone street to a lamp post and hung him. Abraham's corpse swung from the unsteady jerking of the rope. Then someone started a chant and the crowd yelled gleefully for the Southern President, "*Jeff Davis! Jeff Davis!*"

Peter Heusen, a Mohawk Indian who had lived in the city for two years and worked as a whitewasher, wandered by the commotion. His bronze skin had darkened through the sunny days of summer and he had cut his black hair short. Heusen approached the raging mob with curiosity then stood in shock at Abraham hanging and swaying. Someone yelled, "*There's another 'un!*"

"*I'm Mohawk!*" Heusen screamed but the blood-thirsty mob wouldn't listen. They struck him down and continued to beat him until he was unconscious. After the crowd moved on, an Irish bricklayer picked up Heusen and carried him to the hospital several blocks away.

Not far from the docks, William Williams, an African American sailor approached a little white boy, who stood on the street corner. Williams asked the boy where the nearest grocery store was. While the boy gave directions, the crowd descended upon Williams, who tried to explain he only wanted directions to a grocery store. A laid-off Irish dockworker made a fast jab with his knife, caught Williams in the gut, and his blue sailor's uniform became wet with dark blood. He doubled over in pain and his deep red blood dripped onto the cobblestones. Another quick stab and then another were followed by kicks and the mob pummeled Williams to the ground. A poor white stone cutter jumped in with a blackjack and smashed his skull until it was a pulpy, lifeless mess. Then the mob moved on, looking for any dark-skinned person to vent their fury.

~ ~

After the battle of Gettysburg, because the term of service had expired for the nine-month Vermonters, many of them went home. George did not know how to deal with his turmoil at home, of being divorced, and he wanted to continue serving his country. He decided he would not take leave with the Vermonters.

He was ordered to report to General Harvey Brown at the military headquarters at New York Harbor, where his duty would be to deal with the riots in New York City. He thought for a long time if he should take Charger with him then decided it may be better to stand with the soldiers and to be among the people in the rioting to break-up any fistfights and Charger may be jumpy around so much chaos. He also felt his time in New York City should be relatively brief before restoring order, at which time he would return to the Army of the Potomac. He decided to leave Charger stabled with the officers' horses in Camp Boredom.

As he rode the train to New York City, he wondered what would await him. He had never seen a riot but thought, What could be worse than the horrors of the battle of Gettysburg with tens of thousands wounded and dead?

~43 ~

After a full day of rioting the officials of New York City again read the names of the men chosen by the Draft. Many selected were Irish. A growing rage festered in the crowd and some went to the pubs, drank all night, then let their drunken rage spill out into the streets at dawn. Women and men yelled, fistfights turned into beatings, someone stabbed a Draft official, another man fired a pistol at a running African American boy and soon the angry mob was another full-scale riot.

The federal government sent in New York's 65th Regiment, recently from Gettysburg, and a flotilla of Navy ships docked near Wall Street trained their big guns on the rioters and their houses. The federal soldiers, armed militia, and two rival police forces, the Metropolitans and the Mayor's Policemen, roamed the streets in an attempt to restore order. New York's 65th Regiment was composed mostly of Irishmen. The police were mostly Irishmen. The rioters were poor whites and mostly Irishmen. Many times the policemen looked the other way while some joined in looting. One policeman explained in the next day's newspaper, "I can't step in if'n I see a friend giv'n an uppity Colored their come-uppance."

George arrived in New York City to find a chaotic mixture of panic, fear, and anger. Buildings had been burned and looted, African Americans were viciously beaten and some killed and hung by lampposts, and some rich white men were also clubbed and beaten to death.

His first thoughts were for the people he knew in New York City—Dottie, the children at the Colored Orphans Home, Father Kelly, Sisters Margaret and Catherine, and Molly Selzer. First he reported to his commanding officer General Harvey Brown.

General Brown, the officer in command at New York Harbor, assigned Colonel Henry O'Brien to the 65th Regiment with orders to march through the streets and stop the troublemakers *now!* If necessary they could "shoot to kill" anyone who resisted.

Across the city more fistfights broke out and more Federal soldiers entered into the rioting. Here and there fires were set, flames engulfed the wooden structures, and homes and offices burned. The volunteer firemen, mostly Irish brigades, were either depleted from the rioting or refused to fight the flames that burned the homes of the rich Draft dodgers who had paid their way out of conscription. Southern spies saw their opportunity and lit more fires to the homes and offices of the rich and powerful. The greatest city in the North burned.

On Thirty-fourth Street and Second Avenue Colonel O'Brien and the soldiers of the 65th Regiment met an angry group of Irish dockworkers and shipbuilders. The seething mob had gathered in front of Oliver's Livery Stable and created a barricade on two sides. O'Brien moved his regiment of about 150 Zouaves into position around the screaming troublemakers, who wouldn't leave. The rioters would not back down and threw stones at the soldiers. Then O'Brien ordered his men to set-up the howitzer canon to disperse the crowd but some soldiers glared at him reluctantly.

"*Aim over their heads!*" O'Brien hollered and a few soldiers complied. O'Brien noticed their timidity, which enraged him. Then some rioters charged at the line of soldiers and swung sticks or blackjacks, and fired their pistols.

The howitzer was ready. O'Brien was furious and screamed, "*Fire!*"

The howitzer sprayed grapeshot above the crowd, uphill, and struck a group of children further up the street. Seven fell to the paving stones. Horrified men and women ran back to the fallen children and mothers screamed in anguish. Blood spilled onto the cobblestone street. Fathers and neighbors carried the dead and wounded into their homes then slammed doors behind them. The rioting crowd on this block was dispersed but they were even more enraged and a personal revenge seethed in their hearts.

O'Brien and his Zouave soldiers dispersed the remainder of the angry mob. After it had quieted down O'Brien and Corporal

Pense left his troops to walk up the avenue to a nearby drugstore. O'Brien ordered Pense to stand guard while he went inside.

The infuriated mob had reformed with a personal vengeance in mind, remembered the loud voice of O'Brien, and went looking for him. They found Pense standing guard outside the drugstore, pushed past him, and charged inside. A large dockworker named O'Sullivan saw O'Brien in his colonel's uniform and greeted him with a haymaker, then wrestled him and grabbed his arms. Another barrel-chested man, an Irish shipbuilder who grieved with red-hot fury for his slain eight-year old daughter, beat O'Brien about the face and stomach. They dragged him outside onto the sidewalk and more rioters attacked O'Brien with violent blows to the head, arms, and body. Pense, at attention on guard, stood in wide-eyed shock then walked away, glancing over his shoulder then ran in fear. O'Brien called out for Pense but fists pummeled his jaw and his shouted order twisted into a scream of agony. O'Brien lost his balance and fell to the sidewalk.

One of the rioters pounced on O'Brien, took a sharp stick and rammed it down his throat. "Order your men to fire, will ya! Now whadya say?"

The stick was repeatedly jammed into O'Brien's mouth, ripped apart his throat, and punctured his jugular vein. Blood poured out, choked him further, and more blows from the angry mob beat his listless body. O'Brien was kicked, bashed with stones, hit with blackjacks and lost consciousness. Saunders Jordan, a local resident who ran a nearby bakery, tried to help O'Brien but was violently pushed away by another dockworker named Michael Kilkenny, who had lost a son to the howitzer's fire.

The mob's attention was drawn to watching Kilkenny, the enraged dockworker yelling at Jordan, who was dressed in his powdery white apron. While they screamed at each other, O'Brien regained consciousness and leaned up from the sidewalk. Then the crowd noticed O'Brien again, gazed at his bloodied face and pulsing throat in stunned amazement, and regained a level of sympathy. For a moment the crowd questioned each other as individuals, on what they were doing and what they should do next. Then another man tried to give O'Brien water from a canteen but the intense fury of the rioters returned, shoved away the water bearer, and picked up O'Brien. They carried him off, where he was further beaten and tortured. The next morning soldiers on patrol near the livery found Colonel O'Brien's mutilated and dead body in the gutter.

General Brown had O'Brien's body taken to Bellevue Hospital and called together his officers for a staff meeting in his office at the harbor. In the meeting George was introduced and Brown received reports from Major Hanratty of the 65th Regiment, plus the other regiment colonels, from the previous day. The 65th Regiment had killed 18 rioters and arrested hundreds more. Brown received the reports of the day's events with distress and muttered, "This is terrible. This must stop. I don't know how to be any clearer, or what more we can do. It must stop!"

George had seen ineffective commanders groping for leadership before and had vowed to never allow this to happen in his presence if he could help it. He stepped forward from the line of officers and, despite being new to the scene, spoke boldly, "I request a series of regular pickets march through the city to arrest the troublemakers. Instead of having our boys 'shoot to kill' anyone who resists arrest, they should arrest them *as calmly as possible* to avoid increasing the violence, or firing their weapons. If it's a matter of self-defense, yes, then respond. But *we* must resist harming citizens."

Brown huffed with a sideways glare then paced in front of the standing officers, stroked his beard, and sat down behind his very large desk. "We must be firm with these lawless hooligans! Many are Southern sympathizers!"

"As far as we know," he said, "without a trial or evidence, they're citizens of New York. Our boys should alter their time and direction, break-up any fights, and arrest any loitering ruffians. We must do this *as calmly as possible.*"

Brown shook his head, pushed aside the reports then shook his head again. "Okay. We'll try this method *one day.* But if the rioters want a firefight, give it to 'em!"

On the first day of patrols, 232 more rioters were arrested, including several policemen and firefighters, including a few dozen women. The soldiers did this calmly, almost on an individual basis. Many of the Federal officers, including General Brown, were astounded. The second day saw 63 more ruffians arrested and by the end of the week relative order was restored to the city.

George then went to Molly Selzer's Moon Star Inn, where he found she was fine and spoke with her briefly. He then hurried over to the Colored Orphans Home and saw the ashen remains burned to the ground. He stood among the ruins, shocked and horrified at the destruction. He was sick with worry for Dottie and the children, Father Kelly, and Sisters Margaret and Catherine. Then, from a nearby building, Father Kelly and Sister Margaret came out followed by Dottie sprinting for him. Dottie pushed past her caretakers and hugged him tightly. He breathed a huge sigh of relief. Miraculously they had all survived. After hugging Dottie for a very long time, he held her at arm's length then said, "I'm so glad you're okay. Say, would you like to play some jacks?"

Tears streamed from Dottie's eyes and ran over her face. She could only nod yes.

The result of three days of rioting, burning and looting had taken a horrible toll with 184 buildings torched with some fires still burning, 12 city officials dead, 32 soldiers killed, and 67 African Americans beaten, lynched, burned and killed. More Federal guards were stationed at the docks but over time ship captains were able to unload their cargo with growing confidence. Soldiers roamed the streets similar to picket duty to create a calm military presence. By the following Sunday, women once again paraded through Washington Square Park.

The city had been restored to order and once again he felt he had simply done his duty but he had witnessed horrors inflicted on innocent, ordinary citizens. He wondered, Why had the violence spread among the angry citizens? What did this say about the role of African Americans in society? Should they be given full, equal rights? If African Americans were emancipated and given inalienable equal rights by their creator, why weren't they part of the Draft?

It was perplexing and he had other troubling thoughts about the war. Why should rich people be allowed to buy their way out of service? Was this to be a poor man's war, a war of Irish and other immigrants to do the "dirty work"?

He loved his country and was proud to serve but these thoughts of horrendous violence on ordinary citizens caused him many restless nights. He tried to stop thinking of the vast inequity of the African Americans, the poor, the Irish, and of how their struggle in society had resulted in awful horrors.

He forced himself to turn his thoughts elsewhere. He thought of Helen despite himself—her lovely blue eyes, her charming laugh, and how far apart they were in divorce. New York City and the entire country were in a dreadful, dire situation, but his personal life was also awful. He wondered what Helen thought of him, if she thought of him at all? Despite trying to think of pleasant times, of Helen, again his mind returned to the recent god-awful sights he had witnessed. He was haunted in particular by a burnt corpse swinging from lamppost. The gruesome sight made him wonder, How could people do this? Where was their humanity? How could a just God let such horrific atrocities happen?

~44 ~

It had been a quiet night in New York City. Dawn broke hazy and thick with the stench of smoldering fires and he awakened from his tenuous sleep to the smell of smoke. It reminded him of the burnt corpse he saw but also reminded him of the awful fire at the foundry when a charred stench remained in his nostrils and lungs for days.

The new day held little promise. Heavy, dark rainclouds and smoke hung on the horizon with a threatening sense of more trouble, if that was possible, after the hell of rioting, arson, looting, and lynching.

The citizens of New York cleaned up the ashes and remains of the burned debris and a great sadness and remorse descended on the people. The burned bodies of Henrietta and Abraham Franklin were taken down and made ready for burial. Peter Heusen lingered near death at the hospital, where his condition was grave. A soldier was posted at his bedside for protection.

George wrote a long letter to Aunt Amelia to explain he had been stationed at New York Harbor then copied it to Helen. He received a note in return from Mrs. Turner, who wrote she had read in the Burlington *Free Press* of what had happened at Gettysburg, of how most of the Vermonters were coming home, and also the article stated he had been assigned to New York Harbor. Mrs. Turner also wrote that her butler, Obadiah, had been killed in service of our nation in South Carolina but gave no details. Mrs. Turner closed her letter by writing Helen was also in New York City and resided at the Prescott Hotel on Fifth Avenue with a friend she had met named Madison Younger. She scrawled, ***P.S. Helen is often in the company of Captain Henri de La Salle.***

He was very upset by Mrs. Turner's letter for Obadiah's death but he had to re-read the post script about Helen over and over again. Although he was divorced it was very upsetting Helen had left Burlington with Captain La Salle. Even though his marriage was "expunged," he still had deep feelings for Helen, wanted to see her, and needed to talk to her. He set down the parchment letter and went to the hotel on Fifth Avenue.

The Prescott Hotel was a brown, stone structure in the middle of the block on Fifth Avenue not far from Broadway with its lobby a grand room decorated with a marble floor. He approached a mahogany podium where a sign proclaimed the Manager on Duty was Mr. Garland Tosen, whom he asked for Mrs. Helen Stannard. Mr. Tosen, a stout man with a high, receding hairline and full beard, said, "Nope."

"How about Countess Helen Bokowski?"

"Yes, she's, well, we haven't seen the Countess since yesterday afternoon," Mr. Tosen paused and ran his hand down his very long beard, pulled the ends, then continued, "Beg pardon, but some residents noticed she was not at dinner and, well, she was not seen for the remainder of the evening!"

Mr. Tosen went on to explain the Countess was often seen with Madison Younger, her roommate, a pretty debutante from Virginia, who had come north to escape the war and they were also seen in the company of Captain Henri de La Salle. Mr. Tosen then sent a bright-eyed, club-footed clerk up to Helen's room, who soon returned with Madison Younger, wearing a shawl over her long white petticoats. Mr. Tosen smiled politely, bowed and excused himself.

"Hello, I'm George Stannard," he began then stopped because of Madison's clothing and unusual demeanor.

"I know," Madison responded slowly, "the clerk explained your case." She clutched at her flimsy white undergarment then pushed back her dirty blonde curls over her ears. She was so thin the points of her hipbones, elbows and shoulders stuck out. A daze floated in Madison's big hazel eyes and she spoke languorously, "I have no idea . . . where she is."

"It's very important I find her," he said and tugged down his uniform coat. "You see, I was her husband."

"No, no, I don' believe tha'. Oh, yes, yes. . . Oh!" she said. It was almost two o'clock in the afternoon but Madison appeared drowsy with her eyelids drooping heavily. Her eyes were bloodshot and the smell of alcohol was strong on her breath. She let her shawl fall off her shoulders, exposing her small bosom and bony ribs under her lacey petticoat. "D' you know where, I mean. . . I coul' use some food."

He glanced around then motioned to the dining area off the main lobby. "Were you with Helen yesterday?"

"Yeah. But afta I lef', how woul' I know wha' she did?"

He gave her a five-dollar, gold eagle coin. "Here. Where did you go?"

Madison took the gold coin, pinched it, smiled then turned away and headed up the staircase until he grabbed her bare arm. He asked again, "Where did you go?"

"Oh," she spoke in a raspy, dazed voice. "I though' I tol' you," she gave a short giggle, "Henri has a ship! A Soush Shree' ship!"

Madison giggled again then added in a confused tone, "They… were goin', um, no. Maybe she's still there?"

"Thank you." Her eyes were dazed and dilated. "What's the name of the ship?"

Madison floated backward on the staircase then came forward and fell onto his chest, grabbing his shoulders. Her smallish bosom pressed against him, she smiled and burped a strong gust of alcohol. "Yo' ratha fo'wa'd, aren' ya?"

"Did Helen speak of me?" he asked.

"Hones'ly?"

"Yes, of course." He had some hope but realized he knew the answer then thought a better question would be if Helen was courting La Salle now. "Never mind. Tell me about you and her. Are you good friends?"

"No. . . An' yeah. We do eve'ythin' togetha'. I jus' *had* to get somethin' ta eat. I lef'."

"What time was that?"

"I don' know, fou', five, sish," she giggled again. "See! I can coun'!"

"An early dinner."

Madison laughed brashly and tried to focus her eyes. "No! In tha mo'nin', silly! *Look*," she slurred some words. "Ya a *niiish* man. Ya shod fe'get he'. She's gone an' I know! Ya know how I know?"

"No."

"Cuz I'm gone, too." Madison turned and stumbled up the stairs, raised her petticoats, grabbed her shawl then clutched the railing, all in desperate clumsy motions, and somehow succeeded. She continued up the stairs, belched alcohol fumes along the way, gained speed on the landing then accelerated for the end of the hallway, opened a door and produced a loud sound of vomiting. He turned, gathered himself after this blow then went in search of Henri La Salle and his ship at the docks at the South Street seaport.

At the landing at South Street stood a large white house, where he spoke with the port manager, a tidy, clean-shaven man in a navy suit, who insisted La Salle might be at the shanty across the street with a blue vase on each side of the door. He crossed the rutty, cobblestone street to a long row of run-down shanties, where he found one with very large blue Chinese vases with a decorative design of dragons. He knocked, knocked again then went inside, where a few soldiers and sailors in uniform lay slumped on the floor on pillows. A tall bamboo plant was in one corner and a string of red lanterns hung across the room, which was very dark despite the low-lit lights. A smell of sweet smoke hung in the air. An old Asian woman came from a back room, through a red-bead curtain, and examined his uniform then said, "All good. Paper good. I get?"

"No. I'm looking for Captain de La Salle because I want to see Helen Stannard." The woman said nothing. A scrawny cat slithered through the swaying curtain and circled the room amid the languorous bodies on the floor. The Chinese woman wore formal-looking black silk pants, a black silk coat, and her face was wrinkled with hardened eyes. She gazed at his uniform, focusing on his brass general's star.

"Henri de La Salle," he said clearly and slowly, in an effort to be understood. "His ship?" The woman was unmoving, a living statue.

"Have you seen a dark-haired woman about this tall—" He put his hand out near his shoulder, "—about five-feet four inches, very pretty blue eyes. Countess Bokowski?"

"Ah-h-h! Oh, no. No, please stay." The old woman raised one hand to signal to stay, turned and went through the beaded curtain. The scrawny calico meowed, a sailor looked up dazed, and from the back room he heard the old woman's voice arguing in Chinese with another man, who also yelled in Chinese. They went back and forth with the woman's voice louder and more emphatic until there was a loud smack.

Then a man came out of the back room and bowed often. He wore a similar formal black silk suit and black skullcap, and had bloodshot eyes and a very long black mustache that went to his thin chest. One cheek glowed red, showing the woman's handprint. He spoke in a low, soft voice full of sadness. "I am so sorry. There was accident by *Josephine.* The woman you seek, she ah, went to hospital. Last night."

"What? Who's Josephine? No, Helen. Countess Bokowski." The man was unmoving so he asked again, "What happened?"

"Fire. Terrible. *Josephine*, yes? They take hospital. I sorry. That all I say. You go hospital. See."

"Not Josephine. Helen. Is she hurt?" he asked. "What happened?"

"I sorry. You go hospital. They know. I do not know."

"It was Helen? Are you sure?"

The man closed his eyes, nodded solemnly then opened his eyes unflinching. "Yes, La Salle ship. Miss Helen, the Countess Borowzee. She come often. Her choice, you understand."

"No, I do *not* understand!" he raised his voice.

The Chinese man remained calm with his voice smooth, almost bored. Perhaps he had similar discussions before? "You do not know her. Not how we know. You go hospital. Captain Henri. Hospital. They say."

"Wait. What happened?"

"Please. Go." The man motioned with both hands toward the front door like he was shooing away the cat. "Please. You go."

He felt incredibly angry, frustrated, and tightened his right fist. He wanted to grab this man by the throat and beat him into talking. "What hospital?"

"Big one. Please. You go!"

He stared viciously at the man, who kept bowing and waving his extended arms. The cat meowed again and strutted back under the curtain. He sensed foul play and somehow this man was involved. He thought he would go to the hospital and then come back with the police to the harbor master's office. Then he looked at the soldiers and sailors on the floor, unmoving like the dead on a battlefield. He shook his head and left.

Outside the shanty the air was refreshing. He hadn't realized how stifling the sickly sweet air inside had been. He removed his floppy hat, wiped his brow with the back of his uniform sleeve, and replaced his hat. He gathered his bearings amid the cobblestone city streets, noted a few buildings, and headed for the midtown hospital, which he was familiar with its location due to the numerous injuries in the rioting.

After marching for an hour, all the time worrying about what injuries Helen could have, he saw the large building with a man helping another man with a bandaged head leave the front entrance. Inside the hospital, he asked the front desk attendant, a short woman with braided reddish-blonde hair, for Helen Stannard then for Countess Bokowski. The very short woman stood, not much taller than the old school desk she used, tapped her hair pins in back, excused herself, and a moment later returned with a doctor, who had blood smeared on his white coat and his hands were still wet with blood. The doctor had a long dark beard and held up his wet hands, apologizing for them, then motioned with his head toward the hallway, wiping his hands on his apron. “Come this way. Are you kin, general?”

“I’m her husband, ex-husband. George Stannard,” he said in an introductory tone. The doctor stopped in the hallway and examined his uniform and brass star.

“I’ve read about you, general. It was in the paper what you did at Gettysburg. Did they send you her to stop the rioting?”

“That’s one way to look at it.”

“I stayed away from the war to avoid all the, ah, the gruesome wounds. The bloodshed,” the doctor shook his head then cleared his throat, “and lookit here. It’s right on my doorstep. Worst five days I’ve ever seen.”

The doctor’s eyes were tired and bloodshot, and he had a gaunt sleepless pallor to his skin. He wiped a bead of sweat from his temple with the back of his bloodied hand and appeared like he expected a compliment for a job well done.

George returned to the point. “Where’s Helen?”

“Oh,” the doctor seemed distracted and gazed at the polished marble floor. His pallor gave him a very unhealthy appearance and he mumbled, “I’m sorry.”

“What’s happened to her?” he said.

“No, you don’t understand. I’m sorry, sir.” The doctor bowed his head in a formal manner then turned and made his way down the hallway. He hurried to catch up to the doctor who pushed his way through a partially opened door to a large room that held dozens of corpses lying on tables with gray woolen blankets drawn over them. “She was deceased when they brought her in.”

He stopped, dazed, and felt an immediate heaviness in his chest. What in the world was going on? How could she be dead? “What? What happened?”

“She was deceased. For some time. Half a day, probably longer. Rigor mortis had set in.”

He adjusted his collar but that did not ease the thick lump in his throat. He felt dry-mouthed and unclear on what was happening. How did she die? What in the world? Dead? It was unbelievable. “I, I don’t understand,” he said. “Can I see her? What do you mean? She’s dead?”

“I’m sorry, sir.” The doctor again wiped his hands on his apron then grasped his shoulders. “She’s no longer with us. She’s dead. I’m very sorry.”

He coughed and cried all in one outburst and held on to the doctor’s shoulders to steady himself. This did not make any sense. Dead? Helen? How? His voice warbled through his tears, “Please tell me, what happened.”

“Come. She’s right over…” The doctor led him to a table where her very thin, slight body lay under a gray blanket that he pulled down to show her face. Helen’s hollow blue eyes stared up fixedly with her mouth slightly open with parched, cracked blue lips. Her long dark hair had bits of debris in it and her skin was a pale bluish-white.

He touched Helen's cheek, soft but cold and lifeless. It was her and it was *not* her. She appeared to suffer with her gaunt skin and a crease between her hollow eyes that stared out expectantly for something that was never coming.

He wiped his eyes with both palms but tears poured out and he leaned against the table, bent over, then collapsed under the emotion and knelt down.

The doctor patted his shoulder. "I'm sorry. At least she's no longer in pain."

After a moment he composed himself, unknotted his fists, stood and again wiped his face. The doctor's expression appeared very kind and understanding.

"Was it during the rioting?" he asked, his throat thick with emotion. "What happened to her?"

"No, no. She drowned but it looks odd. She also had some burns on her skin, on her back. There could have been a fire from the rioting but she drowned. I can't say for a certainty," the doctor said blandly, "but on occasion we get one like her. The thinness, her pallor. To me, in my doctoral opinion, it looks like she had been smoking opium for some time. A couple of Chinamen and Mister La Salle brought her in yesterday."

He couldn't understand it all. Drowned, rioting, fire, opium. After a moment he cleared his throat but his voice still warbled, "So she died of what?"

"She drowned. But *if* she was about her wits, maybe she wouldn't. I know it's not much but she was probably at peace when she departed. She's at peace now."

"This is..." He did not know what to say. "Where is La Salle?"

"Oh, the police took him straight away." The doctor nodded a few times then said something softly and drifted away, leaving him alone in the makeshift morgue.

He thought of what a horrible husband he had been. He had left Helen for the war so, in some way, he was responsible for this. How could this have happened? He had tried to understand her, didn't he? Did she smoke opium? What went so wrong? Why was she with La Salle?

He stood still in the cool room and he did not know what to do. It was extremely quiet and he heard his own breathing then heard his heartbeat. Numerous dead bodies lay under gray blankets on tables. Who were these dead? Where were their families? Were they all victims of the rioting? All these dead people and for what cause? They weren't part of the war.

Then, after a moment, he thought, What was he doing with *his* life? He stood still for a very long time, closed his eyes and tried to make some sense of it all. After a long time he decided: he didn't understand and that was all he could reason.

He took out his wedding ring from his pocket and slid it on Helen's emaciated hand. It was much too large, then he tried her middle finger and it was still too large but stayed on. He lifted her hand, now bearing his ring, and kissed it solemnly then crossed her hands gently over her heart.

After a while he realized there was nothing more he could do here. At some point he had to leave. He shuffled away slowly. In the hospital lobby he spoke with the attendant, the reddish-blonde lady who had met him, and gave her detailed instructions for Helen's body to be returned to Burlington for burial. He would return tomorrow to pay for everything. The woman gave him a consoling tight-lipped nod, took a one-sheet form from a stack and filling it out said, "It's a right good thing what you're doing, general. Tha other fella, the Frenchman, he's worthless. Plus the police got him now."

Stunned, he walked out of the hospital. After several confused moments, confounded by all the buildings, he stopped a man in a bowler hat with a dark beard and asked where the nearest police station was. The man responded with a very thick Yiddish accent. He could not understand a single word but pointed to a building further down the avenue. He thanked him and went there.

Inside the police station, behind a large, old desk sat a beefy police sergeant with brown hair and a wide, bushy beard. He told him the story he had pieced together but also of the doctor's suspicion of Helen's smoking opium. The officer wrote down his name, made notes and said, "General, we got Mister La Salle under arrest."

"Where is he?"

"Right back here." The sergeant motioned with his thumb over his back and looked up from under his bushy brown eyebrows. "Wanna see 'im?"

He was surprised and said 'yes' and the hefty sergeant led him through a door, down a corridor then down a staircase to a series of jail cells. In the third cell, behind bars, was the short Frenchman he had remembered seeing at Lady Eve's in Burlington then at Mrs. Turner's afternoon tea, at various dances, and at the theater. La Salle was dressed in a blue velvet suit and lay on a cot with a navy-colored, woolen blanket over his feet. When La Salle saw him he rolled away, faced the pockmarked cement wall, and showed his exposed bare feet.

"That's him, alright," he said.

"He don't say much." The sergeant stroked his puffy brown beard. "Mumbles in French. He keeps saying, 'A mistake.' Tell the judge, I say."

"Incredible," he said and eyed La Salle, laying still on the cot. His blood pounded in his temples and he clenched and unclenched his fists. "Would you let me in there?"

"No, I can't do that, sir. I'd lose my job."

"My wife died! And he killed her!" He lunged for the keys on the sergeant's belt but his large left hand swatted him off and he turned his hefty body away. He continued, grabbing and tugging at the keys then shouted, "*I want to beat the shit out of him! Let me in there!*"

Captain La Salle stirred on the cot, seeming indifferent to his fate, then used his thin fingers to adjust the blanket over his feet.

He gripped the bars of the cell and screamed, "*What the hell happened!*"

The Frenchman froze then moved uncomfortably on the cot. La Salle was paying very close attention so he screamed again, "*What happened?*"

La Salle continued to face the wall and mumbled, "Fire. She jump and drownded. A mistake."

His rage flared. He lunged for the keys on the Sergeant's belt and screamed, "*Let me in there!*"

"I can't do that!" The sergeant twisted away with the keys and stepped back. He held the keys outstretched in his left hand and raised a blackjack club in his right fist. "Now general, unless you want some of this, you back away! I let you come down here to identify him. Tha's all."

"*Goddamit!*" he screamed, letting out all his frustration and furious anger. He turned to the lethargic Frenchman on the cot, figured La Salle would use his wealth to hire a fancy lawyer to avoid justice for the crime of killing Helen, and knew deep in his gut, instinctually, something was very, very wrong. La Salle was responsible. "You deserve to die! You rotten son-of-a-bitch!"

"Oh, I'll betcha dollar he'll get the noose, alright." The sergeant spat on the floor.

He realized he was breathing rapidly and foaming at the mouth but he didn't care. At this moment he never wanted to hurt anyone as much as he wanted to kill La Salle, *now*, to strangle him in his hands. He clutched the iron bars of the cell and shook them with all his might, thinking of La Salle's thin neck. He rattled the bars more then yelled in a fierce growl of anger, pain and frustration. He hollered again and the sergeant pulled on his arm but he broke free, screamed at La Salle again then the room spun around heavily and he hit the floor in a heap.

He awoke in a chair in the lobby of the police station. The back of his skull ached with a lump behind his right ear and he tenderly straightened up.

"I'm sorry general, I had to take you out," the sergeant said plainly, doing his job. He sat at the large old desk with his boots on top and read a newspaper but glanced at him. "The judge will handle this. You need to go home and get some rest."

He stood and a rush of pain shot up his neck, making the back of his head throb, and he felt hopelessly sad. Helen was gone. Now what?

He wandered north up Broadway then after several blocks realized he was headed in the wrong direction, turned, and walked south for the harbor fort. He made a few wrong turns along the winding, cobblestone streets. It took over two hours to make it back to the harbor area.

In the harsh brightness of the late afternoon sun, the trees were too green, the red roses overblown and sail boats with bright white sails tacked leisurely on the calm green water. A fresh sea-scented wind blew softly. He staggered to the officers' quarters and his stone house, where he saluted to Sergeant Lloyd, who spoke affably with two corporals. He noticed Lloyd's reaction to his depressed demeanor and a concerned expression washed over Lloyd's puffy face and he said, "Sir, what's wrong?"

He went inside and collapsed in the single bed without taking off his uniform or boots. His head hurt and he felt discordant with the universe. He couldn't even bring himself to cry. It was all too bizarre.

~ ~

He had orders to remain in New York until August first, at which time he was to report back to Washington City. The Army of the Potomac needed him again. He decided there was nothing more he could do about La Salle. He sent a telegram to Mrs. Turner and informed her of Helen's death. He expressed his condolences and assured her everything would be paid for in regard to Helen's funeral and any outstanding debts she may have incurred.

He also wrote a letter to his Aunt Amelia and described finding Helen, her sad demise, but omitted all details. He explained he had to report back to Washington City but he did not mention he was not due for another two weeks.

After Helen's death, Burlington was haunted for him. It was corrupt with memories of great joy and dreams of unachievable happiness. All gone. He did not want to see anyone in Burlington over this awful event and did not want people to think poorly of Helen. He preferred to let her rest in peace.

~ ~

Peter Heusen, the dark-skinned Mohawk who stumbled upon the rioters, lay in a hospital bed for two weeks with his body pummeled with various broken bones and punctured organs. Some family and friends hoped and prayed for his recovery, but his wounds were too severe. He died quietly.

President Lincoln reconsidered his call for a Draft. Lincoln knew the nation needed greater protection and decided the Draft would remain.

George received no official mention for his role in calming the riots in New York City except that he did his duty and was reassigned to the Army of the Potomac. As the trained pulled away for Washington he saw the charred remains of the great city of New York destroyed upon itself. The riot was over, Helen was dead, and the healing must begin. It was all a terrible waste, he thought. Why did this happen? Where was God during all this? How could He be so silent through such awful suffering?

The train chugged along the tracks and was soon speeding along the rails for the capitol and the uncompromising surety of the horrors of war. It would be dangerous, bloody, and deadly. He felt he couldn't take any more and he didn't care. Wasn't this Hell? What could be worse?

~ ~

In camp with the Army of the Potomac, he found some solace in the routine of training new soldiers. It was after another long day of drilling that Benedict called out then entered his tent, handed him a letter, and left. The envelope had fancy, swirled writing on the outside and was from Colonel Wheelock Veazey. The letter was on fine parchment and read,

Dear George,

I cannot imagine the grief you are feeling, to have lost your precious Helen. As you are well aware, I also had strong feelings for her although I always considered you the better man. I also understood, from the very beginning, she preferred your company and so I deferred to you. My deep emotions for Helen remained. In my heart I know my emotions are but a drop in the ocean to the incredible heartache you must feel. I want this to be clear to you, that I share my condolences, and I reaffirm my great respect for you, my dear friend George. If you ever need anything, anything at all, I am at your service.

In deep sympathy,

Wheelock Veazey

He dropped the note on his writing desk and cried in great sobbing heaves.

~45 ~

Confederate President Jefferson Davis often stated he wanted more than anything for his nation of secessionist states to live in peace. The War Between the States had now gone on for three years and had been fought almost exclusively in the Southern states. Every day President Davis was given horrible news about innocent civilians killed, lost homes and farms, and businesses burned and looted. Davis was exasperated that such horrors occurred on a daily basis in his nation.

Several proposals were brought to President Davis on how to take the war to the Northerners. Sitting in his favorite easy chair in the executive mansion in the Southern capital of Richmond, he rejected them all. Davis had been in meetings with various politicians, generals, spies, and mercenaries but no one had given him a sure-fire way to take the war to the Northerners without escalating the level of atrocities in the South. A common phrase he used to reject these plans was, "Despite how our enemy behaves, we shall remain dignified."

Despite this phrase Davis had given free rein to various bands of renegade leaders to take the war to the Northerners. This included the 400-man regiment of Colonel Quantrill's Raiders in the western states of Missouri and Kansas, and to smaller groups with plans to attack key positions in the North. After two years of taking blows from the Federal Army in Southern lands, the Confederates were ready to unleash major attacks in Northern states. Many Rebels had years of bloody vengeance roiling in their bitterness and were ready to exact a terrifying blow of revenge.

Some Confederates felt their powers weakening and their chances for peace diminishing. It had been three years and they had not received any international support even from England, which had the strongest economic ties to the Southerners. Several other nations had implied support but each would wait to ensure the Southerners were an independent nation free from the North before they acted. Meanwhile the Confederate treasury was running very low. The various Armies in the Carolinas, the Western theatre, and the Army of Virginia were all running low on armaments, materiel and supplies. They needed money.

In this time of desperation President Davis accepted and worked on a plan to invade the North but with a unique twist. Their plan would be to send a small band of 30 Rebels to attack from Canada, rob a few wealthy banks in a few Northern cities and towns, and then escape back to Canada. They would later return to Richmond via ship and pour hundreds of thousands, perhaps millions of dollars into the Southern Treasury. Several targets were considered where it would be easy to cross over the border from Canada, attack a few unprotected cities far from the Army of the Potomac, and slip away. They considered striking in Michigan but felt there were not enough rich cities, other than Detroit and Toledo, which were almost a day's ride apart with not much to be had. They considered upstate New York, Buffalo or Albany, and Maine. Each was rejected due to lacking in sufficient funds plus those cities were well defended with local recruits and reserve militias.

Then Davis settled on an area near the Canadian border where a small band of men could cross through the woods, rob banks in two cities, and return to Canada by nightfall. Davis tapped the map repeatedly, decided they would attack these two cities, and approved the plan. He pointed to St. Albans and Burlington, Vermont.

~46 ~

It was before dawn when a band of 21 Rebels, dressed in plain clothes to avoid detection, rode horses across the border from Canada. Their plan was to attack the small town of St. Albans first, just after its three banks opened, continue to Burlington to rob more banks, then ride back north through the night and escape back into Canada.

Travis Coleman, a wiry man of 26 from Tennessee, led the group. His brother Wilber, better known as Wil, had been shot in the left arm at the Battle of Bull Run and had vowed revenge on the Yankees. Wil had not been allowed to rejoin the Army of Virginia because he had lost the use of his left arm completely. Now he rode with his brother Travis and held a vengeful bloodlust in his eyes.

With the rising sun the 21 raiders crossed over the border, rode hard for 15 miles, and swept into St. Albans without warning. Local resident William A. Church, who had been in the Ransom Guards militia and had been designated to watch out for Rebel raiders, would have fired warning shots but Church was killed in the battle of Gettysburg. The militia was not prepared to stop the Rebels because most of the Guards joined the Federal Army in 1861 and the few remaining were missing limbs or were too old with failing eyesight. Although many signed up for an additional tour of duty, some had returned home but were no longer of a military mind. They tended to work their farm's crops or work in the machinery shops in town. Only a few members attended meetings and maneuvers, and those meetings were held irregularly. The town of St. Albans was unprepared for an attack.

As the raiders rode into town on the main road everyone could see they were Southern Rebels. They had a rough-hewn look on their faces and wore shoddy clothing. The largest group rushed into the First National Bank and announced they were taking all the money for the Confederacy while two other smaller groups split off for two other banks. They shot their guns in the air and whooped the Rebel yell. When they had every sack of money from all three banks, they robbed the civilians of every penny they carried.

When the Rebels left the banks they continued to fire their guns at random objects. Winslow Upham, a boy of 15 who had just deposited his father's earnings from his general store, rushed after the thieves. The raiders were on horseback and Upham pulled at one of the white canvas bags thrown over the pommel. The rider pulled back and laughed like it was a game. Nearby Rebels also laughed then the rider aimed his pistol at the boy's face and cocked the trigger. Young Upham turned his head and dove away an instant before the rider fired and the bullet grazed his scalp. He tumbled off hard and broke his left arm in the fall.

Emily Clark, who was in St. Albans visiting her grandmother Curtis, was on her way to Brownell's General Store for cooking supplies. Emily drove her grandmother's wagon into town and was startled by gunshots and yells, then saw people and horses screaming through the village green and running out onto the streets. She steered the wagon to the back alley entrance of Brownell's store and slapped the reins on the black-and-gray mare. She felt uneasy, looked over her shoulder and saw a wild-eyed, bearded man on horseback following her. He fired his pistol in the air, fired again, and whipped his horse eagerly.

Emily pulled back on the mare and didn't bother to hitch the reins then jumped off the slowing wagon and rushed in the back door. Her good, blue-gingham dress caught on the door jamb and ripped at the bottom hem but she hurried inside and ran to Hank Brownell, who cowered behind the counter with a shotgun in one hand with the stump of his right arm supporting it. Brownell was thin, wore glasses, and screamed, "*Emily! What are you doing here?*"

She shook her head, confused, and crouched behind the counter with Brownell. A few seconds later the ruffian's boots kicked at the back door. Emily pointed excitedly but Brownell quivered and held the shotgun close to his chest. The back door banged open and Emily's eyes widened. The raider called out, "Here girlie, girlie!"

Brownell didn't move. His jaw trembled and a tear ran from his right eye. Emily pursed her lips and again pointed excitedly toward the back door. Brownell didn't move. Instead he closed his eyes.

Emily grabbed at the shotgun but Brownell clutched it to his chest. She grunted, jerked at the gun again, and again, then he eased his grip on the shotgun and opened his eyes. She stood up, leveled the shotgun, aimed at the raider and blasted both barrels. The buckshot tore into the bearded man's right side and assorted jars of pickled fruit shattered, sprayed and spilled onto the floorboards. The Rebel dropped his revolver, looked down at his bloodied shirt and touched his mangled right side like it wasn't real, then turned around and staggered out the back door.

"*Where do you keep the shells?*" Emily hollered. Brownell trembled and pointed with a shaking hand further down the counter. She searched and found more shotgun shells on the shelf under the counter then reloaded the gun. Brownell gave her an appreciative look then wiped the tear from his cheek. His hands shook and another tear spilled out, then he used his left hand to push up his spectacles, raised his stubby right arm, covered his face, and bawled like a baby.

Emily left the counter and moved cautiously toward the back door. Shards of broken glass crunched under her footsteps. She avoided a small puddle of fruit syrup dotted with the raider's dark red blood and his pistol lay on the warped, darkened floorboards. She angled her way to the door opening, saw no one, and eased the shotgun out the doorway then stepped outside.

The mare and wagon were still there but the raider and his horse were gone. Outside she noticed more drops of dark blood in the dirt and a trail of drops disappeared with the horse's tracks around the building toward the front. She bit her lower lip then went back inside the store and saw Brownell sat crying behind the counter. She went past him and made her way to the front windows, pushed aside a lacy curtain with her left hand, balanced the shotgun with her right and saw women and children screaming and racing about frantically. A middle-aged man rushed at the Rebels on horseback and they shot at him so he turned and sprinted for an open storefront door. Most civilians were unarmed and ran for their lives. The Rebels fired their guns in every direction and several townspeople fell wounded.

As they sacked the town, the Rebels' plan was abandoned. One raider rode after a blonde woman in a tight corset and scooped her up onto his roan horse with his right arm. Another rider maneuvered his gray-and-white horse up onto the wooden sidewalk and kicked in the large store-front windows with his right boot, shattering the glass. Another Rebel stopped to rob an old farmer, who only had a pocket full of coins. The Rebel was mad and used the butt of his pistol to smash the elderly man's forehead, causing a gash above his eye and knocking him down. Blood flowed onto the wooden sidewalk.

Another civilian, Elinus Morrison, a building contractor from Manchester who was making renovations on the Welden House, was a Southern sympathizer. Morrison ran after the Confederates with joy and hollered to them, "*Hey there!*"

A Rebel turned in his saddle, leveled his pistol at Morrison's head and pulled the trigger. Somehow Morrison ducked the shot but the rider fired three more bullets into his abdomen. Morrison dropped over his tangled legs and clutched at his stomach with blood spilling from several wounds, laying on the dusty street and writhing in agony. The raiders rode their horses around and past him.

Travis Coleman whistled in an effort to round up the Rebels but his call was not heard or was ignored in the chaotic pandemonium. One raider kicked over a kerosene lamp and started a fire on the boardwalk. Another rider circled his horse, reached into his saddlebag and used his burning cigar to light a bottle of Greek fire and tossed it into a window of the Vincente Hotel. The bottle exploded and flames spread up the green velvet draperies of the front windows then caught on the side walls and eves. A moment later a clerk, followed by an older woman, rushed out, covering their faces and coughing in the thick black smoke. The woman collapsed sideways in the street and didn't move. The clerk patted her cheeks then fanned her arms back-and-forth in an effort to help her to breathe. The large, overhanging "Vincente Hotel" sign caught fire and flames spread to the second floor. People screamed from inside their rooms, which caught the attention of a few citizens who immediately rushed toward the burning building. The Rebels shot at them to turn them away.

More whoops and Rebel yells yipped through the air mixed with gunshots and more Greek fire, and more civilians screamed in terrified horror. Children cowered in the alleys between the buildings. The blacksmith, Uno Agnello, with his long beard and long hair streaked with gray, limped out of his livery with a shotgun in each hand. Agnello fired the right shotgun and blasted one of the raiders in the back and the man fell off his gray-and-white horse, which bolted away riderless. Agnello's second shot missed a whooping Rebel but now he had all the nearby raiders' attention. Three Rebels turned their horses and fired at him. Agnello dropped the spent shotguns, drew a pistol from his belt, and fired back. He hit one rider in the cheek, who jerked his dark horse sideways, fell off and landed hard against a water trough. The other two Rebels fired and fired again. Agnello's right arm and belly were riddled with bullets. Then he picked up a shotgun and reloaded it, trying to hold himself up against a storefront post but slid to the ground. The two riders spurred away but another Rebel whipped his sorrel straight for him. The Rebel appeared angry with his teeth gritted and he fired his pistol at Agnello again and again, missing each time, then continued past him down the street.

Another Rebel rode past him in the opposite direction with a screaming blonde woman splayed across his lap, spurring his horse at rapid speed and the woman hanging on for her life. Agnello turned on his rump, leveled the shotgun, aimed and plugged the Rebel square in the back. His body leaned forward, then off to the side, then slumped over. The horse slowed down, curled left with its rider's deadweight drawing them sideways and then the man slid off and plopped to the street motionless. The blonde woman jumped off the other side of the horse, and she and Agnello exchanged a quick stare. He recognized Petra Lermontova, who lived with her uncle, an emigrant farmer from Russia. She bled from her hand and dashed into Edberg's Feed and Grain Store.

The Rebels continued their assault on St. Albans into the afternoon and after several hours of chaotic violence they appeared to lose energy and interest. They had long abandoned their plan of travelling to Burlington to rob more banks and gradually assembled around Travis Coleman's more frequent whistles and calls. Then they rode north out of town and headed back for the Canadian border.

The Rebel raiders had robbed three banks in St. Albans of $207,000 dollars, set fire to many buildings, and wounded several people including women and children. The only citizen killed, Elinus Morrison, a building contractor from Manchester, had ironically supported their "noble cause."

~47 ~

George received news of the St. Albans raid while he was in camp with the Army of the Potomac. He requested leave immediately, there was no time to arrange for Charger to also go, and took the next train north. When the connecting train from New York pulled into St. Albans, he was shocked to see the devastation. The quiet little town he had known since childhood had been ransacked and destroyed with several buildings burned to the ground. A few men cleaned up charred debris from what was the Vincente Hotel but very few people walked about. The town felt empty. A little boy poked through the burned, blackened remains of a house. He called out, "*Hey there!*"

The boy clutched a stick horse, picked up a half-burned rag doll then strolled over. It was Hemmings Echols, youngest son of a family he knew from working at the foundry. He said, "Hemmings. How are you?"

"Good." Hemmings' short blonde hair stuck out in every direction.

"What are you doing?"

"Looking for toys. This is Reena's doll," he said and held up the burnt doll by its leg. Then he showed off his stick horse with a carved head and strands of brown yarn on one end and said proudly, “This is my horse.”

“Mmm,” he made an impressed face. “What’s his name?”

“Thunder.” Hemmings straddled the stick horse and grinned.

“Yes. That’s an excellent name for an excellent horse! I once had a horse named Thunder. That was before the war.”

“What happened?” he asked, staring up with his large blue eyes.

“I had to sell him,” he replied. “He was needed for the war, you know.”

“I know,” Hemmings made a frown, registered some experience of making a sacrifice for the war, then changed and looked up pleasantly.

“Right,” he said. “Well. How is your family?”

“Good.”

“Where are they?”

“Church. ‘til we build our new house. Then again we may have to move in with Auntie ‘Rika for a spell.”

”Oh. Is that where they’re caring for the wounded? At the church?”

Hemmings shook his head no, pointed across the village green, and answered, “The schoolhouse.”

He ruffled Hemming’s hair, knelt down and took out his plain white kerchief, unfolded it, and offered some root beer-flavored hard candies. “Things will get better. I promise.”

Hemmings stared in wide-eyed awe, then placed a single candy in his mouth, rolling it around and sucking on it, and smiled broadly. Then he returned to his business, combing through the ashes of what was home.

He wrapped up his kerchief, replaced it in his pocket, grabbed his bag and walked briskly for the red schoolhouse. He thought about his teaching days but was overcome with a sense of impending doom. Who was in town that day? Who would be among the dead and wounded? He knew so many people. He felt horrified and doomed. Mixed in all of his emotions, he also felt the Southerners' sense of outrage.

In the old schoolhouse he saw Mayor Littlefield slumped against the doorframe on the wooden floor. He appeared exhausted and wore his usual suit. Littlefield had put on weight, his vest bulged at the buttons, but he was without his white powdered wig and his thin gray hair stuck out at the sides. He looked over his wire spectacles and shrugged.

Desks had been pushed to the back wall and cots were lined up for the wounded, some of whom were now homeless. Thirty-one people were injured and lay on cots with their assorted wounds bandaged. A male nurse attended them with a tray of tiny bottles of medicine. Many of the wounded he recognized, along with families of the wounded, who sat or stood near their loved ones. Then Aunt Amelia rushed to him, gave him a strong hug, and pulled him by the wrist further inside the schoolroom. He wondered why Amelia was here, how had she come from Burlington? but was grateful to see her.

She rubbed his arms and hugged him again. Then he realized *he* was reacting like *he* had endured this fight. She spoke cheerfully, "We're so glad you're here," then added, "I'm sorry for your loss, for Helen. What a tragedy!"

He nodded, swallowed hard, and again thought, Why was Amelia here? Then he realized this wasn't too far from Burlington and she knew many of these people through his parents. "Thanks for helping," was all he could manage to say, feeling transfixed by the staring, wounded townspeople. He saw elderly Peter Kildee, who lay on his side to keep his wounded arm and bandaged ribs off the cot. Then he saw husky Uno Agnello on another cot, his black-and-gray streaked beard had grown long and his face, usually marked with blacksmith soot, was shiny and clean. Agnello waved with a jolly smile.

He went to Agnello and shook his hand firmly. These civilians had fought to defend their town and he saw the gritty determination in Agnello's eyes. For a few minutes he and Agnello spoke warmly, about horses and things other than the raid, until Amelia tugged on his arm yet again and said, "There's someone else here you should see. She's been quite wonderful."

Amelia led him deeper into the schoolhouse. Then he saw *her,* off to the side in the far corner with a group of children sitting on the wooden floor circled around her. Emily sat in his old teacher's chair and read the children a story. A few feet away Grandpa Clark snoozed in a rocking chair with his mouth hanging open.

He was surprised and relieved, walked to the group and stood by Emily, clutching his bag and hat, mesmerized, until she finished reading the last page of the storybook. Her dark hair was pulled up in a bun and she wore a simple forest-green dress, which accentuated her dark brown eyes, glowing with care and warmth. She smiled to each child. All begged for another story.

He couldn't wait any longer, dropped his bag and hat, and reached out with his hands. Emily stood and he pulled her close then hugged her and said, "Thank God, you're alright!"

"Never better," Grandpa Clark said, startled awake.

Then he burst into tears. It was unexpected and simply happened. He didn't know why he cared so much for this woman but he did, and he held her close. Visions of his life circled in his mind, flashes of war, killing, his love for Helen, their wedding, intense moments of heated arguments, of soldiers grotesquely wounded, more killing, survival in battle, and now this kind, caring woman, here, warm in his arms.

He didn't want to let Emily go. Ever. He let the tears flow and held her for a long time, and when she tried to break free he tenderly held her longer. She embraced him fully, completely.

~48 ~

President Lincoln was yet again frustrated with the Commander of the Federal Army. This time General Meade, after a convincing victory at Gettysburg, had failed by his lack of pursuit to finish off General Lee and his army. Displeased by Meade's lack of aggressiveness to end the war, Lincoln removed Meade and appointed General Ulysses Grant as Commander. Grant had won key battles in the Western Theater, including a bloody conflict at Shiloh then captured Vicksburg to control the Mississippi River. Even Grant's appointment had not swayed the overall result. It had been one year since the Union's decisive victory at Gettysburg and yet Lee and the Confederates fought on.

President Lincoln often requested Grant to proceed to Richmond to terminate this awful war. Lincoln wrote long letters, short telegrams, pleaded eloquently, or spoke bluntly. After several more months, he wrote a brief note to Grant and urged him "to close his hand around Lee's army," which was so close within his grasp. Lincoln finished by writing he had asked this of each of his many commanders these past four years but he was thankful Grant appeared to be making some progress.

George, his staff, plus a few key officers, were re-assigned to the Army of the James. In addition to the Vermonters, he now also commanded the 23rd, 25th and 27th Massachusetts regiments, 9th New Jersey, 89th New York, and 55th Pennsylvania. They were good soldiers, improving, and it helped fine officers like Ripley and Benedict were still with him to train and lead them. With Grant commanding the Army of the James and their forces moved on the Southern capitol of Richmond.

After several days of marching Grant made camp, developed his plan of attack, and issued orders to each brigade commander. Later that afternoon George and Benedict stood off to the side of

Grant's tent while a photographer, Matthew Brady, adjusted the shutter of his camera. Grant stood motionless with his forearm on a sturdy pine tree then placed his left hand on his hip. Grant wore a crisp white neck cloth with a bow tie neatly in place and his general's hat was upturned with an unlit cigar in his mouth amid his full brown beard with an engaging, defiant stare burning in his hardened blue eyes. Despite his formal tie Grant appeared to be a confident fighter, ready to scrap with the devil.

He watched the photographer, who was dressed in a black suit. Brady reached around from behind the camera and adjusted a lens, all while remaining under a short black cape. Then he peered out at Grant, who stood unflinching, retuned under the cape, paused then lifted the lens cap. The moment was locked into a gelatin plate.

George recalled Billy Caldwell said a photograph stole the soul of the sitter and for a moment, while Grant stood transfixed and he wondered if some transition of the soul had taken place. Then Brady replaced the lens cap, lifted the cape, and said, "I'd like to take another, if you have time general."

Grant did not respond to Brady but turned to him and said, "What do you want?"

"If I may have a word, sir?" he asked.

Grant tugged his general's cap "goodbye" to Brady and turned for his tent. He and Benedict followed him inside where a table was covered with maps, papers, and lists of brigades. Off to the side an oak washstand held two crisp white linen towels and a shiny blue pitcher. Next to the washstand was a matching oak dresser with carved rose drawer pulls. Grant's cot did not have any bedding, which seemed unusual, then he realized the bedding was probably being cleaned.

"Yes, George?" Grant motioned to a single wooden chair but he preferred to stand eye-to-eye with him.

He spoke directly, "As you know, my boys have led the assault or been in the thick of every engagement for a long time and—"

Grant cut him off, "I know where you're heading with this."

"If I could finish, sir? To make my point."

"Make away." Grant's tone was a swift counterpunch.

A stout, dark-haired aide entered the tent, balancing three silver trays of meat with bread, soup, and coffee. Grant motioned to him to help himself but he declined then grunted out of embarrassment, knowing this conversation was improper and that Benedict watched him, but pressed on. "Our boys are exhausted and I don't know if they can handle the consequences of another attack. They will follow me into battle but should things prove *exceptionally* difficult, I don't know how my boys will hold up."

Grant paused and waited for the aide to set the trays on the dresser and leave. Then he took his unlit cigar from his mouth and spoke firmly, "This whole Army is exhausted general and that is precisely why I'm counting on you. Your Vermonters are damn fine soldiers and *this* battle could turn the course of the war."

"Yes, sir. That's what they said about the first Bull Run, and Gettysburg, and a lot of battles since."

Grant squinted, acknowledged the past false declarations, and tightened his grip on his cigar. "We're knocking on Richmond's doorstep. If we break through here, Lee will have no place to go. He'll be forced to choose between the capital and his supply base of Petersburg, and then he'll be stuck. Then it will only be a matter of time."

"I'm surprised he's fought this long," Benedict said, quickly realized he spoke out of place and lowered his head, then offered a salute apologetically.

Grant nodded to Benedict. "Yep. A better man would have said, 'Enough!' and saved thousands of lives. But he's got his orders and he has to do something. As long as he has men with fighting spirit, he'll press on until he sees there's no use. And, after this battle, Lee will see that."

"Yes, sir," he said and Benedict echoed him, "Yes, sir!"

He saluted crisply, turned abruptly for the tent opening, and Benedict jumped to follow him. Grant called out, "Your point was made, George."

Outside Grant's tent he walked briskly, stopped, removed his hat and wiped the sweat from his forehead, and Benedict caught up. He was annoyed, tugged on his floppy hat, and said, "Get our boys ready. We attack Cold Harbor tonight."

"Yes, sir. And sir?" Benedict asked.

He thought he knew what Benedict would say but listened patiently. Benedict's pale, thin face showed his emotions of concern, pressure, and pride. With Grant, he had tried and failed but he was glad Benedict was there to see his effort for his boys. This war had gone on for years, then longer, years more. It had lasted longer than any courageous man could take a punishment. He felt a maniacal scream deep inside himself and took steps to save anyone he could, even knowing this meeting with Grant, his commander, was wrong-headed leadership. A leader follows his commander's orders *without discussion.*

Benedict recognized the strain on his face and rested his palm on his shoulder. They were both exhausted with this awful war yet under his glasses Benedict's dark eyes held empathy and compassion. He spoke with a slight quivering in his voice due to the terrible fighting and killing that would happen soon. "Thanks for trying, general."

~ ~

In the deep of night it felt hot and stuffy. Black clouds covered the sky and enveloped them. No moon rose. Chaplain Dickinson led the Vermonters in prayer in the pitch-black darkness.

Then General Winfield Hancock, who had recovered from his wounds at Gettysburg, led their march. He rode Charger over to Hancock on his new mount, a fine chestnut quarter horse with black points, at the front of the column. They didn't speak.

The Second Corps marched through the night, 12 miles in 10 hours to Cold Harbor. Hancock decided the men were too drained from their long night march to attack as planned and, instead, ordered they rest.

The Southerners had anticipated an attack and had built breastworks and defensive earthworks. The Northerners did not scout the area or do any reconnaissance of any kind. After their rest, they would attack at 4:30 a.m. but they had no idea of what lay ahead. The Confederates were well-fortified in trenches and behind breastworks on Turkey Hill, and along the low ridges that sloped to the west like an inverted funnel with a myriad of swamps and open fields below, which was the only manageable route to attack.

In the pre-dawn darkness George sensed trouble but it was an indefinable wrong. His instincts screamed a warning through the deep blackness with the moon and stars obscured. The blindness bothered him, not knowing how many men or how many guns waited ahead. He sat high on Charger, tried to observe what would unfold, to see if there was any path, any weakness to exploit, and the first wave of Federals attacked.

The Union forces moved up the sloping ravine and into a deadly crossfire from the wooded ridges above them. Still they pressed on, advanced through the swampy ravine toward the low, wooded ridge, where the Southerners blasted a sheet of blazing fire into the bluecoats. The Confederates shot down at them from 40 yards, from behind breastworks of fallen trees and in shallow trenches, and were impossible to hit even by the best Vermont marksmen.

When the soft light of dawn illuminated the overcast sky to a gun-metal gray, he saw the rising smoke clear. Now he could see over the clearing to the base of the hill, where a few young men still tried in vain to move forward and were cut down in seconds by another shower of lead from the Rebels, who poured a killing crossfire into the remaining Union soldiers. Then smoke again billowed across the open ground and obscured the area and he heard the sound again, yet another volley, and the mini-balls struck his boys with a lethal thwack and more soldiers fell and cried out, followed by more horrible slaps of bullets against flesh and bone, followed by more screams, some in small cries and some in deep grunts, or stumbling to the ground followed by yells from the wounded, calling out with their sharp shrieks of pain and begging for mercy.

He sat on Charger from the protective woods, looking up and down the Union line. His Vermont boys and other regiments were ready to follow him. Then he was surprised to see Private James Freehan of St. Albans and figured Jim had re-enlisted. He dismounted, handed the reins to Charger to Freehan, whose blonde hair had grown long and was tucked behind his ears and ordered, "Hold 'em here, Jim," and the boy saluted but gave a twisted frown.

He unholstered his pistol, felt the engraving for "luck" and knew there was no such thing, and hollered, "*Forward!*" A flare of bugles sounded along the line, then he led the second wave of Federals marching in even strides behind flag bearer Corporal Hicks and filing out of the woods into the clearing.

He was immediately struck in the right hand then the left middle finger. He tightened his bleeding hand on his pistol and led his boys, yelling, "*Onward!*"

Then Hicks was shot. He stumbled and fell to his knees but clutched the pole of the First Vermont Brigade flag for support but did not fall, not completely, while another private came to steady Hicks and led him back to the woods with their colors. Then from out of the smoke in front of them some bluecoats returned, survivors of the first wave, lines that were now gone. Across the field through an occasional clearing in the smoke, he saw bodies everywhere. He glanced behind him, saw his Vermonters holding together but not advancing, instead they crouched here and there, and moved their feet like nervous stallions ready to bolt. He waved his right arm in a circular motion then forward, and a drop of blood flew off his hand. His boys cheered, responded in a gutsy display of courage, and marched forward en masse. He raised his pistol and shouted, "*Forward!*"

They moved steadily up the rising slope toward the far woods, toward the great mass of guns that waited atop the ridge behind timber and behind assorted stones in a breastwork of protection. The Vermonters and his regiment began to pass the first wave of young men, some of whom now turned and joined their advance while others lay flat, hoping to survive behind a fallen comrade or covered themselves.

They struggled on. His boys were shot left, right, behind him, and nearby again. A bullet clipped Sergeant Lloyd's shoulder next to him but they moved forward, onward, for another 20 yards amid the chaos of death, amid wounding of fine officers and young privates alike, then a bullet smashed into his right thigh. The bullet collapsed his leg and made him fall onto a dead private and he rolled behind his still-warm body. He noticed a larger pile of soldiers nearby with a big major on top of another poor soul and quickly crawled behind them. He wondered if this was Major Samuel Pingree of Hartford, no it was someone else, thankfully unknown. Then a bullet hit the corpse of the major with a thudding sound and startled him because it was so close, so filled with death, and he felt the bullet's impact move the major's thick chest. Then it happened again and again, and he slid down further and tucked his head lower.

After a moment he holstered his pistol then squeezed his bleeding thigh. He tore open his pants at the hole created by the mini-ball and examined the bloody wound, using his two right forefingers to press above the gouged flesh and felt the bullet lodged deeply. He noticed his blood was already beginning to thicken, to slow down, and figured the bullet had missed his artery. He thought he would be okay *if* he could get out of this killing field.

Then the third wave came, more Union soldiers stoked the battle, blindly into the vicious hail of bullets, and many more men fell. Most were behind him but a few farther ahead, but no one made it even half-way to their objective of the far woods atop the hill. From some distance behind him he heard another Federal officer holler "*Forward!*" but the order was impossible to achieve. Thousands of Southerners held the wooded high ground on three sides in front of them, behind fortifications, with plenty of ammunition.

It was gruesome. The Federals died en masse, 1,000 soldiers in 15 minutes, a platoon of 50 killed in seconds followed by a company of 100, followed by another company, and in every moment another wave of bloody death. Scores, followed by hundreds, fell two and three deep on top of each other. The Confederate soldiers fired so much and so often the barrels of their guns became too hot to hold.

With each charge the Federals moved with less speed. Instead of advancing through the clearing, up the slope for the far woods, some soldiers stopped petrified by their fallen comrades and searched for cover. In the midst of the chaos, a single soldier, Captain Alexander Beattie dashed out from the protective woods, made his way through the fallen soldiers, and helped an officer to stand then rushed with him to the cover of their woods. Then Beattie returned and the Rebels focused on him, fired at him, but he helped a lieutenant stand and limp back to the safety of the woods. Beattie started out again but Lloyd, bleeding from his shoulder, tackled him and held Beattie down.

After one hour, the Union officers stopped trying to advance through the clearing but not because they refused the order and not because they were afraid. With piles of corpses two and three bodies deep, there was no place to run without stepping on a fallen comrade. After several attempts, General Hancock, General Smith, and General Wright relayed their overwhelming losses to General Grant, who ceased the order to attack. The battlefield was still.

The low rays of early dawn sunlight cut through the trees and lit the gruesome masses of fallen soldiers. He lay still on the bloody field behind the bodies of the hefty major on top of a smaller private and desperately tried not to look at them. They were alive a moment ago, with families and cares of their own, with loved ones who missed them, unknowing they lay dead. It was impossible not to think of them, their loved ones, but who were they? By mid-morning the sun inched higher above the tree line, burned the dew off the bodies of the fallen, and turkey vultures swooped in, circling overhead then settled in the trees. Then more vultures came circling.

His right hand throbbed with pain and he couldn't move his left middle finger. It must be broken at the second joint. His right thigh became numb around the wound and his left hip held a dull ache from bearing all his weight but he dared not to shift too much at the risk of his movement calling attention to himself or exposing himself to be shot again. Flies buzzed around his wounds, took tiny stinging bites of his flesh, and suckled his blood. He shooed them away then saw them settle on an unmoving corpse. Other flies returned a moment later with swarming insistence.

Then a corporal rose from a pile of dead and sprinted for the rear with a slight limp. The crack shot of a Rebel sharpshooter cut him down in mid-stride and the corporal slammed head-first into a tangled mass of bodies in blue uniforms. Nearby another soldier leaped up and ran, this time a captain without a hat, with dark hair and an athletic build. He hurdled over a group of dead soldiers with his left arm flopping uselessly. The captain scooted left then sprinted right while shots rang out and he zigzagged around the fallen. Then another shot wide, two more behind him, and then the captain's head was ripped apart and he sprawled over a dead private with his legs flying up over himself and slammed into the heap. One last shot sounded and the bullet slammed into the captain's backside. He did not flinch.

He sweat in the mid-day sun. The turkey vultures waited no longer, swooped down and pecked, then pecked and tore strips of flesh from an unmoving bloody corpse and swallowed in voracious gulps.

He felt nauseous, his throat was parched and he needed water, but he didn't dare call out. Back in the Union line in the woods he vaguely saw Jim Freehan holding Charger's reins taut. A few officers milled around several horses and an unknown private held the Vermont First Brigade guidon. He realized he did not see Chaplain Dickinson in his black habit and thought, Yes, this is a god-forsaken place. It occurred to him he could slowly bleed out and die here on the warm, red Virginia earth.

Twenty yards away, across the field of fallen soldiers, all in blue uniforms, he saw a man who looked like Colonel Ramses Garthwaite from Boston, who led the New Hampshire boys. He had met Garthwaite earlier in the week and found him to be a cheerful, steady soldier. He made a low horizontal wave to encourage Garthwaite, or maybe to encourage himself, all would be well. Garthwaite didn't move. He had a fixed gaze in his direction. That soldier was dead. Yes, his chest was not moving, he was not breathing. Now he hoped it wasn't Garthwaite.

The stifling heat was oppressive and grew hotter. Catcalls came from the Southerners, followed by shouts of bravado from the Union side but far to the rear. Some Union soldiers yelled to their fallen comrades to sit tight, they would be rescued soon, only to be followed by more taunts of gruesome humor from the Rebels to "Come get 'em now!"

He tried to think of something pleasant like riding Charger on a crisp autumn morning when the leaves had changed color, or Emily's bright brown eyes and her warm, engaging personality, or her cheerful smile when they spoke on the porch. It was all impossibly far away.

He let himself doze off, told himself he could awaken and defend himself if a Rebel tried to capture him, but knew he couldn't defend himself, not with three wounds. Still, he allowed himself to collapse into a deep sleep.

The hot sun on his face woke him. He felt his skin becoming sunburned and wiped crusty sweat off his face with his sleeve. Time dragged torturously. He tried to rest, to stay calm, but heard the prayers of the wounded, "Dear God, let me live!"

"*Please God! Let me die now!*" another soldier cried out. "*Please dear God!*"

It was a throbbing, nightmarish hell of near-dead, of corpses, including the major and the private he lay behind. Then he saw a movement from the direction of Garthwaite. Something moved on his belly. Was he breathing? Then it moved again. A brass button popped from its mooring on his uniform, from his big belly and dangled by a tattered thread. Garthwaite's face was glazed grayish-white, absent of any rosy glow. How was it his button moved? Then it happened again and this time he saw the swarm of flies take off from his bloated corpse to set the waistcoat button swaying like a pendulum on the frayed thread. Garthwaite's lips were swollen open with his mouth a cave for any insect to buzz in or out and feast on his unmoving flesh.

Again he felt he was going to be sick, closed his eyes, and tried to bear the blazing heat and growing stench. After many long hours the sun inched nearer the western horizon and crickets and cicadas chirped incessantly. The sliver of a copper moon crept over the horizon and illuminated the ghastly field where exhausted, wounded men bled, moaned, gasped for water, wheezed for breath and cried for this life to be over.

He recalled Bear Brisken, shot by a sniper in the lingering moments of dusk and decided to wait longer until it was completely dark. A few wounded boys rose from the field like ghosts of the dead giving up their corpse. No gunshots sounded from the Confederates. It appeared safe.

He pulled himself over the dead, stood up straight with pain shooting through his wounded right thigh and stretched his sore left hip. He roused a wounded soldier, encouraged him to come with him and soon a few more stumbled for the Union line. They groped through the pitch-black nightmarish hell of thousands of corpses. They endured the pitiful obstacles, often accidentally kicked a boy in the torso or head, or nearly fell over a raised arm or a stiffened leg. More wounded rose and helped others more severely wounded. Then Captain Beattie and others rushed out to bear off the wounded and the dead. Each was a close comrade they couldn't stand to leave to the god-awful hunger of the wild.

His wounded thigh throbbed painfully and now both hands oozed blood. He felt lightheaded from the loss of blood and nauseous from the foul odor of decaying dead and the vile images of the day but he continued to wind over and around the piles of corpses. When they came closer to the Union line soldiers ran to them, their shapes barely discernible in the heavy darkness, and two boys helped him stumble into their lines. He did not see Freehan with Charger, or Benedict, or Lloyd or Ripley, or Chaplain Dickinson or flag bearer Hicks. He hoped they were all alive. He leaned on a private he didn't know, a stout young man with an oval face and an odd-shaped brown birthmark on his cheek, who gave a grim smile.

He was taken to the field hospital, where several doctors tended to the wounded. It took only a few seconds for a doctor to remove the bullet from his right thigh while another aide used thread and patched up his three wounds, then another aide wrapped him with gauze and bandages. Compared to the many dead and so many severely wounded comrades, his wounds were very minor. He knew he was one of the lucky survivors of the battle of Cold Harbor.

Over the next few days he recovered from his wounds in the field hospital and learned Lloyd, Benedict, Ripley, and Hicks were all wounded but all had already been released. Chaplain Dickinson remained, milling through the hospital and offering comfort and prayers to the wounded, then he gave George several newspapers that depicted various accounts of the battle of Cold Harbor. Over 6,000 men were killed in 45 minutes. He had been in vicious firefights, several times, but he was stunned by that sentence in the newspaper and had to read it again. Over 6,000 men were killed in 45 minutes.

One reporter wrote, “It was the largest, most vicious slaughter in the shortest period of time in the history of mankind.” The northern newspapers reported the losses on both sides but there were very, very few Confederate losses. When journalists described the battle of Cold Harbor they used words like “slaughter” or “senseless.” Many expressed concern that Grant was incompetent like his predecessors. One newspaper repeated the horrendous losses under his command at the battle of Shiloh, proclaimed “his apparently callous disregard for life,” and called Grant a “butcher.”

President Lincoln examined the Union losses at Cold Harbor in detail, which he always did after every battle. Lincoln noted this battle had horrible losses but it was also no worse than the total dead from Shiloh, Antietam, Fredericksburg, Chancellorsville, or Gettysburg. In fact it could be viewed a victory because Lee was now trapped. Grant had pushed Lee into a tactical loss where he must lose the capital of Richmond or lose the key railroad hub of Petersburg. Now all Grant had to do was keep Lee on the run, make him defend Richmond or Petersburg, and one or the other would fall and then there would be no place for the Southerners to run. The end of the war *was* in sight.

Despite the horrendous losses President Lincoln described Grant as a worthy leader and continued to support him. Most of the newspapers and the people of the North also supported Grant. Some journalists went further and praised Grant as the greatest hero of the

Union, which caused George to raise his eyebrows and shake his head in disbelief.

After reading the newspaper accounts, he thought of his hellish ordeal of lying wounded, all day, between the lines. He recalled the horrendous smell of thousands of decomposing bodies and his sickening walk in the dark over and around the wounded and thousands of dead. He wondered what this world was coming to if the leader responsible for the death of 6,000 men in less than an hour could be called a hero? He had severe difficulty weighing these opposing thoughts and his motivation to fight for his country was now in jeopardy. What in the world was God's plan? Did God exist?

~49 ~

It was very late at night, long after General Grant's staff meeting when he walked into Grant's tent for the second time in four months, now with Benedict and Ripley in tow. Grant had a large tent with plenty of headroom and he sat at a table with a hurricane lamp studying maps of Richmond and the Rebel's defenses. Off to the side was his oak dresser with a half-eaten plate of pork, beans, and a hunk of bread. Grant chomped on his unlit cigar and his dark brown hair was matted down and disheveled. His white collar was open and his typical bow tie missing, perhaps due to the late hour.

George stood at attention and saluted. Grant's bloodshot eyes took in the crisp formality of his stature and he saluted back with a half-raised eyebrow. "Yes, George?"

He knew he should have an unquestioning attitude with Grant, their Commander in Chief, but he felt his men needed rest or at least not to *lead* the charge into the most intense fighting. They had been through several versions of Hell, including Cold Harbor. Should this battle not go well it could be tragic for their Corps in the long run. The war had lasted over four years, with different regiments of nine-month volunteers serving Vermont, but this group had been tested more than the others. Most of the officers had been with him from the beginning but everyone in this brigade was exhausted. This time they were being asked to attack the key, frontline defensive fort outside Richmond with the bulk of 30,000 Confederates that remained fighting for their homeland, ready to viciously defend it. The whole situation gave him a sense of foreboding disaster where they would lose many, many fine young men.

"It is an honor to be chosen to lead the attack on Fort Harrison," he began, "My boys have led every charge since Cold Harbor, and some before, but I don't know if they can take any more. They're exhausted."

Grant stared up at him from his desk. Both recalled having had this conversation before Cold Harbor. Grant did not seem any different in his demeanor and he appeared he would not allow that tragedy to sway his thoughts now. His hardened blue eyes spoke volumes of his gritty determination. Simmering underneath it all, once again, both knew they should not be having this conversation at all.

He continued, "I don't ask this for myself but for my boys, that you reconsider our *position* in the lead."

Grant stood with some strain, showing his fatigue, and rolled his hand tiredly toward the map. It showed a series of forts protecting Richmond and the most forward and prominent was Fort Harrison. It was *the* key fort in a series that formed a ring of seven forts protecting the Confederate capital. Grant's plan was a multi-pronged attack from the south and required taking Fort Harrison first.

"General, it is critical we take *this* fort," Grant said, with his index and second finger encircled around his cigar then jabbing at the map, "and simultaneously General Butler will take Fort Williams, here, and so on. This is the *key* fort and that is precisely why I called on *you.*"

Grant pointed at him with his first two fingers, still holding his cigar, and his eyes were cold and unrelenting, "Because I know *you* can take it."

"Yes, sir." He stood silent, taking in the gravity of the situation. He could not question Grant's plan despite the disastrous outcome of Cold Harbor. He knew this battle *may* be the critical moment to begin the ending of the war and also knew, before he had entered Grant's tent, he must accept the lead. He maintained his level-eyed stare and locked bold determination with Grant until each man's eyes watered.

Grant's bloodshot eyes blinked and he returned to the map, cleared his gravely throat, only to look up and lock eyes with him again. Grant spoke with gruff frankness, "George, we're not silk scarf leaders from some romantic book. We're warriors with a tough, hardened core. We do our duty. I know you and your boys will do this. That's why I called on you."

He saluted and with that action his sense of a horrible, foreboding doom was sealed with a tremendous loss of life. Yes, he thought, into the breach again, this time with horrendous results *guaranteed.*

Grant stood, walked over to his oak dresser with carved rose drawer pulls, where his plate of food was unfinished. He set down his cigar on a green glass ashtray, picked up the small bread roll, glanced at Ripley, Benedict, then him, and began chewing. He grunted something akin to "Dismissed!" and returned to the map but now examined it from the side, hoping something new may be discovered.

He walked out of the tent and his brothers-in-arms Benedict and Ripley followed. Benedict appeared weary from a long day of issuing orders and double-checking details and his voice was tired, "It was good that you tried. Again."

"We need to take this fort as soon as possible," he said. Ripley, who preferred his well-worn kepi to a new colonel's hat, focused his brown eyes with resolve as campfires flickered, illuminating Ripley's rosy, oval face. Over the course of the war, very similar to Benedict, Ripley did not need to speak. They understood each other very well. Both knew this was another opportunity they had spoken about back in Camp Douglas as prisoners. They had their orders and they were placed in a position to fight. Ripley merely saluted and walked for his tent.

"Wake the men, let's get started," he said. "The sooner we attack, the better our chances."

"Yes, sir!" Benedict saluted but added, "One more thing, sir."

"Yes?"

"New recruits have arrived. Reinforcements. They're from Vermont, sir."

"Right. Mix them in with other veteran companies and—"

"Of course, sir," Benedict cut him off, which was unusual then motioned for one private in particular to step forward from near their campfire. The young man was the spitting image of Sergeant Bear Brisken. The private was big-boned, blonde-haired, and grew a short blondish brown beard. A dimple popped in his right cheek when he grinned, then he saluted and said, "Willy Brisken of Saint Albans, reporting, sir!"

He recalled Bear Brisken's tragic death at the hand of a sniper after the Battle of Bull Run and figured Willy to be Bear's younger brother. He gave a grim look to Benedict, who continued without pause, "Private Brisken will be assigned to the supply wagons in reserve, general."

Before he could respond, Private Brisken spoke up, "Sir! I'd rather be with Colonel Ripley. I've heard good things about him. And you, too, sir. If I'm to be reassigned, I'd rather be with Colonel Ripley. In the action. Sir!"

"You'll shut-up when you're in the presence of an officer, *Private* Brisken!" he snapped at him. He was sick of youthful, naïve boys wanting to test their manhood. He also felt indebted to the

Brisken family, for Bear's heroic action to save his life, and didn't want another life lost from this fine family. "You'll also follow orders without comment. Is that clear?"

"*Yes, sir!*" Brisken bellowed, clearly from the same strong stock as Bear.

"Alright. Put him with Ripley and inform the colonel of *our* intentions."

"Absolutely!" Benedict saluted and hustled off for Ripley's tent.

He took a moment to reflect on Benedict. They were good friends going back to the Canadian Revolution where they had both known Bear Brisken. Then he came to know Benedict better through times of peace, through the years of training with the Ransom Guards militia, through more training near Burlington, in Camp Boredom on the Potomac, followed by several battles over the years of this bloody war. Each could speak the other's mind. Benedict always carried out his orders immediately regardless of his feelings. He was steadfast, extremely bright, intuitive and responded unquestioningly. He was a very good friend and damn near a perfect soldier.

He turned for his tent but Ripley returned, put his hand on his forearm and said, "I'll keep Willy Brisken out of harm's way, to the extent that's possible. And thank you, George, for speaking up for all of us. Maybe next time General Grant will reconsider."

"It's good to know he thinks highly of us." He patted Ripley on his shoulder then shook it. "Edward. Let's not let him down."

"Yes, sir!" Ripley nodded once then saluted sharply.

He took out his pocket watch. It was 2 a.m.

~50 ~

With a flare of bugles their brigade of 2,000 young men rose and gathered their rifles, haversacks full of ammunition, tents, and gear. Some ate hardtack but the boys fell-in to columns of four behind their flag bearer Corporal Hicks, who had a slight hitch in his wounded left leg from Cold Harbor. They were assembled at 3 a.m. He sat up in the saddle and ordered, "*For-ward!*"

They marched quietly, under an order of no talking, through the thick Virginia woods under a moonless, dark night. They came to an area known as Aiken's Landing, crossed over the James River on a pontoon bridge covered with dirt and hay to muffle the soldiers footsteps and the officers' horse's hooves. He thought of the pontoon bridge at Harper's Ferry, of how they could have crossed over and been of service at Antietam, then shook his head, trying to let go of that thought while they crossed *this* bridge. On the Richmond side he wheeled Charger about, sat still and watched his boys shuffle by quietly, over the bobbing bridge and once again recalled how close they were to escaping capture at Harper's Ferry then surmised how different this war might be if they could have been involved at Antietam. He shook his head again, the past was gone, and tried to remain focused on the present, on this battle to come. Then he fell-in and they travelled four more miles in the pitch black, up the Varina Road.

At dawn he reined in Charger then turned to Benedict and Ripley, each on their fine chestnut-colored quarter horses, with Folio's splash of white on its nose, and placed one finger of his gloved hand to his lips to signal not to talk then raised his palm to halt. Hicks responded by extending his arms with the First Brigade flag sideways to stop. They took a few brief moments of rest without talking. A few canteens clattered then were still. The rising sun gave the grayish sky an orange, bloody-red glow.

His boys and the veteran officers stood still, awaiting his order. Some were old friends, from all over Vermont and New Hampshire, with some new comrades from Massachusetts, New Jersey, New York, and Pennsylvania. Then with resolution he nodded to Ripley, who saluted, paused a moment to review the long lines of soldiers, dismounted from Lightning and gave the reins to Corporal Pinder, his aide, who was his boyhood friend from Rutland. Ripley unsheathed his sword with his right hand then used his left to take out his pistol, then nodded firmly to him. They were ready.

He steeled his eyes then motioned with his gloved, stiff right hand, *Forward, attack!* Ripley quietly led the way on foot. The first wave of 600 marched with determination for Fort Harrison.

The Confederates were surprised. Most were still sleeping and it took them a few moments to gather behind their earthen and pine abutments. They fired at random then picked up their intensity.

The 600 Union soldiers continued a steady march with nothing more to protect them than fixed bayonets, then on Ripley's order they broke into a "*Quickstep!*" jog, three-quarters of a mile over open ground, slightly uphill and attacked the heavily manned fort. The Rebels fired their 22 canons down at them, fired more canons from two gunboats moored in the James River less than a mile away, and fired an occasional huge, barrel-sized 220-pound shell that came screaming down on them from Fort Gilmer two miles away. The Rebels poured heavy musket fire from the fort but the Union soldiers carried on.

Then they reached the base of the small earthen hill, a blind spot in the Rebel fort's defense where the canons could not be pointed any lower, and the first wave of soldiers caught their breath. Ripley lay on his back, his cheeks flushed crimson, then he leaned up and his dark brown eyes flashed a quick review up and down their line. He glanced at his pistol and flicked off a piece of the red Virginia clay from the barrel. Then he stood with his left hand clutching his pistol, slashed his sword downward and yelled, "*For-ward!*"

They stood en masse and charged up the earthen wall, past the pine abatis and into the fort. The Confederates fired and fought fierce hand-to-hand combat. Then, for the first time, many of the Federals used their new Spencer repeating rifles, having traded in their single-shot Enfields earlier in the month. The Confederates returned fire again but when they saw the startling Spencer rifles fire, then fire again and again, and again, and again, they ran. They left behind their breakfasts of eggs and bacon fat, sizzling in greasy black pans. It happened so fast some Rebels had no time to run. They simply surrendered.

Five minutes after the first wave, George led the second wave and attacked the fort. He rode Charger in a slow gallop alongside color bearer Manning Hicks of Montpelier, who held their flag leaning forward. By now very few Rebel shots rang out. Charger climbed the slope easily, much of the fighting was over, and after another moment the shooting stopped. Thousands of Rebels had run out the open back of the fort and dashed up a slight slope to escape into the pine woods 90 yards away.

He turned his attention to the captured soldiers. They were half-clothed, half-starved ragamuffins, young boys in their early teens and elderly men well over 60. Here and there were able-bodied soldiers but even those few had worn uniforms with holes in the knees, frayed cuffs, or stood barefoot. He thought, *This* is what remains of their fighting army. Perhaps the end *is* near.

He was proud they had captured the fort but knew there would be hell to pay when the Confederates counterattacked. He removed his gloves and ordered Corporal Pinder to gather the officers' horses and stake them just inside the southern wall they had just scaled. Then he ordered loudly for everyone to "*Reload and gather ammunition!*"

Next he focused on how to fashion a makeshift defense out of Fort Harrison, which was without protection in back. It was the outermost post in a series of seven forts protecting the southern approach to Richmond, five miles away, and had an odd construction of three sides of earthen walls and pine abutments but with one side to the north open for a quick escape, which was the direction the

Confederates had fled. It was the most logical place for their return attack because it was also the easiest and closest area for their cannons to support.

He saw the Confederates gathering in the woods, 90 yards away, and thought of what needed to be done next, how to strengthen their position, and how to repulse an attack here or an attack there. It required fast-thinking, quite different than Harpers Ferry two years earlier when Stonewall Jackson and his Rebel army felt their way through the Shenandoah Valley and the Federals had several days to prepare a defense. The Rebels were reloading their guns to mount an immediate, desperate counterattack *now*.

He commanded Benedict to disperse his orders: most of the soldiers were to defend this open side, dig a trench and build an earthen wall. Then, seeing eight small barracks the Confederates had built to house their troops, he ordered Ripley and his company to tear down the shacks and to use the boards to reinforce the mounds of earth to the north. Then he conferred with General Hiram Burnham, who split off a company of New Yorkers under his command, and they spread out along the eastern and western walls in case the Rebels tried a flanking attack. After 15 minutes most their brigade was entrenched in the open northern area behind their makeshift wall and stared out over a short field of 90 yards to a belt of pine trees that ran along the slight ridge to a white-washed farmhouse called Chaffin's Farm.

From those distant pine woods the sound of the Confederates clanging their bayonets onto their muskets followed by what sounded like a Herculean effort to wheel canons into supporting positions was heard. They made as much noise as possible.

He again surveyed the battlefield in case he overlooked any oddity of terrain, any dip where they might be vulnerable to the Rebels pooling and holding, but no, there was nothing. It was a nearly level open field with a slightly rising slope to the fort.

Their brigade totaled almost 2,000 soldiers and most crouched in the shallow ditch behind the newly formed earthen wall with wooden boards and pine abutment, no more than two feet high. He walked tall, behind his boys, unafraid. He noticed the resolve in every face, from Benedict to Ripley, who now commanded the New Hampshire boys, to Colonel Roberts of the 139th New York, to General Burnham also of New York. Then he heard a familiar sound, similar to the shrill piercing call of a gull floating over Lake Champlain, melding with the screeching scream of a nearby soldier. A rocketing shell whistled down on them from the Confederates' "Big Bertha" cannon from Fort Gilmer two miles away and blasted into the eastern wall. It sent dirt, pine splinters and human body parts flying. Horses reared up and pranced in fear and Pinder tried to calm them. Then more Confederate artillery blasted away from the woods.

"*General!*" Private Sawyer screamed, "*I'm scared somethin' fierce!*"

He rushed over then squatted next to the boy, Frankie Sawyer, who fidgeted and trembled wildly. Sawyer had a boyish tenderness in his face that made him appear younger than his age of 18 and he stared into the boy's darting, brown-and-bloodshot eyes then spoke calmly, "You'll make your family proud. All of White River Junction will salute you. Your country is counting on you. But most of all, you'll make yourself proud, Frank Sawyer."

Sawyer's eyes glanced about wildly, everywhere. He grabbed the trembling boy by the shoulders, shook him hard once then spoke harshly, "Look at me!"

Sawyer fixed his gaze on the pale blue calmness in his eyes. Then George remembered his father, Samuel's dark brown eyes, staring down at him with resolve and with reassurance while he saddled one of their best horses, a beautiful black mare named Midnight, to travel to Montreal for supplies for the first time. Then he repeated the same words his father had said, "*We're counting on you. Don't let us down!*"

Sawyer said nothing but gave a slight nod. He plucked his cheek, held the base of his neck, and said proudly, "You're a good man, Frank. It's my honor to serve with you."

He stood and motioned to flag bearer Hicks, who rushed over, planted the flag in the earth next to Sawyer then checked his pistol.

George continued down the line and told his boys to pile rocks, dirt, anything higher. He calmed them with his raised, firm voice and commanded them, "Take aim slowly. *Take your time!*"

Then the Southern artillery stopped. A brief moment later came the howling Rebel yell. It rose into a loud a fierce cry of 15,000 men from the Amy of Virginia under the command of General Richard Ewell. The Rebels, in their gray, brown, or odd uniforms in the distant woods started their Rebel yell while still under the protection of the band of pines that ran across the far ridge near Mrs. Chaffin's farm. Then they charged out of the woods, at first a company then scores more, now hundreds more, and they kept coming, now several hundreds, thousands, out across the open field and up the gentle slope to Fort Harrison. More and more poured out, several thousand soldiers appeared to rise from over the ridge, out of the ground, dead already. Their terrible scream sounded louder, a fierce cry of violence, the blood curdling Rebel yell from a whole brigade of blood-thirsty killers. He thought, How in the world could they hold against so many? Then he hollered with all his strength, "*Fire!*"

Rebels crumpled amid the smoke but on and on they came. A squad of 20 stopped in formation, knelt and fired. Several Union soldiers were hit and crumpled on the line. Here and there a Confederate was felled in a frayed uniform, another punched backward and their red hacksaw colors fell to the ground only to have a thin boy scoop it up, advance 10 yards before being shot in mid-stride and fall apart all loose, tripping forward over his legs and landing hard onto the ground over their flag. The boy's bare feet were the same brownish-red color of the earth.

A bullet nicked his coat. It reminded him of his farm when a swallow bird dipped low and brushed his shoulder. He knew he would not survive this day but wanted to fight with his brothers-in-arms, here, *now* and hollered, "*Give 'em hell, boys!*"

Some shot their old Enfields, tested and true from the battles of Gettysburg and Cold Harbor, but 200 of the boys on the north wall had the new repeating Spencer rifles and fired from now until Sunday without having to be reloaded. They fired, fired, fired, and fired again, picking off the thin Southerners running over the field. The Rebels shot back and fought bravely. Here and there a cry of pain, of fear, but everywhere a steady resolve to kill that soldier, right there, to put a bullet in him, to stop him *now*.

The battle raged on. Union soldiers fired their rifles and pistols with urgency. Private Aaron Orenson of St. Johnsbury trembled but mumbled aloud, reloaded his Enfield, and prayed, "Dear Lord make my actions swift and let Carver Oakley next to me continue to fire, to hold this sanctuary of ground for a few more seconds!" Orenson finished his prayer with a swift "Amen!" rose, leveled his Enfield, steadied his shaking gun with a minor miracle of calmness and pulled the trigger. A Rebel 30 yards away fell. Then Oakley, also of St. Johnsbury, finished loading the Spencer, rose, and fired again, again, and again.

George picked out a leading Rebel, an officer in a gray uniform, and fired his pistol. The man twisted, fell, pawed at his chest, rolled onto his back and reached up helplessly, trying grasp something in the air then collapsed.

Alvan Rowley of E Company called out, "General, something hit—" but was struck in the chest, knocked backward off the line, and rolled sideways into the soil with his mouth open, jamming his face into the dirt and leaves.

A rain of bullets chipped at the trees and thudded into the short earthen wall. Benedict shouted something from nearby and

George turned, adrenalin pumping in his heart at Benedict's urgency, and saw Sergeant Lloyd move out, ahead of their line, wielding his empty Enfield like a club. Lloyd slammed down one then a second Rebel in quick succession. The immense noise of screams and yells amid the god-awful, vicious, hand-to-hand fighting was too great to hear any singular voice.

Then he saw him, off to the side but angling for them, a Confederate sergeant led a group and breached their low wall. George raised then slashed his sword downward and split open the Rebel's ragged uniform, his chest, and blood sprayed out of the opened wound. Then another Rebel was on him from the right. He turned, fired his pistol into the man's face at close range then slashed at another Rebel who raised his arms to dodge his sword. He fired his pistol into that man's chest, covered in brown sackcloth. The man crumpled, stunned with his very light blue eyes opened wide and his mouth oozing dark blood, now spewing vomit then his eyes rolled back and his body collapsed, falling face-first with blood and puke splashing onto him. Then another Rebel charged at him, 15 yards away, and he shot him in his chest, causing the man to fall flat, motionless.

Then the Confederates were not as thick, they appeared to be moving back, still firing but much slower, at random, with their fleeing shots poorly aimed and the bullets whizzing overhead or slamming into earth and low timber wall. Sporadic muskets popped in a whimpering finale and the few remaining Rebels turned and hustled for the safety of the far woods. Smoke drifted away, leaving a choking stench of blood, guts, vomit and shit, and revealed the horror of hundreds of Southerners wounded and corpses of the dead scattered in odd positions everywhere.

"*Reload!*" he called out, standing tall with his hot pistol in his left hand and his bloody sword in his right. He wiped then sheathed his sword and reloaded his pistol, noting the inscription and thought of his father's gift. Somehow the word "*Justice*" now had a more elusive definition. What *injustice* had these young men, these boys that he had killed just now, done? Because they fought for their village, or their state? Did they own slaves? Did anyone try to peacefully resolve this bloody conflict? He knew he must stop thinking about this. *Here* was not the place and *now* was definitely not the time. He had to ready his men then realized with shock he had to ready *himself.* He had a job to do and cursed, "Goddammit!"

He surveyed the horizon and across the distance to where Fort Williams stood, appearing calm and serene. He stared at its bleak silence, felt a crawling uneasiness, and recalled Grant's multipronged plan of attack yet Fort Williams was quiet. Here, they could *not* hold 15,000 Rebels on a singular mission to retake Fort Harrison. Where in the hell was General Butler?

Colonel Roberts of New York, excited by the last rush of fighting, hustled to his side and spoke in a frenzied tone, "General, I'm not sure how much more we can hold."

His quick temper was lit, now furious, and he bellowed his reply for everyone to hear his resolve, "*We'll give them hell 'til they stop!*"

"*Damn right!*" Private Sawyer yelled, his face showing some surprise, perhaps at his foul language or his tenacity. Then Sawyer held up his hot Spencer rifle and claimed his new-found confidence. Hicks reloaded his pistol, patted Sawyer on the back, and gave him a slight, grim smile.

Ripley hurried over, his anger showing in his jerky strides and he spoke through clenched teeth, "Where's Butler? His brigade should have taken Fort Williams an hour ago! We're up against the whole damn Reb army!"

"We can't worry about Butler!" he snapped. "Our orders were to take this fort and *hold it!*" This was not to be debated, with zero doubt in his mind. He spoke harshly, "And that is *exactly* what we will *do!*"

"Yes, sir!" Ripley said, and Roberts echoed him, "Yes, sir!"

He again turned his thoughts to what his boys needed, if they were positioned correctly, and what could happen next, and after that. Then he was distracted by Ripley. His right forearm bled through his blue uniform, dribbled down his hand, and dark red drops fell off his wrist. "You're shot."

"Yes," Ripley said with his gritty anger at Butler still seething, "I believe I am." Then he looked at his right forearm, feeling it with his left hand like the wound wasn't real, and watched his blood run and drip onto the red-clay ground. Then Ripley seemed to realize what he thought, to take him off the line, and he grew even more hostile. "I'm fine goddamn it. *Leave me alone!*"

"*Benedict!*" he called out and Benedict dashed over. "Get Captain Swann to form a detail of ten men. Pull the wounded off the line, back to that far wall near the horses."

"What if they attack from that direction?" It was the approach they had scaled earlier in the morning but Fort Harrison only had three walls.

"They'll keep coming from this direction, or maybe the east or west in a flanking move, but we'll need to re-form in an area, to fall back if needed. That southern wall is the only place I can figure." Beyond the far wall was the steeper slope and open field they had attacked from, and a few miles beyond the Federal Army of the James waited with 80,000 men, languishing in the hot Southern sun. "Do you have another idea?"

"No, sir."

"Fine. Get Captain Brydon to form a squad of ten and go for an ammunition wagon back at camp. Then take inventory of how many rounds each soldier has left." Benedict, who had grown very thin by this long, exhausting war, stood waiting for any other orders. They stared at each other, had the same thought, but there was nothing more they could do. Each knew they may not survive another attack. "That's all."

"Yes, sir!" Benedict was off with haste and yelled the instant after he saluted, "*Captain Swann! Captain Brydon!*"

Then from the southern approach, four Union soldiers rode swiftly on horseback. All four were excellent riders. When they came closer it appeared the lead rider was General Grant on a dark quarter horse with black points with three officers. They raced into the fort and Grant expertly reined in his horse. Corporal Pinder, who was in charge of the officers' horses, ran up and grabbed the reins tossed to him and Grant dismounted. Two of his aides also stepped down but one remained mounted on his winded chestnut quarter horse and his forequarters.

General Burnham jogged over with his field glasses bouncing around his neck and saluted Grant a moment before he arrived. George raised his eyebrows at Burnham, who had sweat running down his temples, then nodded at his drawn pistol, and he holstered it.

Grant saluted casually and looked around the oddly-built fort with an open escape toward Richmond, strengthened with a trench and a short earthen wall and reinforced with the weathered boards from the Confederates' barracks. Grant understood everything all at once and nodded his approval. Next he took Burnham's field glasses and scanned over the open expanse to the Rebels massing at the edge of the pine woods, then turned to the east and searched in vain for Butler's overdue force on the Varina Road, late to attack Fort Williams. He snarled and handed the field glasses to George, who returned them to Burnham. Grant reached into his coat pocket, took out some crumpled paper and the stub of a pencil, then wrote an order and handed it to the mounted aide, who saluted, wheeled about, spurred his horse, and rode off swiftly.

Then a huge missile screamed down on them, bouncing in the fort's interior, rolling across the trampled mud and came to rest 10 feet from Grant. Most of the soldiers hit the ground and covered themselves in a fetal position. One of Grant's aides, a lieutenant, dashed for the bomb, losing his cap and threw himself over the shell. It fizzed and smoked under his blue uniform. A long, tense moment passed, waiting for the explosion. Then, amid the stillness, nothing happened.

The aide swept aside his long dark hair, chuckled nervously then laughed until he doubled over in tears, crying and shaking. The other soldiers got up one by one, including the heroic aide who wiped his tears. Another aide clapped him on the back and said, "Thanks just the same."

During the excitement Grant had calmly written another order and now gave it to an aide, a pale, big-eared lieutenant who hopped up onto his sorrel, pulled the reins to the side, dug in his spurs, slapped the sorrel's rump and raced out of the fort, heading back to headquarters.

Grant turned to him, rested his right hand on his shoulder and spoke in his rough, worn voice, "Fine job, George. Hiram, well done. We'll get reinforcements up here."

"Thank you, sir," Burnham said, brushing away sweat with the back of his leather-gloved hand, and searched for words then offered, "We're doing our best."

"We *must* hold this position." Grant took a fresh cigar from his coat pocket, bit off the end, and appeared to know what George was thinking then answered his thoughts with equal exasperation, "I have no idea where in the hell Butler is! When Millston, that's the lad who just rode off, when Millston gets a-hold of him he has my direct order to place his boot squarely up his ass! We need Fort Williams! In the meantime, this fort is *critical* to our advance on Richmond. Hold it at all costs!"

"Yes, sir!" he saluted and waited. Nothing more was said.

Grant took back the reins from Pinder, mounted his dark quarter horse with two white socks and a flash of white on its nose then stroked its neck. Grant took his time, walked his horse before each officer and stared each man in the eyes sternly, from Burnham to Roberts to Ripley and Benedict then stopped in front of him. He nodded, brought his hand up slowly then gave a sharp salute. Then Grant pulled the reins, wheeled about, and slapped his horse once with the reins and dug in his spurs. The last aide followed and they were gone.

Pinder, who had held Grant's horse, approached Ripley with a shy shuffle then spoke with awe, "Was that General Grant?"

George said, "Yep. Benedict, get all the officers here, *now!*"

In less than two minutes all 37 officers were gathered around. He disliked giving speeches but he spoke loudly for all to hear. "We are to hold Fort Harrison at all costs and that is what we *will do!* That is all."

Their reaction was like he had announced a grand party. All the officers had a variety of positive reactions from simple large grins to saluting to nodding to huzzahs and hearty calls of "*Yes, sir!*"

They returned to their positions and a moment later the Confederate artillery began again. Shells rained down, blasted around the fort, and took its toll on the Union soldiers. They bombed the fort for 20 minutes, smashed holes in the walls, ripped more young men to shreds and made the 20 minutes seem like 20 hours. Then it was over but everyone knew what was next.

He took this moment to walk among his boys, stopping to pat a friend on the back, gave words of advice to a young man, offered proud reminders of how their particular town in Vermont looked to them, and reinforced their bravery to each of these brothers-in-arms. Without exception each young man relaxed and rebounded under his encouragement. Here and there a grim smile came or their anxiety showed in their troubled eyes but everywhere a sense of honor and duty bolstered the battered blue line.

Then he saw a detached leg out in the short grassy field without a body nearby. It was odd, grotesque, clothed in brown pants, a Southerner with a white sock and a black shoe tied down in a bow. Where was the man? Most of the brown-panted leg was clean but at the top the deep gashing wound oozed drops of blood into the rich Virginia soil and stained it dark maroon, soaking it with blood. The detached leg had a disordering effect on him. He felt directionless amid the chaos of battle, the wounded, the dwindling ammunition, Ripley wounded, Grant's visit, reinforcements, and this horrible sight, a detached leg, there, 10 yards away. What was next?

He turned away and saw Thomas Jenkins from Brattleboro, one of the first volunteers, a young man he had known for four years, lay slumped against the short earthen wall and blood trickled from his mouth. His already milky eyes were glazed over and he stared at nothing in particular. He stepped over, bent down, and smoothed his palm over Jenkins's boyish forehead to close his soft eyelids.

Then he heard loud sobbing from Private John Twindertus from Montpellier. He had noticed Twindertus before the most recent attack but did not have time to go to him and indeed had noticed him *not* shooting his Spencer when they charged together earlier in the day, 1,400 hundred strong in the second wave to capture Fort Harrison. Now, three hours later, here was Twindertus trembling in violent spasms and crying uncontrollably. He was done.

"*Benedict!*" he called then squatted next to Twindertus, pushing his long hair off his face and drying his eyes with his puffy palms. "It's going to be alright."

"I, I. . . " Twindertus's voice sputtered and trailed off. He rocked back and forth, and cried, "I don't, I mean, I, help me! *Look out!*"

"It's okay. You're alright," he rubbed the boy's back. Twindertus looked around nervously. "Come on. Stand up, John. Let's get you off the line."

Colonel Roberts watched with stunned amazement. Benedict ran up, announced the results of the inventory, the wounded and dead, and summed up the desperation of their position. Then Benedict slipped under Twindertus' armpit to help him stand.

He handed Twindertus's Spencer repeating rifle to Roberts then spoke to Benedict, "Help John get to the rear to rest. Maybe later he can assist with the wounded. When he's up to it."

"Yes, sir," Benedict said, escorting him off the line and Twindertus held on to Benedict like an elderly woman after church.

"Why'd you do that?" Roberts demanded. "We need every man. There's nothing wrong with him!"

"That boy's filled his course. It's also for the others. Cowardice is contagious. We don't need anyone giving our boys any idea of failure."

Roberts shook his head sideways in disagreement then turned and walked away. He called out and pointed, "*Roberts!* Get a shovel and bury that damn leg."

A Confederate officer hollered from the woods, "*Hey thar boys! Why don't y'all surrender? We don't want to kill* all *y'all.*"

Cicadas whirred a fast rattling hum in the hot sun. Several boys in blue looked to him for a response while the veterans took this time to inspect their guns or to dig deeper into the Virginia clay and pile more dirt onto the small wall.

The Rebel continued, "*Don't y'all know we got the* en-tire *Army of Virginia here? And Marse Robert E. Lee* his-self *is comin' down to whup ya!*"

"*Let General Lee come!*" he hollered back. "*We'd be happy to give him the same welcome we've given you!*"

The Federals laughed and cheered. It grew into a rallying cry, louder and louder still with hurrahs. Then the Confederates fired on the ammunition wagon being pulled by four mules, with Captain Brydon and 10 young men rushing alongside, over the exposed Varina Road on the southern approach to the fort. The Rebels continued a withering fire at the squad, who flinched and pushed the wagon faster. Then a mule went down then another but their rigging held them tight to the wagon. Brydon raced around and unhitched the two shot mules on the right side.

General Burnham hollered, "*Put some fire on those woods closest to the wagon!*" The boys in blue lay down a heavy protecting fire and the Rebels retreated back behind the trees and deeper into the cover of the woods.

Brydon and his squad again moved the heavily laden, low-slung wagon toward the fort but now with only two mules pulling and most of the boys pushing from the protected left side and two more pushing from behind. They again had it rolling up the slight incline nearing the entrance, then Private Roderick Greene at the back was hit by a bullet in his right shoulder and his rifle fell from his grasp but he stayed with the young men heaving at the wagon. Then Greene's face seemed to register his need and he dashed back for his rifle. Mini balls pelted the area around him, kicking up puffs of dirt, but he grabbed the gun with his left hand, then ran back and caught up with the wagon entering the fort. A great cheer went up from the all the Union soldiers.

Benedict met and conferred with Brydon, who soon had his squad dispatching boxes of bullets for the Spencer seven-shooters. He felt a surge of pride at how Brydon continued his task, knowing their brave deed to retrieve the ammunition wagon was not completed until they had distributed its precious cargo. They were still unloading when a Confederate officer emerged from the woods, slashed his sword downward and hollered, "*Charge!*"

Another huge wave of graycoats swarmed out of the pine woods, out into the open field toward the northern wall-less approach. They charged in large companies and regiments, hundreds at once, now thousands, and screamed their damn Rebel yell louder, fiercer, and with them came a low rumble like thunder booming from behind them, booming from the ships on the river, booming from Fort Gilmer, and blasted with direct hits around the fort's exposed area, smashing against the nearest wall with deafening explosions, and peppering the interior. Then with perfect timing the cannon fire stopped, the Rebel yell continued louder still, and they rushed with determination for the wall-less area, sprinting for the exposed underbelly of their defense.

"*Fire!*" he yelled and Ripley echoed his order and a great din of gunfire filled the air. Union and Confederate soldiers screamed and the fierce battle raged again.

He aimed his pistol on a gaunt Rebel straight ahead, who ran hatless with a scruffy beard that grew in patches with a shrill, piercing shriek howling from his emaciated skull. He ran left then right, and scampered further ahead. He pulled the trigger but the man cut right again and a puff of dirt popped near his next step. He lowered his aim to the man's midsection, saw the man's coat oddly pulled together with twine, and fired. The man stumbled over his legs, falling in mid-stride then struggled from the ground, grappling to raise himself with pursed lips of determination. Then another bullet slammed into his forehead and his head snapped back violently, wiping all expression off his face, and he crumpled sideways onto the ground.

Next he focused on a hardy youth, jogging next to the Confederate flag bearer. He was an officer with a tailored coat and a ruddy face with a fine mustache pointed at the ends. The Rebel officer stopped to yell encouragement to his men, and he aimed at his chest and fired. The shot went high but bore a hole clean through his neck and blood spurted from his throat as he fell to the ground, clutching at his wound desperately. The flag bearer stopped and went to the officer, bent over him, then someone else shot that young boy, now falling across the officer he had stopped to help. Their red hacksaw flag bounced across both their bodies then rolled off them to the ground. Another Rebel scooped up the flag and continued with yet another group charging at them.

The Federals crouched behind the short earthen mound and fired, but here and there more Union soldiers were hit. Private Koosbeck, a young man from Bradford, was shot in the head and blood ran out of his left eye and nose, and down his face gruesomely. Colonel Cullen of New York's 98th rallied that part of the line but was shot in the lower abdomen and sagged down, unable to stand. Throughout the furious noise and intense struggle, death found the brave of heart, the misguided, the pure, the timid, and they fell equally silent. The immense horror of the battle raged.

He knew ammunition was low on the front line and hollered, "*Captain Brydon! Bring up—*" he was caught in mid-order, knocked down and fell backward on his arm. His torso slumped heavily, useless, and he saw his blue coat already stained by his right arm with his dark blood pumping out generously on the ground. This is bad, he thought and shut his eyes.

"*General Stannard is down!*" Brydon screamed. A quick murmur went along the line but the gunfire and roar of the fierce battle continued.

"*What?*" Private Sawyer yelled from across the way, then fired his Spencer again and again.

Private John Popovich, further away, halfway down the line, hollered the news. "*General Stannard is dead!*"

"*Keep firing, boys! Heave at 'em!*" Burnham screamed, the soldiers responded, and the battle rose in pitch to an enormous cacophony of anguish amid rifles firing and pistols shooting with smoke and dust rising among the wounded and dead.

Again a call came from the eastern wall, "*What happened to General Stannard?*"

"*General Stannard is dead!*" Sawyer yelled back.

Sergeant Lloyd, an immense man, enraged, screamed then ran out of the wall-less area toward the charging Confederates. Two, three, now six Union men rallied after him, fired their rifles again and again, and killed Rebels in a push of terror. Lloyd moved to his left, swinging his Spencer rifle like a club, turned and fired it to protect his right, and killed Rebels in an ever widening circle around him. Lloyd's fury was palpable, deadly, nearly out of control but winning the moment. Then the Rebels in that area turned, a man here, a boy there, and scampered back across the field for the woods, running from this huge unstoppable fury. Those left behind on the battlefield felt the tidal change and more Rebels turned, retreated, and left their wounded comrades behind, crying in pain.

The Union soldiers slowed in their firing until Ripley yelled, "*Stop firing! Lloyd get back here!*"

The bulky sergeant with dark hair and a dark beard stopped then turned and stared back at Ripley with his light gray eyes as if he didn't know how he had come to be outside the fort. Then Lloyd gazed at his fellow soldiers then at Ripley again. The horror of General Stannard's demise washed over his reddened face and he fell to his knees, a giant slamming to the earth. His rage burst in a loud, deep cry that screamed out over the fallen, over the wounded and the dying and the dead, out to the far pine woods and above the rising smoke to the sky. It was a powerful, furious, bellowing moan, then Lloyd caught his breath and cried a keening mournful wail, "*He's dea-a-a-a-d!*"

~51 ~

It felt like someone as large as Sergeant Lloyd had punched him on the shoulder with all his might. His right arm was numb, he couldn't move it, and the right side of his chest hurt. He felt dizzy and sank back into darkness.

Now the sun burned his eyelids and he was floating, bouncing with several angelic hands supporting his arms and legs, and more hands lifted his body upward toward the sky. He opened his eyes and saw Benedict's warm eyes under his spectacles, his thin face grimy with black gunpowder and dust. Benedict said something excitedly and trickles of sweat cut rivulets of cleanliness over his temples, then ran down his anxious face.

Now Ripley's reddened boyish face was in front of him, becoming larger and larger, then he moved his lips and said something. It was Greek with words falling in and trailing off in indistinguishable phrases. Why would Ripley speak Greek? Was he testing the old teacher? He tried to sound convincing, "That's Plato."

The children stared at him obediently. They believed in him wholly, unquestionably. Except for George Benedict, a tall, thin, young man among these school children. "Yes, it could be Plato," Benedict said. "I've read his work but it reminds me of Socrates. The fight for free will in mankind."

Now Ripley said something else and patted his chest but even his tender tapping felt like a heavy weight smacking down on him. The sky was incredibly beautiful, very high with puffy clouds gently pulled into wisps, and he felt a sense of wonder and awe. He felt he could melt into those grand clouds, fly up and be part of the vast horizon. Then he felt slammed down onto a hard surface. Dining chairs were off to the side. He must be on a dining table but somehow he still saw that magnificent blue sky with wisps of feathery clouds. Someone jerked off his coat and mind-numbingly fierce pain shot through his right arm, dangling useless out of his coat sleeve. The hot pain flowed through his shoulder and chest, and he felt dizzy again. Then the clouds swirled faster, darker, losing light and now deep-red black.

He felt back-and-forth shaking, as when his father tugged at his shoulder to wake him for a pancake breakfast. Was it time to wake up? The tugging felt rugged, sharp, painful. He tried to see but couldn't. What was happening?

Then he opened his eyes and all was clear. It was the doctor's saw ripping apart his flesh, back-and-forth, hacking across his right arm! He raised himself at the neck and turned to Ripley, who had tears in his dark eyes with his face flushed deep red. Ripley's hands trembled but pressed down on his chest over the wound. Tears and sweat ran down Ripley's face, then dropped onto his face.

Doc Thayer finished sawing, his wounded right arm clumped to the earth and blood spurted out. Doc pushed his fingers down on the artery, pinched it then deftly closed the artery with suture and knotted it. Another hand poured liquid from a pint of whiskey to douse the wound.

Incredible pain shot through his right arm. But wait, wasn't his arm gone? Pain flooded and throbbed throughout his chest and pounded and throbbed in his head. The high Virginia sky spun around, pushed into the earth and spun around the waists of the officers, around the table, then spun wildly faster up to heaven now, red-hot and white. He ached for a cooling white balm like snow and dreamed of snow falling gently down, gently over the fields, gently, quietly on the soft sloping hills of his Vermont farm.

A long black train of carriages with thousands of riders in black and women in black mourning dresses slouched to the funeral of someone very important. A solitary bugler wailed a mournful "Taps." He made his way up the cemetery hill, through the immense mass of Federal soldiers mourning, to the open gravesite. The casket was open but he could not see the face, made his way closer through the front row of mourners, who were all Union generals. He peered into the coffin and saw General Grant, still, with his blue eyes fixed—shouldn't they have shut them?—but he appeared lifelike with a cigar stump in his tightened lips. He turned to one of the many generals standing at attention, a stout man in full uniform with tears flowing over his cheeks, and asked, "How did this happen?"

"Cigar got him."

He chuckled but the general was not laughing. Was he serious? This fierce warrior who had fought tens of thousands of soldiers in bloody battle, time and again, was felled by a cigar? "No. Honestly?"

"Yes." The general eyed him up and down, noticed he was also a general, and saluted. "Look after yourself."

He stood stunned by this important warning. A shroud of mist clung around the trees and over the mossy hillside. Then he saw another open grave and curiously walked toward it. A solitary priest mumbled something, walked away, and left the open grave unattended. There was no one. A crow cawed a shrill cry in a large oak nearby. The gravestone was etched:

GEORGE J. STANNARD

BORN IN VERMONT

SLEEP SOLDIER, THY BATTLE'S O'ER

He stumbled backward, fell down then crawled to the marker. Yes, it was his name. Where was everyone? No family. No parents, aunts or uncles. No wife or children. No friends. No one.

He wiped his eyes and looked around again. No one. All was silent. Then the crow cawed again and the enveloping mist grew thicker.

He coughed then violently coughed again. A choking fluid filled his lungs. This was it: he was dying. The grave was ready and he was dying. What was there to show of his life? What would become of him? Is this how it ends? He coughed again and felt he couldn't breathe. He couldn't breathe. Is this it?

~52 ~

After word spread General Stannard was dead, the rumor was put down as false. He was severely wounded and an ambulance wagon brought forward, and they used a stretcher to load him into it. In the latest Rebel attack General Burnham was killed and his body was slid into the ambulance next to him. It was quiet for some time, perhaps he fell asleep, and then Ripley said, "Lloyd! Get eight of your best men to escort this ambulance back to headquarters!"

It seemed like an instant later they were moving, jouncing along, and astounding pain shot through his right arm. The terrible pain continued with all the jostling and soon he was unconscious again.

Doc Thayer had administered morphine for his pain, which gave him some weird dreams. He saw Helen riding a large fire hose, like some mythical beast spraying fluid out of its mouth, undulating up and down, spraying white foam everywhere. Then Helen was calm, floating above him, smiling, and cooed seductively, "Come, join me!"

He awoke, unable to rise up, but Benedict was there patting his chest and said, "Please. Lay back. Rest."

He closed his eyes and saw Helen's curvy body under a Grecian robe of sheer white muslin. She smiled sweetly, her high cheekbones pointed, her bright blue eyes beamed, and she held out her open hand then whispered, "The play has started but I've been waiting for *you!* Come, George! Join me!"

The jostling, pounding wagon awakened him again and a thickness of fluid choked his chest. It felt like someone was standing on him and he could not breathe. He struggled, leaned up and coughed, and Benedict propped his hands under his shoulders. He fought, took a tiny breath, and squeezed out the words, "Can't breathe."

"Is this better?" Benedict shoved a folded blanket under his back then gave him another shot of morphine. He breathed more deeply, relaxed, and was soon asleep.

~ ~

The Federal soldiers with the Vermonters defended yet another attack on Fort Harrison, which was renamed Fort Burnham in honor of their fallen, deceased General Burnham. They withstood vicious fighting and established a foothold to Richmond, which they held despite several more counterattacks. Then Southern General Lee, seeing that there was nothing worthwhile to this ground, withdrew his troops.

More battles were fought and the Vermonters continued to lead the way in General Grant's advance to capture the Confederate capital. Then Lee decided the city itself held no more importance than Atlanta or New Orleans. It was the Confederate Army that must survive to fight. Key railroad junctions, roadways, mountaintops, and bridges were important to hold but not this city despite it being their capital. Lee and his army retreated from Richmond and set up a defensive position around Petersburg, where they held the railway station and crossroads.

Southern politicians and ardent sympathizers abandoned the capital. It was a ghost town. Confederate President Jefferson Davis was one of the last to leave and reportedly snuck out by wearing a woman's dress and shawl as a disguise.

The toll of the war had been immense. Every Southerner knew someone who had been killed, or lost a relative, or had their entire family wiped out. Farms were plundered and businesses sacked. Very few citizens stayed in Richmond, mainly because they had businesses that held too much value and could not be moved, or they had lost *everything* so there was no point to go anywhere else.

Newly promoted General Edward Ripley was the first Federal officer into the fallen capital and led the Vermonters, as usual at the front of the army, into the destroyed city. President Lincoln was interested to see the fallen capital and was escorted by Ripley. There was little left of Richmond except the crumbling shells of buildings, bombed out by artillery, with very few buildings intact. Ripley informed the President of various assassination plots he had uncovered from prisoners and Southern sympathizers, and advised him to take greater precautions. Lincoln declined.

Union General Grant used his army of 100,000 men to tighten its grip on the Confederate Army of 35,000. The Rebel army was exhausted, ill clothed for the winter, running out of ammunition and supplies, and their will to fight was diminished. There was little to do except negotiate a surrender, hopefully with dignity. When and where they would surrender would depend on General Lee, who continued to maneuver his army and fight through the winter months of 1864, at the cost of tens of thousands of lives of Northerners, Southerners, citizens, young and old.

The end was in sight but Lee and the Southerners fought on. They fought around Petersburg in several engagements. The Rebels built elaborate trench fortifications and Grant maneuvered the Union forces, wheeled around and attacked Lee's flank. The army in tattered gray, butternut or sackcloth retreated and entrenched themselves again, only to see the soldiers in blue maneuver and arrive on their flank again. Lee would somehow escape to another hilltop, be attacked again, only to escape across the river and into the woods. The maneuvering, adjusting, attacking, and evading continued. The end of the war was in sight but the fighting went on day after day, through the battles of Cedar Creek and Marion, to be repeated again with more wounding and death on both sides. It lasted weeks, months, and through the long wet winter of 1864 and into the spring of 1865.

Thousands more were killed. They fought at Fort Stedman, Five Forks, the Second and then Third Battle of Petersburg, with thousands more dead and thousands more wounded. The Union dead were carried by train to join the thousands before them and buried at Robert Lee's doorstep at his home in Arlington. The cemetery, renamed Arlington National Cemetery, would be Lee's reminder of his decision to *not* support his country but to rebel against it in their noble cause.

~53 ~

It had been a very long difficult year despite the war ending, followed by the tragic assassination of President Lincoln. The South needed to be rebuilt and many had a plan, or a wish for retribution, or a dream to make a fortune in the rebirth of the national economy. Lincoln's plan for amnesty, along with a kind, helpful reconstruction with forgiveness at its core, died with him. His successor, President Andrew Johnson, imposed retribution. The Southern states reaffirmed restrictive laws called black codes, which greatly limited freedom and civil rights for African Americans.

George had seen astonishing mismanagement from leaders during the war and wanted to avoid those same men after the war. He served out his term of enlistment with a position behind a desk for the Sanitation Commission, where their chief aim was to provide for the contraband, freed Negroes, quality health care and tent housing near Washington City. Even that effort ran afoul through dissenting leadership and a lack of long-term planning and outside political maneuvering, which seemed to corrupt almost every initiative after the war.

When his term of service ended, he returned to Vermont and continued to court Emily Clark but something was very different. She remained cheerful, warm, and kind but he held so many wounds—his missing right arm, one wound in his thigh, two wounds in the fingers of each hand—that he felt incapable of giving of himself because he was unhealed in whole. He let Emily know he cared for her very much but he needed some time alone to heal. He returned to Georgia to focus on his farm and his horses.

He managed, with some help from the Lonegran boys, to care for his horses and to train the animals left-handed. He also started drinking whiskey, at first to ease his discomfort from his wounds then more heavily in an attempt to chase away the awful visions of sights he had seen and actions he had committed. If he drank enough, the eyes of the ghosts would blur, the piercing blue eyes of a Southern lieutenant shot at arm's length, the haunting hazel eyes of the foul, sausage-breathed Kentucky sergeant, his chest split open by his sword, the pleading brown eyes of the redcoat on the hill in Canada asking why, my God *why?,* and a dozen more ghosts, sometimes different, often the same, each day, where he had hoped he had forgotten them but they hung ever-present, unatoned sins floating in memory. The bottle helped wash them away, temporarily at least. Some days he barely got out of bed and sometimes only then to take up a bottle of whiskey on the dining table.

It was during a sharp cold spell Charger developed fluid in his lungs, shuddered in his coldness despite an extra blanket and stared at him with passionate, unblinking eyes. He then staggered, fell over onto the hay, kicked twice and that was all he suffered. Charger passed away from pneumonia and old age.

He hitched long ropes to Jupiter and Victor, and dragged Charger up the hill to the clearing in the woods. It was difficult work left-handed but he preferred to be alone. He dug a grave and buried Charger on the other side of the meadow, not far from his mother's grave. He was surprised at how much he cried. For four hours he sobbed. At times Jupiter nuzzled him and Victor stomped a forefoot. He and Charger had shared so much together that his loss was more difficult than he cared to admit.

The day after Charger's passing he stopped drinking and was mostly successful. Sometimes he had dark days when he remained in the house. He continued his courtship with Emily but something was still not right. It was in talking with her he felt he had broken a promise, although an unstated promise, and decided he needed to take action to make it right. He rode Jupiter to Beck's Livery in Burlington, stabled him, and took the first train to New York City.

It was an overcast day, threatening heavy rain when he arrived at the institution where he asked for the authorities. Like many places after the war, the administration had changed. He filled out the paperwork then met Sister Constance with an older, short nun with pale-white skin and tiny veins across her petite nose, who escorted him to the playroom, where he saw her playing with another little girl. He stood patiently.

"Dottie, there's someone here for you," Sister Constance said while her eyes flashed with annoyance. A tight frown creased her pale face and she cracked a switch. "*Come here!*"

Dottie approached cautiously with downcast eyes but glanced at him.

"Do you remember me?" he asked. It had been two years. Dottie didn't speak for a long time then looked over her shoulder at the other girl, who was about 12, thin, and held a rag doll. She pretended to cook a meal on a table that served as a stove and laid out paper circles for dinnerware. It seemed Dottie preferred to return to playing.

"He asked you a question!" Sister Constance's switch smacked Dottie's arm. He noticed Dottie had marks on the backs of her hands and forearms.

"Yes, ma'am." Dottie continued to look down.

He had made a mistake. This was all romantic hogwash. Then he thought of a frightened, difficult colt, and of how patient he must be, and knew people could be much more complicated. He relaxed, squatted down to her level, raised his eyebrows and reached out with his left hand.

Dottie glanced at him out of the corners of her eyes, wheeled about, then with all her might slapped him hard on the face.

Sister Constance gasped and raised her switch but he stepped between them, grabbed the nun's wrist with his left hand and said, "No, it's, ah, it's okay. I deserved that. I've been away too long."

"You should go," Sister Constance said, twisting from his grasp but not before he took the switch from her, folded it over, and stuffed it in his pocket. Then he turned and knelt on one knee and said, "Dottie. Hey, Dottie."

She glared with sulking eyes. "Why you here? I don't play jacks no more!"

He focused on her fiery eyes and spoke firmly, "That's the last time you hit me, do you understand?" She frowned with shame, turned away but continued to look at him, then nodded. He held out his left hand again and waited but she wouldn't come. He kept his hand out and said, "How about if you show me what you do play now? Okay?"

She walked over to her friend then said, "We plays house now. This Becky," the other girl waved, "and this Amma. She our doll-baby."

"It's almost a whole family," he said.

"The daddy coming home soon," Dottie said, then she seemed to have an idea and looked to him. "Less you wants to be the daddy."

He smiled broadly and Sister Constance gazed heavenward and crossed herself. He said to Dottie warmly, "That's why I'm here. Not just today. Always."

Dottie stared hard and her eyes expressed the growing miracle of what he had said. She gave a broadening smile then said to Becky, "He don't have no right arm so we gonna pass food to the left."

"Okay," Becky said. "Here a cup. What you drinkin'?"

He felt very self-conscious of his drinking problem, knew he must stop completely, and vowed he would. "Water. Or juice, if you have it?"

Becky said, "Today is Monday so we have apple juice. That good?"

"Yes, that's one of my favorites," he smiled.

Dottie again looked around at the children playing assorted games, then returned her gaze to him. She couldn't resist her emotions any longer, ran to him, and hugged him strongly.

It was the happiest he had been in a very, very long time.

~54 ~

Dark gray clouds rolled low and heavy over the Vermont landscape, released a sifting, heavy white snow that fell like white ash from a censor for the fallen. Snow fell silently over the white fields of buried grass, piled high in large white mounds of fallen angels in mass graves at Gettysburg, a growing mound of white sallow corpses at Cold Harbor, a long white ring of faint, lily-white bodies piled high at Fort Harrison.

He watched the snow gather in the corners of the window pane and heard a mysterious noise. Was that a faint crying? A woman keening to soothe the pain of a distraught soul?

He used the thick base of his left palm to wipe the glass but his warmth had no effect. The snowflakes fell, stuck and piled higher. A raven stared at him from a pine bough covered in heavy snow, then cawed a screeching, faint cry.

He had arrived home very late at night in the snowstorm, stabled Jupiter in the barn then tread lightly through the house in order to not wake anyone. He disrobed to his sleeping britches and slipped into bed next to Emily. They had not spoken.

In the morning's first light, she rose and tried not to awaken him, knew he needed rest but he was startled awake, which happened with almost any little noise. She moved softly to start a fire in the fireplace of the living area. Its warmth spilled out from the center of the house to the dining room, the bedrooms and the growing sound of the crackling firewood brought comforting warmth. He rose, gingerly avoided his right side, eased into a heavy woolen robe then went to the small back room and relieved himself in a night jar. He heard Emily stirring in the kitchen area with pottery bowls and wooden mixing spoons but also heard a distant piercing cry. He used the palm of his left hand to wipe the window pane, watched the snow pile up in the corners like ashes for the dead, and recalled ghastly sights of once good friends now gone. He stood dazed for a moment, even after he had finished, realized he was statue-like then bundled up and moved through the house toward Emily, now cherishing every article in their home—the oak dresser from his grandmother, the large dining table he and his father had built together, the porcelain china and tea set his

Aunt Amelia had given them as a wedding present, only two weeks before she passed away at age 81, last January 3rd.

He stared after Emily, his devoted wife, making coffee in the kitchen of their home, which was once his father and mother's house. He was so overcome with various emotions he did not know what to say or how to approach her. In their courtship, she had accepted him despite all the horrendous acts he had seen and done, and had accepted his adopted daughter with open arms. He was grateful for her loyal and accepting spirit, and overwhelmed with a boundless love for her, and sometimes these emotions overwhelmed him and he did not know what to say or what to do.

A red shawl covered Emily's shoulders, wrapped over her simple, best blue cotton dress. He wondered what occasion would require her to put on her best blue dress, allowed the thought to pass, and focused on her dark brown eyes, lively and quick, then an easy smile touched the corners of her small mouth. She was busy in the kitchen yet appeared skittish, like a colt let out to the corral after a long spell. All he wanted to do was to hold her, be soothed by her calming acceptance, and be lost in her embrace.

The house was very quiet. Dottie was sleeping late as usual and he felt an awkwardness with Emily. He had heard other soldiers say when they returned home from the war their wife had changed. It was the woman who was different, distant, and their marriage ruined. Of course it was the soldier who was different, who wouldn't be, but it was also the woman who had changed. He was worried.

"Come, let's sit by the fire," Emily said with her voice lowered to not awaken Dottie. Her dark brown eyes showed a touch of sadness and he wondered, Was that for him and his condition? Then she smiled warmly. They walked into the living area and the way the firelight caught the red wool of her shawl it reminded him of a bloody shoulder wound but he said nothing. He was often quiet now, other than his great outpouring of words in Washington City. Perhaps he had said all he had to say about the war to the reporters and journalists at the hospital during his recovery? There was nothing more to say on the subject. He would rather have a drink than talk about it again. What would be the point of more talking? Is anyone truly listening?

He moved to her, stood by the fireside and gazed at her face, her sweet smile, round cheeks and bright brown eyes. He noticed she had fixed up her auburn hair in the special way he liked it, in a braided bun.

She said, "You're very quiet this morning. Was your return okay?"

"Yes, I suppose I am. I'm thinking, having a lot of flashes today."

"What's the matter? Did the sale of the Burlington house go okay?"

He nodded but again recalled the horrific sights and sounds of war. He thought of the incredible number of young men, some well-known, most new volunteers, arranged in haphazard array across the battlefield at Bull Run, strewn in awkward positions but some lying peacefully, all dead. Then Sergeant Bear Brisken, stocky but swiftly rushing out to club an attacking Rebel with his musket, the Rebel's head smashed like a busted watermelon then afterward, Brisken walking casually next to him only to be shot by a sniper and collapsing next to him. His blonde, bearded face and determined brown eyes showed he was ready to serve or smile, then the slow, eerie sound of his last breath leaking from his chest when he expired. He thought of the sudden stillness of Gettysburg before dawn of the second day of battle, standing with Abner Doubleday and hearing through the darkened night the low moaning of the wounded and near-dying, calling out for help with parched throats for hours. He recalled the awful, hot day when he lay wounded at Cold Harbor behind the dead bodies of two other soldiers, piles of corpses all around him, young men once alive with families and loved ones, while thousands of swarming flies and vultures suckled essence from their corpses in a squishy, pulsing, nauseating sound while he waited for darkness to come with an end to that interminably long day so he could rise, retreat, and survive. He remembered the terrible, high stack of limbs outside the field hospital at Gettysburg, then at Fort Harrison the grotesque single leg unattached to a body without anyone in sight. Also many of the Rebels he had killed. Young men charging full speed, shot in the head or throat, or the young man clutching at him with vengeful desperation to kill him, an instant before he slashed open his chest with his sword. How could he begin to describe any of this to Emily? He had told her, several times, he had "suffered unmentionable horrors." Need he say more? What would be the point?

"Well. Are you going to tell me?"

"No," a quiver of emotion warbled in his throat. He stood by the mantle and gazed across the room to the icy window and the vague whiteness outside. "I can't."

"Are you feeling okay? I know you came in very late."

"Yes, I'm fine. 'Healthy as a horse,' Doc Thayer said." He shrugged then nodded at his empty right sleeve. "More or less."

"You're not catching a cold, dear?" She stepped closer to him at the mantle and tenderly wrapped her shawl around his shoulders, careful to avoid touching the stub of his right arm under his robe near his shoulder. She took his left hand and led him to sit down in the large maple rocking chair, the one his father had received in a trade with a traveler from Carolina. He eased into it and once situated smiled up to her.

"Do you remember the day we took our marriage vows?" she asked softly then went over to the serving table and poured coffee into a cup of their special porcelain china. Although the question was straight-forward, it had thrown him into a spell of soft reminiscence. Their wedding had been small and intimate with only family and a few very close friends, in a cozy white-steepled church in Vermont in the middle of winter two months ago. It was a simple day of incredible beauty surrounded by loved ones.

The fire crackled and hissed. She said, "I'll take that as a 'yes'."

She removed a stack of books by Emerson, Wadsworth, and Longfellow from a table to the left of the rocker then set down his cup and saucer on the tabletop. She had learned he could not drink it if she handed him the cup *and* saucer.

"I'm sorry I'm a special case," he said, trying to explain his awkward silence.

"Don't fret," she said. "When I took our vows I promised to be with you forever in the kingdom of God and He is not looking down on you any differently today because you're a little different physically, or because you have thoughts of your *trials*." He noticed she swallowed hard and tears of emotion filled her beautiful brown eyes. This was difficult for her. "And neither do I."

"Oh sweetheart, I don't mean to test you," he said, followed by another long pause. The grandfather clock ticked in the corner. He wanted to say more but again, he did not know where to begin then lifted the cup with his left hand, tipped it back and tasted the strong, smooth coffee. Every action was a new complication and required forethought to manage the movements left-handed. He remembered when he was seven and thrown off his first horse, a big, dark thoroughbred named Thunder. He had landed hard and slammed into the ground on his right side. His father ran across the riding ring and pulled him to his feet but his right wrist was sprained and a small, jagged rock opened a gash on his right palm. He was mid-way through learning cursive writing at the schoolhouse but with his right hand wrapped and his arm in a sling, the other kids teased him and said he was faking because he wanted to avoid learning to write. Back then he had to do everything left-handed for a week, which was like a game at first then a discomfort in every action. He took off the bandage two days early because he hated the feeling of being less than his best, of being this left-handed person the other children ridiculed.

Emily rebounded some and continued, "You need some time to heal and you'll be fine. What do you need your right arm for that your left can't learn to do as well?" Then as soon as she had spoken those words she began crying, a muffled whimper at first then not being able to hold it back, a great sobbing rocked her. He wanted to comfort Emily yet knew she was avoiding the truth. Things *were* different now and he wanted to say everything on his mind but waited, not knowing where to begin with the war horrors, his trials, then heard the sounds of Dottie stirring in her bedroom, off the living area that was his old bedroom and now hers. The moment passed but he had received Emily's meaning, that she loved him and supported him, yet needed his affection. She needed his love and his actions of everything that made him who he was.

Throughout the day he reflected on his life and thought of how much more difficult each event would be single-handed, left-handed: roping horses, baling hay, hunting, fishing, birthing horses, feeding chickens—well, that was easy left-handed—pouring molten iron at the foundry, clearing trees and thick brush, fist fights with bullies, idiots, drunks, commanding men in the militia—that should be okay—raising Dottie, and courting Emily. Sweet Emily. The redeeming, crowning jewel of his life. Their life together would be different, *was* different. Now he needed to act. After their wedding and for three months now, he had avoided romantic intimacy with her because he felt less than himself. He had often wondered what would happen in tender private moments? During the war he had suffered various wounds and injuries, including extremely hard falls off Charger, plus the draining, twice, of his swollen right testicle. How would those wounds be approached? Would Emily be eager to engage? Or would they need to wait until they both had the spirit and he could be himself, now less than whole?

~55 ~

After a very long, difficult winter's day, after he had finished farm chores in the dim graying light and after Emily had maintained their house in Georgia, after she and Dottie had cleaned and put away the dinner dishes then stoked the fireplace for the night, after he put Dottie to bed with a book of Shakespeare's *Romeo and Juliet*, they met in the their bedroom, both weary and exhausted. They had not been together romantically, not even on their wedding night three months ago, but their bedroom was still comforting and restful. He handed Emily a birthday present, unevenly wrapped in brown paper with a piece of old twine around it.

"You wrapped it yourself," she said. Two candles flickered on the nightstand and two more shone on a marble-topped dresser.

"I thought you would enjoy it more if it was wrapped."

She held the object, about one inch think, five inches wide and seven inches long. She said, "I think I know what it is."

She unwrapped it slowly with dulled expectation in her tearing eyes and found a leather-bound volume of poetry by Elizabeth Barrett Browning. “It’s very nice, George,” she paused, “but you have collections of poetry.”

“This is for you.” He remained joyful, “Can one have too much poetry?”

“No. It’s grand.” A sorrow washed over her face, came through her eyes and her lower lip quivered. “I’d hoped for something more personal.”

“Emily. Look on page seventy-four.”

She opened the book, flipped the pages carefully and admired its gilded top. Inside were two roses, one red, one white and both still moist with life, pressed flat between the pages. On the page was a love poem. She read it in a soft whisper,

“How do I love thee, let me count the ways
I love thee to the depth and breadth and height
My soul can reach, when feeling out of sight
For the ends of Being and ideal Grace.”

She was overcome with emotion and couldn’t continue reading aloud. Her eyes filled with tears, spilled over onto her cheeks and fell onto her dress with white lace covering her bosom. She continued reading and he joined in from memory. Both trembled with joy until they came to the end and she closed the book. She gently hugged him then with all her strength and said, “It’s beautiful, thank you!”

He was incredibly happy yet felt he had to say more to express why he had done this. “I needed to show you, so you understand, you have *all* my love. This was the closest thing I could find to express my emotions and show my faith in our love. It’s all in this one poem as a symbol of my love.” Now his pale blue eyes welled up with tears. “I’m sorry if you wanted something more substantial.”

“Oh no! It’s beautiful.”

“We said our vows to God and our families, and I gave you a gold ring as a symbol of that vow. I’ve wanted to give you something more and, well, I’m not very good with words or emotions. This poem comes close so I’m letting these words speak for me.”

She cried with love-filled joy, held him tightly then said, “I don’t know how I got so lucky.”

“I believe in those words with all my heart. And more.”

“Be quiet, dear.” She held him close and kissed him softly. Then she unbuttoned his clothing and continued gazing at him as she gracefully undid her clothing. She took the hairpin out of her hair and shook her head gently, letting the dark braids fall then fluffed out the curls, spilling down onto her shoulders. She looked into his teary, light blue eyes, gently rubbed them dry then kissed him fully on the mouth. They collapsed onto the feather mattress and he felt the softness of the downy quilt. Their warm bodies pressed against each other in a beautiful dance of love that grew more and more passionate with each passing moment.

~56 ~

He sat in the maple rocking chair holding little Emily. He bounced her on his knee and held her tenderly yet firmly with his left arm. Her big round eyes were open wide and she stared at her father in wondrous amazement. He made cooing sounds to her and was delighted and awed when she gave a toothless smile.

He had risen early to take care of his six horses, with Dottie shadowing him, then handled the other farm chores. He wanted to have time with little Emily before he went to the Reunion luncheon. Even now, he hesitated in leaving. It was very comfortable here and even the simplest moments gave him great joy.

"You better march if you're going," Emily said, standing in the doorway to the kitchen and admiring him even though he had put on 20 pounds since the war ended and took naps in the afternoon. He was also melancholy sometimes but when Dottie or little Emily was around he smiled constantly and played with them. He also told Emily he wanted more children.

"They'll miss you if you don't go," she said and took the baby from his lap then carefully handed little Emily to Dottie, who fussed and cooed to her. "Then most of them, scores and scores of them will come here. Is that what you want?"

"No, I'm going." He put on his boots and noticed the spurs his father had given him so long ago, small, five-pointed rowels with short shanks. They had indeed lasted a lifetime. Then he thought of Samuel's death. That gruesome image was followed by the thousands of men attacking at Gettysburg, where the young men in gray had no chance, and then at Cold Harbor, where the young men in blue had no chance. Good young men dying uselessly and each battle a slaughter. At last he spoke quietly, “I’m more than a little sad for those who won’t be there.”

“That’ll include you if you don’t get started!”

He stood and pulled down his coat with his left hand. Emily had spent the past few days adjusting the waistline of his military pants and took out the seam of his coat, and made the worn uniform fit perfectly. She brushed off his lapels and shoulder straps then patted down his graying, dark hair in back where a cowlick stuck up.

“It’s not a beauty contest, dear,” he said, “otherwise you should attend.”

“Very funny. March!”

He kissed her on the lips, gave Dottie then little Emily a hug and kiss, and went out to the barn where he passed the empty stall where Charger had lived. Since his passing from pneumonia and old age, he couldn’t bear to put another horse in his stall. Then he chose Jupiter, a dark quarter horse and saddled up.

On the ride into Burlington he thought about himself, once a youthful boy of 17 eager to fight in the Canadian Rebellion and now a wizened veteran who had still more to learn, even at age 44 at the end of the Civil War. He was saddened by so many deaths, so many were the result of the many incompetent leaders in the Union Army, plus so many more because the Southerners fought on long after they had any hope of winning and long after their political leaders knew there was no hope.

In Burlington as he approached the very large hall for the reunion he saw 50 or more horses on several very long hitching poles and several scores of carriages stopped by a huge barn in back. He eased off Jupiter, looped the reins over the hitching pole and stretched. After sitting in the saddle for two hours he was stiff and sore, affected by his various war wounds plus middle age.

Each man looked to him, some smiled and others nodded hello. He made his way to the front of the building with his coin-sized spurs jangling and he felt somewhat odd because his uniform felt comfortable again.

Inside the reception hall was decorated with white linens and red, white, and blue bunting. Centerpiece flowers decorated the long tables every six feet with fine china and silverware in place. The American flag was displayed front and center next to a podium along with a stand of 17 Vermont regimental infantry colors, artillery, the 1st cavalry and navy flags with many labels sown on to proclaim which battles each had fought. Several veteran flag bearers stood nearby including Corporal Hicks, who was much heavier and nearly bald. Hicks smiled broadly and stood proudly by the stand of flags.

Gregory Sutpin, who was one of their buglers during the war, had grown into large man with curly dark-blonde hair. Sutpin sat in a chair near the entrance with a small band, including Wallace Derry, the heavily freckled red-haired boy who was now a short, confident man who performed on the coronet with the band playing "Tenting on the Old Campground Tonight" to welcome the soldiers filtering into the hall. Sergeant Lloyd gave a quick salute with his angled smile and lively gray eyes. Lloyd said Doc Thayer recently moved his family and practice to Boston, where he was kept very busy and doing well. It was great to see so many familiar faces, now old veterans. Sergeant Cohl, who had stowed the Vermont 9th regimental flag under his coat at Harpers Ferry, was still very large but unlike most of the others he had remained fit and smiled jovially. Judge Wheelock Veazey, tall, handsome, with his dark features turned white with age, wore his general's uniform. Edward Ripley was still red-cheeked but his dark hair had receded high on his head and had turned white, although his soft brown eyes glowed warmly and he also appeared fit and vigorous in his general's uniform. The two generals stood next to each other and George Benedict, who had put on much weight but somehow still fit into his well-worn lieutenant's uniform, poked fun at Veazey then Ripley by saying the other one's stars were larger, or shinier, then reversing it when the other turned to shake hands with an old friend. Benedict wore his Medal of Honor, along with Veazey, and Nichols, and Brown, all from their courageous acts at the battle of Gettysburg. Then he saw DeWitt Clarke, who he met in Camp Douglas after he had lost his right arm in the fighting at Harpers Ferry. He matched empty right sleeves with him but Clarke was not in a uniform and instead wore a very nice navy-blue, three-piece suit. A few other veterans were also not in uniform but wore their Sunday best. Clarke said he had been "working the law" in Montpelier and enjoyed it very much. Burt Cromartie joined them and shook his left hand vigorously then clapped him on the back and thanked him "for putting up with a petulant youth." There was a lot of laughter, hugging, and a great sense of camaraderie.

He spoke warmly with many comrades-in-arms and watched the men filing into the building by the score. Efficient waiters ran about in their white cotton coats. Some of the men toasted each other with beer or drank shots of whiskey. Champagne stood ready with glasses filled but untouched, with more bottles chilling in buckets. Cigar smoke filled up the hall. He felt himself becoming overwhelmed with emotion and stepped outside for fresh air.

Outside he strolled to the shade of a large elm tree and gazed at the puffy white clouds rolling in from New York. It had been two years since the end of the war but a flood of vivid memories filled with intense visions hit him hard. It felt recent and brutal. He tried to focus his thoughts on the tedious times in Camp Boredom on the Potomac, then studied his overall experience in the war. Because he had been through military training and exercises, and had experienced the heat of battle, he was able to rely on his instincts in each situation and knew he had made the right decision time, after time, and again. He had been right in leading his boys to stand firm at Bull Run, knew the Vermonters could break through at Harpers Ferry but he was right in following orders to return to the fort, saw the opportunity for a flank attack at Gettysburg and ordered it, felt the folly of attacking uphill at a fortified position at Cold Harbor, and knew the deadly consequences of holding Fort Harrison without reinforcements against what was left of the Confederate Army. Still, he performed his duty on each occasion. Yes, he was comfortable with what he had done.

He took out a new white kerchief and gazed where Emily had sewn her initials 'ECS' in gold thread then wiped the perspiration from his forehead. He recalled using her first kerchief as a tourniquet to save General Hancock's life at Gettysburg and how Hancock repaid him by stealing credit for his order during the battle. The shrill notes of trumpeter Sutpin's "Call to Reveille" sounded and he replaced the kerchief in his coat pocket and walked up to the hall with his boots crunching pebbles on the gravel walkway.

The hall was remarkably quiet, especially since a moment earlier it was rowdy with drinking and laughter. He ascended the wooden steps, crossed the porch, and went in through the open double doors, where hundreds of men in blue milled about. Lieutenant Stephen Brown, who stood by the entrance with a long white, walrus-like mustache drooping over his jowls, saw him and called out, "*Ah-ten-tion!*"

All the men looked to him then moved to attention, although not briskly. Some were missing a limb and some were less than perfectly upright but each man saluted. Each man faced him with their drinks down on the tables and here and there a hardened smile beamed. Then Veazey stepped forward gracefully with his handsome features now accented by white hair and white eyebrows, clicked his heels, and snapped a salute to him. Veazey's clear, practiced voice boomed, "*The men are ready, sir!*"

As a reflex he waved the empty sleeve of his right arm, out and back in a salute. Great emotion overwhelmed him and he paused a moment to swallow hard then said, "At ease, gentlemen."

They all stood motionless, watching him, and he felt uncomfortable. "You know I'm no good at this kind of thing. I'd rather face General Lee again."

Many of the men laughed and Ripley called out, "*We'd whip him again, sir!*"

The crowd yelled "*huzzah!*" and buzzed with excitement. From the front of the room near the podium someone called out, "*Speech! Speech!*"

"No," he said humbly but, as usual, Benedict was by his side and pushed him on his back toward the podium. He turned and spoke in a lowered voice, "No, I can't."

Benedict, who had put on weight and moved more slowly, had the same confident wisdom flowing from his dark brown eyes. He adjusted his new, stronger bifocal spectacles, patted his upper back and replied, "Many of these men traveled for days and some for weeks to see *you. . . Sir!* Give them *something.*"

He nodded then moved the remaining distance to the podium and looked out over the sea of expectant faces. Men in blue uniforms or their best Sunday suit, and a few waiters with white aprons, all stood still with fixed attention. He saw so many brave soldiers, men who would do anything for their fellow comrades in the room, and his heart again swelled with emotion.

"It was my great privilege to lead you," he spoke softly yet his voice carried to the back of the quiet room. "There is no finer group of men in all of Vermont."

The men cheered, yelled huzzah!, and cascades of boisterous cheers continued for a few moments until Veazey rapped his scabbard on the floorboards. When it quieted down, he continued, "People ask me all the time, will the South rise up and fight?"

He paused, steeled his eyes at the thought, then continued, "And if they did, would I lead the men of Vermont into battle again?" He looked at the wise, veteran face of Sergeant Lloyd with his light gray eyes, the bookish spectacles and dark-brown determined eyes of Lieutenant Benedict, and the firm chin and white-hair of General Veazey, and the reddened cheeks and soft brown eyes of General Ripley. Each man was older but stern and ready. "Yes, if the South were to rise up again, the men of Vermont would be there to *'Preserve the Union!'*"

"*Here, here!*" The men cheered loudly. Several raised glasses in a toast and downed the entire contents. They clapped, hollered, and stomped their boots on the wooden floor.

"Let me relate a story to you," the room became quiet again. "Something that happened right after the end of the war. I was in Washington City and I met General Grant at Willard's Hotel." Some of the men cheered at the mention of Grant's name but more than a few grumbled in remembrance of Cold Harbor.

"General Grant and I spoke of many things that afternoon. We began by talking about our common love for horses, of how he wanted to bring Arabian horses to America, and of our equally intense loathing of horse's asses, also known as politicians." Many of the men laughed. "We did not speak of the war for quite some time. Then he put his hand on my shoulder and said, 'I heard of what your boys did simply to get to Gettysburg—one hell of a long march in the blistering sun. And then the fighting. Plus I know first-hand what your boys can do and I appreciate your sacrifice at Cold Harbor. You and your men were exceptionally brave in taking and holding Fort Harrison. So it is with all sincerity that I say, there are only two things the Vermonters can do: They can outmarch and outfight any regiment in the Union!'"

The men cheered wildly and gave a thunderous ovation. He stepped away from the podium and lifted a champagne glass and everyone in the room followed his lead. The rowdy cheering went on, they would not stop, and it lasted for many, many moments until he raised his champagne glass higher with his left hand. All around the hall was an unbreakable bond gleaming in the eyes of his comrades.

"To those who could not be here," he paused, felt the absence of Bear Brisken, Doc Thayer, Private Milne, Mrs. Turner's butler, Obadiah, Vincent Caravaggio, Billy Caldwell, the African Americans killed in the New York Draft riot, Ramses Garthwaite, General Burnham, Alvan Rowley, Thomas Jenkins, Private Koosbeck, Captain Male, Abner Doubleday, and many, many other soldiers. President Lincoln. His father. "And to each of you. . . the finest men in all the land!"

He drank it all, in long, slow swallows.

~57 ~

He rocked slowly in the maple rocking chair and held Jeddie, his son of six months. Clara played on her toy stick horse and galloped around the room. Little Emily, now eight, baked bread and canned tomatoes in glass jars in the kitchen with their mother and Dottie, now 18, and courting an occasional suitor.

Earlier in the morning he had received a letter of invitation in the post to be the keynote speaker at the 10th Reunion of Vermont Soldiers in the Civil War. It was to be held later this month in Burlington at the same hall it had been held for each of the past nine years. He knew most of the men would be there, if possible, except for Judge Wheelock Veazey, who had died of a heart attack last spring. Lieutenant Brown was away to Europe to promote his new business related to farm machinery but many, many others would be there, including Benedict. They would talk of the battles once again, of how they had given their all, of how they would do it all again because they loved their country, and even more, each would do anything for their fellow comrades.

He nuzzled Jeddie, his baby boy, bounced him in his lap and thought of all the needs of his children, of what he could do to make more money before the winter snow came. He was very, very happy with his home life and wanted nothing more than to provide a world of comfort, wonderful gifts, and fine opportunities for them.

The appendage where his right arm had been sometimes throbbed with dull pain. On occasion his old groin injury felt prickly hot without reason. He stood, gently placed Jeddie in the nearby red cradle, and shook his tingling legs. When Clara saw him do this she giggled and he improvised a little dance for her. She dropped her stick horse on the floor, rushed to him, put her stockinged-feet on top of his and held on to his belt. His waist had become portly. They waltzed around the room in a slow, sliding motion and he hummed, "The Moonlight Tonight."

When he stopped, Clara said, "More Papa. Please!"

He started up again, in spite of the numbing sensation in his left hand where he was shot at Cold Harbor, and soon they hummed together, sliding around the floor. Jeddie was wide-eyed and quiet in his cradle. Emily came into the room, smiled, and radiated loveliness, admiring them from the doorway. He felt very, very happy.

Dottie called out from the kitchen. "Momma, they're done! The bread looks good."

"I need to feed Jeddie now," Emily said, the remains of a slight smile on her face, then called out to little Emily, "Did you finish canning the tomatoes?"

Little Emily stepped into the living room to answer, a miniature copy of her mother, thin with long auburn hair and a dimple in her right cheek. She was growing fast. He admired her composure, grace, and willingness to help.

"Yes, Momma. It's all done. Papa, can we ride this afternoon?"

He did not want to be away from Jeddie for too long because it would inconvenience Emily. "Would that be alright, dear? If we rode over to the lake?"

"If you're back in time to care for Jeddie this afternoon that would be fine."

"*Yea!*" Dottie shouted. Little Emily cheered and triumphantly raised a wooden spoon wet with tomato paste.

"Can I go, too, Papa?" Clara asked and pulled repeatedly on his belt.

She was still standing on his feet with her big blue eyes pleading. She was almost seven, physically able to take care of herself, had followed him around the horses, and rode well in the ring with him nearby. She had always done her chores. He weighed all this then said, "Yes, I think you're ready!"

"Oh, Papa!" little Emily said, clearly upset. "I like it just you, me, and Dottie!"

"It's okay. We can ride with your sister. She's old enough."

"She'll slow us down!"

He looked at her evenly, which was all it took for her to understand 'no.' "We'll all ride together. Come on, it'll be wonderful."

Emily lifted Jeddie from the cradle and strolled to their bedroom. Little Emily put on her boots, Dottie had already disappeared into her room and would be ready in an instant, she was always one step ahead of her sisters, while Clara still celebrated and jumped up and down with joy. When they were all in their riding clothes with light jackets, they went out to the stables together.

A slight breeze of cool autumn air felt invigorating and the horses bobbed their heads when he approached. He stroked their strong, muscular front quarters, patted their necks and prepared four horses, Victor, Daisy, Sunny, and Regal to ride. They walked the horses out of the stable then out of the corral. He examined the sky again. The weather should be lovely, although it could change quickly.

The large oak by the side of their house stood strong and fully matured with thick, sturdy branches shooting out in various directions. Its leaves were still on although beginning to turn various autumnal colors of red and golden brown, shimmering in the late morning light. He admired the old oak and reflected on his family with a feeling of great joy and fulfillment.

He helped Clara knee-up onto Regal, a thick-boned mare, then watched little Emily almost effortlessly swing up on Daisy, a chestnut sorrel, and Dottie was already up on Sunny, eager and ready. Dottie smiled then raised her eyebrows with a look that said, “Let’s go!” He mounted Victor, highly aware of his various hindrances but even with one arm, like many things, it had become almost routine.

Across the meadow and rolling hills the trees on the far mountains were ablaze with color. He felt very good, riding with his three girls. He enjoyed these moments with them very much. Puffy white clouds rolled over the high blue sky. They watched cows grazing through the fields of grass, munching on shoots of clover, then stopped in a field by the lake to gather black-eyed susans and daisies.

The sun blazed gloriously high above, and over the great, calm blue of Lake Champlain, Harney Peak and the mountains of eastern New York stood majestically. He loved those great mountains on the far shore and viewing them gave him a sense of strength, dignity, and serenity. They continued their leisurely ride and the day passed like a magical dream.

In the afternoon they returned home to their two-story, white farm house and eased their horses down the slope of the last low hill. He handed the picked flowers to Clara to give to her mother. He, Dottie, and little Emily stabled the horses and spoke enthusiastically of their fantastic ride and of how mother and Jeddie would join them one fine day.

When he entered the house he again saw the Reunion announcement on the table where he had left it. He had not thought about the Reunion all day and the formal invitation had not been moved from the table. Instead of attending to the note, he went to see Emily and Jeddie.

~ ~

Some say the old Vermont general died of his wounds, albeit 18 years later. Others say George returned to his own country and "that was that." All agreed the old soldier had at last found some measure of peace.

The End

www.ingramcontent.com/pod-product-compliance
Lightning Source LLC
Chambersburg PA
CBHW070823020826
48982CB00014B/441
9780988459779